RICH GIRL

RICH GIRL A NOVEL

HALEY WARREN

imPRESS Millennial Books
Greenville

imPRESS Millennial Books
Greenville, SC

First imPRESS Millennial Books paperback edition January 2023

For information on imPRESS Millennial Books Consulting, please contact imPRESS Millennial at publisher@impressmillennial.com or visit our website at www.impressmillennial.com.

Printed in the United States of America

ISBN 9798843656720 (Paperback)

To Benjamin, who believed in Charlie from the beginning and for being Deacon's number one fan.

And to Kelsi, who told me not to give up, and who has the same affinity for morally gray characters as I do.

RICH GIRL

CHAPTER ONE

I was sliding my heel up and down the seam of David's suit pants as he sat across from me at the conference table. My father was standing at the head of the table, talking incessantly and looking perpetually serious as always. It bored me to no end. It was very balmy for an early spring afternoon in Chicago and I used the weather as an excuse to wear my favorite leather jacket that my father hated. I should have known then my day would take a turn. Early spring in Chicago was always misleading; it was just a late winter.

It was supposed to be casual Friday. Casual Fridays were something my father had insisted on since he inherited his company from my late grandfather a few years after I was born. No one really listened and most people just took it to mean no suit jacket. Sometimes, if he was feeling particularly loose, my father wouldn't wear a tie. He thought it made him more relatable and younger, just like his ill-conceived casual Friday. My father still looked young. He was in his late-fifties and probably could have passed for mid-forties to anyone on the street. He was also exceptionally fit, which was funny to me because he wasn't staying fit for anyone and really didn't seem to like working out. He started joining me at Soul Cycle classes every morning when I moved home in what might have been an attempt to reconnect with me.

Somehow it sort of worked and became our thing, but it was probably just so he could be seen in public with his only daughter at least semi-regularly.

On this particular Friday, I was clearly not paying much attention to the weekly executive briefing. I had already provided my weekly update about the status of the charitable fund and where in the world I was off to next. My father had finally convinced me to move home to Chicago and join Winchester Holdings by dangling a carrot in front of my face. The carrot being that he would allow me to start a community development-focused charitable fund, and he would make me director. When I finished school, much to his chagrin, I took the two degrees I held in international development and economics and left Chicago—left the country—to volunteer in various community projects across the world before settling in Sri Lanka for a year to work at a community health center.

Everyone else around me at the table was a vice president of something or another. My father had been very clear that my director status was temporary, as long as I could prove to him this was a worthwhile venture and could be successful. I wasn't sure exactly how he expected me to define success for him when grant funding didn't generate us direct revenue, but he was probably advised by the Board of Directors that something like this would set WH apart and be a good PR move. It really did seem sometimes like my father was trying to run his company differently. He always said that my grandfather had this saying that it was a family. I wasn't sure I bought that, but I played pretend when required.

When I had finished my briefing, everyone else around the table gave me the green light to continue vetting the shortlisted grant applicants. I had promptly resumed my seat and continued to rub my heeled foot up and down the suit pants of the man sitting across from me. David Kennedy was the vice president of acquisitions, only two years my senior, one of my brother's best friends and someone I had recently begun secretly seeing. I smiled mischievously at him, tempted to toss him a wink, but I didn't push my luck. He arched a dark eyebrow at me and ran a hand through his disheveled dirty blonde hair, leaning back in his plush leather chair. He swiveled slightly to look as if he was paying more attention to the VP of marketing, Rowena, as she delivered their most recent social media strategies for various portions of the company and our subsidiaries. But really, he was giving me a better vantage point to slide the point of my Jimmy Choo farther up his leg.

"Thank you everyone." My father smiled curtly as Rowena sat down, shuffling his papers before knocking them against the table in front of him like he always did at the end of meetings. She simpered, tucking a dark curl behind her ear. She was incredibly kind and younger than my father by only a few years. My brother and I had always held out hope that she and my dad might get together after our mother died. She seemed like she might be good for him but my father stopped having interest in anything to do with family the second our mother stopped breathing.

"As you know, we are looking for a new VP of sales, as Carter has left us to go to medical school." The previous VP, Carter Marks, had a crisis of conscience and decided suddenly to leave the corporate world to become a doctor. "I was hoping we could take a few minutes before EOD to chat about potential candidates. Is there anyone who might be available? Who might be looking?" There were murmurs around the table.

Working at WH was highly coveted by young professionals. My father was incredibly well-connected and always happy to serve as a stepping stone for many portions of corporate America. It was his way of ensuring he had connections across multiple industries and across the country.

I was busy eyeing David, who was sitting around a table full of Hugo Boss, Armani, and Tom Ford suits, and he was more than happy to wear a suit I had made for him at a small tailor when I was in Vietnam. We locked eyes and I felt my pulse quickening. I wasn't sure if it was entirely a secret that he and I spent time together, but we had never broached the subject of what it meant. A small seed of fear and doubt had grown roots and begun to blossom in me every time I wondered whether someone like him would ever be really interested in someone like me. The thought of asking him made me want to vomit. We did, however, have a standing after-work drinks' date on Fridays that had begun when we were first colleagues, so it never seemed entirely suspicious to anyone when we were leaving together, his hand on the small of my back as he held open the elevator door.

I bit my lip slightly, in awe of how wonderful I found his features. The planes of his face looked like I had imagined them. I could vaguely hear the names being tossed around the table, but I was much more interested in studying the way the sunlight reflected against his eyes. I was certain of one thing: I had grown very quickly, irrevocably, enamored with him.

"I hear Tripp Banks is available," suggested Ash Reynolds, a long-standing friend of my father and the CFO of the company. That broke my reverie. A bucket of ice water would have been less shocking to me at that moment. I could vaguely hear murmurs of support.

"We are NOT hiring Tripp Banks!" I sputtered, jerking my heeled foot back so quickly I sent my chair careening backward from the conference table. I caught myself suddenly, grabbing the arms of my chair to steady myself from spinning. I braced myself as my brother, Deacon, had a hard time controlling his laughter and ended up fake-coughing into a fist, simultaneously clapping David on the back as he shifted in his chair uncomfortably.

"And why not?" My father arched his dark eyebrow. His tanned skin rose, revealing lines of age on his forehead.

I sat there, vaguely aware of all the eyes on me. I chewed my lip and exhaled before surveying my brother, whose coughing fit had subsided. He was leaning back in his chair, head cocked to one side, tapping his pen against his notepad. "Yeah, why not Charlie?"

I jutted my lower jaw out before pursing my lips and closed my eyes quickly. "Because Tripp Banks works in Investment Banking." I shuffled on my heels against the polished hardwood to come back to the table and hopefully salvage my dignity.

"We invest. Or do you need me to familiarize you with the general workings of a holdings' company?" Deacon patronized, his smile wide and his eyes glowing with mischief, incredibly unhelpfully. "I know Tripp. Ash knows Tripp. Ash was just running down WHY he would make a great VP of sales. Did you not hear that?"

"I believe she was too busy making eyes at David to be listening, Deacon." My dad interjected, folding his arms and shaking his head slightly as his blue eyes narrowed in on me. I swallowed. This was my absolute nightmare. I grimaced, imagining my female colleagues who were clawing their way up the corporate ladder, desperate to earn an ounce of respect. Here I was in a position of power, respect readily given due to sheer dumb luck of who I was born to after having been practically dragged back from another continent to sit in these leather chairs that probably cost more than some rental apartments, and I was busy giving a foot-job to the closest available bachelor.

"Sorry Steven," David interjected on my behalf, an easy grin sliding into place. He was well liked by everyone at this table, his employees, and by my father. "My fault. But I do know Tripp Banks, quite well actually. We did our MBA programs together at Harvard."

Not as well as I do. I lowered my head, cheeks burning. I had gratitude for David's bailout, but the embarrassment and anxiety that rose up in me the second I heard Tripp's name eclipsed any thankfulness I could feel.

"Hmm." My father glanced at me quickly before dismissing my indiscretion with a wave of his hand. "And? What do you think of him?"

"Charlie is right, obviously he works in investing strictly. But I also happen to know his sales and trades percentages are the highest of anyone at his firm. He would be a steal for us." David folded his hands on top of his legal pad casually, as if we hadn't been called out in front of the entire executive team.

Of course his percentages were *the highest of anyone at his firm*. I could barely contain my eye roll. The Tripp Banks I knew was not to be outdone by anyone. I folded my arms across my chest, hoping my leather jacket would swallow me and I could disappear. What was once a promising afternoon was suddenly turning into my nightmare.

"Alright. Why don't you three," my father gestured at myself, Deacon and David, "take him for dinner and drinks tomorrow. Take him to the Supper Club. He's around your age."

I tensed, tempted to open my mouth to protest but expected it was best to stay quiet. I sat back while David and Deacon discussed it further, until he dismissed everyone else but signaled for me to stay behind. I attempted to hold my head high, keeping my pointed chin raised prominently. I felt a hand on my shoulder and looked up to see Ash. His green eyes were crinkling with a slight laughter. His salt-and-pepper hair was pushed back from his face. "We were all young once Charles, don't sweat it." He tipped my chin with his finger affectionately, almost like you would to a child. It didn't help that Ash used the nickname Deacon had given me when we were children. He told me that our parents were hoping for another boy, and that Charlie was actually short for Charles, not Charlotte, like everyone assumed, and would run around the house screaming that my real name was Charles at the top of his lungs. Unfortunately, the nickname stuck and all these years later, I couldn't shake it. "See you on the green tomorrow, Steven."

Once the room had emptied, I swiveled my chair forward to face my father. He was busy stacking his papers, as he waved in his executive assistant, Damien, to gather his notes. Damien came in, his wire-rimmed glasses having slid down his nose slightly. Once upon a time, seeing Damien might have made my heart swell. It would have endeared me to my father, that he had hired a male to work as his executive assistant as opposed to some young girl for him to have an affair with. I imagined now it was likely some form of PR stunt or that no one else could stand working for him. Damien was exceptionally good at his job and somehow managed to make my father laugh on occasion. Who would have thought?

"Charles," he winked at me. He was only two years younger than me, and I had adopted him as something of a friend the second he started at WH. "Drink after work?"

For the first time in the last forty minutes, I broke a smile. I smoothed down my black leather pencil skirt. "Absolutely, David and I were–," my father cut me off.

"That'll be all Damien. I need to talk to Charlie before she leaves for the day." He narrowed his eyes on me. He was very supportive of office friendships—surprisingly so. I think it had something to do with those bizarre familial notions he seemed to think he should be instilling.

Damien pulled a face at me behind my dad and mouthed "maybe next time" before grabbing the papers and practically sprinting as fast as his ostentatious leather brogues would take him. I turned back to face my father. Steven Winchester is many things: businessman, avid golfer, a yachtsman, a widower and a father. He is also a man with a temper. He sometimes remembered to be a father first, but looking at this steely gaze, I was quite unsure which I was going to get.

He pushed off the mahogany conference table and loosened his tie as he made his way to the wet bar in the corner of the room. It was mostly for show, but I did know that he kept a few bottles back there for particularly intense or celebratory meetings. "Vodka?" He inquired, already pouring scotch for himself. I rolled my eyes. He knew very well I preferred soda—but he would make it with tonic anyway. "Sure, Dad. Now when you come back over here, can we just get this over with?"

I heard him sigh audibly as he mixed my drink. He turned, looking resigned and weary. "You know I can't be seen showing favoritism to you or Deacon. What do you think would happen if some of my other staff was caught flirting with one another instead of paying attention?"

I accepted the drink and ran my fingers over the crystal detailing on the glass. I swirled it quickly, enjoying the sound of the ice clinking in the glass. I took a sip and hid my grimace. Tonic grossed me out. "Would you fire them?" I asked dryly, arching an eyebrow.

He rolled his own eyes, crossing his arms. "No, they wouldn't be fired. But they would be disciplined. I don't want you and David sitting near one another or working on any projects alone. Got it? Look cowed if someone asks you about it. Maybe run out of here and pretend to cry. Just do me a favor and make it look like I laid into you.

I gave you free reign to create this portfolio and body of work here, and I need you to demonstrate that it works and that you can handle it."

He swirled his scotch, too, waiting for me to speak. A family trait, I guess. I swallowed my shock, fully expecting that this would certainly be one of those times he forgot to be a father first, but it thankfully wasn't. "I know, Dad. I know. Don't...don't punish David. He was just trying to cover for me." The fear I felt bubbled in my stomach, turning into worry that this would push David away. I had intended to tell my dad and Deacon if there ever was something more to tell. "He's good at his job, Dad. He fits here."

"I'm not going to punish David. He is incredibly valuable, and I don't want to give him any reason to leave. He has a future here." He took the first sip of his drink. "However, I need to know if there is something going on with you two."

I sighed, gulping back half my vodka. My cheeks were burning. Did he count regular sex in this very office as something. "I...it's new. I don't know. I wasn't ready to make the official Winchester debut, yet. Not until we had figured it out. I haven't had the chance to ask him." I made air quotes with my fingers when I mentioned our last name, resisting the temptation to roll my eyes again. I didn't need to remind my father that dating a Winchester was a full-time job in itself. Dating into one of the wealthiest families in America required a particular skin. Finding a suitable partner was something I had consistently failed at. So had Deacon, if we were keeping score. But at least all his partners were very happy to be photographed with him.

"David is a good man. A good match." He said gruffly. He had told me on several occasions how he worried I would never find someone who fit into this life, or who knew what it meant. "He's from a good family."

"He's a fucking Kennedy, Dad." I laughed out loud. He wasn't related to THE Kennedys but was from a very wealthy family in North Carolina. He had told me his entire family was made up of lawyers. He was the outlier. We had that in common.

My dad managed to laugh at that, as he drained his scotch. "Just remember Charlie. You're a woman in this world and you will have to work—"

"Three times as hard to earn their respect. Got it Dad." I drained my drink as well, standing and gathering my papers. He had drilled that mantra into my head for as long as I could remember. It's a good thing Deac is the one interested in finance, not me. Old staunchy white men don't tend to be interested in community development. "I'll get you those briefings on my top choices for the foundation project grant by EOD Tuesday. Sound okay?"

My father grunted, staring down into his emptied glass. "How do you know Tripp Banks? Is there something I should know?" *There it was.* My mind began to race. There were a million things I could say. I could make something up. It wasn't unlikely I would know him, as there was a small crowd of young professionals like us across Chicago who all ran in the same circles.

"We went to Brown together. Just someone I used to know." He looked at me appraisingly, running a hand through his salt-and-pepper hair, quite aware this was likely not the entire story.

"Have a nice night with David, will you? Tell him to join myself and Ash at the course tomorrow morning. Tee off is at 9:15 sharp."

I smiled knowingly. Steven Winchester golf invitations were not just for anyone. David would be thrilled. It gave me a sort of ironic thrill, too, knowing my father approved of David. I read somewhere that no matter what, children always desired their parents' approval. I turned on my heel and made my way out of the conference room, hoping somewhat naively to leave Tripp and his memory behind permanently.

––––––––

I was sitting across from David, leaning back slightly in my chair, enjoying the warmth that was wafting off the nearby heat lamp setup on the rooftop patio we were on. We had decided to meet down at Mullen's—a popular après-work members only, known for their expensive cocktails and beautiful views. The balmy Friday afternoon really did turn into late winter, hence the blazing heat lamps lining the rooftop bar. I silently vowed never to be fooled by a Chicago spring again.

A server came by with our drinks; David had ordered a Modelo, something about him I enjoyed immensely. I could picture him, hair mussed from the saltwater, twisting the cap off of a beer to watch a North Carolina sunset from the deck of his family home. It was his exclusive Friday evening drink. I smiled graciously as the server handed me a double Vodka soda. "Thank you." David looked up briefly, smiling.

He turned back to me, messy hair pushed off his face. His brown eyes surveyed me over his perfect nose. It was broad and set off his face nicely. His skin was even, except for the few lines that started to pull around his eyes when he laughed. But I liked how it reminded me of his smile. He had a five o'clock shadow coming in. I found that I liked I knew enough to know he only grew his facial hair out over the weekend. "Thanks for jerking me off with your goddamn foot at the meeting today. I had to keep my legal pad over the front of my suit pants when I was leaving with Ash and Deacon." He shook his head and took a sip of his beer. A woman looked at us, shock coloring her features, as she glared at us from a nearby table, and I snorted loudly into my drink. I liked this about David. He was fun. His eyes widened, and he choked a laugh into his drink.

"Actually, it must have paid off. My dad wants you to join him and Ash tomorrow morning for golf. 9:15." I pulled my jacket tighter around my shoulders. The breeze off the water was unforgiving.

David looked taken aback. "As an employee he's trying to groom, or as someone who asked out his daughter?"

"I think the latter. I didn't let him know that we've hooked up on almost every available surface in his office, though." I winked at him, smiling over my drink as the woman at the nearby table made a loud noise of disapproval. I should probably be careful. My name was not exactly unknown in Chicago. The second a server said the last name Winchester, it would be all over the tabloids.

David's brown eyes grew darker momentarily and his pupils widened. He smiled slightly, looking at me like he wanted to grab me across the table. "Don't tell your brother, either. Deac is my friend."

"I know, I know." I waved him off. "Your VP club and all that. Actually, did he tell you where he was going tonight?" I resisted the urge to roll my eyes. My brother's conquests were simultaneously something I enjoyed discussing for endless entertainment value but was absolutely disgusted by.

"You don't want to know." He laughed again, taking another sip and reaching across the table to stroke his thumb across the back of my right hand. It stopped short of the diamond wedding band I was wearing on my ring finger. It had been my mother's. Somehow, this was a topic we had never broached. "Oh, I meant to ask you. How do you know Tripp Banks? You kicked off like a fucking rocket when you heard his name and almost stabbed my dick with your damn heel." I distinctly heard the woman beside us inhale sharply, as if in shock by such slanderous words. It distracted David long enough for me to gather what was surely a look of horror on my face. Tripp fucking Banks, finding a way to ruin my life seven years later.

"We uh, we went to Brown together." I shrugged non-committal and drank the rest of my vodka as quickly as I could, my throat burning. I gestured to the bartender with a smile for another round.

"He's my age, though...he would have been finishing up when you were in your second year or so, no?" David asked, his broad hands wrapping around the sweating bottle of beer in front of him.

"He was the president of the fraternity that my sorority did the most work with." It seemed almost like a lie slipping off my tongue, but it was actually true. It was sort of how we knew one another.

"You were in a sorority?" David was laughing now, leaning back in his chair, unbuttoning the top few buttons on his dress shirt. I had it made to match his suit. "I mean, I know you're a Winchester but I just can't picture it for you. You seem more the type to have been protesting unfair animal treatment outside the science labs."

I noticed a knowing glance from the woman beside us when she heard David mention the name 'Winchester.' So much for waiting for the conversation. This would be all over Chicago Business Monthly's salacious gossip columns. Society News, they called it. "Charlie Winchester and David Kennedy: A worthy match?" I turned to look at her, trying to smile gently. I hoped to convey to her in that smile that this man was new and valuable to me. However, she was busy texting. Great. Probably turning in the story to someone she knew. My father would love this.

"Yes, I was in a sorority. No, I am not telling you which one!" I batted at his hand, as it playfully snaked across the table to inspect for any lingering sorority rings. "Are you trying to tell me you weren't in a frat, Princeton?"

"No, no I was." He held a hand to his chest in mock outrage. "But I was a dick back then. For someone so decidedly different and so...good, I'm just surprised." He thanked the server again who brought over an additional round, smiling broadly. This was another thing I liked about David. He never forgot to be kind.

"I'll have you know, I actually joined for the public service and charity work." I tucked a loose piece of brown hair behind my ear. "I have a hard time believing you were ever a dick."

"If that were to be anyone's motives, I believe it was yours, Charles." He winked at me and took another thoughtful sip of his beer. "Seems a strong reaction not to hire Tripp, though, no?" Fuck, how did we get back here again? I steeled myself for some sort of lie. I felt the vodka burning my cheeks. I didn't want memories of Tripp to derail my Friday night with David. I looked forward to having him to myself all week. I enjoyed our playful and friendly banter, and I liked that he never seemed to care who I was.

"Well, I probably overreacted. He was horrible and a douche when I knew him, and I don't want that kind of energy at work. It's why I avoided coming home for so long."

David shrugged, running a hand through his hair. This just accentuated his muscular forearms. Irrational anger at Tripp for somehow derailing my night when he was practically a figment of my imagination at this point spiked through me. "Well I was in a frat, and so was Deacon. Anyway, I guess we can figure it out tomorrow. Where do you want to take him?"

"Have you already talked to him?" I asked begrudgingly, hoping that Tripp might be too busy or perhaps occupied with an Instagram influencer like my brother typically was.

"Yeah, I called him when I stepped out. Asked him if it was true he was looking. He said he was, and I told him we might have something. I asked him to meet us at the Supper Club like Steven suggested tomorrow evening around seven. Told him it would be me and the Winchester twins." David shrugged. Deacon and I weren't actually twins, but for some reason, everyone in the corporate world referred to us as a unit. "He said he was looking forward to seeing Deac again and hadn't run into him since a weekend in Vegas last year, allegedly. And that he thinks he went to Brown the same time as you. Clearly you had quite the impression."

David was laughing, as I seethed inside. Leave it to Tripp Banks to destroy someone's very being and barely remember. "Well, I'm sure between the three of us, we can give it a good sell." I smiled in what was probably closer to a grimace. I was suddenly very tired of this. I wanted nothing more than to not be talking or thinking about Tripp Banks. In fact, I didn't want to be talking at all. "Let's get out of here." Somehow this rooftop had become yet another place Tripp had invaded like some kind of locust. I had a sneaking suspicion there were many more Tripp-like plagues to come.

CHAPTER TWO

David and I relocated to my townhome in Lincoln Park. After leaving Mullen's, I had already received a text from the WH Publicist, Rebecca, saying a story was going to be run in Society News about David and me. I had no desire to be out in public, a sinking feeling accompanying pits of fear and worry that were monopolizing my stomach.

My father was not a fan of my townhome. He much preferred Deacon's living arrangement—a penthouse in a high rise overlooking the river. It had security, and he said he was concerned that I would be robbed as a single woman living alone. But I loved it. It felt like home the second I stepped foot in it. The place was spacious and full of exposed brick and a beautiful rooftop terrace.

I shouldered the glass door that led to the terrace, a bottle of wine in one hand and two stemmed glasses in the other. I had left David out there to turn on the heat lamps that lined the glass railing along the edges of the roof and pull the many wool blankets from a storage bin nestled in the corner. He had spread them out across the ground and was lying on his back surveying the sky. He sat up on his forearms, which emphasized the muscle under his long-sleeve button-up shirt. Neither of us had changed out of our work attire. "I would have helped you." He went to push up to grab the bottle and glasses from me.

"I can grab beverages, David," I rolled my green eyes. Maybe this is why people thought Deacon and I were twins. We had identical forest green eyes. "I might be a Winchester but I'm not useless."

David eyed me curiously, pushing some of his dirty blonde hair off his forehead. "Oh, you're anything but useless, Charles." He reached forward and grabbed my legs, bringing me down on top of him. I came crashing down, knocking the bottle of wine against his head. I shrieked, holding up the glasses.

"These are crystal, DAVID!" I shrieked again, as he grabbed my waist, rolling me backward onto the makeshift bed he had created with the blankets on the terrace.

"Not the crystal!" He cried in mock outrage. "How will you ever afford more, billion dollar baby?" He buried his head in my neck, biting at me playfully. "You knocked me in the fucking head, Charlie!"

I was laughing uncontrollably as I pushed away from him, trying to maintain my grip on the glasses. I crawled forward, tossing them onto the nearby patio sectional, praying I wouldn't hear glass shattering. I was still wielding the bottle of wine, as I pushed myself into an upright position and settled back onto his lap. David resumed his grip on my waist and was looking up at me, his dirty blonde hair falling everywhere and his collar askew.

I struggled to uncork the bottle and ended up grabbing it with my teeth, pulling hard. I looked down at David, who hadn't taken his brown eyes off of me. "Not your billion dollar baby teeth!"

I grinned, taking a swig of the wine before tipping it like I meant to pour it into his mouth. "Would you like some, Mr. Kennedy?"

David looked up at me, his thumbs massaging into my hip. "You're amazing, Charlie Winchester." His eyes were growing darker by the second and his thumbs were moving slow, deliberate circles over my hip bones.

Most people tended not to see this side of me, who I was behind a closed door. I couldn't remember the last time I had shared laughter with someone like this. To be honest, I tended not to get this far in dating in general. It was either all about being a Winchester or men tended to be very intimidated by me. It was easier for Deac.

"Do you really think so?" I waited for his answer, growing quiet. I was keenly aware of the hum of the heat lamps and city noises rising from the street below. I met David's eyes. I had not expected this when I started fooling around with him. I thought we would have fun; we had been friends first, but we had been keeping this secret for months now, and slowly, it evolved into something more. I could feel the energy passing between us as we maintained eye contact, and memories of us rose up in me, wrapping around me and reminding me of all the ways he saw me.

I was shaking hands with him the first time we met, his eyes sparkling already and never leaving mine when he asked me in earnest about my new portfolio. David was sitting beside me courtside at a Bulls game, but he was turned toward me, leaning forward like every word I had to say was of the utmost importance.

I was sitting around the executive's table while my father droned on and on incessantly, and David caught my eye, widening his own in exasperation before pushing a legal pad toward me discreetly, a game of hangman ready, with a question posed for me at the top. What would Deacon bring to a deserted island? The answer was a new tan suit, and nothing was ever more funny to me; so much we both fell into peels of silent laughter and were asked to excuse ourselves by my father until we could act like adults.

I blinked, realizing I still had the bottle of wine tipped precariously over David's face.

"What do you mean do I really think so? Are you kidding me?" He surveyed me, cocking his head to the side, his shirt collar still uneven, brushing his neck. "You spent a year volunteering all over the world, Charlie. You worked at a community health center in Sri Lanka. You take your money and try to do something good with it. You claim you joined a sorority to give back, not to find a husband. You're funny and crass, and you drink Vodka instead of champagne when we go for drinks. You are more than any North Carolina debutante and Princeton princess I have ever met. And you have the audacity to shove your Jimmy Choo up my pants at company meetings."

I squinted my eyes and felt a burning sensation. No one had ever described me like that. I don't think I had ever been anyone but Charlie Winchester to any man I had ever been with. Unsure of what to do with myself, I brought the wine to my lips, as David sat up, sliding me off his lap gently in front of him, his eyes boring into mine and said, "I know who you are, Charlie. And I don't mean that I know your last name."

I pulled back, even more unsure of what to do with that admission. We had never really moved beyond the fun and the physical, despite the shift I felt between us and the way my heart was hammering against my ribcage at his words. "Would you like some wine, Mr. Kennedy?"

David laid back down, his eyes still on me. I could barely discern his pupils from his dark brown irises. "Sure, Miss Winchester." I began deliberately pouring the wine into his mouth, giggling slightly as it splashed all over him and as he gulped, his Adam's apple moved down his throat. I chewed on my lip before broaching the subject. "I think that woman who was sitting beside us at Mullen's called a Society News columnist. She must have heard you call me Charlie Winchester."

David knit his eyebrows together, sitting up suddenly again. He exhaled heavily, grabbing the bottle of wine from me and set it down beside the bed of blankets. "Shit, I'm sorry Charlie. I should have been more careful. I know we hadn't talked about this or what we might be. You haven't had a chance to talk to your dad about this being something serious...I should have talked to him–"

"David, it's okay. I don't mind. This would happen eventually. But I guess...I just want to give you an out. If you don't want that part of me...if you don't want a Winchester." I stopped, continuing to chew my lip and the inside of my cheek. My dark brown hair had come entirely undone from the low bun I was wearing it in. Steeling myself, I continued. "You're either all in or you're out, David. We're either going to give this a try for real or this is the last night. I'm feeling myself...I think I'm falling for you, and I can't keep doing this if you aren't in."

David flipped me over and positioned himself above me, his rough hands running through my hair. "I'm all in, billion dollar baby."

———

David and I stayed on the terrace until it was almost dawn. The bottle of wine, and two more, had emptied. At around four-thirty in the morning, shrieking with laughter, we stumbled back downstairs to my bedroom. David had been there before, of course, but he never stayed over. There were floor-to-ceiling studio windows, and the gray light of dawn had begun to creep in. I had forgotten to make my bed that morning, white sheets tangled in a ball in the center of my California King with pillows tossed all over. For some reason, it seemed endearing to David.

"Charlie, don't you have a maid?" He laughed, kneeling in front of me and planting kisses across my stomach. He grabbed the zipper at the back of my leather pencil skirt and yanked it down to reveal a pair of black lace boy shorts. He groaned, grabbing me under my thighs and picking me up, tossing me on the bed.

"I have a cleaner that comes once a week," I laughed, wrapping my hands around his neck, running my fingers through the curls at the nape of his neck. I leaned up and started biting his trap muscles. "Deac has a maid that comes daily to launder his things."

"I know, billion dollar baby. Where did you come from and why are you so different?" I looked up at him. His eyes were almost black, and his hair was sticking up in all directions. He had shed his shirt somewhere and was standing in front of me in the pants that match the suit I got him. "I used to think it was bad...I guess I still do. That I was so different from everyone else. That's why I left. I never wanted to work at WH...I just wanted to live the way I wanted to."

David hummed against my neck. "Charlie, you are one of a kind."

"Don't rip your pants!" I cried suddenly, leaning forward with tender care to make sure they were carefully unbuttoned and set aside. "The woman who made those was a fourth-generation tailor." I could feel David smile, as he continued to kiss any inch of skin available to him. He laid me all the way back flat on the bed. I arched my back, meeting his mouth with mine, as the remaining clothes between us were shed. I hadn't felt this at home in my own skin for as long as I could remember.

The sun was shining by the time we closed our eyes.

————

I heard David groan imperceptibly, the sunlight was beating mercilessly through the windows. On mornings unlike this one when I was not horrifically hungover, it was one of my favorite ways to wake up.

"My fucking head," David groaned, grabbing me and bringing me closer to him. "What time is it? No wait. Don't tell me."

I opened my eyes the tiniest amount possible, afraid of what I would see on my cell phone beside me. Other than multiple missed calls from Rebecca, I noted that it was seven-forty-five in the morning. "I think you need to get up soon to meet my Dad."

David moaned again. "I didn't bring my golf clothes here. I don't think I have time to go home."

"There is some of Deac's stuff in the closet in the spare room. He keeps some here for whenever he stays. It should fit."

"I cannot show up to golf with your dad and Ash like this. I will reek of booze and of I-just-fucked-your-daughter all night long. What am I going to do?" I watched him roll onto his back, forcing himself up on his elbows before grumbling again, like the world was ending before.

I snorted. He wasn't wrong. I could spot long, deep scratches down his back. "David–" I started, before he cut me off.

"Charlie, I meant every word I said last night. I want to give this a real try. What followed after was just the icing on the cake. You are incredible, and I cannot wait for this round of golf to be over to spend all day in bed with you." He leaned forward to kiss my exposed shoulder.. I heard his phone buzz on the nightstand. I sat up, finally grabbing my phone. Five missed calls from Rebecca and seventeen texts. Jesus.

"What is it?" David asked from behind me. I felt him crawling over the bed to reach me. He tucked his chin into the crook of my shoulder. "Are you having an affair with Rebecca? Why else is WH's publicist texting you non-stop?"

"Very funny!" I pushed his face off with my free hand. "No...Society News is running a story. In exchange for our good faith, or more information, they've given Rebecca an advanced copy before it goes to print tomorrow. She's asked my father and I to review it."

"Fuck, I'm sorry Charlie. I should have been more careful when I said your last name." He snaked his arms around me, bringing me closer to his chest.

"No...no, it's okay. You shouldn't have to worry about those things. The tone of the article is okay from what I can tell, but I think it's better we get ahead of it. They mentioned that we were having a 'lewd conversation' at the table. So it was definitely that woman." I set my phone down and leaned back, closing my eyes slightly.

"I can't believe I'm golfing with your dad and Ash in an hour." He buried his face in my shoulder.

"Can I give them your name?" I craned my neck backward to see him. "They don't name you...it just says that 'Chicago, and maybe America's, most eligible bachelorette is off the table.' You didn't say your name and Mullen's definitely wouldn't release which members were there. I think we can get them to strike some of those notes if we trade them that."

"Yeah, of course Charlie. Whatever you need to do." I closed my eyes as he kissed my neck and nuzzled my hair. This is exactly what I had been trying to tell him last night: what the price of being with me would be.

"I have to call my dad. Stay quiet if you know what's good for you." My dad was under the impression last night was our first date. He did not need to know we had been secretly sleeping together at the office for about four-months' time. I chewed my lip thoughtfully. It was usually Deacon getting into this kind of trouble. I typed in his number and he picked up before the first ring had finished.

"Morning, Dad."

"What part of 'have a nice night with David' did you think meant being overheard speaking lewdly at a public restaurant and which one of you was dumb enough to announce yourself to the entire bar?" He barked sharply. I could vaguely hear birds chirping. He must be outside. He lived on his waterfront property in Lake Forest, a wealthy suburb of Chicago. He often looked down his nose at Deacon and me living in the city.

"Well Mullen's is members only. I would have assumed they had rules about this sort of thing! We were just joking around. We didn't say anything serious." I stood up and looked over at David, who was momentarily lying on his stomach with his head in his hands across the bed.

"Do you know who it was? I will be calling Christopher myself. This is absolutely unacceptable. Winchesters have been members of Mullen's since prohibition." I rolled my eyes. I could clearly picture my father's expression right at this moment. I made my way toward my chest of drawers, pulling out various pairs of lacy underwear. I threw them at David mouthing, "You pick." He groaned audibly into a pillow on the bed after I told him to keep quiet, and I picked up a pillow off the floor, tossing it at him. He wasn't usually this dramatic. These were the sort of theatrics Deacon was prone to, though. "Yeah, okay, Dad, calm down. I have a plan. Other than the 'lewd' comments piece, the article isn't that bad. It's pretty standard stuff about our family and the company. I'm thinking we trade them David's name and ask them to strike that. The name of the man who 'took me off the market' is more important to these people than the tone of the conversation." I made air quotes with my free hand and hit the speaker button before I turned to David, holding the phone out.

"Well that's...wait what did you say?" I heard my father's voice catch. "Did you say 'took' you off the market?" I locked eyes with David, a small smile playing on my lips. I felt more seen and at home than I had since I set foot back in Chicago. I chewed my lip and felt my stomach stir. He was looking at me, his brown eyes barely visible behind his pupils. His dirty blonde hair was disheveled as usual, and he was breathing heavily. He really was perfect: broad shoulders that tapered inward and ridges defined his abdomen. He broke into a wide smile that was slightly crooked. I smiled in return, having difficulty believing I could touch him any time I wanted.

"Yeah. We had fun last night. I really like him, Dad. David is a good man, and I think he has the right skin for this. Don't you?"

"Charlie, I–" he cut off. He actually sounded choked up. I was tempted to roll my eyes. His emotion likely had more to do with David being a suitable match for our family than anything else. "I don't think I could have picked a better match for you. Your brother loves David, I love David, and your mom would have–" he stopped speaking abruptly. Oh. *Oh*.

I immediately looked down and chewed the inside of my cheek. My mother was the one topic we hadn't discussed and one that was practically forbidden by my family.

"Well, it's about time. I was afraid Society News would be

writing up a story about how you were turning into a spinster at the age of twenty-seven when I saw the email from Rebecca." He cleared his throat, any lingering memory or mention of my mother seemed to evaporate. I narrowed my eyes and cocked my head to the side. David raised his eyebrows and mouthed the word 'spinster' back to me.

"Anyway Dad, I can take care of this. Just be glad I didn't get caught with an Instagram model and a bunch of drugs like Deac did when he was twenty-three." I shimmied into the pair of panties David threw back to me.

My dad, in spite of himself, laughed. I found myself smiling. It was a rare sound, and it reminded me of being a child. "No, you had just taken off to work like a peasant God knows where. Anyway, I would like to get a quick row in before I meet David and Ash at the club. Tell David I said thank you for giving up his name for the story. And that I'll see him at the club in about an hour. I assume he doesn't have his clubs at your house, so I'll bring him a spare set of mine."

"What are you talking about? David isn't here." I pressed a hand to my mouth to keep from letting out a laugh. I might be twenty-seven but for some reason this felt like getting caught making out with my prep school boyfriend in the pool house all over again.

"I wasn't born yesterday, Charlie." And with that, he hung up the phone. I bursted out laughing.

———

I was sitting outside, wrapped in a blanket and holding my coffee, as I looked out over my terrace into Lincoln Park. I could see people beginning to move around the streets, heading out to enjoy their everyday lives. I was reading through the Society News' story Rebecca had sent me. I recognized the author on the byline—Jessica Wilkes.

She was often writing about Chicago corporate and high society. I'm pretty sure she was the one who broke the story about Deacon being seen on a yacht with an eighteen-year-old model about two years prior. Our father had loved that one.

The article had the tone I suspected it would; it painted me as a vaguely mysterious figure who didn't often date, although I wondered why that was. Because I was so busy as a woman in the working world, climbing up the corporate ladder now that I had returned to Chicago? There was a picture of me on assignment in Nicaragua the year prior. And the title was exactly as I expected: "Charlie Winchester—Taken at last?" I rolled my eyes. Why did these people care so much about whether or not I was taken? As if my worth was cemented when I had a rock on my finger.

After a long argument with Rebecca, she had finally given me permission to call Jessica directly. Strictly speaking, I wasn't allowed to talk to the press directly, but I had a sneaking suspicion Rebecca wouldn't have minded portraying me as some vapid little rich girl who just wanted to be married. Society has been wanting to get something on me since I came back from Sri Lanka and started working at WH. I took another sip of my coffee, wishing desperately the hangover wine headache would disappear before dialing Jessica's number. She answered immediately. "This is Jessica Wilkes."

"Jessica," I began. "it's Charlie Winchester." There was a belated silence on her end.

"To what do I owe this pleasure?" She asked, and I rolled my eyes.

"I've read the story, Jessica. My publicist passed it on to me and my father. I don't get left out of decisions at WH. That's not how my father works." A partial lie. My father hated cleaning up our messes. More silence. I imagined she had been hoping to deal solely with Rebecca. But that's not how Steven Winchester worked, either. He didn't delegate his dirty work. "It's really not a bad article. I only have one problem. I need you to strike the line about 'lewd conversation.'"

"And why would I do that?" I heard shuffling. She was probably grabbing a notepad.

"Because I'm trying to get a foundation off the ground, Jessica. I don't need to tell you what that looks like when I'm trying to get people to donate their money to charities and all they have in their heads is that I have 'lewd conversations' on rooftops. Come on. You're a woman in this world. You know how this works."

She paused, her next words bitter. "But my dad doesn't own the company I work for, Charlie."

I pursed my lips. "No. I suppose it's not quite the same. But I don't also have to remind you that whoever broke that to you was eavesdropping? Doesn't that somehow come up against journalistic integrity?"

"Not in the state of Illinois," she clarified.

I held up my hand, like she was in front of me. "Honestly I don't care. I need you to strike it. But not for nothing. I'll trade you something." I took another swig of my coffee, closing my eyes against the morning sunlight.

Silence.

"I'll give you his name. I'll even send you a photo of us together. But you need to tell me on the record that you'll strike that." There was a pregnant pause. I could tell she was weighing her options. The story of me as someone who engaged in 'lewd' behavior with random men was likely much more interesting than breaking that I was 'taken at last,' to use her words. But that would be a bigger story and I was giving her an exclusive.

"I'll let you quote me," I stated, offering her the card I had been holding in my back pocket.

"Done. On the record, I'll strike it. Now give me his name and make something up about how blissful you are. Tell me when you knew." Jessica was like a rabid dog but I found myself respecting her for it.

"His name is David Kennedy. He's VP of Acquisitions at Winchester Holdings. He's currently golfing with my father and Ash Reynolds at the Widmore." We're just one big happy family, I thought, and I laid my head back against the pillows on my outdoor couch hoping to paint a picture for her. I felt something poke into my back. I reached behind me to pull out one of the Crystal wine glasses from last night. I smiled widely.

"And give me a quote...something the young girls and housewives will love. When did you know he was different? When did you know you would date him exclusively?" I paused. When did I know? When had I realized I had fallen for him? David and I were friends for months before it escalated late one night over a bottle of my father's liquor at the office. It was torrid, fun and sneaky. He never even stayed the night and I had never seen his apartment. Now, there was nothing that thrilled me more than his laugh or his smile. Now, he felt like a possibility. Now, he felt like *home*.

The words tumbled from my mouth before I could stop them, a smile stretching across my face as I told Jessica how I had been away and returned with a tailored suit for him. Sneaking into his office like a child who had candy they weren't supposed to have, I handed him the garment bag with a shy smile. I remembered the exact way his eyes lit up when he realized I brought him a gift, how his hand shook slightly when he unzipped the suit bag, and the laughter that fell from us both when he stripped in his office in broad daylight to change suits.

Jessica emailed Rebecca and I back shortly before noon with an updated copy of the story that would go out the following day. She had stuck to her word and struck the line about our conversations at Mullen's. She included the photo I shared with her of David and me from the recent WH Christmas party. We had just started seeing one another, and in retrospect, I could see how charged the photo might look under a different context.

My head was still pounding and I had relocated to my living room. I was lying backward on my couch with some senseless Netflix show blaring in the background. I was tempted to call Hydra-V. My brother was a frequent client of theirs. It was one of those hangover IV companies that were popular in Vegas. They would do house calls for a cost around the downtown core of Chicago. I hadn't heard from David—or my father—but I assumed they must be on the back nine now. Lying down alone with my head pounding more than it had in months, I remembered the meeting with Tripp Banks. In about five hours, I needed to start getting ready to see him, my brother and David at the Supper Club.

It was another private club down by the waterfront and was my father's favorite meeting spot. He often took prospective clients and investors there. It had an old-school Chicago feel and kept many prohibition area elements that had been built into the building, like hidden doors. I saw Tripp there once before. I had ducked down one of the hallways hidden behind a door for an inordinate amount of time until I was certain he was gone. I was never even sure how he ended up in Chicago. His family was from the east coast. I didn't think there was anyone I hated more in the world than Tripp. Hearing his name made me feel like I was twenty again and brought back some of the worst moments of my life. Things I had never shared with anyone.

The fact that he acted like he didn't even remember me caused bile to rise in my throat.

My phone rang and I fumbled my hand across the soft leather until I reached it, grunting out loud in a way that would have made my father shudder. I opened one eye to see Deacon's name and a photo of the two of us at boarding school popping up in the background. I skated my fingers across the screen to hit the speaker button.

"What?" I growled, keeping my eyes closed. It hurt to keep them open.

"Jesus, you sound awful." Deacon was clearly out in public, as I could hear voices mumbling behind him. "What's happened to you?"

"Have you not talked to Dad?" I assumed that my father would have confronted Deacon immediately after the meeting yesterday, assuming he would have known about David and me.

"No, but I called David. What's he doing at Widmore with Dad and Ash?" He paused. "Yeah. A little shorter in the leg."

"Are you at the fucking tailor Deacon?" I hissed. I would have rolled my eyes if it wouldn't have taken more effort.

"Yeah, we're meeting with a prospective new VP. Of course I'm getting a new suit. What do you think I am, some kind of animal?" Deacon bought a new suit with custom changes at least once a month. He was nothing if not predictable.

"Fucking Tripp." I muttered, swinging my legs forward off the back of the couch. A wave of nausea swept through my stomach.

"What is your problem with Tripp? Do you even know him? And why is David golfing with Dad and Ash?" Deacon was insistent. I could picture him, standing in his underwear in the backroom at the tailor. His chocolate hair mussed to perfection, skin bronzed all year long from the tanning bed he had in his apartment.

"Uh. Nothing. We went to Brown together. Sorority...fraternity stuff. He was an arrogant asshole back then." I pushed myself forward off the couch. Another wave of nausea, accompanied by the feeling of someone hammering a nail behind both of my eyeballs swept over me. "David is golfing with Dad, because Dad invited him."

"Did your date go well then?" His voice sounded strangled. Deacon was many things, including being incredibly protective of me and often had great distaste for any man in my life. "You know if he was going to ask you, I would have preferred he ask me first."

"You're not my keeper, Deacon." I managed to successfully roll my eyes this time, as I started shuffling toward the kitchen.

"Yeah but he's my friend, and when you inevitably don't want to go further with him like you do with every other guy, it's going to be weird for me and weird in the office. Don't shit where you eat." He was terse. I heard him muttering about sleeve lengths.

"Coming from you? You have slept with every summer intern over the age of eighteen since you were in college."

"Yeah, and they don't stay. So, are you going to tell me or not? Did he get the royal CW treatment where you had one date, maybe even let him into bed and then kicked him to the curb?"

"No, Deacon." I resented my dating history being referred to as the 'CW Treatment.' "I've actually been seeing David since before Christmas."

"What?!" He bellowed. "You have been fucking one of my best friends since Christmas and never told me? What is he just a fling to you? A good lay?"

"Thank you for that. You make it sound so romantic. Aren't you at the tailor?" I cringed. Leave it to Deacon to describe it that way.

"It's just me and Josie back here. She won't say anything." I could picture Deacon flirting with the middle-aged seamstress, skating through life as he typically did.

"No. That's not what it is. I mean I will have you know, David is actually phenomenal in bed. Nowhere near as selfish as I am sure you are." I paused while Deacon began to interrupt. "We're going to try this. For real. I...I really like him, Deac. And I think he really likes me. And knows me. Who I actually am. Not who people want me to be."

There was a pause. Once, after a failed date with a family friend, who had made it incredibly clear they were only interested in dating a Winchester, I had ended up spectacularly drunk, crying and puking all over Deacon's penthouse. I sobbed to him, lied in his lap while he stroked my hair about how it felt to be the only female Winchester left feeling like a pawn in the games played by our father and what it felt like when someone preferred the idea of who they wanted you to be versus who you actually are. He knew in some ways what I meant. Plenty of women used him for his name—but the power dynamics were different. He knew there were things about my position in our family and our future that he would never understand. For years, Deacon was the only thing that kept our father from forcibly dragging me home.

"David is a good man, Charlie. And you're the most amazing woman on the planet. I'm not surprised he can see that. It's everyone else who is blind, you know." His voice was uncharacteristically soft. "I would give you the typical speech about what I would do to him if he hurt you...but to be honest, I'm more worried about you being the one to hurt him."

Months later, I would finally understand what Deacon saw in me that I couldn't at the time.

CHAPTER THREE

I caved around two in the afternoon and called Hydra-V. I was sitting on my couch in the living room with the AC blasting, wrapped in yet another wool blanket. I could feel my eyes continuously closing, as the nurse checked on my IV.

"How much longer?" I mumbled. I had reached the point in my hangover, and in my dread for this meeting with Tripp, that I wanted to curl up under a blanket and disappear. There was a mountain of work waiting for me to do before Monday, and my father likely expected some sort of sales pitch for this evening. I'm sure the fact that I hadn't prepared a PowerPoint would disappoint him.

"You've got about twenty minutes left. Seems like this is a rough one," she laughed. She was a pretty woman. She had shoulder-length blonde hair and crystal blue eyes. "What did you in?"

"Three bottles of wine and some stiff vodka sodas." I had given her a fake last name in an attempt to avoid another issue like the Society News debacle that had usurped half my day, though I did have it on good authority from Deacon that they were incredibly discreet. My father usually requested for Deacon and I to ask most services like this to sign an NDA, but unlike him, neither of us kept a handy stack of non-disclosure agreements kicking around our homes.

The nurse laughed and ran a hand through her hair. "Celebrating something? Or maybe drinking to forget?"

I smiled slightly, the memory of David biting at my neck on the terrace and pouring the wine into his mouth coming back to me. "Definitely celebrating."

Silence fell and I closed my eyes, sinking further into my blanket cocoon. I was developing a sick feeling in my stomach that I did not think had anything to do with the hangover. I could feel the dull thump of my headache fading as the IV fluids made their way through my veins. I knew it was because I was now at about four hours until our meeting with Tripp. I did not relish seeing him at all, let alone in the presence of Deacon or David. I had started to hope what David said was true: maybe he really didn't remember me. He was a senior at Brown, and maybe I was truly inconsequential.

I must have fallen asleep, because I felt a gentle shake on my shoulder. It was the nurse. "You're all done. Just a little pinch while I take the IV out."

I nodded, keeping my eyes closed. "Thank you," I mumbled as I could hear her packing up. "Sorry...I'm so rude. I didn't ask your name?"

She smiled at me as I opened my eyes, which I could only assume were devastatingly blood shot. "Melissa. It was nice to meet you. We're all done. Payment will be charged to your credit card on file. I hope you're feeling better soon."

I stood, remaining wrapped in my comfy blanket and shuffled behind her so I could lock the front door. If my dad found out I had allowed my door to remain unlocked while I slept a mere five feet away on the couch, he would have killed me. I shuffled back to the couch and flipped sideways, tugging the blanket closer around me. Two hours to Tripp.

I woke up to David bent over in laughter in the doorway to the living room. He was still wearing Deacon's golf clothes I lent him that morning. His hair was perfectly windswept, and he was holding a suit bag over his arm.

I moaned, pushing myself upward. I noted, with delight, that my hangover had subsided entirely. It had just been replaced with more dread in the pit of my stomach. "What's so funny?"

"The beautiful Charlie Winchester, lying sprawled out, hungover on what is probably a priceless antique leather couch with a thrift store blanket and a receipt from Hydra-V on her coffee table. Do not tell me you called Hydra-V..." He was laughing so hard he was crying.

"I know. I'm pathetic. I spent all morning dealing with Jessica Wilkes and Society News, and I forgot to do anything that would cure my hangover. How was golf with my dad? How was Ash?" I sat up, feeling some of the tension leave my body when I looked up at David. His skin was glowing from being outside all day and the collar of his Ben Sherman golf pullover was slightly ruffled.

He had stopped laughing the second we made eye contact. I noticed his pupils expanding again and his eyes growing dark. I had briefly wondered what it was about David that made me so drawn to him. Enough to stick with it for four months. Deac was right about one thing, I usually gave up pretty early. I looked at him again, watching as the flecks of amber and honey in his eyes danced in the sunlight that was streaming through the window. There was nothing to wonder about. If I squinted, I could vaguely see a shape of myself huddled with the blanket on the couch reflected back in them, and I thought I liked what I saw. "They put me through the ringer but we had a lot of fun. They rubbed me mercilessly for the executive meeting incident but your dad couldn't stop smiling. It felt good. They introduced me to a lot of the other members they know."

I patted the buttery leather beside me. I didn't want there to be any space between us any longer. "Did he ask you back?" David closed the space between us in no time and pulled me onto his lap.

"They actually recommended me for a membership. He told everyone who would listen that we were together." I had a hard time believing my father would brag about my new relationship for any purpose other than one that suited him.

"Huh, are you not a member already?" That was odd. Most VPs were or their families were, but David's family was from North Carolina. His father owned a law practice. I shrugged the blanket off my shoulders, revealing the Calvin Klein bralette I had been in all day. David's breath hitched.

"Never had a reason. I usually go home to play golf. No offense but Widmore is nothing in comparison to the courses at home." He had placed his hands on my waist, his thumbs rubbing small circles into my hips.

I snorted. "None taken. I have never actually set foot on the course there. I've only been to the club for weddings. I'm glad you had fun, Mr. Kennedy."

David exhaled a deep breath. I had taken to calling him Mr. Kennedy at work after we started sleeping together and he had drunkenly told me it drove him nuts. "When do you have to start getting ready? It's only three-thirty."

A small smile broke out across my face. I was exceptionally glad that at that moment I hadn't overslept.

———

I was tracing patterns over David's broad chest with my nail. We hadn't even relocated to my bedroom. We were lying on the high-pile rug in my living room. I pushed myself up, noticing that he was looking at the prints that decorated the hallway. They were all from my time in Sri Lanka or volunteering, as I avoided Winchester Holdings.

"Where's your favorite place you've been, Charlie?" He had his arm wrapped around me and was drawing circles against my shoulder blade.

I chewed the inside of my lip. "Does right here count?" I buried my face into his neck.

"I'm serious...you're always gone from the office, out somewhere doing something good. Where's your favorite place?"

I paused. David was right. I was traveling internationally and quite frequently 'roughing it' as my dad or Deacon put it. I had seen some of the most untouched and most beautiful places on the planet. But none of them were my 'favorite.' "Actually...none of those. Nowhere I went after grad school and nowhere I've been with work. My favorite place is actually Cape Cod."

"Cape Cod?" I felt him pull back slightly and push up to look at me. I flipped over so I was lying my chin on top of his chest, meeting his eyes.

"Yeah. We have a house there. We haven't been in years but...it was my mom's favorite place. It's...it's actually where she died." I kept my eyes on David but I could feel my vision cloud over. I didn't speak about my mother very often.

"I'm so sorry, Charlie. She was beautiful. Your dad still has that photo of her in his office. You look like her." He tightened his grip around me. "You and Deac don't talk about her."

"No. No, I guess we don't. It was seven years ago." I felt the tears begin to spill over my eyes. David moved his hand to cup my face and was stroking my cheek with his thumb. "She died when I was twenty and Deac was twenty-two. I was halfway through Brown, and he was finishing up at Yale."

David didn't press me any further. But I felt him gently planting kisses across the top of my head. "I don't want to talk about her anymore." I said in a small voice, as he tightened his grip around me, uncomfortable with the offering he had laid before me. I couldn't remember the last time anyone spoke to me about my mother.. I wasn't even sure where I would begin.

————

I was shrieking, running through the halls of my townhouse in a mint green matching Petit Macrame La Perla lingerie set as David chased me, fully dressed in a navy Armani suit. The built-in Bose sound system in my ceiling was playing music from my phone.

"David! Stop, I need to put my dress on, or we are going to be late!" I wheeled around the corner running into my bedroom, crawling over the mess of sheets on my bed to place myself on the other side.

David stopped himself in the doorway, his hands bracing on either side. His suit jacket was undone and had a plaid dress shirt underneath, top three buttons open. It was tucked into the matching slim fit pants. His hair was still messy from the wind at Widmore. "We have an hour until we need to be there."

"You're going to mess up my hair and my makeup!" I grabbed the duvet off the bed and wrapped it around myself.

David narrowed his eyes and laughed. "Billion dollar baby who doesn't mind sleeping on the dirt of the Serengeti but can't mess up her makeup or her hair?"

"We aren't going to Applebees! This is the Supper Club." I tightened the duvet around my neck.

David leaned forward, his hands still gripping the door frame. "That duvet doesn't help you. I've already seen what's under it. I know what's going to be under that dress all night. Am I supposed to sit at dinner with your brother with a raging hard on?"

"You've been doing it at meetings for months, you're going to be fine!" I began to take tentative steps toward the closet, where my dress was hanging. It was a strapless black bodycon dress that went just below my knees. I planned on wearing it under my favorite leather jacket, despite the fact that it was frigid outside.

David checked his watch. It was a Vintage Rolex Submariner that had been his grandfather's watch. It was his most cherished possession, as David really loved his grandfather. "The town car is coming in forty-five minutes. What did you suggest we do with the other forty-two once you've slid into that dress?"

I slowly started to inch the duvet down either side of my shoulders. I noticed David's dark eyes on me. "I was going to suggest we have a drink. I bought you beer. You know they only serve overly expensive bottles of wine and top shelf liquor at the Supper Club. Why don't you go downstairs and have one while you wait for me? You clearly can't be trusted to be up here." David grinned, and I dropped the duvet and met his eyes before turning to the closet.

I actually needed a moment alone. Being near David distracted me enough to forget about the knot that had been twisting tighter in my stomach since this afternoon. I stood in the mirror of my bathroom. My dress was hung off the back of the door, and I was ready to slide into it at any moment. I leaned forward, bracing myself against the granite countertop. I breathed in and out, repeating to myself in my head that Tripp didn't remember. He didn't remember me. I was inconsequential. I could go back to pretending. I would be with David and Deacon. I looked up.

I had tied my hair back in a tight, low ponytail. It set off my cheekbones that I contoured extensively. My lips were colored with a light pink gloss, and I dusted highlighter across my nose and forehead. I met my own green eyes in the mirror. I wasn't twenty years old anymore. Tripp Banks was just a person. I was a director at a multi-billion dollar holding company. I worked with community organizations across the world. I summited Kilimanjaro. I led a clean-up of Everest base camp. I swam with Great White sharks in Guadeloupe on a research trip. *I was not twenty years old anymore.*

I came down the stairs, walking to the living room. David was leaning back on the leather couch, drinking a beer in one hand and furiously answering emails with the other. He turned when I stepped off the last stair. I had shimmied into the dress and was holding a pair of strappy Jimmy Choo heels I had for years in one hand. I smiled slightly at him—the knot in my stomach loosening as he met my eyes.

He dropped his phone mid-email. This was also a rarity in our world, or at least in mine. "Jesus Charlie," he exhaled sharply. "You look incredible." He stood up to grab my jacket from the closet in the hallway and brought it over to me. David stood behind me holding out one hand to grab the shoes from me and the other to guide the jacket over my arms and onto my shoulders. He bent over to set the shoes down, his hands tracing the nape of my neck, twirling my ponytail around his fingers.

"Do I really get to touch you?"

"If you'll still have me, Mr. Kennedy." I turned to face him, tilting my chin upward. His hand was still tangled in my hair. "I know you only signed up for salacious office sex with the boss' daughter."

David smiled, reaching his other hand down around my neck. "You are much more than the boss' daughter, Charlie."

———————

The ride from my townhouse to the Supper Club took about twenty minutes. I had been aggressively jiggling my heeled foot the entire time, to the point David had asked me what was wrong and I had pretended I was cold.

David held the door open for me, as I smoothed down the front of my dress and stepped out onto the raised sidewalk. I stood under the awning as he walked around to the driver's side to tip. I was aggressively rubbing my arms up and down the sleeves of my jacket. At least I looked cold. I felt David's hand on the small of my back, and I relaxed slightly as we walked up to the doorman together.

"Miss Winchester, Mr. Kennedy. Lovely to see you this evening." Tim was at the door this evening. He had been a doorman at the Supper Club for as long as I could remember. I had watched him age alongside my father, and his warm smile and dark eyes were surrounded by lines of age.

"Hi Tim," I smiled. "How many times do I have to tell you it's Charlie?"

"You'll always be Miss Winchester to me." He smiled graciously and held open the door. I noticed David reached out to shake his hand and ask him how he was.

I turned and smiled at David, his hand had returned to the small of my back. There was a younger girl at the desk who I didn't recognize, but I noticed a blush creeping up her face as she studied David. The manager of the Supper Club stepped out from behind a swinging door and looked up, his grin broadening when he saw us.

"Miss Winchester, Mr. Kennedy! You're meeting your brother and Mr. Banks, correct?" He subconsciously adjusted his tie clip.

"Hi, William," David reached his free hand out to shake his, vigorously. "Yes, we're here to meet Deacon and Tripp." I leaned back into David, feeling his broad chest behind me, attempting to ground myself before I stepped into the proverbial lion's den.

"They're in one of the private rooms. I assume you're here on business?" William gestured for us to follow, as we wove in and out of the tables in the dimly lit main hall. I was determinedly staring at the polished hardwood floor, putting one foot in front of the other. *I was not twenty anymore.*

"Yes, I think we would appreciate it if you didn't mention to anyone we were here if someone we know comes in." David stopped with William on the side of an open doorway. The private rooms of the Supper Club weren't actually closed off but were down short stone hallways. I could vaguely remember the owner telling my father that at one time, they had all been hidden behind secret doors during the height of prohibition. David clapped William on the back, who gestured his hands forward, indicating we should go down the hallway. I could vaguely hear two voices down the hall. One belonged to one of my favorite people in the entire world, and the other I hadn't heard in seven years.

CHAPTER FOUR

We turned the corner, and I saw Deacon immediately. I grimaced, immediately noticing his new tan suit. He looked like a dick. Directly across from Deacon was a head of messy black hair. If Tripp was the same person he had been, I suspected there were hours spent in front of the mirror making it look just messy enough. Tripp turned in his seat, the back of his gray suit jacket buckling slightly as he went to stand up. I blinked as he stood. Looking at Tripp, being near him, felt sort of like looking back in time. Though he was older, and age had changed him—with lines around his eyes and his shoulders broader—it was like a glimpse into my past, like I was looking at who I used to be. Who I was before my mom died.

"DK!" He smiled widely. Revealing his perfect row of white teeth. Probably ready to sink into and tear the heart out of another young girl. I had forgotten how shockingly blue his eyes are. He has a square jaw that looked like it could use a good punch. He leaned forward, grabbing David's hand and hugging him roughly. "How long has it been?"

I was frozen in place at the interaction.

David smiled brightly in return. I schooled my expression to keep the sour look off my face, thinking about the fact that David and Tripp were in business school together just a short few months after the last time I had seen him. He wrung Tripp's hand. "I think since Kyle's bachelor party in Amsterdam, last fall."

Ew. An Amsterdam bachelor party and Tripp Banks. Sounds like a perfect combination. Tripp turned to me, grinning broadly. Our eyes locked and I immediately felt my blood begin to boil. Seven years later and he was still under my skin.

"Chuckles!" He reached forward to grab me into a quick hug, kissing my cheek. I wiped my hand across it quickly, inspecting my palm for residue. "I haven't seen you since senior year at Brown."

"Chuckles?" David asked, cocking his head as he pulled out my chair. "I thought you said you didn't remember Charlie from school?"

I felt my teeth beginning to grind. This was fucking typical Tripp, always needling or poking at a pain point. "Yes, Tripp. Why don't you tell them why everyone in your sweet frat called me Chuckles?" I said, sliding into my chair, making a point to let my hand linger on David's forearm as he sat beside me.

Deacon narrowed his eyes and knit his eyebrows. "Wait a second...didn't they all call you Chuckles because–"

My cheeks flushed with embarrassment. This was not a good story, and it had clearly been a rhetorical question. Leave it to my brother to pick up on all social cues but mine. I immediately held up a hand to silence him. "Deacon. This is a work dinner."

Deacon held both his hands up in response, leaning backward in his chair. "Sorry sis."

One of the servers entered the room. "Would you all like something to drink?"

David looked at me expectantly, running a hand through his already disheveled hair. Of course he was expecting me to order first.

I turned my head, grateful to have a reason to look anywhere but Tripp. I could still taste bile in my throat. My veins felt like they were on fire. "Just a Vodka Soda for me, thank you." The server nodded, hands still folded behind his back. They were expected to remember everything at the Supper Club.

"David can share with us." Deacon reached forward and began to pour a third glass of scotch from the bottle of Johnnie Walker sitting in the middle of the table.

"Yes, that's great. Thank you," David placed his free hand on my knee and slowly began to draw circles with his thumb.

"No wine for you?" Deacon raised his eyes at me. "We almost ordered you a bottle for the table."

The mention of wine almost brought my hangover screaming back. "No. I have had enough wine this weekend to last me a lifetime."

Tripp leaned back in his chair, unbuttoning his suit jacket. His blue eyes surveyed me with vague disinterest. "Late night?"

I rolled my shoulders back. I am not twenty anymore. "David and I drank a bit too much last night, but that's besides the point."

David snorted into his scotch. "Charlie and I went through three bottles last night. I was not feeling my best when I met your dad and Ash at Widmore this morning."

Deacon laughed and swirled his scotch. "I'm sure Dad and Ash loved that. Spent the night with his daughter and showed up reeking of booze to his tee time. Classic."

"Actually, the best part was when I came home, Deac. You will never guess what Charlie did this afternoon." David turned to me grinning playfully.

"Oh, fuck off David–" I began, rolling my eyes and reaching out to pinch his arm playfully, but Deacon cut me off.

"Oh, this is my favorite game. What was Charlie doing?" He leaned forward pushing the sleeves of his suit jacket backward, a gleeful expression painted across his face.

"She had to call Hydra-V." David almost choked on his scotch when Deacon burst out laughing. Even Tripp looked vaguely amused, the story earning a smile that didn't quite meet his eyes. I snatched my drink and shook my head at my brother.

"Oh, come on. Charlie the next time I do that, you absolutely can't say anything to me." Deacon continued to laugh, leaning back and swirling his scotch. He looked eerily like our father.

"How long have you two been together then?" Tripp leaned forward as if he was interested. I noticed a five-o-clock shadow invading his jaw. He looked like a movie villain.

David smiled easily, looking over at me and winking. "Not long enough. But she's not an easy catch. It took me a few months."

"Well I wouldn't imagine it was before Kyle's bachelor party? At least I hope not." Tripp glanced at me knowingly, a small smirk playing on his lips. "I seem to remember you breaking the bed with some blonde you brought home from the bar."

I felt David clench my knee after Tripp's comment, as Deacon coughed loudly. "Jesus Tripp!"

I leaned forward on the table, making direct eye contact with Tripp, as I ran my hand along David's forearm. I wanted to unsettle him, the way he always unsettled me. "That doesn't surprise me at all."

———

I was on my third drink and switched to an Espresso Martini after dinner had finished. Our plates had been collected, and Deacon and David did the majority of the talking through dinner to overview what we were doing at WH at the moment and how all the subsidiaries did last quarter. I was leaning back in my chair, one hand toying with the gold hoop in my ear lobe and the other scratching the nape of David's neck, twirling chunks of his hair between my fingers. It was unprofessional, but I didn't care. Touching him was the only thing keeping me grounded and preventing me from reaching across the table to scratch Tripp's eyes out.

David was finishing his overview of a recent acquisition. He and Tripp would be working side by side. Tripp suddenly turned his attention to me. It reminded me of a hunting dog sniffing out its prey.

"And what about you, Chuckles? Still trying to save the world one turtle at a time?" He drained the last of his scotch and began tapping his finger against the rim of the now empty glass. I narrowed my eyes. I had spent one spring break at a turtle rescue in Costa Rica, much to my father's chagrin. I felt David clench his hand against my knee again, and I noticed Deacon cock his back slightly as if he was surprised by Tripp. He went to open his mouth.

I am not twenty anymore. I steeled myself. "Actually," I started coolly, pausing to sip my drink, "I've started my own branch within Winchester Holdings. I'm working to establish a charitable funding arm. So, if you call that saving turtles, then sure. Still saving the world one turtle at a time."

"Only a director?" He cocked his head to the side, a feral grin taking up residence on his face, as he helped himself to more scotch.

"No family member starts out at the top. That's something our dad prefers. I only came to start at WH about a year ago. David and Deacon have both been there since finishing business school. The only reason I am at this dinner is because my father thought you might get a sense of what the company is like for people around your age." I shrugged. Leave it to Tripp to point out that I was technically a lesser title. I wasn't going to even get into the fact that my father had been clear it was sink or swim with the foundation.

David cleared his throat. "I would actually argue that Charlie has more responsibility and that Steven trusts her more. She reports directly to him and oversees her own fund and department to support the foundation. She oversees all of the groups that receive grant funding."

"Well I'm not surprised he trusts her more than Deac over here," Tripp split into a wide grin, switching his attention back to Deacon and David. I felt my face searing from when he had been making eye contact with me.

"Why don't you tell us why you're looking Tripp?" Deacon poured more scotch into both his and David's glasses.

Tripp narrowed his eyes slightly, likely weighing his next words carefully. He was young and wanted to switch careers. "Honestly, I'm looking for more growth and responsibility. Being at the firm has been great. Investing has been a challenge, and I have had the absolute time of my life, but it's kind of stale to be honest. There's nowhere for me to go. I'm a senior broker. None of the VPs are going anywhere, they're all late forties. And you know that crowd. I'm not challenged anymore. I could make a trade in my sleep."

Tripp shrugged. Of course he was leaving because he considered his talents to be far too advanced. I resisted the urge to roll my eyes. David resumed tracing circles more urgently across my knee. I could tell by the way he was shifting in his seat that he was ready to leave.

"So are you interested?" Deacon capped the empty bottle of scotch and ran a hand through his chocolate hair. It was usually gelled to perfection but a few wisps were falling across his face. I personally thought he looked better that way.

"I'd like to continue this conversation. Let's meet again and we can talk about what the role would look like." Tripp raised his ice blue eyes and met mine from across the table. "But I would definitely say

I'm interested." A chill that had nothing to do with the temperature ran down my spine.

———

I was teetering on my heels on the curb outside the club, pulling my leather jacket tightly around me. Deacon, David and Tripp were inside at the front desk sorting the payment out. Tripp couldn't have WH pay for the dinner while he was still at his firm. It was against his contract. We all had respective family or individual accounts, but Deacon and David had made a big show about Tripp not having to pay for his dinner and were inside sorting it out. Any gathering was usually put on one membership, but it didn't seem likely that they would object.

I huffed. The knot in my stomach was loosening and tightening, rolling over constantly in my stomach. It was clear that, unfortunately, Tripp was absolutely the right person for the job. My stomach turned at the thought. But this was business. My father would not care about ancient history.

Tripp was tenacious in all the ways that Carter hadn't been and would likely be able to take the sales division in an entirely different direction. I heard the door open and laughter spill out. Deacon was without a doubt telling a charming story about some young woman he was off to see. David met my eyes and winked at me, and I felt my stomach drop in an entirely different way. I bit my lip and smiled at him, as he closed the distance between us. He slipped his hand under my jacket onto my lower back and planted a kiss on the top of my head.

"Can you not maul my sister until you're in the town car, Jesus." Deacon had taken his phone out and was typing furiously, either answering an email or updating a date about where he was going. There were three town cars lined up against the curb.

Tripp walked up behind Deacon, his hands shoved into his gray suit pants. "I'll expect to hear from your dad on Monday then?"

"Yeah, man. Charlie and I are having breakfast with him tomorrow out in Lake Forest, so he might call you before. I'll send you a text and let you know." I had forgotten about that. "Anyway Charlie, say thank you to Tripp."

I narrowed my eyebrows in confusion. "What are you talking about, Deacon?"

He looked up at me, mischief pulling at his green eyes. "Oh, Tripp paid for your dinner personally when we were sorting everything out. David paid for Tripp's, and I put mine and David's on the WH account."

I felt a sour taste rising in my mouth, and I knew I was visibly grimacing.

"Just for old time's sake, eh Chuckles?" He raised his eyebrows and reached over and clapped David on the back before raising two fingers in a salute and opening the door to one of the town cars, disappearing into the backseat. David's eyes narrowed, almost imperceptibly before his usual grin slid back into place.

I turned immediately to Deacon in hopes of diffusing the situation. "What are you doing tonight? Do you want to come over for a drink?"

Deacon usually spent one or two nights a week at my place. I was eager for a sense of normalcy in my life after spending so many hours in the company of Tripp.

Deacon looked up from his phone, looking backward between David and me, a shit-eating grin on his face. "Oh no, no no. I'll let you two lovebirds be alone. Besides, I have to work tonight. Ash just emailed me some financials to review. I need to approve them before they go to accounting. But I'll see you at Dad's tomorrow morning? You coming DK?"

David reached out to clap Deacon on the back. "No, I actually have to go into the office tomorrow. Your dad asked for some updated figures on a few things by Monday."

I stepped forward and hugged Deacon, uncharacteristically hard. He was the only thing from the Tripp era of my life I looked back on with any fondness. A small smile pulled at my lips, as I remembered sitting at our mother's funeral with him, sneaking a flask of scotch in the bathroom at the visitation.

He stiffened slightly in my grip. He wasn't used to affection from me. He wrapped his arms around me and planted a kiss on my temple. "You're the best, Charlie, remember that." He whispered in my ear before ducking into his own town car.

The second David closed the door to the car, he said thank you to the driver but indicated we would like some privacy and raised the partition.

I shrunk slightly in my seat, feeling infantile all of a sudden.

"Are you going to tell me what that was about Charlie?" David turned to face me, speaking softly and calmly.

His hand remained on my knee. I looked down and exhaled. "I told you. That's just Tripp. He was an asshole back then and he's clearly an asshole now."

He cocked his head to the side, not quite buying it. Which was smart, because I wasn't telling the entire truth. "I know Tripp, he's a bit of a dick, you're not wrong. But that was an entirely different level."

"Well, have you ever seen how he treats women?" I deadpanned. "He destroyed half the girls in my sorority." *Including me.*

David paused. "Actually, I've never known him to be in a relationship."

"No, because he's a misogynist pig." I turned to face David, leaning one arm up over the headrest of the seat. "You men in high society and these positions of power, you don't see what women do. You don't even know the half of it, David."

He smiled sadly. "I guess you're right. Do you want me to tell Steven I don't think he's a good fit?"

My heart swelled. The truthful answer was yes. But this was business. "No, because unfortunately he is a good fit. I think he can take sales further than Carter ever did. This is business, David. My father doesn't care that Tripp was a dick to me in college. But I appreciate the offer. I don't need you to take care of me. I can handle men like Tripp."

David laughed, running a hand through his hair. "You're no one's fool, Charlie. I know that much about you. I also want to apologize for his comment about Amsterdam. It was crass."

I rolled my eyes. "You don't owe me an apology for Tripp's behavior. That was probably the least surprising thing he said all night."

David exhaled, unbuttoning his suit jacket. "No, but I also wouldn't want to hear about a one-night-stand of yours at dinner."

"Wait, you weren't a virgin when we met?" I clapped my hand to my chest and dropped my mouth in mock outrage. "Just promise me I'm the best you've ever had."

He grinned and ran a hand through his disheveled hair. He reached across the seat and grabbed the back of my neck. "Oh, you're unlike anyone I have ever had."

———————

Deacon was right; I rarely got beyond the date stage with men, and when I did it was usually a one-night-stand, and I tended to try and kick them out before morning. Up until last night, I hadn't even let David stay the night. I had attempted to keep things as casual as possible. I'm sure if I went to a therapist they would tell me it was some sort of protective trauma response.

But I think I loved waking up with David.

The early morning sun was streaming through the studio windows in my bedroom. David had his face nestled into my neck, and one arm tucked around me protectively. When we had returned from dinner, I had successfully pushed Tripp out of my mind. David had barely shut the door behind him, and he was unzipping my dress, chasing me up the stairs toward my bedroom.

I reached across the bed for my phone, bringing it close to my face and hoping not to disturb David. I knew he had to go into the office soon. It wasn't even eight in the morning. I could see from my screen that I had multiple notifications and missed calls. I furrowed my brow. Shit. It was Sunday. Society News was published every Sunday. I opened my email to see a copy of the digital issue sent to me by Jessica and another from Rebecca indicating I had done a great job with the line negotiation. There were about a dozen additional press requests. Neither Deacon nor I ever pressed, and our father rarely agreed to be quoted, let alone interviewed.

I opened the digital article to see what Jessica probably considered a catchy new title: "Charlie Winchester—Won at Last?" The article opened with a typical synopsis of my family and how the Winchesters had amassed their wealth quietly until my grandfather started the company. A commonly shared family photo of my Dad, Deacon, my mom and me at our house in Cape Cod took center stage. I felt a pang in my heart, as I looked at the traditional Nantucket-style architecture and the smile on my Mom's face. Her brown hair was blowing in the wind and out to the side while she looked adoringly at my father. Her hand was latched onto Deacon's shoulder, and I was clinging to my father's forearms.

I quickly skipped over the few sentences about her sudden death and scrolled to Jessica's introduction of David; it was quite scant on information about him. I had specifically asked her not to do a full family biography on him. I hadn't met his parents and didn't feel that it was appropriate. She spoke mainly about his professional achievements and what was a matter of record: how he went to Princeton, where he completed his degree in economics, and completed his MBA at the Yale School of Management. She spoke briefly about his role at WH, and as per my instruction, she made it very clear we had not started dating until long after he was hired, so no one could assume it had anything to do with me.

And then came the picture I had sent her. It was taken at the WH Holiday Party this past winter. David and I had kissed the first time only about two weeks prior to that. In the photo, I was wearing a plain garnet-colored one shoulder gown that our family stylist demanded I wear. It was tame by her standards. My hair was tied in a sleek, low bun. My arm was tucked around David's back. I distinctly remembered that I was tracing my finger underneath the waistband of his suit. He was smiling broadly, his messy hair pushed off his face and gelled to perfection—likely by my brother. His hand was resting on my waist, but his fingers were angled down toward my hip.

We also slept together for the first time—the night we kissed for the first time.

We had been in the office late every night for about three weeks prior, living off take-out food and sneaking drinks from the wet bar in the conference room. David and I had been assigned to create materials for our investors and subsidiaries to overview the new funding arm and showcase the value of community development programming. My father had been very clear that we needed to emphasize the non-monetary value of being associated with something like that. I had returned from Sri Lanka only a few months prior, and upon meeting David, I immediately registered how attractive he is, but I had long since decided most men in the corporate world were not for me. They all seemed like younger versions of my father.

We were sitting on the floor of my office, our backs against my desk, surrounded by poster boards with various statistics and sticky notes, a plethora of Chinese food containers and a bottle of scotch I had taken from my father's office. I was laughing so hard that I was clutching my stomach, doubled over. David had done an impression of Deacon attempting to get bottle service at a club when he was too drunk. He had reached up to wipe the tears from his eyes and began to loosen the knot on his tie and we fell into silence. I hadn't realized how funny he was. I turned my head to look over at him, and I noticed he was staring at me. I hadn't felt the urge to kiss anyone in a long time. Impulsively, I reached out and grabbed his tie pulling him toward me. We stumbled upward, pushing everything off my desk and our clothes were gone in a matter of minutes. Over the next two weeks, we had found increasingly creative places to hook up at the office—once in Deacon's coat closet.

I felt David shift beside me, as I scrolled through the remainder of the article. I could hear his phone vibrating non-stop. "I think you're getting a call." I set my own phone on the nightstand, aware that I had multiple missed calls and texts to return.

"Who is calling me this early on a Sunday?" He groaned and pushed himself up into a sitting position, fumbling for his phone.

"Jesus, it's my mother."

I sat up, gathering the duvet around me, watching as he propped himself up against the headboard, his bare chest exposed.

"Hey Mom...everything okay?"

I began thumbing through my own phone, attempting to look like I wasn't eavesdropping. I could hear his mom screaming, voice shrilly. He didn't talk about his mom much. I knew she had also been a lawyer but retired after she had his younger sister. I got the impression she was basically the grown-up version of a debutante, but those might have been my own judgments.

David sighed heavily, running a hand through his hair. "Mom...I'm sorry. I don't really think my dating life is any of your business until there is something to tell. I'm almost thirty years old." I could distinctly hear her saying the words 'Society News' on the other end of the line. Yet another thing to blame on Jessica Wilkes. I wasn't sure how David's parents would have seen the article, but it was a small world.

"Mom, I would have told you. I'm sorry you had to find out from people you went to law school with. I didn't even know you had friends in Chicago." David paused, shaking his head at whatever she was saying in response. "Well, our hand was kind of forced yesterday! Someone at a restaurant saw us together and gave the information to Society News. Who Charlie and Deacon date is a big deal, as I am sure you can imagine. Charlie and I hadn't even had a chance to tell her dad or talk about whether this was even a real relationship before the WH publicist was given the details."

I reached for the robe that was hanging off the side of my headboard and began to wind it around my body. This was exactly what David didn't sign up for. I stood and grabbed my phone and mouthed the word 'shower' to David, as I could see him sighing in frustration, grabbing at the ends of his hair. I padded into my bathroom, guilt gnawing at my stomach. I had been too preoccupied with making sure I didn't get raked across the coals for making lewd remarks and thinking what it would do to my Dad's business or my professionalism to realize what reading the story would mean for David and his family. I ran my hands across my face, as if I could wipe the guilt off.

I wondered briefly what it was like to have a mother who cared about your dating life. My father had only ever been concerned that any prospective suitors would be able to handle my fortune, respect the fact that I would one day be a part owner in WH, and make him and our family look good in the process. Deacon was always going to run it, but my father had ingrained in us since we were young that it was meant to be shared. That had never bothered Deacon, and he had always looked forward to the day he and I would take over WH together. We had been a team from the time we were kids—and even more so when mom died. Deacon flew out to visit me four times when I was in Sri Lanka, and like little kids, we would stay up late into the night talking about our hopes and dreams.

Swinging the glass door open, I turned the knob to the hottest setting possible. I had the sudden urge to scald all the Winchester off my skin. I would have given anything to be anyone else. My father hadn't always been like this. I think he used to love us more genuinely before our mother died. At least, that's how I remembered it. I tossed my robe aside and stepped into the shower. I immediately regretted my decision to turn the knob that far toward the heat. "Shit," I muttered, stepping backward out of the way as the water cooled off.

"Charlie?" David knocked on the already foggy glass. "May I?"

"Sure." He stripped down quickly and I stepped out of the way, directly under the rainwater shower head that had mercifully cooled significantly. "I'm sorry about your mom. Was it something I said in the article? I shouldn't have told Jessica that story about you stripping in your office."

"What?" He wrapped his arms around me, his usually messy hair now pasted to his face. He reached up to push it back. "No, she thought that was funny. And she thought it was sweet you had me a suit made. She was just upset I hadn't told her. She takes that sort of thing personally. It's nothing you did, Charlie. She asked me if I would bring you to Figure Eight for my Dad's sixtieth birthday in a few weeks. I hope you'll come with me." He was pushing my hair off my face. For some inexplicable reason, I had begun to cry at the suggestion. "Charlie, why are you crying?"

I gulped, inhaling an alarming amount of shower water. I gave a shaky laugh. "I was just wondering what it would be like to have my Mom call me." *To have a family to spend a sixtieth birthday with.* The unspoken words hung in the air around me.

David held me closer and tucked my head into the crook of his neck, letting the water stream down around us.

———

Deacon picked me up at around nine-thirty that morning for the forgotten breakfast with our father out at his house in Lake Forest. He had just gotten a new car and was eager to drive it farther than fifteen minutes to work. I stood on my step rummaging through my bag, aware that my phone had been continuously vibrating all morning.

After The Society News article was released, a fury of texts from my friends and acquaintances were annoyed to have read about it in the Sunday section of the paper but were desperate for more information.

Deacon honked furiously and I looked up, raising my giant aviator sunglasses to indicate I was rolling my eyes at him. I pushed them back down on my nose. The sun was brighter today than it had been in months. I was wearing a slouchy, oversized sweater and a down vest with worn jeans. I had hastily shoved my feet into a pair of ancient Stuart Weitzman boots I refused to part with. David had whimpered when he saw me come down the stairs.

"You know what most girls like you would wear to breakfast with their dad right?" He reached for my hips to pull me down onto the couch with him.

I batted his hands away and laughed. "Yes, because Deac will probably show up wearing the male version."

Deacon laid on the horn again. I could faintly hear *The Life of Pablo* playing from inside the car. I made my way to the door and threw it open to a loud objection from him.

"Just because you drive a Bentley and live in Chicago doesn't mean you need to like Kanye West, too, Deacon." I immediately pulled my boots off and sat crossed legged on the seat, slamming the door shut.

"Jesus, Charlie leave it on the hinges!" Deacon looked affronted under his Ray Bans. He had just bought that car, a brand new Bentley Continental GT and had an outrageous amount of upgrades and customizations put into it. He leaned over and ruffled my hair affectionately. "How was your night?"

I smiled slightly and looked down, aware that a blush was creeping across my pale skin. My body felt warm where I could still feel David's hands on me and where his lips had been the night before. "It was good."

I could make out Deacon's arched eyebrow, as he pulled away from the curb. His hair was floppy and natural, slightly pushed off his face. I thought he looked best that way, not when he was done up and had it styled just so. "How exactly did this start, anyway? You know, I'm not an idiot. I noticed you guys went out for drinks often, and I always saw you flirting, but I obviously don't know the details."

I reached forward and turned the stereo down slightly, gliding my hands across the piano wood finishing stereo system. I heard him mutter about streaks. "Deacon, we both know you're going to have this car cleaned at least once a week." I inhaled, looking out the passenger window to the streets of Lincoln Park and temporarily ignoring his comment. I smiled, as I saw the green on the trees. There was nothing like a Chicago spring when it actually decided to arrive. I pulled my thoughts together. "It started a few months ago. Remember when I had completed my first round of successful funding? Dad assigned David and me to create all those materials to describe the new funding arm?"

Recognition dawned on Deacon's face. "Oh yeah, you two were always together and 'working' so late."

"I mean we did actually do work!" I smacked his shoulder playfully. "But it was after we had finished. I took a bottle of Hennessy from Dad's wet bar, and we were sitting on the floor of my office and it just happened. I remember thinking I hadn't realized how funny he was."

Deacon raised his eyebrows and nodded. "I am happy for you, Charlie. I can tell how much he cares about you. And he's a good match for you. He's got the same sense of humor, and he seems to have the same disdain for wealth that you do."

Deacon had always teased me that I didn't really belong in our world, and in some ways he was right. I enjoyed the privileges and the comfort as much as the next person would, and I dressed to play the part. But whereas people like Deacon relished and enjoyed their wealth, with new cars and suits, I took part in none of that. My townhouse was nice but modest. Nothing like the sprawling monstrosity of Deacon's. I didn't own a car; I walked to work or took the subway. When it was freezing, I used a town car service.

"That's why I like him." I shrugged, toying at a fray in my jeans. "He never looked at me like I was Charlie Winchester." Deacon and I had significantly different experiences in life in the dating department. He understood, in principle, why it was different but also acknowledged that it was something he would never experience.

"When you came back to work at WH, he had been there about a year. The night after you came back, remember when I took you out for drinks? Taylor was there, Carter when he worked at WH still, and David came?" Deacon ran a hand through his hair, eyes on the road, and I nodded. "David and I went to the Bulls game the next night. And he wouldn't shut up about you. 'Charlie is so funny, you never told me your sister was funny Deacon. She is brilliant. You never told me that your sister was so smart. I find it fascinating she spent a year volunteering all over the world. I can't believe she summited Kilimanjaro alone. I can't believe she's been in the water with a great white shark. I can't believe she was in Sri Lanka.' He was relentless. He never saw you for anyone but who you are." Deacon took his eyes off the road momentarily to smile at me affectionately.

I looked down, smiling broadly at his words, until I heard my phone vibrate again and a sharp realization shot through me. "Fuck! Taylor!"

Taylor Breen has been my best friend since childhood. We went to day school together before splitting up to go to separate boarding schools. She had gone to the West Coast, and Deacon and I had gone to school in New York. She had moved back to Chicago around the same time I did to begin her residency at Northwestern Memorial. Aside from my brother, Taylor is the only person in my life who has ever really, truly, *seen* me. She knew who I was right down into my soul.

Deacon looked gleeful. "Have you not told her yet? Oh please put her on speaker!" He turned his stereo off and looked at me expectantly. I closed my eyes and grimaced before answering her call. Deacon reached across me and hit the speaker icon, grinning like a small child.

"David Fucking Kennedy?!" Taylor shrieked. "You're dating a VP from your father's office and I had to find out from my mother who was reading a Society News article? What the hell Charlie!"

Taylor had finished admonishing me when Deacon pulled up to the gate of our father's home. "Taylor, I have to go. Deac and I are having breakfast with our dad shortly. I promise I will make it up to you. Let's go out Friday. You said you weren't on call this weekend, right?"

Deacon waved at the person in the security booth. I couldn't make out from my angle who it was but leaned forward to smile and wave. Most of my father's staff had been with our family since before our mom had died. I hung up on Taylor, before she had a chance to tear another strip off me. I'll give her all the dirty details she wants over drinks on Friday. Girls only.

Deacon pulled around the circular driveway, stopping in front of the steps leading up to the house. We had both grown up here with our mother and father. It was a sprawling estate—much too big for four people, in my opinion. I looked up at my father, as I shoved my boots back on. He was sitting on the steps between the imposing stone pillars that surrounded the door smoking a cigar. Deacon had turned off the car and came around to my side to open the door for me.

"Is that the new car? How much did that set you back?" I saw my father arch an eyebrow at Deacon, as he handed him a cigar after he darted up the steps to meet my father.

"Probably more than some countries make in a year," I muttered under my breath, as I also walked toward my father. I bent down to kiss his head and ruffle his short hair.

Deacon shot me a look, as he lit his cigar. "Not much." I was pretty sure he had spent upward of $100,000 on upgrades alone.

"No David?" My dad turned to me. I noticed a third cigar in his pocket. A small smile tugged on my mouth and a creeping hope spread through me.

I shook my head, my dark hair falling out of the messy top knot I had hastily tied it in. "He's actually at the office, Dad, you run a tight ship."

My dad nodded and began to draw on his cigar. "Did the meeting with Tripp go well?"

Deacon puffed out smoke, attempting to make a ring and failing spectacularly. "Yeah it did, but you might want to ask Charlie. Are you going to tell us what that was about?"

Tripp fucking Banks. I felt my cheeks burning, shrugging and feigning innocence. "Tell you about what, exactly?"

Deacon arched an eyebrow. "He was kind of vicious with you. I didn't think you guys knew each other that well."

My father's eyes narrowed and he gave a sharp glare to Deacon. "What do you mean he was vicious with her?"

I felt bile rising in my throat. "It was nothing, Dad. He's just like that. We went to Brown together. I told you all this. He was a dick then and he's kind of a dick now but would truthfully be a really good addition to WH." I noticed Deacon's eyes lingering on me. My mouth was suddenly very dry.

My dad studied me for a few moments before putting his cigar out in a glass ashtray he had sitting beside him. "Well, this is business, Charlie. I don't really care if you don't *like* him. I'm asking you if you all think he would be a good fit."

"I just told you I do, Dad." My voice was flat, confident in that moment I would never be able to tell them the truth. It was business, and I knew enough to know business came first. I felt Deacon's eyes on me. I sometimes thought he knew me better than I knew myself, and he could absolutely tell when I was withholding the truth from him. He studied me shrewdly before turning to our father.

"Yeah Dad, he's a good fit. David will back me up, I'm sure." He clapped him on the back and stood with his own cigar. "Did you see the Cubs game?"

———

Deacon and I stayed at our dad's until late in the afternoon. At some point, both had disappeared to take a call with Ash. I was curled up in a ball on a chaise lounge outside, my eyes closed under my sunglasses. I knew I should be working, too. I had five separate proposals and research backgrounders to have on my father's desk by the end of day Tuesday but the sun beating down on my face was too enjoyable.

I felt my phone vibrate against my leg, and I reached down to grab it. It was a text from David asking if he could make me dinner at his apartment tonight. I had never seen it. I realized that would mean spending three nights in a row together, but I didn't mind. The old me might have run screaming for the hills. Everything about him was exciting, and I wanted to know everything there was to know. David told me he would call me when he was finishing up at the office. As I was sliding my phone back into the pocket of my vest, I felt a hand on my shoulder.

I craned my neck backward. Deacon had come out of the house and was looking down at me over his glasses, "You ready to go?"

I nodded, reaching up to stretch. "Where's Dad?"

"On the phone." Deacon was swinging his keys around his fingers. "Trying to close the Halton deal."

Our father was currently in the process of becoming the majority shareholder of Halton Entertainment. It was the largest family entertainment company in America, with sprawling mall complexes, and arcades and cinemas across the country. It seemed futile to me. He already had more money than anyone could dream of having. I took this to mean my father would not be coming out of his office to say goodbye to me. Both Deacon and I were used to this. I followed Deacon back through the glass patio doors to where I had abandoned my bag on the other side.

I was happy to leave. I didn't enjoy staying at my dad's house for longer than necessary. There were a lot of ghosts there. Neither Deacon nor my father had ever exhibited any desire to speak about our mother, so I had remained silent, too. I found it difficult, and at times unbearable, to be in the house where she spent her short life, not being able to share her memory. I inhaled a lungful of air before following Deacon through the front door and down the steps to his car. I had been hoping since I was twenty that I might find some trace, some scent, of my mom in our home. But I never did.

CHAPTER FIVE

Deacon suggested we go for a drive around Lake Forest, desperate to test out various features on his car, claiming that we didn't spend much time together one on one, which was an absolute fabrication. I had arched an eyebrow at him skeptically, sure he had ulterior motives but pulled my boots off and moved the seat backward to stretch out.

"I know you're lying to me, Charlie." Deacon wasted no time. We were barely past the security gate.

"About?" I asked, feigning confusion, as I scrolled through social media.

"Tripp. Something happened between you two." I noticed Deacon's knuckles were clenched on the steering wheel. "He didn't do anything to you, did he Charlie?" *Well, that would depend on your definition of anything.*

"What?! Jesus, Deacon, no," I said, very aware I was not likely to get away with pretending there was nothing else to the story as far as Deacon was concerned. "I told you. Nothing happened between us at Brown. We knew one another. That's it. I don't want to think about it. It reminds me of when Mom was alive. Dad hiring Tripp is a smart business decision and not something I am about to interfere with. Drop it." I turned, looking out the window determinedly as the trees blurred together, unable to stop the memory from sinking its claws into me.

————————

I am twenty years old again, sitting on the third floor of the John Hay library by the window of my favorite spot, studying for my upcoming Development Economics final. I love this library. The only problem I have with Brown is that the libraries are uninspired compared to some other Ivy League colleges. Most of them feel like regular old buildings you would find anywhere, not home to secret alcoves or winding spiral staircases. I feel my phone begin to vibrate on the table, and I notice that it is my father. I knit my eyebrows in concern. It's two-thirty in the afternoon on a Wednesday. I grab my phone and move between the aisles of chairs and desks to go answer the call in the hallway outside the room.

"Dad?" I whisper. "Can this wait? I'm studying. Is everything okay?"

"Charlie..." His voice is all wrong. The usual stern and steady tone of my father is choppy and broken. "It's your mother."

And then my world comes crashing down.

I sob silently into my hands, as my father tells me my mother has been found dead at our house in Cape Cod. Instinctively, I reach out for Deacon, and I remember he is not there. He is miles away. Has my father told him yet?

"Charlie, I'm sending the plane for Deacon as soon as it comes back tomorrow morning, and then it will come for you okay?" His voice is steady again, as I sob into the phone. "Charlie, you need to tell me you understand, sweetheart. You need to say something."

"I understand," I whisper and slide down to the floor.

I go back into the room, my head down and tears streaming steadily down my face, as I pack my bag. I bite my lip to keep from sobbing loudly. As soon as I reach the door, I run out of the library building as fast as I can. I'm gulping in fresh air, as I head in the direction of my sorority house only five blocks away.

"Chuckles?" I look up to see Tripp Banks coming out of the student center, before I can get very far. "Chuckles, why are you crying?" I tell him my mother is dead through my steady stream of tears. I have known Tripp for two years now. He's my friend, and no one makes me laugh like he can. We kiss at parties when we've had too much to drink, and he playfully tells me I'm a tease, then he sleeps with all the girls in my sorority.

He puts his arm around me and I sob into his shoulder. He asks me if I want to be alone. I want my brother. I don't want to be alone. He wipes my tears and asks if I would like to come over. He will take me home later. I nod.

Tripp brings me upstairs to his room, somewhere I have been many times before. I'm sitting on his bed sobbing, wishing I could be anywhere. Anyone else. He is looking at me sadly, trying to make me laugh or smile.

I meet his eyes. They are so blue. I feel a jolt go through me. I am going to miss Tripp. He is a senior and is leaving soon. He tells a joke, and I laugh in spite of myself. I ask him for a drink. He goes to the fridge and brings us each a bottle of beer.

We drink for the next few hours. We lay backward on his bed, laughing together about memories we've shared over the last two years. He is incredibly handsome. His black hair is ruffled, and he has stubble growing in over his defined, square jaw. I impulsively reach out and pull on his hair, giggling.

"There's my Chuckles," he whispers quietly. We are staring at each other. My body feels like it is on fire being this close to him. I think I would regret it if I didn't kiss him again. I set my drink down and lean

forward. He meets my lips with his immediately and grabs the back of my neck.

We are kissing furiously, and I feel numb to the world around me. I tug his shirt off over his head and run my hands across his broad chest.

"I've wanted this for so long Charlie," he whispers into my ear as he kisses my neck. I feel loved and wanted. I forget my mother is dead. There are no clothes between us, and I think nothing of it when he spreads my legs. I want to be devoured. I do not want to think about anything else.

We are moving together, and I understand what all the other girls are talking about when they said he knew what he was doing. I bite into his shoulder to keep quiet. I feel his ragged breath against me, as we move faster. He buries his face in my neck.

It's over, and I still feel nothing. I roll to my side, as I feel him get up off the bed and leave the room. He was gone for a while. I drift off to sleep, my eyes tired and sore from crying.

I wake up later. I can see that it's nighttime through the window. I reach for my phone. Missed calls and texts from my father and my brother. I no longer feel 'nothing.' I feel everything. I hate myself. I am disgusted with myself, and I want my mother. I want to be her little girl again. Instinctively, I know nothing will ever be the same. I stifle a sob, as I extract myself from his bed. He's now sleeping next to me again, his back turned. He's my friend, and I will never see him again.

I dress quietly, tears streaming down my face, as I gather my bag and leave. He lives on the top floor. I sneak down the stairs to the main landing. I see the door to the living room is open and a light is on. I go in to turn the light off. I don't like the idea of the electricity being wasted.

As I step into the living room, I see a large poster board on the wall beside the television. I study it for a moment, confused, before I see my name. It is a list of women from my sorority and others. Beside each of our names, there is a list of activities. I see that each is worth a certain amount of points, and I see that beside each name, there is a corresponding name of whoever completed the activity first. Tripp's name is now beside mine and sex with me is worth fifteen points.

I clap my hand to my mouth. I feel the urge to vomit as my stomach churns. I turn and run out of the house. I forget to turn off the light. He is not my friend.

Days later, I am wearing a black shift dress for my mother's funeral. We have to leave in ten minutes. I chew my nails, my phone pressed to my ear. The ringing is endless, until it goes to voicemail. I leave him a message, but I am not even sure why I called.

Tripp never calls me back, and I don't see him for seven years.

CHAPTER SIX

Deacon mercifully dropped the subject of Tripp and insisted we go on a tour of our favorite spots in Lake Forest; there weren't many. We drove past Lake Forest Academy, where we both attended until we reached ninth grade and went off to boarding school. He insisted on driving through the winding side streets, revving his engine unnecessarily and blasting Kanye West.

"Let's go to Forest Park," Deacon flicked his signal briefly, before swinging the car around a corner aggressively.

I frowned. Forest Park was a public beach with a walking trail. It would be swarming with people today. "Why? That is not one of my favorite places in Lake Forest, is it yours?"

"It is the last stop on the Deacon Winchester tour of Lake Forest, and do you want to know why?" He took one hand off the steering wheel to ruffle my hair. I leaned away from him. "I lost my virginity on the beach there."

I burst out laughing. "No you didn't Deacon! I know for a fact you lost it when you were a freshman at boarding school! Because when I started, you took me on your 'The Hartford School, Deacon Winchester Experience' tour and showed me the dorm room it happened in!"

Deacon grinned at me sideways, exposing his perfect teeth. He was classically handsome in a way that you would expect a son of a billionaire to be. He would never have to work another day of his life for anything. And I loved him more than I loved anything. He is an absolute perfect version of himself. Deacon is frivolous and funny. He is irresponsible and carefree. When he was younger, had made a good show of being the quintessential bad—and rich—boy. But he is also the person I loved most in the world. The person who had cared for me in the worst moments of my life and had defended me and taken the blame for my wrongdoings when we were kids. He never failed to tell me how special I am.

"Not that kind of virginity, Charlie." He laughed, as he drove past the turn off for the park. I made an overexaggerated shudder, horrified to imagine how my brother classified levels of virginity. "I won't bore you with the details. I assume David is coming over when he leaves the office, so I'll bring you home."

"I'm going to his place actually. I've not been. Have you?" I looked out the window, watching the trees whip by as Deacon accelerated, catching glimpses of Lake Michigan over the cliffs.

"Yeah, a few times to watch the Bulls play and shit. It's nice. It's your style. You'll like it." He shrugged. I took that to mean it wasn't lavish, and David did not use his home to make a display of his wealth. "Lots of those studio loft-style windows you like so much. Big balcony that overlooks the river."

I nodded, chewing my lip thoughtfully as I thought back to David asking about our mother, and my failed attempt to find any trace of her in our family home that morning. "Do you ever think about Mom, Deac?"

I noticed that his knuckles whitened on the steering wheel, and the car sped up slightly. "Honestly Charlie? I try not to. She obviously wasn't the person we thought she was. To do that to us." I surveyed Deacon sadly. I didn't think that was how he really felt; I thought he had a lot of unresolved grief, but I was not one to talk. "I don't think that's fair, Deacon."

"What she did wasn't fair Charlie!" He raised his voice suddenly, taking one hand off the wheel and smacking his palm against the leather. "I was a senior, it was supposed to be one of the most exciting times in my life. You were only twenty. What she did was fucking selfish, and she is obviously not the person I thought she was."

I recoiled in my seat slightly, taken aback by the sudden outburst. I cocked my head. His chocolate brown hair was falling in messy waves around his head, wisps across his forehead. His dark eyebrows were drawn in frustration, as he watched the road. I noticed he was grinding his teeth, his jawline popping under the three-day old stubble. We had the same nose. I think it was called a Greek nose—a straight bridge. I had always envied those women who had slightly upturned noses. I thought it was more elegant.

"I'm sorry I brought it up. I only asked because David's mom called him this morning. It made me wonder what it would be like." I shrugged and turned away from Deacon to look back out the window. I typically regretted bringing her up, and this was no exception. I had done my best to commit her to memory and hoped that it wouldn't fade.

Deacon said nothing for the remainder of the drive, and I pressed my head against the glass in an attempt to shrink as far away from him as possible. He pulled up to my townhouse and David was outside, leaning against his car. He raised his hand to us. Deacon stared ahead, one arm propped up against his window, running his hand through his hair, the other was gripped on the steering wheel. He made a sort of strangled two-finger salute with the hand that had been running through his hair.

I shoved my feet into my boots and held up one finger to David through the window. "Deacon?" I turned to face him, leaning my head to the side. "You know there is no love for you like mine." He put both hands on the steering wheel and stared determinedly into his lap. "See you tomorrow morning," I shut the door gently before he peeled away from the curb.

I felt my shoulders sag involuntarily, and I shoved my hands into the pocket of my vest. I could feel my eyes burning slightly, and I was glad that they were shielded from David. He had pushed himself up off his car and his lips were pursed in worry. The dark chrome of his car glinted in the sunlight. He drove a more practical car than Deacon, albeit slightly. He had a BMW 4 Series Gran Coupe. It was about two years old. He had mentioned buying it when he made JVP, because my father had told him he couldn't continue to show up to meetings in Ubers.

"What was that about?" I couldn't see his brown eyes beneath his own Wayfarer sunglasses, but I was sure they were dark with concern.

"We just had a stupid arguement." I shook my head, feeling my top knot bob loose.

"Huh," he looked as if he was going to reach out to me but changed his mind and shoved his hands in the pockets of his khakis. "You guys don't really argue or fight, do you?"

"No, we don't." I could tell my voice was strangled. Guilt was gnawing at my stomach. I knew better than to bring up our mom around Deacon. Or my dad, for that matter.

On the anniversary of her death, I had attempted to organize a dinner for the three of us. I was going to cook my mother's favorite meal. Deacon had taken off to Vegas two days before and ended up getting caught with a model and about a pound of cocaine his first night there. My father had followed his lawyers to bring him back, and the day passed with no acknowledgement and it had been that way ever since.

"Are you okay? You don't have to come over if you don't want to." David inclined his head toward me, running a hand through his perpetually disheveled hair.

"No, I want to see your place! Do you live in rich boy bachelor squalor?" I leaned forward, smacking his hard abdomen playfully with the back of my hand.

"I think my cleaning service comes more often than yours," he smiled widely. He gestured a hand behind him, "Did you want to grab anything? I know it's three nights in a row, but I was hoping to make you dinner."

"And he cooks!" I smiled, parting my pink lips. "If walking into the office with me tomorrow morning doesn't freak you out, I would love to get a glimpse into what a regular Sunday night looks like at the Kennedy residence."

David reached out to grab my hips, spinning me around to pin me against his car. He buried his face in my neck, biting at me playfully. "I don't plan on there being anything regular about this night."

———

Deacon was right. David's apartment was full of floor-to-ceiling loft-style windows. It was an open concept apartment with concrete flooring. It was sparse, but I doubted he was going for a minimalist look. He probably worked too much to even bother being at home.

He had taken my coat and Louis Vuitton Keepall to his room. It had been a gift from Taylor when I had gone off to Sri Lanka. I kept it in storage at my dad's house, as there wasn't much use for a luxury leather duffel bag in rural East Asia.

He had immediately cracked a beer open for me, running his hand across the small of my back before making his way to the kitchen, and I surveyed his apartment. There were some indications that David lived and breathed there: a worn UNC Tarheels hat was hooked onto the back of an industrial-like chair that was pushed into some sort of wooden table. Live edge maybe? I wrapped my knuckles on it and furrowed my brow. It felt different.

"It's driftwood." David raised his eyes to me, while his hands were busy preparing dinner. I crinkled my nose. It was spicy and felt familiar. "It was the largest piece that washed up one summer at my parent's place in Figure Eight."

"Did you have someone make it for you?" I ran my fingers across the soft wood, appreciating the knots and edges.

"No, I made it." He laughed slightly and shook his head, hair falling onto his forehead. He raised his beer to his lips and nodded his head toward the table. "Check out the legs."

I bent down quickly and stifled a laugh. Four metal rods with a flat base had been haphazardly drilled into the side of the wood. I stood up, biting at my lip and taking a sip of my beer before continuing to survey the room. There was a large, dark gray sectional pushed against the opposite wall with a plain concrete table sitting in front of it on four much more secure-looking iron legs. I made a mental note to check to see if the dining table would hold any weight.

I stuck my leg out to test a flat, woven rug that was under the table. I arched an eyebrow thoughtfully. It seemed very feminine and un-David. I flicked my eyes upward. There was a large print above the couch; it was a black-and-white single wave curling in. It took me a minute to realize there was a person in the barrel of the wave, crouched low on a surfboard. It was hard to tell who it was. Their hair looked dark but was obviously wet, and their body was covered in a wetsuit. I pointed the end of my bottle at it. "Where is this?"

David looked up, brushing his hair out of his eyes with his shoulder. I couldn't see what he was cooking as he was standing behind the kitchen bar.

"Back home...the Outer Banks."

"Someone you know?" I smiled. David didn't talk about North Carolina much, but when he did, he spoke about it fondly. Pieces of his upbringing were littered across his personality: southern manners, a slight tilt to his voice when he drank too much and evidence of what home meant to him across the apartment.

"It's me, Charlie," he laughed, looking up to make eye contact with me. David and I were from the same worlds, technically. But sometimes he looked at me like I was from an entirely different one. He didn't do it with judgment; it was often said affectionately, as if he found certain things about my upbringing and my complete ignorance to be endearing.

"What!" I did a quick glance back at the print. "How high is that wave! When was this?"

He shrugged and cocked his head, as if the fact that he could cruise through the barrel of a wave was nothing. "That was about six feet. It was pretty big for the Outer Banks. I was seventeen."

"Baby David Kennedy!" I smiled widely, examining the print closer. I could see David in the photo now. The way his face was knit in concentration, the floppy slightly overgrown hair. "Do you miss it?"

David brought his beer to his lips and surveyed me. "Every day."

"Were you good? Was it just a hobby or something? David was an enigma to me in so many ways.

"I was *okay*," he smiled modestly, which led me to think that he was likely better than okay. "I used to compete. My parents put an end to that, though, around the time that was taken. I could never go much further than local competitions. I had an offer to join a circuit team with a brand when I was sixteen but obviously, that was not an option for a Kennedy."

He shrugged as if it was no big deal and went back to simmering whatever he had in the pan.

"Surfing to the big bad Corporate world, who are you David Kennedy?" I tipped my head. I had released my hair from its unruly top knot on the drive over. My hair was naturally pin straight and sometimes a top knot would allow for some waves for a short period.

"Oh fuck!" David stepped back suddenly from the stovetop, as I noticed an alarming amount of smoke begin to whirl. He turned to me, laughing and running a hand through his hair. "I'm the guy that just burnt our fucking dinner." I laughed hysterically.

———

I was wearing an old sweater of David's, my socked feet kicking in his lap and the hood pulled up over my head. The minimal waves I had gotten from the top knot had since disappeared and my middle part was just a sheet around my face now. David had attempted to make Lentil Dhal for me—something I missed greatly from my time in East Asia—and had ended up burning the oil so badly all the ingredients shriveled up in it. The empty take-out containers on the coffee table were slowly being accompanied by empty bottles.

"You've got a great laugh, Charlie," he reached out to grab my feet to try and contain the mini kicks I was making.

I stopped abruptly. "Really? It's not too loud?" My laugh was something I had always been insecure about. My father had told me once it was too 'boisterous' for a young lady.

David shook his head, taking another sip of his beer. "Not at all. It's so big coming from such a tiny person."

I impulsively pulled the strings on the hood of the sweater as tight as they could go, trapping my face in the bunches and bursted out laughing again. David smiled earnestly and watched me, his usually dark eyes dancing. It felt like there was no side of myself I couldn't show David. I had been told by more than one man in my life that the way I acted and these sides of my personality were not fitting for a woman like me. I felt my phone begin to vibrate in the pocket of the sweater and fished it out. I loosened up the neck of the sweater and looked down. It was from Deacon.

I shouldn't have shot you down like that today.
I'm sorry Charlie. I love you.

I put the phone away, turning it to silent. Deacon would show up at my desk tomorrow morning with some sort of apology gift, I'm sure. We didn't fight much, but sometimes he was a proper asshole, usually when he was hungover or stressed. He'd bring me coffee, sometimes flowers to apologize.

"Everything okay?" David grabbed both of my feet in his hands again.

"It was just Deacon. Saying sorry." I shrugged and began to pick at the label on my bottle. Fighting with Deacon left a weird hollow feeling inside me.

"Do you want to talk about it? Obviously it's still bothering you." He set his beer down and turned to face me, bringing more of my legs onto his lap.

"You have siblings, David. You know how difficult they can be." What Deacon had said about our mom was ringing in my ears. I didn't think she was selfish, and it broke my heart to hear his pain and to hear him say it.

David began running his hands up and down my calves. "Yeah, I have siblings. But to be honest, we aren't as close as you guys. I mean…we're close and I love them, but you two are best friends." David had two brothers and a sister. He was the second oldest.

"It was just a stupid disagreement, David." I could feel an edge creeping into my voice, and I wasn't sure why. I took another sip of my beer and I could see him eyeing me thoughtfully. "I'm sorry. I shouldn't speak to you like that."

David raised his hands, showing me his palms as if offering a truce. "Look Charlie, I'm not going to make you talk about anything you don't want to."

I was quiet. I could hear the low stereo he had put on in the background and vaguely still smell burnt onion and garlic, despite the many windows we had opened in an attempt to air out the apartment. "It was about our mom. I should have known better than to bring her up. *They* don't like talking about her."

I could feel his eyes on me. "You're not wrong to be upset, Charlie. I can imagine your brother would likely feel like the safest person to talk about your mom with."

I felt myself chewing on my lip. My thumb nail was worrying at the label on the beer bottle. "He just said some shocking things about her. It was upsetting. I mean…I know he and my dad are still mad."

A brief look of confusion passed across David's face. "I don't know what it's like to lose a parent or anyone close to me like that, but I would imagine it's normal to be angry about it. Especially when you were so young, and she was so young."

"They're not angry at God or at life, David," I scoffed, taking another sip of my beer. The bottle was almost empty, and I would have given anything for another. "They're mad at *her*."

The look of confusion that passed over his face earlier had come back, and this time it stayed. "Charlie, I don't think that can be true–"

I interrupted him, raising my eyes to meet his. "Do you know how my mom died, David?"

He shook his head, running a hand through his hair as he usually did. "Actually, no. I saw they wrote that it was sudden in that Society News article."

I stared at him blankly, about to say something out loud I had not repeated since I was twenty. "She killed herself. She drowned herself in our fucking family pool at our house in Cape Cod."

I felt cold, my stomach was churning. I could picture it clearly any time I thought about my mom. What it might have looked like to see her floating in the water. The pool was lit from underneath, and I imagined she must have looked ethereal in some ways. Her pale skin likely blue, with her brown hair floating around her. I always pictured her wearing a red dress.

David was silent. He was staring at me intently, his eyes dark. I could hear him breathing through his nose, as if he was working to make the least amount of noise possible.

"They're mad at her, because they still don't know why she did it." I closed my eyes. I could taste bile in the back of my throat. My brother and father's inability to forgive my mother disgusted me at times.

David cocked his head back, his thumbs rubbing into my calves. It was grounding. "They have no idea why she did it?"

"She didn't leave a note. There was nothing. Investigators thought it might have been an accident, or that she had been killed." I shrugged, studying my fingers. It sounded like I was recounting a storyline of a bad teen drama. "She had never given any indication she was depressed or unwell or unhappy. Nothing in her medical records, nothing in her emails, in her phone calls, texts. Nothing to friends. Nothing in her journals. It was really out of fucking nowhere."

"How do you know it wasn't an accident?" David's voice was soft, and he was rubbing his thumbs softly along the tops of my feet now.

"No." This was probably my least favorite part of the story, if there was one. "They were originally treating it as a suspicious death, because the landscaper found her. But we had security cameras and CCTV. By the time they had pulled it, it had been about seventy-two hours. There's footage of her swallowing a bottle of pills and going out and getting into the pool. Obviously because of the nature of it, they did an autopsy. She had overdosed and then drowned. It wasn't an accident."

There were silent tears running down my face. I hadn't said these words out loud since I was twenty. I don't think my father and brother were embarrassed. It wasn't a secret to our extended family or to family friends what had happened. But it was like they had sealed the door on that part of our lives and had never experienced a desire to open it. I didn't want to meet David's eyes. I felt childish and exposed, like my skin had been flayed open and all my nerves were exposed to the cool air coming through the window.

David pulled my legs toward him, bringing me closer and folding them around his waist. "What did Deacon say to you?"

"He said he tried not to think about her. He said she was selfish. Selfish to have done that to us." I rested my forehead against David's chin, feeling hot tears dripping down onto his lap. "I don't really want to talk about this anymore, David."

I felt him nod. "Okay, we don't have to talk about it."

———

My head was laid on David's bare chest and I ran my hands across the raised ridges in his abdomen and along his ribs. We were lying in his bed, plain dark gray sheets tangled around our bodies. My hair was tied in a loose braid over my shoulder. His bedroom was much like the rest of his apartment—bare and practical. The floor was bare concrete, with one high-pile rug at the edge of his bed, which was in the middle of one wall. There was an ensuite bathroom and a walk-in closet, and one long black dresser that took up a chunk of the opposing wall. There were more floor-to-ceiling loft windows that looked out onto the balcony and ran the length of his apartment. He had two plain black nightstands on either side of the basic black bed frame. It suited him.

The glow from the city was pouring into the room, and I could see streams of light falling across the sheets. My clothes for tomorrow were hung up in front of the closet, balanced precariously on a dresser. I had packed a plain black Brooks Brothers sheath dress that I could pair with any of the heels I kept in the office. It was a staple of my work wardrobe.

"Your ass looks phenomenal in that dress." David had noticed me looking. I bursted out laughing, feeling his chest shake beneath me as he laughed silently. He had been working overtime to make me laugh for the remainder of the night.

"Tell me something about yourself." I continued to run my fingers up and down his chest. "I feel like since Friday, we've spent multiple days airing my dirty laundry and my family secrets. Tell me something I don't know about you. About your family."

David nestled his head against the top of mine. "Well, you know I have three other siblings. I'm the second oldest. There's my older brother, Jackson. He's thirty-two and he's a lawyer at my dad's firm. He will probably take over the practice. Obviously, there's me, the best-looking Carolina Kennedy."

I laughed and slapped his chest playfully. I had forgotten they were often known as the Carolina Kennedys to distinguish their lack of relation to the other Kennedys. "Of course, Mr. Kennedy."

He groaned slightly, and I felt him push up against me. I braced my hand against his thigh to stop him. I liked hearing him talk. "And then there's Ryan. He's twenty-five, and he just finished up at Harvard Law. He will also be starting at my father's practice in the fall. He's a bit, I don't know...wild maybe? He really plays the young rich boy from prep school act. He's kind of an asshole. I think he's going to be traveling for the summer."

David might be referring to his younger brother as an asshole, but I sensed it was similar to the way I told Deacon he was a douche. "Maybe I can give him some travel tips."

David laughed, his chest starting to shake again, as he brought me in closer. "I don't think he's interested in staying in your villages and community homes. Picture Villas and Full Moon Parties in Thailand."

"Ew!" I squealed.

"Didn't think so. And then there's Sophie, she's twenty-one and going into her last year at UPenn. She will probably go to law school, too." David laughed slightly, trailing his hand across my arm. "She's not wily like you. She was a debutante and did pageants, but she's not vapid. She's kind. She was certainly too kind growing up, and we absolutely tortured her for it. Mostly Ryan, because they're closest in age."

"Why didn't you go to law school?" I looked up at him and noticed he was staring out the window.

"I think that's what my parents wanted. But I hated the thought of it. Being cooped up articling for a year and reading depositions. I interned at my dad's firm and worked there all through prep school and college. But I could never wait to get out at the end of the day to get to the water. It was too monotonous. I think that's ultimately why my parents put an end to my little 'surfing hobby,' as they called it. I mean my parents were going to support me no matter what, but I think they drew the line at me bumming around beaches trying to make it as a pro surfer."

I pursed my lips thoughtfully. I could never imagine this David to be a disappointment. "Were you serious about it? To go with that brand and their team?"

He shrugged, the pads of his thumbs stroking my skin. "Yeah, I mean, at sixteen? Sure. I loved it. I still love it when I can go out at home. I don't think I ever would have done it for longer than a year, though. I had always intended to go to college, get a job etc. But I would have taken the time off if non-traditional pathways were welcomed in my family. I'm sure you know what that's like."

I laughed slightly. My father hadn't given me that hard of a time. "Honestly, my dad was...not disappointed when I came home and told him I was leaving to volunteer and my first position was in Albania. After that, I went to Ghana and Nepal. He said it was very pedestrian of me and that he expected me back in at least two years. I mean, I obviously dipped to Sri Lanka after so he wasn't thrilled when I told him about that."

"I was at WH when you were in Sri Lanka. The things your dad and Deacon used to say about you were so funny. Kind and clear, they were proud of you. Whenever someone like Ash would ask where you were, your dad would always sigh loudly and say something weird like 'she's probably feeding beans to a malnourished child in a field with no phones.' But then he would smile." David's hand was snaking around my waist. I slapped it away. His comment about my father struck me as odd. It never occurred to me that my father was *proud* of me.

He groaned but his body was shaking with laughter. "You're killing me, Charlie."

"I want to talk! I like knowing about you. I feel like I've been talking non-stop about myself since we said we were going to do this for real. I don't really like talking about my family, if you haven't noticed. I want to know more about your family!" I laughed, resting my hand at the band of the sweatpants he was wearing.

"Charlie." David flipped over and was on top of me in a second, his arms on either side of my head. His hair was falling onto his forehead and his voice was gravely. "You are the most beautiful girl I have ever seen. I am done talking about my family. I have about five hours before I get ready to sit at my desk in my office for twelve hours, as you'll walk by me many times in that dress. I spend every day with fucking blue balls. Now shut up and let me defile the boss' daughter."

My shoulders were shaking with laughter, as David began kissing and biting at different parts of my body. His hands had made their way down to my rib cage, his thumbs gripping against me. "You don't have blue balls all day, David! Those aren't even real!"

"Charlie," he moaned, raising his eyes to meet mine. His eyes so dark. Long gone were his dancing irises. His chin was resting in my belly button. "Shut the fuck up."

I shrieked again, kicking my legs in laughter. David grabbed my thighs with his hands and pushed them apart and down into the bed. "So serious, Mr. Kennedy!" I was still laughing as his hair tickled my lower abdomen. I felt his weekend stubble rub against my inner thigh. Suddenly his head was between my legs and my breath hitched. It wasn't funny anymore.

CHAPTER SEVEN

David's alarm went off at five. I heard him groan and turn it off after two rings. I don't think we went to sleep until well after midnight. I felt him push up off the side of the bed. My eyes were closed, but I could picture him running his fingers through his hair, pulling on the ends. His broad shoulders hunched forward slightly, as he rubbed his hands over his face. I smiled through my closed eyes, feeling the early morning sunlight come through the windows.

I felt David's wide hand on my shoulder. His thumbs stroked my skin softly. "Charlie, I'm going to go workout. It'll be about an hour. Help yourself to anything, okay? If you're not up, I'll wake you up when I get back."

"No, I'm up." I pushed myself up off the bed, gathering the sheet in front of my chest. "I usually get up around now anyway."

"Do you want to work out with me?" He was as I pictured him, running his hands through his hair as he stood, stretching his long arms across his body.

"No, I usually go to SoulCycle with my dad at lunch on Mondays." I turned to survey David. The sun was streaming in, stripes of light across the broad planes of his back.

He turned, the sweatpants he had fallen asleep in were hanging down, revealing a thick deep V of abdominal muscle. He was smiling wickedly at me. The sun was making his brown eyes sparkle again. People say brown eyes are boring, but David's certainly are not.

"Wait for me to shower then?" He asked, and I nodded yes.

He stopped briefly at his closet and grabbed what appeared to be gym clothes off of a shelf before stepping out of the room. I flopped backward, staring up at the light patterns from the sun on the ceiling. I felt around for my phone. I usually wake up early to get a head start on my emails. I received monthly reports from all the programs we worked with about their current status and financials, and I stayed connected with most of the people who were running the programs in a more informal way. I liked to make sure I kept these conversations going and often used the morning time to do so, because it simply wasn't an option during business hours.

In addition to the emails of the personal nature, I had five financial reports to review and approve: three funding extension requests, five complete backgrounders to review from the research team before I turned them into formal proposals for my Dad, and a bunch of boring legal documents to review.

The looming deadline for my father on Tuesday would mean I was in the office all day and likely into the night, as I had done zero work this weekend. Unless you counted drawing a map of David's abdomen with my tongue as work? Some might.

I was sitting at the kitchen island, my hair falling like a sheet around my face. I had my hand cupped around a glass coffee mug I had found in David's cupboard. The fresh coffee I had poured into it had wisps of steam trailing upward.

I was making adjustments to my calendar for the next two days, attempting to clear it of meetings so I could focus on the proposals for my father, then I heard the door open. David was wearing the Tar

Heels hat I had seen on his chair last night. It was turned backward and likely kept the sweaty mop of hair off of his face.

"Good workout? I made coffee." I spun around to face him. I had thrown on the oversized sweater of his I was wearing last night while I made coffee.

David had a can of Folgers; it was disgusting and probably still had the blood of migrant workers in it. I made a mental note to give him a bag of coffee beans from one of the first organizations we worked with when I came to WH. It was a women's cooperative in Guatemala. I paid to have three bags a month shipped to my house, because it is the most delicious—and sustainably sourced—coffee I had ever had.

David took his hat off, running his hand through his hair, which was damp with sweat and curling slightly, before putting the hat back on his head. "You didn't shower, right?"

I snorted and took a sip of the coffee. "Do I look like I showered?"

A grin broke out on his face, and he darted across the landing to grab my thighs, picking me up. "Thank god."

I shrieked, dropping my coffee mug. It shattered on the floor and hot coffee began to seep everywhere. "David! I broke your mug!"

"Did you do that on purpose because I threw your crystal glasses around, Charlie?" David asked, biting at my neck. I smacked his shoulder, wrapping my hands around his neck and laughing wildly. He buried his face in my neck as he began walking us toward the bathroom at the end of the hall and said, "House cleaning service is coming today. I'll get the glass later."

David drove us to work, keeping one hand on my thigh the entire time. The inside of his car was spotless; I wasn't surprised. He obviously didn't have a hair dryer, so I had tied my hair into a low bun at the back of my head. My eyes were burning from lack of sleep and caffeine. I was hoping to keep them hidden behind my aviators for as long as possible.

It was only seven-twenty by the time we pulled into the WH parking garage. It was quite chilly, and I was pulling my leather jacket around me, as we walked into the building, my tote bag hanging on my shoulder. David had his hand under my jacket on the small of my back, as he held the door open for me. His own sunglasses had fallen down his nose, as he looked down at me.

It was already a poorly kept secret that something was going on with David and me, especially amongst the building staff. Security always saw us leaving together at various times, and a member of the custodial staff had caught us in a compromising position, putting our clothes back on late one evening.

We both swiped our badges to walk through the security scanner. I turned to smile at the man behind the security desk, who I didn't recognize. There was often a turnover in staff positions like that. I felt David raise his hand beside me "Morning!"

I turned to look at him, smiling as I pushed my sunglasses up to the top of my head. "You have excellent manners."

"It's called being a human." He reached his arm out to hold the elevator door for me. Winchester Holdings took up the top five floors of a building in the downtown core that overlooked the river. My father owned this building and rented out the remaining fifteen floors to various companies and corporations. The revenue for this single building alone was in the millions. The elevator doors closed, leaving David and me alone. He slid his hand down from my lower back, grazing his fingers across my ass, as he reached down into his pocket. He leaned over and winked at me. We had decided it was best not to walk into the office displaying any sort of affection, although everyone at WH had probably read Society News over the weekend.

The top floor of the building—and of WH—is the executives' floor. It is an open concept and seems like a giant hallway, with offices on either side. Each VP or chief officer has an office side by side, the conference room at one end of the hallway, and my father's office at the other end. All of the executive assistants have desks in front of their respective offices. There is a kitchen off to the side of the conference room, but no one ever ate their lunch there. Most people just used the expensive coffee machine.

The elevator is directly across from my office, and as I predicted, Deacon was already waiting in one of my chairs, tossing a tennis ball up in the air. We were usually in earlier than anyone else on the floor; my father tended to roll in around nine and often accompanied Ash or anyone he might have had a breakfast meeting with. He left around five-thirty or six in the evening most days unless he was looking to close a deal or coming up against a deadline. Whereas Deacon, David and I—and Carter before he left—tended to work until seven or later.

David spotted Deacon and smiled crookedly. "I'll leave you to it. I'm in meetings all morning, but I'll see you later?" David let his hand brush across my back, as he made his way across the floor toward his office. It is in the middle of the floor, right between Rowena and Deacon's offices. I watched him as he raised a hand to Bethany, his and Rowena's shared executive assistant. She is a middle-aged, mousy sort of woman. She doesn't speak much and is incredibly efficient. Her brown hair is streaked liberally with gray and pushed off her face with what I was pretty certain was a velvet headband. I noticed a blush creep up her neck, as David waved and stopped by to say 'good morning' to her before going into his office.

I lingered in the doorway of my office, watching as Deacon leaned farther back in my leather desk chair. My office was covered in artifacts from my life before coming to WH. There were blown-up photos of my time volunteering as well as various photos of me traveling. There were pieces of art or sculptures I had collected hanging on the walls. Behind my desk, both of my degrees were hung up alongside a photo of our family at my graduation from Brown. My desk itself was cluttered. You could barely see the shiny white lacquered surface beneath it. I frowned. I needed to tidy it up. It was covered in sticky notes, various legal pads and phrase books for various languages.

"Morning Deac," I set my tote down on the leather couch that was sitting against the longest wall, and I shrugged off my leather jacket. I hung it on a painted gold coat rack I found at a thrift store. Deacon caught the tennis ball in his hand and set it down against my desk. "Hi Charlie." His hair was gelled off his face, and he had propped up his tan Cole Haan dress shoes on a free area of my desk. He was wearing a dark blue and brown-checkered wool suit I recognized from the most recent Hugo Boss catalog. On anyone else, it would probably look stupid. But somehow Deacon looked like he should be on the cover of Forbes.

"That suit makes you look like a dick." I supplied, unhelpfully. I removed my sunglasses, knowing my eyes were likely bloodshot and sunken.

He looked down in concern, studying the fabric and the pattern." Really? I thought that–"

I rolled my eyes and snorted. "I'm kidding, Deacon. Only you could pull something that preposterous off and look good."

He looked mollified. "I can tell you stayed at David's you know, you might want to suggest he at least invest in a blow dryer. Is he a wild animal?"

"Deacon, can I help you? I need my desk. I have work to do." I pushed the rolling chair out of my way, knocking his feet off my desk. He took some of my Post-its with it. Yanking the bottom drawer open, I pulled out a pair of nude Louboutin pumps. I hobbled sideways, bracing myself against my desk as I slid them onto my feet.

Deacon pushed against the arms of the chair, raising his body out of it. He looked down at me as if he was studying me. "I just wanted to say sorry in person. I would have brought you a coffee as a peace offering, but I assumed David would have done that. But still, I'm sorry. Didn't even have the decency to make you one this morning?"

I felt my cheeks growing red, picturing the shattered coffee mug on the floor of his apartment, followed by forty minutes in the shower which almost made us late. "Thank you for the apology. And we didn't really have time for coffee this morning..."

Deacon pulled a face immediately, squinting his eyes and parting his mouth in something that resembled disgust. "Spare me the details. I'm with the guy in meetings all morning, I don't need to think about him railing my sister."

"You make it sound so romantic, Deacon. It's a wonder there are so many women who vehemently despise you. Now seriously get out of my office. I'm swamped today." I grabbed the chair out from behind him and rolled it back to the desk. I felt him lean over and plant a kiss on my forehead.

I was about to sit in the chair when I noticed all the sticky notes that had fallen off my desk when Deacon's shoe had come down. Annoyed, I dropped to my knees, aware that my calves and Louboutins would be the only thing visible peeking around my desk if anyone walked by my office. I didn't even remember writing half of these, and to be honest, I was not entirely sure what half of them even meant. I was the only person on the floor who did not have an executive assistant, and that was by choice. It struck me as odd to show up here after years away and mold my portfolio the exact same way as every other one—to delegate tasks to someone else, such as simply reaching out to community groups, when I should really do them myself. I wanted to do something different; I wanted to be someone different.

"What the fuck do any of these even mean?" I breathed. I had a sticky note per finger on my left hand. I squinted, barely able to discern even my own writing on some of them. I picked up the final sticky note that had fallen facedown. I flipped it over to see two clearly written words: Mexico City.

"Oh fuck." I pushed myself upward, shaking the sticky notes off my fingers, clutching the one that read Mexico City like it was a lifeline. I brushed off the front of my dress, peaking my head out of the office to see where Deacon went. I was scheduled to be in Mexico City on Wednesday to review and approve changes to a community art program we were funding there. I did not have the time to sort out my travel and accommodations. I was hoping that Deacon would allow me to borrow the assistant he and Ash shared.

I heard laughter coming from down the floor, able to easily pick out Deacon's laugh amongst them. So much for starting work on-time. I held up a hand in greeting Bethany and Damien, who were the only two EAs in the office. I could hear Deacon and David, and another voice coming from David's office. I leaned around the corner of the doorway, holding it with my hands. David was leaning back in his chair, the buttons of his dark blue suit jacket opened. His hair was pushed back off his face, tossing the tennis ball back and forth with

Deacon, who was sitting on the edge of the standard WH Mahogany desk. Christian, someone I recognized as a friend of Deacon's from legal, was sitting in the leather chair opposite to the desk.

David caught the tennis ball in his right hand and looked up, winking at me. "To what do we owe this pleasure?"

Deacon turned to look at me, furrowing his brow slightly. "You're not still mad at me, are you Charlie?"

"No, I was actually wondering if I could borrow Nika whenever she comes in—" I held up my finger with the Mexico City sticky note.

Deacon raised his hands and started making a cutting gesture across his chest. "Get your own assistant Charlie! This is fucking ridiculous. You are a director of an entire portfolio and you keep yourself organized with fucking sticky notes! Does that say Mexico City?! What does that even mean?"

I frowned, removing the sticky note from my finger and crumpling it up. "Sorry if my notes offend you so much. Anyway, I don't need her all day. I just need her to book my travel for Wednesday. I, uh, something came up and I need to be in Mexico City to check on one of the programs." A lie. I had known about this trip for three weeks.

"Take the jet," Deacon waved a hand at me as if he had solved world hunger.

"No, I'm not taking the company jet to check in on a community art program for youth who were previously street involved. I don't even fly first class when I travel for work, Deacon!" I shook my head and began to unwind my hair from the low bun it was in, hoping I would achieve messy waves as opposed to wet, straggly hair.

"Jesus Christ, what is the matter with you?" He undid the button on his jacket and narrowed his forest green eyes at me. "Fine, borrow Nika so you can continue your peasant lifestyle."

"People are dying, Deacon." I responded flatly, turning on my heel, getting ready to return to my office.

I heard Christian speak. He had a faint British accent. "How did you get so lucky, Kennedy? Fuck, what half of the men in this office would–"

I heard both Deacon and David raise their voices in protest and what sounded like a tennis ball making contact with a body. Deacon followed through on his offer, and Nika came by my office shortly after she arrived to find out the details. She also tried to make the suggestion that I at least should be booking a first class ticket. "It's not even a five-hour flight, Nika. If I can't hack it in coach, I have some serious problems." I smiled at her, as she took notes on her phone. That seemed like a more sophisticated system to me. I should ask her what app software she used. "I won't say no to extra leg room, though."

Nika smiled at me and ducked her head, as she turned to go back to her desk outside of Deacon and Ash's office at the end of the floor. I turned my attention back to my computer, where I was combing through the financial reports sent to me by one of the programs we were likely going to fund. There was a timid knock on the doorframe. I raised my eyes to see Olivia, one of the four researchers employed in my portfolio. My portfolio was structured very differently than the others at WH. I led the portfolio and had a small department team reporting to me. I had four researchers, most of whom were fresh out of college and had some varying levels of expertise across the areas of community development we typically funded: health programming, environmental programming, social programming, and STEM Community Programming. Olivia had been with my team for just under a year and was headed off to the London School of Economics in the fall to pursue the same master's degree as I had. I had actually written her a recommendation.

"Hey Olivia," I smiled brightly, gesturing for her to sit in one of the cushioned chairs across from my desk. I noticed her immediate hesitation to enter, and that she was clutching a manila folder with her manicured hand like it was a lifeline. A flush passed over her olive skin, as she looked down at her heeled feet. She was kicking the point of her suede heel into the corner of the doorframe. I arched an eyebrow and pushed back from my computer desk, folding my arms inward. "Olivia? What's wrong? Are you okay?"

I studied her as she gulped visibly and looked up at me, her dark brown eyes brimming with tears, as she pushed a stray curl behind her ear. "There was a mistake with one of the programs we...I...suggested..."

I felt cold suddenly. I had already passed the suggestions along to the executive team and had been in contact with the individuals leading the groups. It clearly was not a small mistake that was easily fixed, like they were receiving funding from another program and we would have to decrease our funding.

"Which groups and what kind of mistake Olivia?" I closed my eyes, a million possible worst case scenarios running through my head.

"Play for Everyone..." She looked down again, leaning against the doorway for support. She stopped kicking her feet and was hugging the envelope across her chest. Play for Everyone is a community sports group that the research team had discovered in Venezuela that worked to give children who had lost their parents to violence an outlet through sports, and in turn, employed the children when they came of age to coach and referee various sporting events. "They are a community sports program, but they've made some questionable political donations..."

"What questionable political donations? Wait. Don't tell me..." I shrieked, vaguely aware that my door was wide open and everyone else on the floor would be able to hear us. I was too angry and shocked to care at the moment. "Olivia, how did this happen?" Our team did an extensive vetting process for every organization we funded to ensure they met all of our criteria, and truthfully, to avoid anything that could potentially be a liability. This included extensive conversations with local community members. This took months.

Olivia looked up, her brown eyes meeting mine. Tears were spilling over and her voice shook. "You trusted me to do the vetting process myself...you said I didn't need you breathing over my shoulder or re-reading everything. I'm so sorry, Charlie, you trusted me! One of the emails from the locals in the community...it was in Spanish and–"

"You speak Spanish, Olivia!" I bursted out again. I saw beyond her, that several of the EAs had stopped what they were doing and were looking in our direction curiously. "You know what, come in and close the door. I'm probably going to keep yelling."

Olivia gratefully stepped in and shut the door behind her. She handed the manila folder to me, and I began to flip through the pages. It was a series of emails back and forth between Olivia and the various community members she had been in contact with to find out the impact of the program.

"I speak Spanish at home with my extended family...it turns out I speak it better than I read or write it." She was looking down, picking at her fingernails. She was going to ruin what looked like a new manicure.

"Stop that Olivia, manicures aren't cheap." I swatted at her hand with the folder. I leaned backward in the chair, putting my face in my hands.

"How did this come to your attention?" I didn't vet Olivia's work. I had thought it was a good growing opportunity, a chance for her to have autonomy in her work. And she was right, I had trusted her.

"One of the community members called me back this morning, and they brought it to my attention that I had misunderstood their email about the program's affiliations..." She looked up at me, tears streaked liberally down her face, running tracks in her makeup. "I'm so sorry, Charlie. I'll tell Mr. Winchester...it was my fault."

"You will do no such thing. If you tell him it was you Olivia, I can't protect you. He will yell at you, and he will fire you on the spot. It will be humiliating, and there will be a gap on your resume." I shook my head and tucked a piece of hair behind my ear. "This was my fault as your director. From now on, everything you do comes through me. Everything. Got it?" She nodded, and a small hiccup escaped her mouth. "I do not care how late you have to work tonight, but you will be finding me a suitable replacement. Do you understand? You are not to have any communication with any of the staff from Play for Everyone. I will deal with them and with legal. Now get off the floor before my father sees you and figures out you did this." I turned back to my computer, a sense of dread bubbling in my stomach.

Steven Winchester rarely remembered to be a father first, and I was pretty certain this would be one instance where he would not. "Close the door, Olivia." I laid my head down on my desk and resisted the urge to begin smacking my own forehead. I lifted my head and ran my hands across my face repeatedly as if trying to scrub the conversation and revelation from my memory. I exhaled and pushed myself up off my desk. I could hear my heels clicking against the ceramic tile, as I made my way across the floor toward Damien's desk. I could see my dad was in his office with Ash and Helen, head of the legal division.

"Damien, I need you to tell my dad I'm coming in, it's urgent." I looked down at Damien, puffing out my cheeks.

He crinkled his dark eyebrows, beneath his trendy, wire glasses. "Everything okay, Charlie? He has a meeting after this one, but you could probably wait and squeeze in–"

Damien reached down and buzzed my father. "Steven, Charlie is out here and she says she needs to come in."

I made my way to the glass door, knocking before drawing it back. Ash and Helen both turned to me, and my dad's brow pinched together. He folded his arms across his chest. "Is everything okay, Charlie? We're in the middle of a meeting, as you can see. This can't wait until–"

"No. Unfortunately, it can't wait. I apologize, Ash." I turned to smile at him, as he began to gather his papers. Helen also went to stand. "Helen, you should probably stay." My father exhaled sharply. I noticed his eyes were narrowing. He did not like being interrupted, and he was not going to like what I was about to tell him. Anything that required legal was never good. He folded his arms and leaned back in his leather armchair.

Ash brushed past me and leaned in to whisper, "Good luck, Kiddo." I closed my eyes, exhaling and steeling myself, as I crossed the room and settled into a chair.

"Talk, Charlie." My father's fingers tapped a steady beat on the table, as Helen watched me apprehensively.

"At our briefing on Friday, I pitched to you the five selections for our next round of funding. I had been in contact with all of the organizations, and they had sent through their proposed budgets and financial information. As you know, we select our top choices through an extensive research process–"

"Spit it out, Charlie." My father interrupted me. His eyes were growing darker by the second, and I could see he was gritting his teeth.

"One of the organizations we have been in contact with...and that we approved for funding...they've made some unethical political donations." I looked up and met my father's eyes. Looking demure and weak by staring into my lap would not help me. I heard Helen mutter beside me, as she leaned her head into her hands.

"I know you signed the formal proposal last week but we haven't made the official announcement about who we are funding yet, so there is nothing in the press tying us to this–"

"Are you fucking kidding me, Charlie?" My father's voice was deadly even. It felt like it was slicing through my skin.

"I really wish I was, Dad."

"How did this fucking happen?!" He stood so fast that the papers in front of him flew across the desk. "Who is responsible for this?"

I closed my eyes briefly while inhaling. "You know I'm not going to tell you that. It's my fault. I take full responsibility."

"You're fucking right this is your fault! You are the director of this portfolio! Again, how did this fucking happen?!" He was leaning forward on his desk, screaming at me.

"Steven, calm down," Helen began. "If there is nothing in the press yet, we can work with this. We can file the appropriate paperwork that allows us to cite a breach of contract. It's work, yes. But it's possible... we will serve them a cease and desist and–"

"Helen, do not make excuses for her!" My father barked, rounding back on me. "Answer me, Charlie?"

I made a mental note to send Helen a thank you email later. "I was trying to be a leader, Dad. I was trying to give my staff some autonomy. I trusted them, and I didn't do the final vetting myself. I should have looked it over."

"You're absolutely right you should have looked it over! That's your job as a director. Who did it Charlie? If you don't tell me someone else will. Whoever it was, was obviously on the floor earlier. I will go down there and yell at every single one of those kids of yours until–" my father was standing, pointing his finger at me.

I resisted the urge to roll my eyes and looked forward to the ceiling, exhaling—this was a typical Steven Winchester display of toxic masculinity. "No you won't, Dad! They're just kids!"

My father steeled himself, his eyes narrowing in on me again. He glanced briefly toward Helen. "Helen, you can go. Charlie will be down to legal later to let you know how we will be proceeding."

Helen gathered her things. She briefly raised her hand as she walked by me, like she wanted to reach out and stroke my shoulder in comfort but made the decision not to. She wouldn't dare touch me or say anything. "But leave the door open so no one can ever say that I 'favor' my children," he continued shouting, as Helen left the glass door open. Everyone on the executives' floor heard him now—if they couldn't before.

"No one would ever accuse you of that, Dad," I said evenly, doing my best not to break eye contact with him. I could hear voices in the hall and the noises of others in the office.

"No, I suppose they wouldn't. What the fuck were you thinking, Charlie?!" He was still leaning over his desk, oblivious to any of his team members out in the hallway.

"I told you, Dad. I was trying to allow autonomy. They took responsibility. I took care of it. I told you immediately. We are obviously going to work all night until we have a suitable replacement. I am not telling you who made the mistake. I took care of it. I will end this relationship with this company myself. I will personally be reviewing everything that comes up from research–"

He cut me off again. "Oh, you bet your ass you will be reviewing everything. I don't give a flying fuck how long it takes you. I don't care how many hours it adds to your day. And on top of that? Every single thing you do comes through me. *You* have zero autonomy."

"I understand," I nodded, keeping my hands crossed in my lap. Steven Winchester admonishments could go on for a while. I hoped by staying quiet it would end sooner. I had seen him and Deacon go at it for almost two hours when he had spoken back to him.

"This is your family business, Charlie. Your family legacy. Your grandfather is probably rolling over in his fucking grave. Do you know what it would have done to this company if that funding deal had gone through?" I resisted the urge to point out that I had caught it before it got to that point. My father had paused and yanked the knot of his tie down. There were beads of sweat lining his forehead. "I don't know what the fuck you were thinking! Has David screwed all the sense out of you?!" He gestured aggressively with his hand, and I turned slightly in my chair to see Deacon, David, and Tripp. David was visibly cringing, and Deacon looked gleeful. Tripp was leaning against Damien's desk with his hands in his pockets, and an impossible-to-read expression on his face. They must be his next meeting.

I turned back to my dad and raised my eyebrows, cocking my head slightly. "Wow. I guess no SoulCycle at lunch. May I please be excused?" He threw himself back in his chair and began to tighten the knot of his tie again. He waved toward the door to let me know he was done. I stood, smoothing the front of my dress. I turned on my heel, resisting the urge to give my father a withering glare. I tipped my chin upward and walked out of his office in an attempt to return to my office with whatever dignity I had left.

Deacon bit his lip, choking back laughter. His eyebrows flew up his head. "Screwed the sense out of you? Jesus, Charlie that's–"

"Suck dick Deacon." I rolled my eyes and hissed out of the corner in my mouth, shaking my head. I heard my dad yell for the three of them to come in, as I slid the glass door to my office closed.

––––––––––

Leaning forward on my desk, attempting to get closer to my computer screen to read the small fine print, I could vaguely see someone approaching my office in the periphery. Great. I pushed back and looked up, gathering my hair into a low ponytail. It kept falling in my face, as I was trying to read. I had been reading and re-reading everything the research team sent me in order to avoid any more 'I guess I speak better Spanish than I read it' conundrums.

Tripp was leaning in my doorway, his hands shoved into the pockets of his black suit. His hair was artfully tousled and his ice blue eyes were cool and unfriendly. "Is that what it's always like here? I might reconsider signing that contract." Of course he had just come over to let me know he was going to be working here.

"Well, I guess congratulations are in order. Welcome to Winchester Holdings. Don't worry, even if you massively fuck up, I will be on the bottom for some time to come." I grabbed the oversized Oliver Peoples black frames sitting on my desk. I wore them sometimes when I had a lot to do on the computer. My eyes were burning.

"You should have just told him who did it, Charlie. That's what I would have done." He arched an eyebrow at me, hands still shoved deep in his pockets.

I rolled my eyes, folding my arms across my chest. "That is the least surprising piece of news I have ever received. Of course that's what you would have done."

He held his palms up, "I was just saying. You could have avoided that embarrassment."

I exhaled and rolled my eyes. "Tripp, you don't work here yet. So, with all due respect, get the hell out of my office."

Tripp snorted and put his hands back into the pockets of his suit. "See you in two weeks, Charlie."

I looked up and met his eyes. I felt my breath hitch and my stomach drop. The last time we had held direct eye contact was seven years ago, and he was moving inside me. He gazed at me intensely before dropping his eyes to do a onceover of the portion of my body visible above my desk. He grinned slightly and turned on the heel of his black dress shoe and walked out of the office. I was sure I could hear him whistling.

CHAPTER EIGHT

The salad I ordered from a local cafe was taking the brunt of my frustrations as the formal workday drew to a close. I was stabbing madly at a particularly tricky piece of lettuce, as I chased it around the compostable bowl in the oil-based dressing. I frowned as I tossed the bowl onto the stack of papers on my desk, admitting defeat.

I pushed my glasses up on my head, pushing my hair off my face and rubbed my hands aggressively across it. My eyes were burning. I had been glued to my computer screen all day in an attempt to find another group to replace Play for Everyone. My research team had been running back and forth between our floor and the research floor below all day.

Mid-afternoon, we brought in a Spanish interpreter to mediate the call Helen and I had with the contact at Play for Everyone. It was excruciatingly painful to sit there while Deacon made a point of strolling by multiple times, whistling gleefully, probably because no matter what mistakes he inevitably made in the future, none would even come close to this one. Helen had already drawn up the cease and desist, as well as hired a translator to create the document in Spanish. The interpreter and translator had to sign several non-disclosure agreements and be read their rights by one of the Winchester Holdings attorneys, more specifically Helen, when they arrived at our office, which was perhaps the most embarrassing part of it all.

There was a knock on the door frame, and I looked up to see Ash standing in my doorway. He was wearing a black suit, clutching his ancient mahogany briefcase that I knew his wife had given him. I sighed heavily, folding my arms across my chest. I had known Ash since I was a child. It was almost as embarrassing to have made such a mistake in front of him than it was my father. "Hi, Ash."

He smiled, his green eyes surveying me sadly. "That was a rough day. You know your father loves you, right kiddo?"

I resisted the urge to roll my eyes at Ash. "I know he does, but he loves his business more. I made a mistake." I didn't think I deserved to be told I had the sense screwed out of me by a fellow colleague but did not feel quite like bringing that up in front of someone who had fed me as a child.

"So did he, Charlie. It was not appropriate, what he did or said. I won't defend that. But I've known your father a long time. This business...all this," Ash gestured around, as if the entire worth of Winchester Holdings could be found within my office, "this is his legacy. But it's also the way he is going to ensure that you and Deacon are set for life. You should have heard him going on after David left Widmore last Saturday. Charlie, he's so happy you're sharing your life with someone."

I looked upward, feeling tears burn at the back of my eyes. I blinked rapidly. If that revelation was true, it was a surprise to me. I brought my head back down, making eye contact with Ash. His green eyes were cloudy with concern. "He has a funny way of showing it, you know. He's always saying to me that as a woman I will have to work three times as hard to earn anyone's respect. And today, he screamed at me in front of our entire office that I had the sense screwed out of me by a man, Ash. It was demeaning."

He set his briefcase down and crossed the threshold of my office, coming to rest his hand on my shoulder and looked down at me. So many memories of my childhood and my parents were intertwined with Ash and his wife, Serena. They never had children, so it was always my parents, Deacon and me, and Ash and Serena on globetrotting family vacations. "I didn't say what he said was okay, Charlie. But he loves you and Deacon more than anything in the world, remember that." I leaned sideways, pressing my head against his forearm. He was unseasonably tan and his skin had a rough quality to it I always associated with hypermasculinity. He and Serena had a home in the Virgin Islands they frequented. I closed my eyes and inhaled. Sometimes, being this close to Ash reminded me of my mom. I could almost sense her, like she was just out of my grasp. I felt him reach across with his free hand and ruffle my hair affectionately.

"Serena is over the moon about David. She hopes to meet him soon." He removed his hand from my shoulder, stirring me from my reverie.

I looked up, smiling tightly. "I would love for them to meet sometime."

Ash's eyes twinkled and he ruffled my hair one final time before heading to the door to grab his abandoned briefcase. "Hang in there, kiddo."

I looked up as Ash began to walk toward the elevator where my father was waiting, his steely gaze on his Blackberry as he typed furiously, clearly not bothered to look in my direction. I snorted, exhaling a puff of air through my nose. Eyeing my salad, I slid my arm in a sweeping motion across my desk, knocking the compostable bowl into the adjacent garbage bin. The plastic fork hit the side and fell to the ground.

I began to bend down to pick it up when there was a hesitant knock on the wooden doorway. I raised my eyes to see Olivia alongside the three other members of my research team, residing in the doorway laden down with papers. I pushed up off the corner of my desk, beckoning them in with my spare hand, leaving the oily fork where it laid beside the trash can.

———

The setting sun casted shadows through the large windows across the marble floor of my office, which was strewn with papers, discarded heels, and coffee cups. Olivia, along with the other researchers, had been with me in the office since the end of the formal work day—around five-thirty—going through all new funding suggestions with a fine-toothed comb. We were attempting to fit months of research and consultation into a few hours.

I was sitting against the front of my desk, my legs out in front of me like sticks, holding my nude Louboutin in one hand, pointing the heel around the room to emphasize the various points I was making, or to address any of the others in the room.

Ruhee, one of the first researchers I hired, was sitting directly across from me on the worn mustard leather couch I bought at an auction and shoved against the empty wall. She was leaning forward, flipping through her yellow legal pad to read back notes from a conversation she had earlier that evening with a community member. "Yes, it's right here. So they are working to re-employ fishermen through conservation and responsible tourism. The community members are engaged in clean water provision and education."

"Yes! Ruhee!" I waved my Louboutin and pointed the heel at her aggressively as I smacked my free hand against the cold marble. "This is the one. Thank God for the time change that you were able to get a hold of someone in the community. Okay, leave anything and everything you all turned up with me."

"You all did great work today. I want to say thank you so much for your energy. I couldn't ask for a better team." I smiled sincerely, sighing slightly, then I looked over at Olivia, who was scuffing her toes back and forth on the floor.

"Mistakes happen and we are only going to be better and more vigilant moving forward." I smiled again and set the Louboutin down beside me. "I know this technically falls under that piece of your contract where you may have to work additional hours as required, but I would like you all to pick a day over the next few months that you can quietly take off. Off the books entirely. As a thank you for the work you did today individually and as a team."

I paused as they all began to state their thanks, giving special attention to the pink hue that was overcoming Olivia's brown skin. I felt it was best to continue. "This isn't going to be the last time someone makes a mistake on this team, or in their career. We are just playing with a lot of public money at the moment, and we need to be careful. I am absolutely positive none of us will make this mistake again."

I clapped my hands together, feeling weary as the last of the sunlight disappeared from the view of the windows. "Okay, everyone leave what you have for me from our new selection and get out of here. Go have a drink and relax." I noticed Ruhee rub her hand across Olivia's shoulder affectionately, as they began to gather their discarded papers. I tried to catch Olivia's eye, but she seemed determined to look at her legal pad and various notes. I raised my eyes, as there was a gentle knock on the door frame.

David was leaning against the doorway, his tie undone haphazardly and his suit jacket gone. His hair was pushed back off his face and there was a shadow coming in along his jawline. "May I come in? I don't want to interrupt."

I beckoned him in with my free hand as I was accepting a stack of notes and papers from Ruhee. "Hey, Mr. Kennedy. Did you have a good day?"

David snorted as he bent down beside me, his arms resting on his knees. His eyes grew dark at the mention of his name. He was still a bit above my head even crouching. "Better than you all did, I think. I'm going to head out soon. I wanted to check if you needed a ride."

I laughed loudly and set my slim hand on his kneecap and met his eyes. "I'm going to be here a while longer. To be honest, I might as well sleep here."

David drew in his eyebrows, as he started playing with my fingers that were resting on his knee. "Do you want me to come back and pick you up later? Don't walk home Charlie, it's still freezing after dark and this is Chicago."

I rolled my eyes. "I'll probably just go to Deacon's. It's only two blocks away." Deacon and I made a point to spend usually one or two nights a week at one another's houses, and we kept a variety of clothing there.

"You sure you don't want to spend the night? I'll come back and get you." David lowered his voice to barely a whisper, as his eyes grew darker and a smile tugged at the corners of his mouth. "I'll see if I can screw some of that sense back into you."

I laughed in spite of myself and quickly bit my lip. "No, I really shouldn't. Now get out of here before you get me in more trouble. David grinned wickedly and leaned forward, stroking his thumb roughly across my pointed chin. He pushed up off his knees, looked down at me one last time as he pulled to further loosen the knot on his tie and winked, before turning around and saying goodbye to the rest of my research team.

Olivia and Ruhee turned to me, their eyes wide, each looking as if they were biting their tongues to keep from commenting. I arched an eyebrow as I began to slide my Louboutin's back on my feet, bracing myself to stand after having been on the ground for a few hours. "Go home ladies."

CHAPTER NINE

The wheels of the plane touched down roughly onto the tarmac, jerking me forward and out of my reverie. My neck snapped uncomfortably as I reached back to rub the nape with my hand. All the joints in my body felt stiff. Perhaps Deacon had been on to something about at least sitting in first class.

I peeked out the window beside me—the sunlight streaming through caused me to blink rapidly. I had been in Mexico City for the past two days. Leading up to that, I worked non-stop to rectify the 'Play for Everyone' mistake, having only slept one evening on the couch in my office.

I turned in my seat to stretch slightly, smiling at the man sitting beside me as I invaded his personal space. Reaching for my phone, I turned off airplane mode. Deacon always insisted that I did not actually need to turn my phone off and that there was no such thing as scrambling the signal for the pilots, but there was something in me that never felt like I could break this rule. A new text message from my father appeared at the top of my inbox reading, "Nicely done on your new proposal. All good to go for next steps." I exhaled loudly, tucking a stray hair behind my ear. He had maintained a stony silence, even when I handed the proposal to Damien before heading to the airport on Wednesday. That was likely as good as I was going to get.

Swiping up, I scanned the work emails I had missed during my four-hour non-stop flight. They were all fairly mundane, nothing I needed to rush in for. After returning home, I usually worked from home that day or the following day, especially if there was a time difference. I was physically exhausted. Both of my days had been 15 hours in the field, but nothing energized me more than this kind of exhaustion.

Returning to my text messages, I saw several missed from Deacon about the new suits he was having made, asking me if I would come to the tailor with him this weekend and another from David in response to a photo I had sent him of a sunrise hike I had gotten up three hours early to do before heading into the city.

I wasn't used to missing anyone but Deacon when I was away, and I found a genuine excitement and yearning in myself to see David again. A smile crept on my face as I responded to him. Seeing him would have to wait until tomorrow. I promised Taylor we would have drinks, and after returning both David and Deacon's missed texts, I found a flurry of texts from her where she indicated she had the afternoon off from the hospital. She had gotten my flight information from Deacon and would be picking me up at the airport, and she expected me to blow off the afternoon.

My father usually forgave me if I skived off after traveling, but I wasn't sure he would be in a forgiving mood this time. Deacon had called me the night I landed in Mexico to let me know he was still storming around the office, having yelled at both him and David on separate occasions. I planned to avoid him until Monday morning. Damien had put an hour-long meeting between the two of us in my calendar for nine in the morning. However, given the fact that my father was handedly ignoring me all week, the likelihood of him finding out I wasn't working from home was quite unlikely.

I shifted uncomfortably in my seat as the night air bit at my exposed arms despite the heating lamps that were spread across the rooftop.

Taylor hissed at me through expertly painted lips. "Stop fidgeting. You look great." I rolled my eyes before narrowing them at her, as she leafed through the menu.

Her dirty blonde hair looked as though her roots had grown in, but I knew she paid quite a bit of money for the appearance that this swath of colors was natural. She sat across from me, her muscular shoulders poised beneath the thin straps of her dress. I watched keenly as Taylor pursed her lips again. They were painted some shade of deep red I would never have been able to pull off. She flicked her eyes upward at me. They reminded me of David's. They were like warm honey and felt like home. Her nose ended in a tiny ski slope—it was fake, but I had also held a bit of a grudge that she *stole* my dream nose. My father forbade me from having any sort of face-altering plastic surgery, not when my face had been known since I was a child. I felt like I was constantly somersaulting between not caring what he thought and then desperately seeking his approval the next.

"Want to split a bottle?" Taylor rained a nail down the page of the leather-bound menu. Her nails were the only thing about her that didn't scream high society elegance. They were cut almost to the quick and appeared dull in comparison to the rest of her that sparkled. She wasn't allowed to have long nails or paint them as a surgical resident, and she spent more time in the hospital than out.

I was tugging absentmindedly at the neckline of my dress; Taylor had convinced me to buy this ridiculous Herve Leger bandage dress. "I don't think people still wear these," I hissed, reaching forward to pinch her arm.

"I saw it in Vogue," she said absentmindedly, snatching her arm out of my grasp and lifting it to gesture to the bartender. I sat back, crossing my arms across the too-tight dress that pushed my boobs up to my neck and narrowed my eyes at her. My hair had been straightened to perfection and was split like a curtain down the middle.

"No you didn't," I leaned forward to pinch Taylor's exposed arm, before turning to the server. "Yes, the bottle. Thank you so much."

She reached forward to press her credit card into the server's hand for the tab. I started forward, snatching it. "No. You can bill me, please."

"Of course, Miss Winchester." He dipped his head slightly, as if I was fucking royalty and handed Taylor's card back to her. He turned on his immaculately polished shoe and headed toward the direction of the prohibition era-looking bar. Everything in Chicago looked to me like it belonged in The Great Gatsby.

Taylor leaned forward grabbing my hands that were pulling at the neckline of my dress. "Stop that, and stop that." She jerked her head toward the bar. "You don't need to–"

I rolled my eyes, leaning back as I studied her. "I know I don't 'need to' Taylor. What's the point of being a billionaire if I can't buy overpriced bottles of champagne for my best friend in the world?"

My only friend really, if I thought about it long enough. Unless I counted Deacon. I had other friends, I guess. People who ran in the same social circles as my father, that I had known for years and belonged to all of the same clubs. But no one who really felt like home the way Taylor did. I had always been the odd one out, never fitting in the way Deacon blended in seamlessly. It wasn't that I couldn't get along with others or didn't even share the same interests; I had just always possessed this sense of otherness. Like I was constantly on the outside looking in. That I never fit anywhere, and a deep-rooted insecurity that I didn't belong anywhere. Our father never understood and tried to force me into social situations that left me deeply uncomfortable. My mother had understood. She had encouraged me and held my hand when–

I closed my eyes briefly and steeled a breath before opening them to look at Taylor, who was studying me with her head tilted to the side, as if I was a particularly interesting tumor sitting on a patient sliced open in front of her. "What's going on in there?" She asked softly.

"Nothing good," I muttered, turning away from her gaze and studying the lights that were strung across the rooftop, blocking out the sky, not that you could see much downtown anyway. There were too many lights and too much pollution. I craned my neck to see if I could get a view of the river.

I felt Taylor tense across the table, still studying me with that maddening expression. She cleared her throat and seemingly decided to change the subject. "So. The elephant in the room. You've been fucking David Kennedy, and I had to find out from my mother when she read the paper. Explain."

She slammed a palm down on the table affectionately and smiled widely as the server returned with a blush, having seemingly heard her. He set an ornate-hammered copper wine cooler down on the table and pulled the bottle of champagne out. I had no idea what Taylor had ordered and was hardly paying attention. I turned and smiled widely as he offered us each a taste before pouring our glasses and ensuring us he would be back to top us up later.

As he turned, I hissed at Taylor and brought the flute to my lips. "We're not *fucking*."

She arched an eyebrow and appraised me, taking a small sip. "So are you making love then?"

. I huffed a small laugh in spite of myself before deadpanning. "Yes, Taylor, he lays me down on the desks at work each night and runs kisses down me, and worships my body, then we stare deeply into one another's eyes as he moves inside me and we come simultaneously."

Taylor grinned wickedly, her pillowy lips widening over her flute. "That sounds boring."

"We fucked in Deacon's coat closet." I bursted out laughing as I met her eyes. She tipped her head back and cackled loudly, not caring who heard her.

"And how is dear big brother?" She leaned forward conspiratorially, her eyes shimmering under the lights strung above us.

I rolled my eyes, adjusting the hem of my dress once more. "Am I meant to believe the two of you aren't in regular communication? That he doesn't swing by your apartment between shifts at the hospital to 'relieve' all of your stress?" Disgusting.

Taylor raised her glass to her lips and arched a single brow, opening her mouth to speak before stopping suddenly, then began to speak after she collected her thoughts. "Charlie," she purred, leaning forward grabbing my forearm again and narrowing her eyes at me, "why did David Fucking Kennedy...the man you are oh so sweetly making love to on a regular basis just walk in here with your brother and some fucking Marvel movie-looking villain in tow?"

My stomach simultaneously somersaulted at the mention of David's name and dropped to the pits of despair. There was only one person I knew who orbited their social circle who would be described like that. I closed my eyes briefly, taking an undignified swig of my champagne before turning in my seat to eye the entrance to the bar. And there they were. Deacon was Deacon, in all of his billionaire boy glory. His chocolate hair was sloppy, falling forward on his face as he shoved his hands into the pockets of his navy suit pants, his green eyes wide looking like a master of the universe. He tipped his head back and laughed uproariously at something Tripp had muttered under his breath. I would know that sound anywhere. He was, in many ways, the other half of my soul.

David stood beside them, raising a hand to run it through his hair, which was also falling messily across his forehead. They all looked vaguely sweaty. Where the fuck had they been? He leaned forward at the hostess stand, smiling widely as he spoke, unbuttoning his dark gray suit jacket to reveal a tight fitting white button up that was open at the top.

Almost against my own will, my eyes swiveled to the last member of the group. Tripp was standing there, his hands in the pocket of his slim fit black suit pants, leaning against the wall as he cocked an eyebrow at something Deacon said and opened his mouth to speak. Surely some snarky remark that would make my brother giggle incessantly. Unlike the other two, he didn't have a suit jacket. A tailored white shirt was rolled up to his forearms and the top buttons were undone. His dark hair was pushed off his face and stubble was lining his jaw. His eyes looked like the fucking Blue Lagoon in Iceland. He surveyed everything with indifference—from the leather-cushioned bar to the glass paneling that surrounded the rooftop and the lights strung up along the metal roof workings—and then they landed on *me*. A feline smile began to spread across his face, as I whipped around in my seat back to Taylor.

"Fuck me. I didn't tell them we were here, Taylor. You've had my phone all day. I haven't even spoken to Deacon or David today." I grabbed my drink like a child reaching for a teddy bear in search of comfort. I was certain Tripp would have alerted Deacon and David to our presence.

She rolled her eyes and lifted her flute to her lips, taking a small sip. "It's fine, but it looks like they're coming over here, so I am guessing our evening alone is getting interrupted. David is looking at the back of your head like he's going to fucking devour you, so I assume there is no chance of separating a lion from his prey at this point. Who is the Adonis?"

Taylor tipped her head as she surveyed them behind me. Her eyes grazing over someone who could only be Tripp. "You've actually met him before," I began, emptying my glass before grabbing the bottle to refill it. That was technically the server's job but fuck propriety. "That's Tripp Banks. We went to Brown together. We used to hang out…"

Taylor's eyes lit up as she let out a cackle. "That's right. You spent a lot of time at his frat. If I remember correctly, he used to chase you around endlessly trying to bag a Winchester. But all you would do is stick your tongue down his throat at mixers and bars." She grinned widely, her red lipstick accentuating her too-perfect teeth. We had both been getting our teeth professionally whitened for years. She didn't know the half of it. Her words rolled in my stomach, the harsh truth of them sinking their claws into my skin. I had only ever been a Winchester worth *fifteen points* to Tripp. I had never told anyone what happened between us. It was too demeaning, too embarrassing, too hurtful. I reached forward, lacing my fingers with hers and squeezing urgently. I dropped my voice. "Don't say anything. David and Deacon don't know."

Taylor's face immediately changed as she surveyed me. Her eyes softened, and she squeezed my fingers back and grabbed my other hand with hers. She examined me with concern, her warm eyes skating across my face. "I won't Charlie...are you sure that's all?" I felt a firm, calloused hand plant on my bare shoulder. I shook my head slightly, the memories of Tripp, my mother, and being alone and forgotten rattled around against the bars of my mind. I schooled my expression to read of enjoyment and turned around to smile widely.

I found I didn't really need to pretend. David's thumb stroked my shoulder, sending warmth skirting across my bare skin. I looked up at him, and he grinned widely. His eyes were bright and Taylor was not wrong. He looked *hungry*. He dropped to a crouch so our faces were leveled, and he continued to stroke his thumb across my skin. "I haven't seen you all week, and the first time I do you're in that dress and we're out in public. Life can be quite cruel, don't you think?" His eyes burned into me, and I hungrily traced his face. He had let his stubble come in all week and I inhaled. I wasn't sure what cologne he wore, but I made a mental note to find out immediately. I wanted to bathe in it.

"Do you like it? Taylor made me buy it. I think it's too tight," I whispered, gesturing to the deep gray bandage dress. His eyes broke away from mine briefly and skated across my cleavage.

"*Like* is an understatement. I think I'm going to fuck you in it later." David brought his mouth to my ear, and his voice was deadly. He moved to brush his lips against mine before his hands wandered to my forearms and he wrenched me up from my seat. His too big, too warm hands immediately found my waist and pulled me to him as he buried his face in my neck. He groaned against me, drawing me closer and brushing his lips against my neck before pulling back and looking down at me. "Hi, Charlie."

I looked up at him, meeting his honey eyes and tipped upward to meet his lips again. Forgetting we were in public and forgetting who I was, I swept my tongue into his mouth until there was a loud smack at our table behind us. I pulled away and whipped around. Deacon had his hand on Taylor's shoulder, but he wasn't looking at us. He had slammed his palm down on the table and was snapping his fingers at a nearby table who had their phones out. His eyes were narrowed, and he looked murderous.

"Uh uh. Do not take photos of my sister and her boyfriend. Have you never seen a couple in love who have been apart for a week? Fucking delete those right now, and if I find a single photo online or in Society News, you'll be hearing from my lawyer. My sister's happiness isn't for sale. DELETE." He barked loudly as Taylor narrowed her eyes at them as well, looking rather predatory herself. She broke her focus before looking over at me, smiling softly, as if she could sense happiness radiating off me.

David craned his head to look at the table behind us that had been documenting the whole thing. It was a mix of young professionals. They looked only a few years younger than us. He opened his mouth to speak as the manager rushed over to Deacon. "Sorry guys," he shrugged, whipping me around so my back was pressed against his chest. He wrapped his arms against me protectively, placing his chin down on my shoulder. "I haven't seen her all week. Got a little carried away."

He turned to the manager. "I'll take their bill for the trouble. You can just send it to me at the end of the night," David looked back at the group, who had all buried their faces in their phones. "But don't get carried away. My generosity only extends so far." My cheeks burned, and I had a feeling their night was likely ending quite soon, as Deacon still looked murderous and the manager spoke in hurried whispers to him. David ran his hands up and down my arms attempting to soothe me. He turned away again and pulled out my chair. Three additional chairs had materialized at our table. Tripp was leaning back, arms crossed in front of him surveying everything with his cool indifference. He arched an eyebrow at me and smiled wryly. "Quite the show, Chuckles."

I rolled my eyes as I settled into the chair. Deacon shook hands with the manager and clapped him on the back quickly as he dropped into his chair beside Taylor, unbuttoning his suit jacket and lazily tossing an arm around the back of hers. She grimaced, turning and picking up the fabric of his suit jacket like it was a piece of garbage and removing his arm from the back of her chair, dropping it in his lap before settling back down. I snorted, as I reached for my champagne.

"You two are fucking disgusting. You're welcome by the way. Dad would shit bricks if he woke up to a photo of David groping your ass in a fucking Herve Leger bandage dress in the middle of a restaurant." Deacon rolled his eyes before turning to Taylor with a sly grin. "Hi, Taylor."

She grimaced, "Hi, Deac. Looking like a giant douche, as always." She turned her attention to Tripp, smiling widely as if she was about to go in for the kill. "I think we met when Charlie was at Brown. I'm Taylor Breen."

She extended a slim arm across the table to reach his hand. Tripp smirked and looked at me briefly before reaching out to grasp her hand in his and shake it. "Yeah, I remember Chuckles bringing you around."

Taylor narrowed her eyes. Withdrawing her hand and wiping it on her napkin like he had left a residue. I loved her so much. "Why are you calling her Chuckles? I'm not sure I like the sounds of that."

I exhaled, my cheeks burning, but I straightened my back slightly and pursued my lips as I took a sip of my drink. "Do you not remember, Taylor?"

She shook her head, as another server arrived with a second bottle of champagne and a bottle of scotch along with three intricate crystal glasses. As he turned to walk away, Deacon furrowed his brow as if searching his memory, too.

Tripp spoke before I had a chance. "When Charlie was a freshman, she gave a blowjob to the frat president and she giggled the entire time. The nickname stuck." Deacon looked torn between anger and laughter as he choked on the sip of his scotch he had taken. Taylor looked less than pleased and a preternatural stillness came over her, as she looked poised to quite literally stab Tripp.

I rolled my eyes and shook my head. "Yeah, it was great for my reputation. Surprised that one didn't make the papers."

David leaned forward and spoke, his hand finding the hem of my dress as he placed his fingers just underneath it on the inside of my thigh. "Well, she doesn't do that anymore. I can assure you of that."

Tripp appraised me, snorting as he swirled his scotch in his glass. "Well you would know, Kennedy." *So would you, you douchebag*. I was seething internally. "I'm sure Deac doesn't want to continue talking about his sister's sexual escapades."

"Not really," Deacon purred, as he turned to Taylor again. I braced myself for what he was about to say. Deacon and Taylor had no boundaries with one another. "Do you have anything you would like to share with the group, Taylor? Perhaps you can tell everyone about the summer I took your virginity in Mykonos?" A laugh escaped my lips before I could stop it. My shoulders began shaking with suppressed laughter. This was in fact true, but Taylor had been ready to attack all evening, and I was certain Deacon would be on the receiving end.

"And now I no longer sleep with men," she deadpanned. I tipped my head back and laughed loudly as David joined me. This was partly true; Taylor did mostly date women but still seemed to let Deacon crawl into her bed upon occasion. Deacon's lip curled back, as he searched for a retort.

"I always had a feeling you were bad in bed, Deac," David laughed again as he swirled his scotch.

Our second bottle came and went, and another bottle of scotch that had shown up was on the last fingers. Taylor's head was tipped back as she laughed loudly at a story David was telling about his younger brother Ryan getting caught with his girlfriend by their parents when he was fifteen.

I placed my hand on the back of David's neck, my fingers tracing the nape and toying with waves of his hair. He stretched his neck, giving me more access, as he brought his scotch to his lips.

The evening had been surprisingly enjoyable. Tripp had been tolerable. He was mostly silent, drinking and adding in the occasional wry remark, which always seemed to send Deacon into fits of laughter. For the most part, his eyes swept past me in cool indifference, as he observed the table, and I preferred it that way. Every time his eyes met mine, my stomach clenched and began rolling uncontrollably.

Taylor leaned back, crossing her arms and accentuating her chest, which I noticed Deacon had been staring at for some time. She turned, her eyes sweeping over David. He was leaning back in his seat, one arm propped up in the chair and the other swirling his scotch. Some rogue waves had fallen onto his forehead and his gray suit jacket had been abandoned earlier, and the tailored white shirt he had on was rolled up revealing his muscular forearms. She seemed to be appraising him, ready to make her final judgment before pointing between David and I. "Okay. I'll allow it."

I arched my eyebrow and laughed warmly. I opened my mouth to speak and was cut off by Deacon.

His hair was falling in his face and his skin was flushed. He smacked his hand on the table again, but he was smiling widely. "If anyone is going to *allow it*, it's me. Back off Taylor. How do you think I feel about one of my best friends and my sister? Look at the way he's looking at her! Like he can't wait to destroy her the second he gets her alone. It's disgusting."

David leaned back, his lips curling in a sideways smirk as his free hand found my thigh again. "That's because it's all I've been thinking about all night. In fact, I think it's time this night came to a close. Want to go home, Charlie?"

Deacon made a retching noise that made him seem like he was seventeen years old, before Taylor smacked his arm and hissed at him. "Charlie could be with someone like you, count your blessings you fucking idiot. Let them go have all sorts of salacious sex and stare deeply into one another's eyes."

I turned to look at David and was about to open my mouth to say I wanted to leave as well when my eyes landed on Tripp. He was leaning back in his seat, his face schooled into an infuriating mask of indifference as always and our eyes met. A small, knowing smirk tugged at the corners of his lips. My stomach dropped and began to knot instantly, as I remembered him moving inside me and whispering everything I had ever wanted to hear in my ears—at that time. He caught my gaze as if sensing what I was remembering and he winked at me. My heart was beating furiously inside my chest. I fucking hated him.

I bit the inside of my lip in anger and tightened my grip on David's neck before turning to him and nodding. I stood abruptly, "I'll be right back," and headed in the direction of the washrooms. They were down a long hallway lit with stupid Edison bulbs mounted into the walls, which were padded in the same leather as the bar. I threw myself into the nearest room and slammed the door behind me, locking it quickly.

I turned to face myself in the mirror and cocked my head to the side, studying myself. What did I really see when I looked at my reflection? My chocolate hair was a sheet surrounding me—not a hair out of place. My green eyes were the same as Deacon's, but where his are bright and sparkling, I had always found mine lacking. They seemed slightly darker and like something was swirling behind them. Loneliness, maybe...uncertainty...self-hatred? I breathed quickly, leaning forward and gripping the edge of the sink with my hands, not wanting to spend a second longer staring into the depths of my own soul to see what might be lurking there. What was lurking in the depths of my mother's soul?

Turning on the faucet, I splashed cold water on my face. I could feel Tripp's eyes on me, feel his hands wandering over my body and his tongue sweeping into my mouth to banish my grief, even if only for a few stolen moments. Even if it was wrong, and I was wrong, I took a steadying breath again before drying my hands and tugging the hem of my dress down again. I turned, unlocking the door and opening it into the hall, my breath caught again. My skin started to warm and prickle across my body. Tripp was leaning against the wall directly across from the washrooms. His arms were folded, accentuating all of his muscles. One of his legs was propped up, his foot resting against the wall. He cocked his head to the side, smiling in that maddening way, like he knew a secret I didn't.

"Something bothering you, Chuck?" The corner of his mouth tilted up.

"*You*. You're bothering me," I hissed, stepping into the hall and turning on my heel to go back to the restaurant.

"No. I don't think I am." He was quicker than me and reached out, gripping my forearm and turning me around so my back was against the wall. He was breathing in my space, before I had a chance to even do anything. He leaned down, his forehead within an inch of resting on mine, and his ice blue eyes surveyed me with some sort of hunger that made dread settle in my stomach.

"What are you? Some sort of fucking vampire lurking in the shadows? Don't touch me." I leaned back, desperate to sink my body as far into the wall as possible and gain space between our bodies, though I could feel the ridges of his abdomen pressing into me.

Tripp smiled darkly and raised his hands to place one on either side of my head, effectively trapping me. "Vampire? Would you like me to bite you, Charlie?" He leaned closer, and I could smell the hint of whiskey on his breath as his nose brushed mine.

"Go away, Tripp, " I said through clenched teeth. My stomach was rolling and every inch of my skin felt hot. "You clearly haven't changed at all. You're the same arrogant piece of–"

He barked a laugh and brought his lips to my ear. "You haven't changed, either. Still the same. You're as hot as you ever were, Chuck. Your boobs might have gotten bigger, though."

I stilled as he brushed his lips back and forth against my ear, his breath hot against my skin and his body rested against mine. I was on fire, and I could not tell if it was shame, embarrassment, or humiliation raking my skin. Or, if I was reacting to him the way I did when I was twenty. "What do you want?"

He paused, tracing his mouth across my ear again before dipping down to my neck with the lightest brush of his lips and stubble before pushing off the wall and running his eyes over my body. I breathed heavily. He turned on the heel of his polished black dress shoe and spoke as he walked away, "Maybe I miss you, Charlie. Looks like you might just miss me, too."

———

I groaned audibly and looked at myself in the full-length mirror in my old bedroom at my father's house in Lake Forest. Our family's stylist, Sabine, had really outdone herself this time—and I don't mean that in a good way. My hair was pulled back in loose waves and tucked into a long fishtail braid that was draped over my bare shoulder. It had been teased beyond belief, giving all the hair at the top of my head more volume than physically possible and was secured in place with more hairspray than should be allowed.

I narrowed my eyes as I moved my head back and forth, my high cheekbones had been dusted with some sort of shimmer that caught the light at every opportunity. I skated over the rest of my body. She had dressed me in a Ralph Lauren sequined cocktail dress. It was form-fitting and fell just above my knees, leaving one shoulder entirely bare and the other arm covered in a full sleeve. It was embellished and the sequins were a light turquoise color. She had paired it with thick, white braided strappy heels and some sort of iridescent YSL clutch that was wider than my ass. I scowled, taking in my appearance once more before turning around to face the doorway.

Deacon was leaning against it, hands in his pockets. His hair pushed off his face, and he was wearing a simple black and white tux. He snorted at the monstrosity of my outfit, "Looking good, Charlie."

"I look like a fucking mermaid," I hissed, stomping forward, attempting to shoulder past him and into the hallway.

Deacon grabbed my shoulders and yanked me backward, grabbing both of my forearms and steadying me, as he peered into my eyes. "Hey, I was kidding. I know you would never have picked something like this for yourself. You look beautiful, Charlie. You always do."

"I look like a fucking idiot Deacon," I whispered as I leaned into him, inhaling the familiar scent of my heart and childhood. "Everyone is going to be staring at me. It's a fucking yacht club members' event. This isn't necessary. They're going to write things about me—"

He wrapped his hands around my shoulders, crushing me against his chest and placing a brief kiss against the crown of my head. "Hey. Stop. I will personally have any storyline you don't like retracted tomorrow, okay? You look beautiful. Young women all over Chicago and the East Coast will be rushing out to buy this dress tomorrow. You just did Ralph Lauren a favor."

I felt tears brimming behind my eyes, but I blinked them away rapidly, not wanting to ruin my own makeup and stain Deacon's shirt. I wrapped my arms around his back, hugging him tight to me. "I look like a Rainbow Fish. Sabine has it out for me."

Deacon breathed a laugh and pulled himself backward, grabbing my shoulders firmly. "That's enough. You'll be the most beautiful Rainbow Fish there. Every single woman at this party is going to wish they were you and every single man is going to wish they were David. Speaking of...I happen to know there is a man waiting downstairs who will probably fall to his knees when he sees you in this dress."

"I look stupid." My voice was smaller than it had ever been. I looked down, biting my lip as I surveyed my feet.

Deacon made a noise that sounded like it was caught between a scoff and a snarl. "I'm only going to say this once, Charlie. I don't know who told you that you weren't enough. I don't know if the things Dad has done make you feel that way. But you are. You are my favorite person in the world, and I will not hear another word. Okay?"

He pushed my chin up firmly with a grasp of his hand and stared down at me. His green eyes were darker than usual as they looked at me. Did he sense part of our mother swirling around in there? I nodded briefly, grabbing Deacon for a hug one more time before taking his hand like we did when we were children and descending the staircase down, down, down into the world.

We walked down the winding staircase together that led into the main entertaining room of the estate. One of my hands was raised and placed against the banister, the other wrapped around my clutch, which I kept at my side as I conquered each step despite the feeling in my heart. He stayed close to me, his hands in the pockets of his tuxedo as he looked down the staircase, an air of preternatural grace around him. A tendril of his hair had snuck down and curled over his forehead. He stopped on the step below me and reached out a hand, which I grabbed, squeezing tightly as I stepped into the foyer. Deacon smiled widely, turned to me quickly and squeezed my hand before letting go and disappearing into the small crowd.

My father had sponsored the new members dinner at the yacht club and had organized a small event at our family home in Lake Forest before the dinner began at eight. The president of the club, alongside his family and other important members were scattered amongst the room. Ash and Serena were there, as were Taylor and her father somewhere in the crowd.

I had been watching my feet the entire time, trying to ensure I didn't make a single misstep. I raised my gaze to survey the room and my eyes fell on David who was leaning against the bar in the corner, next to my father and Ash. He seemed to stop mid-sentence as he caught my gaze. An easy grin broke out across his face, as he leaned forward to shake my father's hand. I stilled slightly as my father turned on his heel to look me over. He turned back to David and clearly said something that made David smile before he clapped his hand on his shoulder, shaking his other hand before releasing him into the crowd.

David returned the gesture before pushing off the bar and threading his way through the crowd to where I stood like a fucking moron poised at the bottom of the staircase. I didn't deserve him. Someone who was worthy of him wouldn't have let Tripp sweat all over her the night before. She wouldn't have stood in their room and almost thrown a temper tantrum over their outfit. She wouldn't be sitting there trembling with anxiety over whatever–

"You look incredible," David leaned forward, dusting a kiss across my cheek. He arrived in front of me, offering his hand and laced his fingers through mine. He was wearing a simple tux like Deacon, clearly tailored just for him. His broad shoulders filled out his white shirt and it tapered downward where it was tucked into his black suit pants. His hair had been left down and unruly, wisps of dirty blonde waves seeming to fall everywhere. He hadn't shaved, stubble coming in across his strong jaw.

I leaned into him, breathing a bit easier as I raised my free hand to place against his chest over his heart. "Do you not think I look like a mermaid?"

David's other hand found my waist as he raised our hands and helped me step off the stairs. His eyes clouded over with concern as he scanned my face. I was seconds from bursting into tears. He pulled me immediately away from the crowd to the corner of the foyer. We were slightly shielded by the staircase. "A mermaid?" He whispered conspiratorially, as he grabbed my clutch and set it on one of the cocktail tables beside us. "Why would you say that? You look fucking amazing . What's wrong, sweetheart?"

Sweetheart. He had never called me that before. I didn't deserve any term of endearment. I deserved nothing. I was an unwanted daughter whose mother had left her behind. I let someone who had destroyed my very soul and marrow paw all over me less than twenty-four hours ago. I felt mollified and justified in my actions. I felt worthy. I lowered my eyes, my vision clouding as I felt both of David's hands come to the sides of my face.

"Hey," he whispered, bringing my face up to meet his eyes. His eyebrows furrowed in concern as his honey eyes searched my face for any sign of what might be bothering me, "What's going on in there?"

Taylor had asked almost the same thing to me the previous night, and I bit my tongue to avoid giving the same reply. Nothing good. Never anything good. I hated being left alone with my thoughts. I think I hated myself. I closed my eyes briefly, taking a steadying breath. I felt the warmth of David's hands against my cheeks, and I prepared myself to lie. Well, a partial lie.

"I don't like my dress," I whispered. "Our stylist, Sabine, dresses our family for events and always picks things that make me uncomfortable. That I would never pick for myself, and I feel...exposed. On display. Like everyone can see everything about me."

I waited for David to laugh or make a comment about his billionaire dollar baby not liking the outfit her stylist had picked for her. But a small, sad sigh breathed through his nose. He leaned his forehead against mine and placed his hands against my waist. "I see everything about you, Charlie. And I like what I see." He placed his lips against my forehead, his stubble tickling my nose. "Do you want me to go upstairs with you and you can pick something else out? You must have other options here."

I closed my eyes, placing my palms against David, and I leaned into him. "Dad will have my head if I change after everyone has seen me. But, thank you. I'll be okay. I just need to get past the fact that I look like a fish from a children's book."

David snorted as he pulled away from me, grabbing one of my hands and pushing it under his jacket, aligning it with his heart. It was beating wildly. "Can you feel that?" I nodded, unsure where he was going with it. "You make my heart do this. And, I guess I have a fish fetish because you in that dress has me hard."

I laughed loudly in spite of myself, louder than I should have in such a small setting. "You're into some weird shit, Mr. Kennedy."

He grinned wickedly and pulled me into his chest quickly before kissing the top of my head. "Come on, let's go get you a drink before we have to leave."

The overheard lights crisscrossing the roof of the reception room at the yacht club beat down mercilessly on me, as I shifted awkwardly in the unforgiving sequined dress. I stood to the left of my father on the raised platform at the front of the room, slightly behind him with Deacon on the opposite side. They both remained the picture of casual elegance. I struggled to control my breathing, feeling like the sequins were tightening around my rib cage with every breath. My lips were pulled toward my ears in some sort of fake closed mouth grin—so forcefully my cheeks were starting to grow sore, and I was gripping the flute of champagne in my free hand like it was a walking staff keeping me upright.

My eyes scanned the crowd spanning out across the reception room. My father had agreed to have Winchester Holding's sponsor the new members' dinner and dragged Deacon and me up onto the stage with him as he gave his toast. I was the only one in fucking sequin. Everyone else was in simple cocktail and evening wear, reeking of old money. I had a sneaking suspicion Sabine often dressed me like this for events to ensure I stood out and would be the center of press attention as the only woman in the family. I had evaded the press for years and had been rarely photographed when I was in graduate school and working abroad, and Deacon was often the central figure of any story about the family.

I noticed a few new younger men and women throughout the crowd who were likely new young professionals in the city, and I knew the second we were off the stage my father would be hounding after Deacon and me to go introduce ourselves. One of his favorite things to say was that Winchesters were "approachable." *So approachable we let ourselves get felt up in dark bathroom hallways. So approachable one of us suffered in silence for years before drowning herself.* I felt my breathing begin to pick up and my eyes quickly found David. He was leaning against one of the cocktail tables that had been covered with an ornate-looking white table cloth and had some ridiculous display of flowers in the center of it. He was standing with Ash and had champagne dangling loosely in his left hand. He met my eyes and winked at me, tossing me a warm, reassuring smile as if he could hear my increased heart rate from that far away.

I lost a breath and rolled my shoulders back slightly as I held his gaze. He was the anchor in the dark that I did not deserve. The yacht club manager was wrapping up his welcome speech that I had not been paying one bit of attention to but the mention of my father's name, along with mine and Deacon's, caught my attention. I turned my gaze back toward him and did my best to smile warmly.

"And we would like to thank and introduce our sponsor for the evening. Steven Winchester and his children have been members of the Chicago Yacht Club for as long as I can remember. I think you might even have a boat or two moored out there yourself, don't you Deacon?" He laughed like they were old friends, as Deacon—ever the perfect billionaire—raised his glass and smiled widely. That was a fact—Deacon had a weird obsession with buying sailboats at auctions, hiring someone to restore them and then acting like he did all the work himself. I think he had three and he only ever used one. We used to sail together when we were younger all the time. Just the two of us on the water with no watchful eyes on us, free to be exactly who we were. Though, I think that had always applied more to Deacon than it did to me.

My father stepped up to the front of the platform and raised his champagne. "Thank you, Harold." So that was his name. I didn't spend much time here anymore other than mandatory appearances at events that WH sponsored. "A toast to all the new faces joining us tonight, we look forward to getting to know each of you over the coming season."

He smiled and raised his glass to his lips. His dark hair was flecked with salt and pepper, and the cut of his tuxedo reminded everyone that despite his age he remained in peak physical condition. As always, he was clean shaven. I studied him for a moment over my flute as I brought it to my lips. We had barely spoken since I got back from Mexico, exchanging brief pleasantries when I had arrived at his house earlier that evening. I was dreading seeing him at work on Monday. He was classically handsome. He had the same defined jaw that Deacon did, and we shared the same nose. Our eyes were our mother's, though; my father's were light blue. The chatter in the crowd resumed, and as he turned to shake hands with Harold, Deacon did the same, and I held out my hand as well.

"Great to see you again, Harold." I met his eyes as my father had always taught me and shook his hand vigorously.

"And you, Miss Winchester." His blonde hair was liberally streaked with gray and was pushed off his head. He had warm eyes and seemed to genuinely mean it, even though I could not remember the last time I had laid eyes on him or spoken to him. "You look as beautiful as ever." Yeah, because I look like one of the fucking fish you probably see off the docks every day, I thought bitterly as I gave him a small, knowing smile.

"Thank you. And please, it's just Charlie."

He dipped his head to me before turning to some of the other members who had come forward for his attention. I turned on my heel, readying myself to step off the platform and into the fray when I found my father waiting for me with his arm out. I cocked my head to the side as I laced my arm through his. "Hi, Dad. To what do I owe the pleasure of this illustrious escort?"

He scoffed in disdain, pivoting his dress shoe toward the small set of stairs that led up to the platform. "You have a mouth on you, Charlie. I have no idea where you got it."

As I rolled my eyes, he stepped forward in front of me to guide me down a few steps, as if I would be unable to manage them unmoored on my own. "Some say these things are inherited traits you know, perhaps you should look to the family tree."

Ignoring my comment, he said, "You look very beautiful tonight, Charlie. How was Mexico?" The simple platitude was as close to an apology as I was likely to get from him. I squeezed his elbow in response, trying to demonstrate my understanding of the offering he placed at my feet. Steven Winchester is a complicated man.

"Mexico was wonderful. It's such a fantastic program. I hope I can fit in a trip back there soon." We wove through the crowd. He stopped periodically, shaking hands with someone and introducing me to those I didn't know. More than one person stopped to simper over my dress, running their hands down my sleeve like I wasn't a person with their own boundaries to be respected. But I supposed, in many ways, I wasn't. Our father had always instilled in us at a young age we were something of a public commodity. As children, people were allowed to ruffle Deacon's hair and pinch my cheeks or kiss my hand,

and we were to sit quietly and diligently—the picture of perfect behavior. Somewhere along the way, my sense of my own boundaries must have begun to blur.

I remember, even then, often feeling like it was too much, too loud, too busy—being preened over and exposed. I would slip my small hand into Deacon's, as we stood beside our parents like perfect china dolls. Him, in the junior version of what he wore tonight with a perfect little bow-tie, and me in some taffeta monstrosity to remind everyone I was indeed a girl. Sometimes our mother would catch my eye, and she would share a small smile with me, as if to tell me she was in on the secret. She understood, and she felt that way, too. I wondered sometimes if she recognized herself in my young and frightened eyes.

My father spoke, interrupting my reverie and I shook my head slightly as I glanced sideways to look at him, finding him studying me intently. "David let me know in a few weeks he's heading home for his father's sixtieth birthday back in North Carolina. He told me his parents had extended the invitation to you as well. He's going home for a week. Would you like to join him?"

I narrowed my eyes at him slightly, unsure what his angle was there. It felt like a trick question in some way. Seeing as I was in deep shit at work and was likely to be for some time to come, it didn't seem like an appropriate time to request vacation. None of us took vacation as it was. I paused and swallowed, accepting another glass of champagne from a passing server.

"This feels like a leading question. I didn't realize I needed your permission to accept an invitation extended to me." He finally stopped our pilgrimage through the crowd, assuming court at a yet unclaimed cocktail table in the center of the back of the room. He raised his fingers at a passing server who cut across an entire line of people to come to him. He ordered a drink quickly before turning his attention back to me.

"I am your boss, so you do, in fact, need my permission to take time off work." He studied me, as if assessing how I'd react.

I snorted, raising my glass to my lips, taking a small sip. "I know you're my boss, Dad. After the whole Play For Everyone debacle, I was going to tell David it likely wasn't the right time for me to be taking off work."

My father had turned away from me, accepting the drink that had returned to him and brought it to his lips, his eyes wandering across the crowd as he took in my response, evaluating if it was the correct one he wanted to hear. "You're correct, Charlie. It's not the right time for you to be taking time off work."

He paused to shake hands with someone who was passing by. I raised my flute to my lips again and resisted rolling my eyes as I smiled banally at everyone who passed by. My father could never just come out and say anything. It was always leading questions to see if you were going to give him the answer he wanted—and the trajectory of the rest of the conversation often changed based on your choices. Every day was like choosing your own adventure with Steven Winchester.

He turned, facing me again and surveying me with his blue eyes, as he set his drink down on the table. "That being said, I would like you to accompany David. The time off is yours if you can promise to be responsive if need be to any emergencies that arise."

What looked like a small smile tugged at the corners of his lips, and I knew in his world this was a gift. He was giving me a gift as my father, not as my boss. I reached out and placed my hand on top of his and squeezed gently before removing my own. He was not a terribly affectionate man and struggled with public displays. "I can do that, Dad. I know this will mean a lot to David. So, thank you."

His eyes were no longer on me as they were back surfing the crowd and before he raised his glass to his lips, he spoke again. "Why don't you two take the jet? Make a week of it."

A smile tugged at my lips, bringing my flute to them as I understood in Steven speak, that was a second gift. A third peace offering of the evening in the only way he knew how. "Sure, Dad. We'll take the jet."

I remained in my father's orbit for the next few hours. Between the endless stream of people who stopped to pay tribute to him and continued to run their fingers across the sleeve of my dress, we spoke occasionally about work, club members and his upcoming golf trip with Ash. They had been going to Hawaii to golf in the spring for as long as I could remember. It was once a family affair—Ash and Serena, my parents, and Deacon and me. I had never been terribly interested in golfing and often just sat in the cart, fighting with Deacon over who got to drive. I remember my mom laughing a lot back then. Sometimes, I tried to close my eyes and remember when the laughter started fading away, and I could never figure it out. In some ways, I wondered if it was like she started to fade away over time and none of us deigned to notice.

My father cleared his throat and swirled the remaining dregs of scotch in his glass before he spoke. "I was hoping the three of us could go to Whitefish for Thanksgiving this year."

I opened my mouth to speak and found myself pausing. The family house in Whitefish had been my grandfather's, though renovated several times over the years. We had gone out there in the fall and winter often enough over the years since my mom had died but never for a holiday. In fact, my father often made himself scarce over holidays—as did Deac, and as did I as a result of not having anywhere to go or any family to be with. We sometimes observed Christmas, but it was usually the three of us spending our holiday at opposite ends of our family home in Lake Forest and meeting only for an exchange of presents in the morning.

"You're not golfing or traveling this Thanksgiving?" This had been my dream for so long after my mom had died—the reunification of our family. I had begged and pleaded with my dad and Deacon for about two years after she died to honor and spend the holidays together and had given up in my fourth year at Brown.

"No. I think it's time we spend it together as a family. David is of course welcome, if he isn't going home to North Carolina."
He turned away to survey the crowd again.

I made a non-committal noise of agreement, as if he was a frightened animal and any sudden movements might send him careening in the opposite direction. I felt my skin prickle and grow hot as I thought of spending a Thanksgiving together as a family without my mother. She was a ghost now—something from a past life that we had all shut the door on. *Was she banging on the door? Hoping to get out of the compartment we had all created for her in our minds?* I felt my breath quicken for the second time that evening as the boning in my dress felt like it was drawing closer and closer against my skin. I blinked quickly and shook my head, as if I could shake the memory of holidays with my mother out of my head. Every time her memory started knocking, I forced it away. Maybe I was part of the problem after all these years.

I placed my palms on the table and the white tablecloth felt too close—and too rough—against my skin. It was sticking to my palms that had grown clammy. Bracing myself, I exhaled quickly and turned to my father. "I'm going to get some fresh air." Snatching my clutch from the table, I turned on my heel and made my way through the glass doors and out onto the deck and into the marina.

———

There was an unseasonably warm breeze blowing off the lake, loosening tendrils of my hair from the confines of that godforsaken fishtail braid. Lying on my back against the slick fiberglass on the bow of the sailboat, I had slipped my legs through the rungs and was dangling them off the side, kicking my feet out like a small child as if I could almost skim the water with my toes. My strappy heels laid discarded across from me. I peered up at the sky, able to see faint pops of starlight. There was too much light pollution in the city. It was one of the things I loved about our family home. It was far enough from the city and looked out over the lake that you could often find so many more stars out there than in the city. The sounds of the party were faint behind me, as I had made my way to one of Deacon's boats—the one that was moored farthest away. It was easier to breathe out there. Everything was quieter and my head wasn't as noisy.

I closed my eyes gently, as I breathed in and out, swinging my legs back and forth, my heels brushing against the smooth hull of the boat. I had always felt so relaxed out there on the water. Maybe I should ask Deacon if I could borrow one of his boats. Faint footsteps sounded on the worn dock and my eyes snapped open as I propped myself up on my elbows to peer around the sail trying to make out who was coming my way.

My heart snagged as I immediately recognized the silhouette. David had unbuttoned his jacket and the bowtie he had been wearing had disappeared, the top buttons of his dress shirt having been opened. One hand was shoved carelessly in the pants of his suit, and the other was wound around the neck of an unopened bottle of champagne. I peeked around the corner of the sail further, studying him in silence as my heart beat furiously against my chest.

I could faintly make out a wicked grin creeping across his face as he spotted me beyond the sail. "I see you over there, Charlie. Are you hiding out here from me?"

"Never from you, Mr. Kennedy. Come aboard," I called, the wind off the lake causing loose tendrils of my hair to whip around my face.

David's dress shoes clicked across the gangplank, as he grabbed the railing of the boat and stepped aboard.

"Whose boat is this Charlie? Are we breaking and entering?"

I grinned mischievously, as he handed me the unopened bottle and settled down beside me. "This is one of Deacon's. He bought it at an auction and worked painstakingly to have it restored." I dug at the foil wrapping around the cork of the bottle with my fingernails that Sabine had filed into sharp points. David snorted, as he shrugged off his suit jacket and laid it over my shoulders before I continued. "I'm sure supervising the contractors was hard work for him. Barking orders and what not."

I tossed the foil beside me and began pulling at the cork of the bottle, as David wrapped his arm around me and pressed his lips to my temple. His hair had fallen forward and brushed against my forehead. I closed my eyes briefly, feeling the wind brush against my face and the warmth of David's lips radiated against the coldness of my whirring thoughts. Bringing the bottle to my lips, I swallowed a small sip before handing it over to David.

He took it from me and set it down on the slick surface beside him and wrapped his free hand around me, pressing his forehead down to the top of my head. "Deac told me I might find you out here. Do you want to talk about what's going on?"

My eyes closed shut again, and I laid my hand on David's thigh. I couldn't tell the truth, not really. And here was this man who was giving me more love and understanding than I ever deserved. "Sometimes everything is just too much and too loud. I used to get really overwhelmed as a kid at functions like this and it got better as I got older, but sometimes I just feel like I don't belong."

David exhaled and began rubbing his thumb up and down my exposed shoulder. "I imagine that would be made even harder when you have boy wonder as your brother. And your dad, I can't imagine he is ever easy."

A snort escaped my mouth before I could stop it. "*Boy wonder*," I laughed again. "That is the perfect way to describe Deacon. Skating through life on his gold-embossed shoes. But he was always the most understanding of them all. And you're right. I love my dad, but he's not...he's not easy. He was better before." *Before she left him. Left us. Left me.* The words hung unspoken between us, and the air felt heavier. I wondered if my mom was somewhere in my mind, pounding against the locked door. Begging to be let out and given life again. *Ashamed of me for what I did to forget her before her body was even cold.*

David's hand wound around the back of my neck, and he angled my head, so our eyes would meet. Even out there with barely any stars, his eyes looked like they were dancing, the warm flecks of honey shining just for me. The strands of his hair that had fallen onto his forehead were blowing in the wind, and I felt nothing else other than the warmth of his fingers at the nape of my neck. His eyes never left mine as he studied my face. "Can I tell you a secret?"

I nodded softly, never taking my eyes off his, as if I was afraid I would miss out on a single moment of being looked at like that. Like I was perfect, and like I was someone worthy of love. Not someone who was left behind by their mother, by someone they trusted.

"I love you, Charlie. I am in love with you. Each and every part of you. Even the parts you think are bad. I wish you could see yourself the way I see you. I think you are my favorite person I will ever know, billion dollar baby." He brought his lips to mine and brushed them gently.

My body was on fire, and my lips were burning where he touched them. I closed my eyes, as they began to burn with tears that leaked out of the corners, surely tracking my ridiculous sparkly eyeshadow down my face. And despite the fact that I could live a million years and would never deserve the love being offered to me beneath the stars, the corners of my lips tugged up in spite of myself. I pressed my lips back to his. "I love you too, Mr. Kennedy."

David groaned slightly, and I felt his lips tug upward and a small strangled laugh escaped his throat, as if he had been holding his breath waiting for my answer. "You are so fucking perfect. I don't think I can even think straight around you. I never want to again."

"Even though I look like a fucking Rockette in this dress?" Tears were streaming down my face more openly now, and David began to kiss them away as they tracked down my face.

"The most beautiful Rockette I have ever seen, and the most beautiful woman in the world." He huffed a laugh again, as he began running his thumb across my jawline before bringing his lips back to mine with more urgency. I yanked on his loose bowtie and removed it from where it hung haphazardly under the collar of his shirt and dropped it carelessly beside me.

"Careful, that's Armani," he whispered, laughing against my lips, as I began to clumsily unbutton his dress shirt and slid my hands under it to expose his broad shoulders. My entire body was on fire, and I needed our skin to be touching. I don't think I would ever be close enough or feel close enough to David. He shrugged the rest of the way out of his shirt, his lips never leaving mine. He removed his cufflinks and discarded them somewhere on the bow of the boat.

"Careful, those could be vintage Harry Winston," I smiled against his lips as he laughed again, and I felt his teeth nip my bottom lip, his hands finding my shoulders. He peeled off the suit jacket he had covered my shoulders with and tossed it behind me, his warm hands wrapping around my ribcage, as he laid me down and pressed into me.

David pulled his mouth away from mine and rested his forehead on mine. His free hand came up to wind into my hair, our eyes so close, and I could still see his irises dancing as he breathed heavily against my face. "I love you," he whispered again, as he began to tug down the zipper of my dress, one hand now braced beside my face on the wood of the boat.

"I love you so much, David. I don't deserve you, but I love you so much." I felt David grumble against my neck, as if that was such an impossibility and soon there was nothing between us. His forehead was now pressed into the base at the front of my neck, as he kissed every inch of skin available to him.

His breath was hot on my skin, the wind whipping around us, and the entire city had gone dark, the stars coming out just for us.

CHAPTER TEN

A resounding crash echoed from outside my office, somewhere along the executives' hall. My gaze flipped up and away from the financial claim report I was reading that had come in earlier that morning. It was the month's end and all of the funded organizations were due to report in the following week. Deacon bursted out of his office, throwing his door open wide and screaming like some sort of eighteen-year-old fraternity pledge who just did a body shot. He clenched his fists and brought them to the front of his body and raised his left knee as he shouted again in some sort of demented football touchdown celebration dance, his chocolate hair askew from all the movement.

My father, Ash, and David followed him through his open office door. I narrowed my eyes, as my father clapped Ash on the back and turned to shake David's hand. I pursed my lips and turned back to the spreadsheet in front of me. I wasn't sure how Deacon's little display was any better or more acceptable than any of the things I had gotten reprimanded for at work but far be it for me to question it.

A knock resounded against the glass door of my office, which had been shut all morning. Exhaling tightly through my nose, I looked up to see Deacon raising his palm to slap against my door, grinning like a fucking Cheshire cat and looking like a supreme douchebag in his tailored tan suit.

"What?!" I barked, gesturing to my desktop, as if the shut door hadn't been encouraging enough to stay away.

Deacon flung the door open, continuing to grin manically as he leaned into my office, gripping the door frame with this free hand. "We just closed Halton. Winchester Holdings just doubled in value. We're going to be billionaires, Charlie."

Leaning back in my desk chair, I folded my arms across my chest and arched an eyebrow wryly. I never even considered the possibility my father wouldn't close the Halton deal. "We're already billionaires, Deacon. Get out." I gestured to the door again before averting my eyes back to my screen.

Deacon let go of the door frame and practically bounded toward me, slamming his hands down against my desk. "We are going to be *billionaire* billionaires."

"Oh, I'm sorry. I didn't realize there were different categorizations. I assumed once you hit that thousand-million mark, it all blended together afterward. Please, sit down and enlighten me about the categories," I deadpanned, my eyes not leaving my screen as I gestured to the empty couch across from my desk. "Seriously, get out. I'm busy."

"Charlie!" Deacon whined, leaning across my desk and grabbing my shoulders, attempting to haul me up from my chair but instead banged my knees against the underside of my desk. He ignored my shriek and bounded around the side of my desk to grab me again. He squished my cheeks and brought his lips to my forehead in an overexaggerated kiss before some ungodly howl emerged from his lips. He grabbed my wrist and began to drag me out of my office. My heels caught on the rug by the couch in my office, and I tripped forward grabbing onto Deacon's forearm to steady myself.

"Jesus, Deacon!" I hissed, ripping my arm away from him and straightening myself. I smoothed down the front of my oversized white button down shirt and checked to make sure it was still tucked into the waist of flared Theory wool pants. My heels slid, as we moved across the tile floor.

My father was still shaking hands with Ash. I arched an eyebrow, as I watched them continue to grasp one another's hand for an extended period. Deacon reached back and dragged me forward with another sharp pull on my arm. I stumbled forward again, before he grabbed both my shoulders and planted me in front of our father.

He dropped Ash's hand, extending his toward me, as if he wanted to share this moment with me as well. A laugh escaped my mouth before I could stop it and offered my hand in the perfunctory manner with which I was expected to respond. "Dad, congratulations."

"Thank you, Charlie. Congratulations to you, too." He gripped my hand with his like I was a business associate he had closed a deal with. I arched an eyebrow and pulled my hand away from him.

"I'm not entirely sure what I'm being congratulated for?" I asked, folding my arms across my chest. Behind our father, Deacon continued to sprint around the office doing bizarre jumps and slapping people on the back and shoulders, howling at the top of his lungs.

Our father's eyebrow shot up, and there was a brief pause, as if he was processing my question. "This is your family business, too, Charlie, your legacy." He shook his head almost imperceptibly, as if my words were so unbelievable to him and turned back to Deacon, who had produced a box of cigars from God knows where.

"I fucking hope not," I breathed, doing my best not to roll my eyes at the back of my father's suit jacket, which was buckling slightly at the shoulders, as he continued to shake hands with every other member of the staff.

A warm hand pressed into my shoulder. I could feel it through the silk of my button down blouse. I knew it immediately to be David's hand; the height of it, the weight of it. His hair brushed against my ear, as he brought his mouth close to it to whisper to me. "It's supposed to be a celebration, Charlie. You can save the righteous indignation for later."

Bringing my elbow back, I rammed it into the hard ridges of his abdomen. David sucked in a breath beside my ear. I turned around, pushing back against his chest with a teasing smile. "I'm sorry, I should be congratulating you. Master of the Universe and all. I know you were instrumental in closing this deal."

David leaned forward and grinned, the corners of his eyes pulling slightly, as the flecks of honey danced in them. "It's entirely thanks to my good looks and charm. Steven always put me front and center on our video calls."

"It would have worked on me," I whispered conspiratorially, then startled when a champagne cork sounded loudly in my ear followed by another scream from Deacon that could only be described as a "whoop!"

Droplets of champagne landed on the side of my face, as he began to shake the bottle, pouring it over a tower of coupes that someone had arranged on Nika's desk. I narrowed my gaze and wiped the side of my face slowly. Opening my mouth to provide a retort, David's thumb grabbed my chin and brought my face upward to his. He was grinning down at me, and a rogue wave had fallen across his forehead.

"Charlie, let's try to have fun. Why don't I make you a deal?" He leaned in, bringing his forehead to mine and lowering his voice. "You enjoy yourself this afternoon, have a few glasses of champagne with your wonderful colleagues here and tonight I will cook you dinner, get you spectacularly drunk, and you can tell me about all the things that are wrong with this deal. We can take a shot for every ridiculous frat boy gesture Deac does this afternoon."

A small smile tugged on the corners of my mouth, and I nodded. Our eyes were so close, but as I looked up at his eyes through my lashes, the sounds of Deacon continuing to shout surrounding us, I could see my own irises reflected in his. I think I liked whoever David saw when he looked at me.

———

Deacon arched an eyebrow at me, as he raised his glass to his lips. "You're wearing feathers." He reached out with his free hand to pull on one of the obscene ostrich feathers sticking out from my shoulder.

I slapped his hand impatiently. My nails had been buffed and filed to perfection, and coated with a light pink gloss by the makeup artist. "Shut up. Sabine put me in it." The Saint Laurent off-the-shoulder mini dress was trimmed with feathers along the cut of the top, but she had assured me they were synthetic. It was actually quite pretty and elegant, but not something I would ever wear on my own accord. When she wheeled her cart into my bedroom at my father's house, I started to have flashbacks to the last time she dressed me, when I ended up looking like a sparkly fish. But given the tone of the event she was dressing me for, she seemed to go toward "understated with a bit of flair." For Sabine, that was probably as good as it would get. My father insisted that I comply with anything she put me in. My mouth had opened to protest when a small smile tugged at the corners of my mouth. I nodded, pressing my forehead to David's. Our eyes were so close, but I could still look up at him through my eyelashes, the sound of Deacon's voice continuing to shout surrounding us, and I could see my own reflection in him. I think I was starting to like whoever David saw whenever he looked at me.

Forbes was profiling our family after Winchester Holding's most recent acquisition of Halton Entertainment. My father had agreed to a cover and three-page spread. Winchesters were notoriously secretive and did not spend our time in the public eye, and in fact never really had. We were always referred to as the "elusive" dynasty of America, though I wasn't quite sure a few generations of wealth denoted a *dynasty*. Each of us was to give a private thirty-minute interview followed by a photoshoot. I was waiting in my father's office, seated on the edge of his mahogany desk, digging my heel into the ground while I waited for Sabine to finish with my father and Rebecca to arrive with our sheets of pre-approved questions for the interview.

"And you like these feathers?" Deacon asked, bringing his glass of scotch to his lips again, coming to stand beside me at the desk.

I turned to look at him and raised an eyebrow. Sabine had dressed him in a classic black-and-white tux. The bowtie around his neck seemed intentionally loose, like she was trying to draw attention to his devil-may-care billionaire boy attitude. "It's better than the fish scales." I shrugged my shoulders.

Deacon snorted, turning away from me to place his glass on the desk. "The dress wasn't that bad, Charlie."

I opened my mouth to respond when the heavy oak door at the other end of the room pushed open and revealed my father standing there, looking like a mirror image of Deacon without the styled hair and loose bowtie. Sabine and Rebecca stood on either side of him, smiles indicating they are pleased with their work. My eyes caught on the dressing racks along the walls in the room. It sat empty and closed up now, saved for occasions like this. Once upon a time, it had been my mother's studio. She was always in there creating something.

As children, Deacon and I would race around the house to see who could make it to the office first. We would hurl ourselves around the corner, grabbing the mahogany paneling that lined the office doorway. The sliding door would be open, music floating from her studio into my father's office, where he sat behind his desk, looking just as imposing as he does now but with fewer lines around his eyes. His tie was usually discarded by that point in the evening, and he'd often have a bottle of scotch opened. One of us would peek around the corner to see what our mother was doing. Sometimes she'd be sitting on a stool, absentmindedly moving a paintbrush across a canvas, or sitting in the corner with knitting needles in her hand, a bottle of wine open somewhere in the room. I often wondered what had happened to all those things she used to create, as they were gone now.

"Charlie, Deacon." Our father stepped forward, and Rebecca held out two identical sheets of white paper, one to Deacon and one to me. I noticed my dad had his folded in his hand. "Your approved questions for the interview."

I smiled my thanks at Rebecca, pushing off the desk and reaching for the sheet. Running my eyes over the questions, I felt my cheeks begin to grow hot. Puffing them out, I exhaled deeply as anger and embarrassment began to simmer in my stomach. My lips popped open as I spoke, "More than half of these questions are about David."

Deacon stifled a laugh, as he looked down at his own sheet before looking at me. "Well, David is an interesting man. More interesting than you, apparently."

Our father's eyes were as sharp as his voice. "Do not start. Rebecca approved the questions."

I narrowed my eyes before whirling on her. "Rebecca," I hissed, tempted to crumple the paper into a ball and throw it at her head, "are you serious? You approved a list of questions about my relationship? There's one fucking question in here about my job, about what I do for the company."

"Well, you really didn't have anything to do with closing Halton, Charlie," Deacon drawled, having leaned back against the desk again, scotch in hand. "David did. Hey Dad, maybe Forbes should be interviewing David instead."

"Deacon, enough," he snapped, slamming the door into the adjoining room before striding forward. "The questions were approved, Charlie. Just answer them, for Christ's sake."

My cheeks flushed and I rolled my neck, attempting to take a steadying breath when I felt Deacon come to stand beside me. He placed his hand on my shoulder and pressed down before speaking. "Dad, come on. I was just joking around, and I agree with Charlie, it is ridiculous. There isn't a single question on my sheet about anything personal. Charlie has single-handedly created an entire portfolio at WH. Rebecca, get the questions changed."

Deacon grabbed the paper from my hand and walked across the room to hand it back to Rebecca. I watched as she looked back and forth between Deacon and our father, as if unsure who she should answer to. Her blond hair was tied in a tight ponytail that pulled impossibly on her forehead. I was pretty certain her forehead couldn't move from all the Botox anyway, but she somehow managed to portray a look of worry on her face. Our father moved to pinch the bridge of his nose and exhaled loudly, as if he was dealing with spoiled children throwing tantrums.

Rebecca turned to me, a look I couldn't quite place in her eyes. Was it sorrow or shame I saw there? "Charlie, they're looking to reach a few different demographics with this feature. They thought that bringing a personal touch to it would increase readership across a broader–"

I held up my hand, closing my eyes briefly as I shook my head, my ponytail swinging with the motion. "I know this is your way of telling me that my relationship will be more interesting to male and female readers alike than my work. Women will want to be me, and men will want to be with me. I'll give them one question about David. One. Change the rest, or I won't answer."

My father had turned his back to us and was pouring what looked to be a double scotch from the dry bar in the corner of the office. Deacon was still holding the paper out to Rebecca, but he had turned to look at our father, his eyes narrowed and a look of something like disappointment was etched across his features. Rebecca looked back and forth between the three of us for a moment longer while my father's silence stretched on. It was safe to say at this point he wouldn't be saying anything further. Pursing her lips, Rebecca grabbed the sheet from Deacon before turning on her heel and stalking out of the room.

Deacon faced me, a rueful smile playing on his lips as he shoved his hands in the pockets of his suit and jerked his chin toward the door. "Let's go get a drink, Charlie."

With a final glance at our father's back, I nodded and followed my brother through the open door, out of the office.

———

I settled into the leather chair behind my father's desk after Deacon and I shared a drink, smiling blandly at the reporter from Forbes who was setting up in front of me. Folding my hands in the demure manner in which I was taught, I continued to look at him, waiting patiently for the first question. I hadn't looked at the question sheet again after Rebecca disappeared to see if it could be changed.

"I'm Adam Lee," he spoke from behind his laptop. "I'm honored to profile your family today. It's great to meet you."

"It's a pleasure to meet you as well, Adam," I responded, the smile still tight on my face. "I'm Charlie Winchester, but I think you already know that."

A good-natured laugh escaped his mouth and he nodded along, quickly adjusting the wire frame of his glasses before looking back at me. "Winchester Holding's publicist, Rebecca, informed me there were some changes to the questions. I'm happy to give you a moment to review them before we get started if you'd like."

I shook my head, keeping my hands in their rightful spot. "No need. Go ahead. Ask away."

"So, Charlie. Tell me about yourself."

I narrowed my eyes, taken aback by the line of questioning and wondering what Rebecca said exactly. This felt like an entirely different tone than any of the questions I read earlier. "Well, I majored in developmental studies at Brown, with a minor in economics. I continued my education at the London School of Economics and completed my Masters of Science in Developmental Studies there. But you know all that, don't you?"

He fell silent, seeming to weigh his next words before he brought the tips of his fingers to his lips, tapping them for another moment before he spoke. "Can I be honest? Rebecca hoped if we took a different approach, you might warm up to some of the more personal questions by the end of our interview."

A scoff escaped me before I could help it. Shaking my head, my eyes flicked over to the closed door of my mother's old study. "Of course she did. Go ahead then. I know a spotlight on charitable funds and development won't feature as well." Embarrassment, coupled with a bitter sense of disappointment, bubbled under my skin as I began nodding along with everything he said, pasting the moronic smile across my expertly-painted features like the good little rich girl I am.

———

My father and Deacon entered the office again, as I shook hands with Adam; our allotted twenty minutes were up. Thank God. Confusion was etched across Deacon's features. He trailed behind our father, hands tucked into his suit pants. He quickly fell into step beside him, crossing the room to stand beside me. I watched his hand twitch in his pocket, like he was tempted to interlace his fingers with mine as we did when we were kids.

"You must be Deacon." Adam pivoted, offering his name and easily switching gears from our conversation. His eyes honed in on them both, like they were the real prize of the interview—which I suppose they were.

Deacon shook Adam's hand, a perfunctory smile dropped into place and erased the lines of confusion that were etched there when he entered the room. "Great to meet you, Adam. This is my father, Steven Winchester."

I watched with narrowed eyes while our father shook hands with Adam, unsure what he and Deacon were doing in there together. Our interviews were all supposed to be separate.

"So, Rebecca let you know about the change in plans?" Adam asked, a genial smile on his face while his gaze shot between my father and Deacon. "We felt it would be great for the whole family to be here to really emphasize that Winchester Holding's is a family-run company."

A scoff sounded from Deacon, who was shaking his head in disbelief. "But Charlie's interview, who is my sister, was conducted separately? Did I miss the memo that she wasn't a Winchester? Have you changed your last name and not told anyone, Charlie?"

"Not that I'm aware of." I said with a low voice, shaking my own head to try and quell the burning behind my eyes. I turned back to them, wanting to look at anyone but our father whose silence pressed down on my shoulders. My heels clicked loudly against the polished hardwood flooring and a childish part of me wanted to stop and dig them in—to scratch and scuff the perfect floor of his office. I steadied my hands against the countertop of the bar before pouring a generous glass of my father's favorite scotch and draining it before slamming the glass against the counter.

Adam cleared his throat uncomfortably, and I imagined him shifting on his feet behind me, afraid he would say the wrong thing in the Great Steven Winchester's presence. "Charlie's questions were quite different, as is her role in the company. Rebecca and I thought–"

"You'll have to excuse my children, Adam. Despite years of etiquette lessons, they seem prone to forgetting their manners." Our father's words cut across the room, causing my skin to burn. It was like I could feel them cutting at all the exposed parts of me, hoping to dig their way in.

Turning back around, I schooled my features, shrugging away from the hand Deacon reached out. "They're very different stories, you two go ahead."

Deacon's eyes darkened and he shifted closer to me almost in solidarity. I tipped my chin toward the empty chair beside our father, indicating him to join. He reached out, gripping my forearm briefly before whispering to me, "Don't leave. Wait here for me to finish this, please."

I nodded, placing my hand on top of his quickly before dropping it. I leaned back against the bar, crossing my arms tightly and flattening the ring of ostrich feathers that surrounded me. My eyes flitted past my father, who hadn't once looked in my direction and quickly over Deacon who looked like he might combust at any moment. I finally decided to stare determinedly at the bookshelf across the room from me. It was set into the wall and laden with textbooks from my father's time at Harvard that he kept for God knows what reason. I could tally that up as another thing Deacon did right that I didn't: followed in our father's footsteps while I traipsed off to Brown.

Adam's voice cut across the room, interrupting my depressing trip down memory lane. "So, Steven, tell me. Winchester Holding's is now a third generation family company, with your son and daughter both there. I believe your great-great-grandfather found his fortune in the Chicago Northwest railway, and it was your father who founded Winchester Holding's. Was it always expected to stay in the family?"

I could see my father shake his head out of the corner of my eye. "No, but it is one of my greatest joys that my children decided to join in contributing to their family legacy." Barely containing my eyeroll, I continued to stare at the bookshelf, the gold embossed titles on the books' spines all blurring together.

"Now, tell us about your recent acquisition of Halton Entertainment. I think it's safe to say that was a deal that shocked the business world. Halton has existed independently for years."

A laugh that I recognized as fake escaped my father before I watched in the periphery as he slapped Deacon's shoulder in a casual, good-natured manner before speaking. "Well, I couldn't have done that without my son, Deacon. In fact, I couldn't do any of it without him."

I jerked my head to look at them, the movement involuntary. Our father's smile was still on his face, despite the sour expression taking up residence on Deacon's. I knew I barely had anything to do with the regular day-to-day functioning of Winchester Holding's, and certainly nothing to do with the deal itself, but his words hurt all the same.

———

My arm was dangling at my side like some kind of drunken marionette, and my legs were crossed at my ankles. The photographer's voice was muffled from behind the camera while he instructed me to pop my shoulder more. I closed my eyes briefly and huffed a breath before doing as I was told. I could feel my father's eyes on the back of my neck from where he sat behind me. He had been sitting in the leather wingback chair behind his desk, and Deacon was standing to his left, one hand on his shoulder while I was propped up on the side of the desk like an accessory.

"This isn't Vogue," Deacon snapped. His mood had gone downhill significantly since the interview. The photographer had begun to poise and draw attention to me like I was a trophy sitting on our father's desk. "She doesn't need to pop her shoulder. Take the damn picture."

"Deacon, leave it. Let's just get this over with," I breathed quietly, continuing to pop my shoulder while my arm dangled uselessly beside me. My other hand was placed across my lap. Our father maintained his stony silence. I was certain he was staring forebodingly at the camera. Rebecca was standing behind the photographer, peering at the photos as they came across the screen whispering instructions to him and pointing at various aspects of the photo. He nodded in confirmation to whatever she had said before bringing his eye to the lens again and the resounding click echoed throughout the quiet room.

He pulled back and examined the frames that had popped up on the screen before murmuring something to Rebecca, "Charlie and Deacon, let's have you two switch and we will do one more take. Deacon, go sit where Charlie is, and Charlie stand right behind your father and rest your hand on his shoulder."

I pushed off the desk, popping up on my heels and chanced a glance at my father where he continued to sit behind the desk. His eyes weren't on me, however. He was surveying Deacon shrewdly as he loosened his bowtie and downed a glass of scotch at the bar beside him before making his way to where I had been sitting on the opposite side of the desk. His fingers brushed along my forearm in a quiet reassurance as he moved to sit. Deacon was the picture of casual elegance, propped on the edge of the desk. One arm was draped on a knee he had raised. Gesturing for them to continue, he made an exaggerated flourish with his hand. My father continued to stare at him, as I moved to stand behind him. I set my hand down gently on his shoulder. Deacon's head turned momentarily, like he might have been shooting a look toward our father.

Looking up, I schooled my features into a mask of indifference, as I had been instructed at the start of the photoshoot while the camera continued to flash, and we were immortalized in the still images. I continued to stare ahead, my hand resting on the soft material of my father's suit, careful not to press down and draw any attention to my presence beside him should he suddenly turn on me with whatever anger he had brewing for Deacon.

I watched as Rebecca leaned forward one more time and pointed to a few images on the screen before nodding at the photographer, a tight smile on her face. Before I could open my mouth to ask if we were indeed done, Deacon had pushed off the desk and turned to me, his eyes pointedly bypassing our father before they landed on me. He jerked his chin at the door and held up his arm for me, for the second time pulling me away from my father. "Come on, Charlie. Let's go get another drink."

"Thank you," I smiled at Rebecca, and the photographer whose name I hadn't caught before brushing my hand along my father's shoulder. I turned to study him, my lips parted as I waited for him to speak, to offer something to either Deacon or myself, to make amends with his children, but he continued to sit in stony silence, opening up his email on his phone. I closed my mouth, as Deacon beckoned me with his hand again, and I realized we were not going to win this one. Today, he is Steven, not our father. I pressed down gently on his shoulder again before speaking, "See you out there, Dad."

He grunted a response from behind me while Deacon wrapped his arm around my shoulder, pressing a kiss to the crown of my head while he steered me out of the office—again.

CHAPTER ELEVEN

The backyard of our family home had been transformed in the few hours we had been inside. When Deacon and I had arrived in Lake Forest earlier that afternoon, the yard had been in various stages of setup with lights being erected alongside a white tent that was covering an elaborate bar. My father had decided to hold a party to celebrate WH closing with Halton and had invited various investors and colleagues to attend the celebration. The timing struck me as odd, as I watched some of the photographers who had arrived with Forbes this afternoon milling around the backyard. I had seen Taylor standing near the bar with her parents before I dropped the curtain and turned back to Deacon. We were waiting for our father to finish whatever he had been wrapping up in his office in one of the sitting rooms that opened onto the backyard.

Deacon was leaning against one of the bookshelves that lined the walls, his arms folded across his chest while he stared pointedly at the ornate grandfather clock across the room from him. "He's really going to make everyone wait for him. How fucking lame is this? We close Halton, and he wants us to make an entrance to the celebration party as a family."

I arched an eyebrow before responding. "I thought you were excited about this. What happened to the Deacon of days past? Spraying champagne all over the office?"

"This isn't what I call a celebration. This afternoon has been painful," Deacon continued to stare behind me at the clock, like he could will our father to deign to arrive sooner.

"Other little boys dreamed of being professional racecar drivers. You dreamed of being on the cover of Forbes, Deacon." I chided, stepping into his path and obstructing the view of the clock. "Don't let what's going on with Dad and me ruin your big moment."

Deacon narrowed his eyes at me, and his mouth pulled into a tight line. "You're making fun of me."

Shaking my head, I walked toward him with my heels clicking on the polished hardwood. "I'm not, Deac. I'm not, I promise. This deal was so important to you. Don't let this ruin it."

"I'm sorry he ruined it for you," he whispered softly, his eyes sweeping over me. "I wish he didn't do things like that."

A small smile played on my lips, and I wrapped my arms around him, careful to avoid his white shirt with my face. I could only imagine what our father would do if I got makeup all over him before the photo ops were done for the evening. "Thank you for saying something. You always look out for me."

I felt Deacon rest his chin against the crown of my head, his arms wrapping around me briefly. "It's me and you against the world, Charlie."

Footsteps sounding from the hallway broke us apart, and I found myself standing beside Deacon, hands clasped in front of me waiting patiently for my father's arrival like a small child. It reminded me of all the times we stood as miniature versions of ourselves exactly like that, waiting while he spoke to adults at events, or presented us with convenient opportunities. I had felt like a doll then, ready to be passed around the room, and as I stood, the feathers trimming my dress moved slightly against some non-existent breeze. It occurred to me that perhaps I was serving the exact same purpose today. A pretty, made-up doll to stand beside him in his moment of triumph who would look onward with a smile on their face, proving to the world that even in the face of tragedy you really could have it all. Though his wife may have left us, left this world, Steven Winchester was still a *family man*.

I smiled tightly at him, staying rooted to my spot. Rebecca and the photographer from earlier trailed a few steps behind him as his eyes passed over us when he stepped into the room. "Shall we?" He asked, rolling his shoulders and adjusting his suit jacket before coming to stand in front of us by the door that led out onto the stonework at the top of the lawn.

Our family home was set on a gently sloping lawn that evened out to grassy ledges my father had inlaid with stones to form a path to walk down to the shore of the water below the overhang, the lake sparkling endlessly beyond it. That day, it had been overtaken by one company or another for the party. Lights twinkled in the early evening dusk, cocktail tables with white linens were placed strategically across the lawn that held giant arrangements of all white flowers: hydrangeas, lilies and peonies, and a large white tent covered an elaborate bar that was set up in the corner by the lawn house, which had also been covered in garlands of greenery. Our father said nothing else, as he threw open the doors. This looked like someone's fucking wedding.

Deacon and I fell into step slightly behind him, all of us resplendent in our swatches of dark designer fabrics walking in unison. We were a well-oiled machine now. When we were younger, we walked directly behind each of our parents at events like this. Deacon behind our father, and I would be steps behind our mother. After she died, Deacon and I had both automatically taken a step to the side and began walking diagonally behind our father. We hadn't been told to do so, it was just like we immediately knew we needed to fill all the spaces she had existed in, as if she had never been there at all.

The evening air brushed over my arms and swirled in the feathers of my dress as I stopped just short of my father who had walked to the end of the stones and raised a glass that had somehow materialized in his hand. A flute of champagne was shoved in front of me by a server that had snuck up behind me. I forced a smile and accepted it. I could see one being given to Deacon beside me from the corner of my eye. Flecks of gray in my father's hair caught in the lights that were swinging gently above us. He was in position in front of us, ready to wow the crowd with what was sure to be an ostentatious speech. My eyes scanned the crowd scattered across the lawn, as the servers wove in and out with trays of champagne until they snagged on David.

The blonde tendrils of his hair lifted off his forehead, after a breeze from the lake swept across the lawn. He was leaning against one of the cocktail tables, a tapered light gray suit jacket unbuttoned. I ran my eyes over him, taking in the white button down that had been tailored to fit him. The collar was unbuttoned, revealing inches of the corded muscles in his neck. His hand was in the pocket of his slim-fitting suit pants. He was holding the flute of champagne that had been passed to him loosely in his free hand. A grin spread across his face when our eyes met and the incessant rolling in my stomach began to quell. A small smile tugged at the corner of my lips, my eyes never leaving his. I swear I could see those flecks of honey sparkling at me from a distance.

David winked at me, bringing the champagne to his mouth and taking a small sip. I tilted my head to the side slightly as I watched him swallow, the muscles of his neck moving. I focused on imagining the heat of his skin pressed against mine. He smiled at me again, almost in an encouraging way. I blinked, realizing I shouldn't be up there looking like I was staring blankly into the crowd. I shook my head, smiling softly at David again before looking across the table where he was standing next to Taylor.

She was leaning forward on the table, her chin propped up on her hand. Her blonde hair had been crimped, which was distinctly eighties but somehow suited her, particularly when she had paired it with some sort of metallic navy blue shift dress I had never seen. Her parents were a few tables back, standing with Ash and Serena. Taylor caught my eye as she rolled hers at whatever my father was saying and began to swirl her champagne around in an exaggerated manner like she was swirling a scotch. Her tongue darted out from between her lips at me in a childlike display. A laugh caught in my throat while she made a yapping motion with her free hand low to the table that I knew was only for me. I was tempted to poke mine back out at her when I saw the flash of a camera go off in the periphery of my vision. A laugh rose in my throat, as I imagined what my father would do if Forbes caught a photo of me sticking my tongue out.

I smiled at Taylor in return instead, finally noticing the other person who had been standing at the table beside her and David. The navy jacket of Tripp's suit was unbuttoned. I couldn't see his legs beyond the gently fluttering white table cloth, but I was sure he was wearing tailored pants to match, with immaculately shiny dress shoes. His dark hair was pushed back off his face, and his eyes glinted with something I couldn't quite place from far away. I narrowed my own as he raised his champagne flute in a mocking salute when he caught me surveying him. He didn't even start working at WH yet. What the fuck was he doing here? Resisting the urge to roll my eyes, I steeled my features and angled my head toward my father whose speech was somehow still going. I hadn't listened to a single word.

My father raised his glass, and Deacon and I followed suit automatically. A well-oiled machine working in perfect synchronicity. I watched with my head turned to my dad, as he finished his toast. "Thank you to all of you. To everyone who made this possible. I look forward to the future of Winchester Holdings. All thanks to each and every one of you. To all of you. To the future."

An echo of his words sounded through the crowd. *To the future.* I found myself murmuring the words with my father and Deacon, along with everyone else assembled across the lawn. Always looking to the future, never looking to the past, even when its voice echoed in every room, in the very foundation of the house that stood behind us. I took a sip of my champagne when Deacon and my father did. Turning to Deacon, my father grasped his hand quickly and said something low in his ear that I couldn't hear. My father turned to me next, kissing my cheek as he spoke gruffly in my ear as well. "Enjoy the evening, Charlie. Try not to spoil it for David. We'll talk later."

A grimace fell into place across my features while I pressed my lips briefly to his other cheek in return. "I wouldn't dream of it, Dad." I responded dryly before pulling back and forcing a smile on my face. My father's eyes were impassive and calculating as usual, but something stirred beneath the surface of them. Like he was troubled by something.

"I meant what I said, Charlie. I want you to enjoy yourself." He said, uncharacteristically soft, his eyes dark before he offered me a tight smile, pivoting on his heel and walked across the stone to where others were waiting to greet him and surely offer their congratulations on his success. The words settled against my skin while I watched him walk away.

Deacon materialized by my side, finding another glass of champagne for himself. He watched with an arched brow while our father fell into step beside other guests seamlessly. Deacon shook his head and rolled his eyes, a wisp of his chocolate hair brushing across his forehead. He slung an arm around me, grabbing a fistful of the ostrich feathers. "Come on, let's go mingle before he tries to get us to pose for more photographs."

A small laugh escaped my mouth, as I leaned into Deacon briefly. He was right; the photographers were still lingering around the periphery of the party, no doubt searching for humanizing shots of the Winchester family. Deacon and I wove through the crowd, smiling and offering pleasantries to everyone we worked with. The entirety of WH had shown up across every department. I was fairly certain there were people here my father likely hadn't seen after they were hired. He made it a point to introduce himself to all staff when they started. I used to think it was proof he was one of the few people like him who truly cared and truly wanted to be good, but I suspected it was probably a PR move that he picked up along the way.

David was still standing with Taylor, smiling as he spoke to her between sips of his champagne. My stomach clenched uncomfortably, as I noticed Tripp was standing at the table with them. A sour expression crossed Taylor's face whenever she glanced over at him. As I drew closer, I realized her eyes had been lined with some obscenely glittery eyeshadow that only accentuated what she must have been going for with this look. It reminded me of something Sabine would put me in to ensure I stood out. She would have been right, people's eyes were landing on Taylor from all over the lawn, and she was drawing plenty of appreciative glances. The spotlight suited her. She winked at me and patted the space beside her on the table between herself and David, beckoning me with her other hand. She shifted her body further away from Tripp like she could form a protective bubble around me.

Deacon was doing that bizarre macho thing all the men I knew seemed to do—shaking hands with Tripp and David as soon as he approached the table, like they never saw one another. Taylor wrapped her arms around me. "Great feathers. Much better than your father's speech," she laughed against my ear.

I snorted, pulling back from her hug. "I don't think I heard a single word. But that was one for the books." I turned, smiling up at David. Leaning down, he brought his lips to my forehead and a hand to my exposed shoulder.

"You look incredible," he said, his thumb tracing patterns on my collarbone. "Do you like this better than the last dress?"

"The feathers are a bit much, but at least I won't be sparkling on the cover of Forbes next month," I answered. "It tones down the utter humiliation marginally."

"Will you sign a copy for me, Charlie? I'd like to keep the cover in my locker at the hospital," Taylor stated without looking at me, her words dripping with sarcasm. She had raised her hand and was gesturing to one of the servers that was winding through the crowd with a precariously balanced platter of champagne and other drinks. She smiled, parting her fuchsia-painted lips as they arrived at the table. "Hi yes, she needs at least two glasses of champagne, but we will also take some shots for the table. What does everyone think?"

Taylor paused and began counting in an exaggerated manner at Tripp, David, Deacon and myself. "I think...tequila. Maybe make them doubles." The server nodded and placed the requisite two glasses of champagne in front of me on the table.

Deacon wound his hands around Taylor's waist and placed his chin on her shoulder, exhaling a puff of air into her ear. "Tequila is a great idea, Taylor. You look incredible by the way." She immediately brought her palm up to his cheek, like she meant to run her fingers down it affectionately. She stopped short of bringing her fingers across her cheek and cupped her hand, slapping him lightly instead. Taylor placed her hands on top of his and peeled them off, but not before I noticed her squeeze each of his hands affectionately.

"You know Dad will freak out if he sees us doing tequila shots with Forbes photographers around, Deacon." I rolled my eyes, leaning into David, who had wound his arm around my waist, his hand applying pressure to my hip bone. He picked up one of the champagne flutes with his other hand and handed it to me.

"It would probably stand to make the article more interesting. Lighten up, Chuckles," Tripp said dryly. I was staring determinedly ahead, but I could practically hear him rolling his eyes as he said it.

"The article is plenty interesting. I'm in it," Deacon supplied, his chin still digging into Taylor's shoulder. She drew her elbow back, looking like she was about to sink it into his stomach when Deacon side stepped, moving to stand between her and Tripp.

The server returned with five deep glasses brimming with the tequila Taylor ordered. I found myself peering over their shoulders to see if I could spot my father or any of the photographers in the crowd while the shots were set out on the table in front of us. He was up the gentle slope of the lawn with this back turned to us.

Deacon reached out, grabbed two of the shots and placed one in front of me, his eyes following where mine had traveled up the hill. "No time like the present then," he said, raising his glass as everyone else followed suit.

I felt David running his hand down the knobs of my spine reassuringly. Arching my back, I pushed into the pressure his palm was providing, and I looked sideways at him. His hair was still damp and curling around his ears, and his amber eyes were sparkling like they only seemed to for me. A smirk pulled at the corner of his lips as he raised his eyebrows, bringing the shot glass to his mouth. Smiling gently at him, I winked before turning back to look at Deacon, who still had his glass raised and seemed on the precipice of some sort of toast. My eyes caught on Tripp's over the top of Deacon's glass.

He was staring at me intently, as if he had watched every moment of my interaction with David, assessing and taking inventory of each movement. The corner of his lip pulled up and somehow the gesture radiated smugness, like he knew something I didn't. Tripp winked at me, his eyes catching the light and somehow becoming even more startling blue. I rolled my eyes before looking away pointedly. Deacon had started rambling, but I could barely hear it over the ringing that had started in my ears. Pressing closer to David, I tried to wash away the feeling of his eyes on me and my somersaulting stomach as the tequila burned my throat.

———————

The waves of the lake lapped quietly against the rocky shoreline. The sprawling lawn of my father's property continued to slope gently down a hill before it evened out to an outcropping of land that had been curated over the years to look like you could walk out onto the lake. I was dangling my feet off the edge, after sitting down on the stones that lined the ridge, bottle of champagne in hand. To my right, there was another slope that had been made into a stone staircase that led to the shore of the water below. I had stepped away from the party when my father had grabbed Deacon and David, demanding to introduce them to someone who was particularly interested in the Halton acquisition. Taylor had gotten a call from the hospital and disappeared into the house not long before that. Tripp had slithered off to God knows where, and I was standing alone at the cocktail table.

And then, it all became too much, just like when I was a child. This time, though, there was no running to hide behind my mother or my father's legs. It was no longer cute to need a hand to hold as I tried to navigate society gatherings and be who I was supposed to be.

Maybe it was childish and maybe my father would scold me tomorrow when he realized I disappeared from the party at some point, but I had taken a bottle of champagne from the side of the bar and walked the back path down the lawn to stop at the lake. I brought the bottle to my lips when I heard footsteps behind me. My heart tumbled, hoping David had come for me like he had at the yacht club. Looking over my shoulder, my stomach began to roll as Tripp strolled down the hill at a leisurely pace, one hand holding a drink and the other tucked into the pocket of his suit pants.

"Try not to look so disappointed. I'm not who you hoped to see?" Tripp asked, a drawling lilt to his voice. It had no place being there—he was from Boston. I bit my tongue at the response that was about to find its way out. He was doing it to make me angry.

"You would never be who I hoped to see." I rolled my eyes as I spoke, whipping my head back around, though this wasn't exactly true. A different me used to search for Tripp in every crowd and used to revel in the times it was just us. It always felt like we were existing alone in some bubble, no one seeing things the way we did. The high, sleek ponytail the hairdresser had styled me in moved with me, obscuring my vision as he drew closer. I watched from the corner of my eye, his polished black oxfords and navy suit pants came into view, as he sat down, dangling his legs over the ledge beside me. I stared straight ahead, taking another sip from the bottle of champagne.

"Well, I'm sorry to say the person I assume you were hoping to come down here is indisposed. Last I saw, he was shaking hands with some very important people from Halton," Tripp supplied, unsolicited. Saying nothing, I took another sip of the champagne, the bubbles tickling my lips. I continued to swing my legs back and forth, the heels of the black patent Louboutin's catching against the stone ledge if I swung them out too far. I studied the shoreline, noticing the occasional boat bobbing along in the waves.

"How come you're out here all alone?" He asked, breaking the silence that had settled over us.

I resisted the urge to roll my eyes. "It was too crowded, too loud, too everything."

Out of the corner of my eye I could see Tripp nodding with a sort of pensive expression that was barely visible in his eyes while he took a sip from his glass. "I remember that. Even back at Brown, sometimes you could leave parties or you would go sit outside alone for a while. Who would have thought? Little Charlie Winchester still doesn't feel like she fits in anywhere. I guess that hasn't changed, huh?"

I stilled, my grip on the neck of the champagne bottle tightening. I used to do that. It was always too much, the pressures of everything pushing on me from every angle even back then. No one ever seemed to care, and no one had ever seemed to notice except the occasional soft, knowing smile from my mother, and a twenty-year-old Tripp, apparently. "You remember that?"

"I always cared for you, Chuck. Even back then," Tripp spoke as he brought his glass to his lips again, pausing to swirl his scotch before knocking it back. His eyes were staring out at the lake, the lines of his throat bobbed as he swallowed.

A scoff escaped my mouth, bringing the bottle of champagne to my lips again. "You only care about yourself, Tripp, always have, always will. We might have been friends, but that was a long time ago."

I turned, as Tripp reached forward and grabbed one of the feathers sticking out of the top of my dress, pulling on it in a childlike display with his large hands. Our eyes met as he began to twirl the feathers between his fingers. His voice was barely a whisper over the sound of the waves as they lapped against the shore. "That's not true. Do you remember when we were responsible for the pledge dinner? You were–"

"I remember," I said, cutting him off and moving to pull my shoulder away from him, the feathers falling just beyond his grasp. That was before my mother had died. When I was a *different* me. Tripp and I had been assigned to host a dinner for all of the potential pledges for our sorority and fraternity. We had gotten so drunk off the Jell-O shots that we were supposed to set out for them and ended up sitting on the roof of my sorority house sharing a bottle of wine I had taken from our family cellar when I had come back from thanksgiving.

"We had fun," Tripp whispered. I had been looking ahead at the waves as they lapped against the shore below us. "Me and you. Back then." Turning to face him, I startled when I realized he had placed his glass beside him and was staring at me intently. His eyes seemed darker than usual; instead of the crisp blue, they were a stormy sea as he looked at me.

"Sure," I smiled thinking of the person who he had known, my lips quivering as I brought the champagne to them once again. "We had fun."

"Have you ever thought of me? Over the years?" He whispered. His voice was low and his face had somehow inched closer to mine. I could see the stubble growing in along his jawline.

I found my eyes locking with his, and my breathing grew heavy. It felt like I was looking back in time, like maybe I could be someone else. Maybe I was someone else. Just for a moment. Some distant part of me, the me who I was now, was screaming in my mind, but it was muffled and quiet as I inched closer to whoever was staring back at me in his eyes. I shook my head slowly. "No, I haven't thought of you, Tripp."

A smirk spread across his face, and his eyes shone under the moonlight. "Liar," he tilted his head, and his lips were on mine before I had a chance to form a thought. My mouth parted almost involuntarily, and Tripp's tongue swept into it as he brought his hands to cup either side of my face.

My momentary lapse in judgment passed as quick as it came when I suddenly remembered whose tongue I was meeting with my own. I pulled my lips away from his and brought my hands to his broad chest to push him backward. The champagne bottle I had been holding fell to the ground and shattered against the stone pathway. The sound reverberated through the night while I continued to stare at Tripp. He was looking at me with something I couldn't quite place. His cheeks were flushed, and he was breathing heavily. I wiped my mouth against the back of my hand, continuing to stare at him. I could feel heat rising on my cheeks and neck, and my stomach clenched uncomfortably at the thought of his lips on mine. The thought of opening my mouth for him like that, like I wanted it.

"Don't you ever do that again," I bit out, my words laced with venom but somehow still barely a whisper above the waves that continued to lap against the shore ahead of us.

"You can't tell me you didn't feel that. Didn't want that." Tripp looked at me while he spoke, his voice low and gravelly.

"One...I'm with David now. I'm in love with David. He is ten times the person you could ever even dream of being. Two...no one has ever disrespected me the way you have." Embarrassment, shame and something like fury began to burn in my stomach.

I could picture myself at twenty, standing in the doorway where I had gone to turn off that light, the tears streaming down my face and my hand clapping across my mouth, staring at the fifteen point-marker beside my name. I pushed myself up hastily, not caring for any sort of grace or propriety and swung my legs from where they were dangling off the ledge. The sharp gravel bit into my palms with the force I exerted. I brushed my hands down the front of my dress, not caring about the integrity of the fabric. Out of the corner of my eye, I could see Tripp begin to stand with much more finesse than I had managed, abandoning his glass beside him. I took a step back, my heel immediately sinking into the soft grass of the lawn.

"Chuckles–" he started, looking like he might take a step toward me.

"Don't fucking call me Chuckles," I snapped, bending forward quickly, as I kicked off my heels. Grabbing them, I turned on my heel, the blades of grass soft against my bare feet. I started back up the hill, forgetting all about the side pathway that would hide me from view, leaving Tripp standing atop the ledge overlooking the lake. The farther away I walked, the more I hoped my heart would stop feeling like it was going to beat out of my chest, and that the guilt ripping at all my organs would fade as I put physical distance between us.

As I came over the crest of the lawn, I saw David standing there with my brother and father; his head was tipped back in laughter, the twinkling lights highlighting the strong planes of his face. I paused for a moment to study him, really observe the man who held my heart in his very hands. It was like I had imagined him, his broad, tapered shoulders that gave way to an easy loping posture that somehow exuded confidence. He brought his head forward again, bringing whatever drink he was holding to his lips, and his eyes landed on me. I could tell, even from a distance, that I was all that he saw. My stomach lurched and a sour taste rose in my throat. I wasn't sure I ever felt worse.

CHAPTER TWELVE

I remained on the precipice of vomiting for the remainder of the night. Tripp had disappeared shortly after he had emerged on the top of the hill not long after I had left him. I wasn't sure where he went, and I couldn't be bothered to care. Taylor had returned from whatever phone call she had gotten from the hospital and was standing by the bar with her parents. Finding her, I immediately slid my hand into hers and demanded that her parents join us in a round of shots.

She looked at me briefly, her eyes narrowed and mouth parted in confusion before the expression passed as quickly as it came when I squeezed her fingers in reassurance. I hoped the tequila would burn the taste of his tongue from my mouth, but shot after shot just increased my nausea and the rolling tidal wave of guilt in my stomach.

Deacon and I decided to stay overnight at our father's, and I had convinced David to stay with me. Each time he had looked at me or ran his hands across my shoulders or my back, the ghost of Tripp's hands found their way into my memories. I pressed myself harder to David, like the warmth of his skin could erase them, too. David and I had crawled into my childhood bed, the ridiculous size of it laughable as we met in the middle, the overstuffed duvet puffing up around us.

We had fallen asleep shortly after Deacon had drunkenly called Hydra-V and paid some sort of ridiculous premium for a nurse to drive out to Lake Forest to provide whatever service he deemed as being the best to prevent and cure an impending hangover. We had whispered to one another, like we were two teenagers who might get caught by my father despite the fact that his room was on the opposite side of the house. We whispered about everyone we worked with, my father's dumb speech, and all the bizarre places David jokingly told me he was going to bring the Forbes cover to.

He had fallen asleep with his hand on my cheek, his breathing slowing and becoming more rhythmic. I laid awake watching him, studying him, while silent tears of guilt tracked their way down my face. My stomach had continued to roll uncomfortably, and I brought my own hand to his cheek. Brushing the stubble poking through, I whispered platitudes of sorrow and apology, beginning his forgiveness until I fell asleep and dawn began to stream through the windows.

I woke up before David, hangover-free thanks to Deacon's ridiculous ministrations the night before, but a sense of dread sunk into my stomach and took root there, winding its way through my entire body. I thought back to the night of the yacht club party, and how I had thought in that moment I could live a thousand lifetimes and never deserve David, never amount to the love he was offering me up beneath the stars. The back of my eyes began to prickle at the sheer irony that it took me two weeks to prove myself right. I studied his face, a ray of sunlight falling ever so perfectly across his defined jawbone. His breathing remained even, and I watched his shoulders rise and fall as he continued to inhale and exhale. I opened my mouth to whisper another unheard apology when his eyes began to flutter before landing on mine.

"Have you been watching me sleep, Charlie?" David asked, his voice still rough as his lips crept up in a grin.

"No!" I blurted, shaking my head resolutely, almost innocently. But I was far from innocent. I opened my mouth, the words rolling like bile on my tongue. I would tell him. He deserved to know. All of it. What happened at Brown, what happened at dinner, and what happened last night when I let Tripp kiss me. David deserved better than me, and I would do everything in my power to keep him. Even if it meant throwing myself at the foot of my childhood bed and begging him to keep me. Begging for forgiveness. "David, I–"

A loud beep sounded to my left interrupting me before I could get the words out. Anger and irritation rose in my stomach, along with relief. Relief that I had been given a reprieve in telling David just how disappointing I truly was; how wrong he had been all along. "What?" I bit out, assuming it was Deacon summoning me through the intercom that sat on my nightstand. We were constantly buzzing one another, despite our rooms being only on opposite ends of the same hallway. The only other time it went off was if we were running late and the driver was ready to take us somewhere.

"Am I interrupting something?" My father's voice came from the speaker. His words were sharp and cold. "Breakfast will be served in fifteen minutes if you think you can all drag yourselves from bed. Deacon hasn't answered me, so fetch him would you?"

My face paled at his words. "Jesus, Dad, no. You're not interrupting anything. I assumed you were Deacon."

There was a pregnant pause during which David was visibly cringing at me before he sat up and began to run his hands across his face, as if remembering it wasn't just my father speaking at us now but his boss as well. "Regardless, please wake up Deacon on your way down. See you shortly."

The line went dead, and I rolled over onto my back grabbing a spare pillow to bring to my face before a strangled scream escaped my throat. I felt David tug the pillow out of my hands, his face appearing above mine. A lock of hair flopped over his forehead as he peered down at me, the corners of his eyes crinkling in concern. Tossing the pillow behind his head haphazardly, David braced an arm on the other side of my head before rolling on top of me. His body pressed into mine, his broad shoulders tapering overtop of me.

"Come on, Charlie, try to laugh about it at least," he said, a lilting tone to his voice as he began playfully nipping at my exposed shoulders.

"I don't know why everything I do is funny. Am I some sort of joke? No one ever seems to find mocking humor in the things Deacon does." I bit out, more harshly than I intended.

David cocked his head to the side before speaking, "I don't think everything you do is *funny*. In fact, everything you do gives me a raging hard-on..."

I rolled my eyes, pushing his face back with my hand while he sunk his teeth into my palm. "I'm serious, David."

"I'm serious, too," he answered, his eyes darkening as he leaned his forehead down to press against mine. "I don't think you're a joke at all. I'm sure Deacon is still asleep. How long until we absolutely have to be there for breakfast?"

"I'm sure he's sitting down there now reading about himself in the business section of the Tribune while whatever spread the staff has planned is being laid out in the sitting room." I pressed my forehead into David's, his hair brushing against the sides of my face. Closing my eyes, I tried to quell the rolling of my stomach and the voice in my head that was continuing to remind me of what I had done. Another silent apology went unsaid followed by an inner promise to make it up to him, to prove to him—and to myself—I deserved him, that I was worthy.

I opened my eyes to meet David's, and despite how close we were, I could see the flecks of light in them as he continued to grin down at me. "Well, seeing as I am sure the Tribune has written a multi-page spread on the astounding success of the Winchesters, I bet we have some time."

David's grin turned almost feral, and he leaned down and began nipping at my neck, pressing into me as his hands traveled down my body with a reverence that I didn't deserve.

———

I usually enjoyed the first days of summer. They were often marked by warm evenings on the terrace with Deacon, or if the water allowed, on one of his various boats. It was also the time I had intended to map out the rest of my community trips for the remainder of the year. Everything I had typically enjoyed about it had been marred by Tripp's new presence in the WH offices.

Aside from the mandatory meetings we attended together, where he would smirk maddeningly at me with an annoying knowing glint in his eye, I spent every waking moment behind closed doors in my office or dodging him by claiming I needed to be down on one of the lower floors with the members of the research team.

This actually led my father to believe I was taking the Play for Everyone incident seriously. I was taking it seriously, and I didn't want anything like that to happen again. But that's not why I skulked around in the shadows of the office, and everytime he mentioned it, I smiled blandly and nodded my head demurely, as if I was still scarred by the incident.

Despite my attempts to avoid him at all costs, Tripp had somehow managed to charm every single person on the executives' floor. He was like a parasite finding its way into every orifice. I focused intently on my computer screen when he passed by. The only thing I was able to make out was his figure at the end of the hall saying something that was leading Damien to laugh uproariously. "What could possibly be so fucking funny?" I hissed under my breath, shaking my head before forcing myself to look back at the screen in front of me. I was pretty certain I had read the same line of the report four times. Every time Damien's brash laughter sounded from beyond my closed office, I felt my stomach clench and found myself looking up in anger and annoyance at the lingering distraction that was Tripp.

"Oh my fucking God, I give up," I muttered. Deacon's laughter had joined the cacophony of voices I could hear through the glass. I made a mental note to contact someone about further soundproofing the office. Smashing my finger down with more force than needed, I sent the report to the printer that sat in the corner of my office. My aggressive movements seemed to continue as I pushed off my desk with more force than necessary, my chair rolling to hit the back of the wall. A frustrated, childlike shriek escaped my throat as I gripped the sides of the chair to steady myself. I steeled my breath.

Fucking Tripp Banks. Ruining everything he came into contact with, including the small piece of my family company I was trying to occupy. I stopped suddenly in front of the printer, irrational anger flooding through me when I saw the blinking red light that indicated there was no ink left. Another peal of raucous laughter reverberated through the glass door of my office, which was distinctly Deacon's. I'm sure he was just in fucking stitches over whatever Tripp had said.

I tapped my heel in irritation, debating what was worse: continuing to listen to that and remain trapped in my office reading the report on my computer, or go out there to print it in the supply room. Neither sounded like enjoyable options. *David.* David would have a printer in his office, and I hadn't heard his laugh, yet. If I had, it wouldn't have grated on me like everyone else's.

I exited my office, tempted to slam the glass door and break up the little party happening by Deacon's office. Tripp was holding court there, his leg kicked up against the back of Damien's desk. I narrowed my eyes, noticing his expression. She was still sitting at her desk with his chin propped on the palm of his hand smiling up at Tripp and Deacon like he was completely enraptured, and like he had nothing better to do. The clicking of my heels against the tile was practically silent amongst their continued laughter. Tripp was the only one facing my direction, and his eyes weren't on me until right before I had raised my fist to knock on David's closed door. His arms were folded across his chest, causing the buttons of his white dress shirt to strain against his muscles. A scowl rose on my face at the sight, and as the memory of his lips on mine stirred—like he could sense it—he winked at me.

My lower lip jutted out and my face grew hot, my hand still held absurdly in the air, poised to knock on David's door at any moment. I was consumed with the childish urge to stick my tongue out and stomp my foot at him.

"Come to join the fun, Chuckles?" Tripp spoke, cocking his head to the side. There was an air of superiority lacing his words that I was certain only I could hear.

I grimaced, lowering my hand and crossing my arms across the front of my dress. "No, I came to tell Deacon he has the most annoying fucking laugh I have ever heard. If you'll excuse me, I have work to do. I imagine the four of you also have much better things to do than listen to whatever vitriol Tripp is entertaining you all with."

I had just raised my hand to knock again when David's door swung open before me. David leaned against the doorframe, mirroring Tripp with arms crossed over his chest. He hadn't discarded his suit jacket for the day, yet. I had never seen the suit he was wearing before. It was a light tan color, and I was certain if Deacon was wearing it I would have thought it looked outrageously douchey, but David looked handsome. Like he was from another era, standing there imposing in the doorway, the hard line of his jaw doing things to my pulse and his brown eyes glinting mischievously as he surveyed us. He had been letting his stubble grow in through the week. I wanted to rub my cheek across his scruff, feel it scrape against my neck.

"Something must be very funny out here, because I've been hearing Deacon's laugh non-stop for the last God knows how long, and it's become quite grating," David said, his eyes sweeping over me gently before he arched an eyebrow and landed on Tripp's little posse.

"It's a horrible laugh, isn't it?" I whispered, leaning into him, all too aware of Tripp's lingering gaze. I could feel the heat from his stare on my neck. He was always assessing David and me when we were together. I couldn't quite put my finger on what he was searching for.

"Shut up, Charlie, my laugh is fine." Deacon's voice sounded a bit whiny, like he would corner me the second we were alone to confirm whether or not his laugh was actually annoying.

David continued to look, a single eyebrow raised. Damien was staring at David and me intently through his horn-rimmed glasses, like he was waiting for us to start mauling one another. I rolled my eyes pointedly at him and jerked my head at the pile of papers on his desk. It was more for his benefit than mine. We both knew what would happen if Steven emerged from whatever meeting he was having and found Damien over here fraternizing—as he would call it—instead of dutifully working at his desk. He turned on his heel abruptly, like I had reminded him suddenly of that fact and scuttled off to the copy room.

"May I use your printer?" I asked David pointedly, turning away from Deacon and Tripp. "Mine's out of ink."

Deacon snorted loudly. "Oh bullshit, Charlie. You didn't come over here to *use his printer*. What's that code for? You sound like you're in a porno."

The corners of David's lips twitched. "Of course you can, beautiful. Come on in." He raised his hand, wrapping his arm around my shoulders and turning me away from Deacon and Tripp before I had a chance to respond. David led me into his office, which was a mirror of my own but furnished in the standard colors of Winchester Holdings: the oak desk, the cognac leather couch and matching chair, and minimal personal effects. All the offices across the executives' floor had oak doors. Only my father's and my own, which sat at opposite ends of the floor, were glass.

He gently shut the door behind him. David removed his arm from my shoulders and propped himself up against the edge of his desk. A grin crept across his face. "So, are you here to service my printer?"

"I hate to disappoint you, Mr. Kennedy," I smiled, moving forward to place my hands on his shoulders, "but I do actually need to use your printer. Mine is out of ink, and Deacon's laughter has been annoying me all day while I tried to review my report. I was going to head down to research or out somewhere." A stab of guilt coursed through me, as David continued to smile in response to my easy lie. Deacon's laugh was annoying, but that's not who I was desperately trying to avoid.

David opened his mouth to respond when his discarded cell phone started ringing on his desk. He leaned backward, both of us noting the photo and name that was displayed across the screen.

"Go ahead," I said. He held up a finger to excuse himself, continuing to smile at me with an easy grace.

I raised my eyebrows in thanks, making my way across his office to the printer. Thumbing my phone quickly, I emailed the report to David's printer as I heard him answer the phone over the whir of the machine. I was about to turn and face David when he spoke.

"Hi, Victoria. I didn't expect to see your name on my phone this morning. How are you? How are your parents?" David spoke with the same easy grace that he had with me earlier.

I knitted my eyebrows, wracking my memory to try and place a Victoria somewhere in David's life. Irritation rose in me, as I continued to stare determinedly at the printer, watching the pages fall on top of one another in the tray. David's laugh cut across the room, a twinge of jealousy flickering to life in the pit of my stomach. The bitter sense of irony that followed almost made me scoff in laughter. David, beautiful and perfect David, was only laughing on the phone, and I was growing jealous. Meanwhile, I had allowed a man standing not more than twenty feet away to paw at me, kiss me, slide his tongue into my mouth with ease, and David had no idea. I took a steadying breath, gathering my papers and turned on my heel to face David, an idiotic smile plastered across my face.

David was propped up against his desk again, the phone pressed against his ear and his other arm crossed over his chest. He was smiling widely and nodding his head at whatever was being said at the other end of the line. "Yeah, yeah. Tonight works. I'll bring them for sure. Just text me the address. See you then." He was still smiling, as he hung up the phone and tossed it behind him on his desk. "You get what you need, beautiful?" I nodded, standing there mutely while my mind continued to wander in far-off directions.

Opening my mouth, I wasn't sure what I was going to say. "Who was–"

The heavy door was thrown open by Deacon, who whistled loudly and snapped his fingers in David's general direction. "Steven needs to see us in his office, David. Something about–"

David held up a hand to cut him off. "I'm not a dog, Deac. You can ask nicely." He pushed off the desk, looking me over as he walked past. His eyes snagged on my face and a look of concern flashed in them. I realized my lips were still pulled up bizarrely. I probably looked like the fucking joker. "Anyway, my friend Victoria just called, and she's in town tonight with some friends. They have a private room at Opus. I said I would swing by, and she invited anyone who wanted to come." He tipped his chin at Tripp, who was standing behind Deacon outside of David's office still, and Deacon, who clearly had not continued any semblance of work while I was in here.

Feral delight rippled across Deacon's face while he nodded in agreement, surely imagining whatever unfortunate soul he would try to sink his teeth into that night. Tripp gave a noncommittal shrug in response, his eyes immediately swinging to me, that look of secrecy and smugness he always seemed to wear somehow tripling over the course of the last few moments. It was like he was taunting me as a grin slipped into place on his features—like we were children and he refused to tell me a secret.

"I can pick you up before we head over?" David asked, stirring me away from whatever was lurking behind Tripp's eyes.

"I'm supposed to go for dinner with Taylor, but we can just meet you wherever you are afterward?" I forced the smile off my face, hopefully settling into a more normal expression.

"Tell her I'll be eagerly anticipating her arrival all night," Deacon called over his shoulder, having turned away and began a leisurely saunter across the executives' floor to our father's office at the opposite end. David smiled at me and nodded in response, exiting his office and following after Deacon.

Rolling my eyes, I stepped across the threshold and out of the office. Tripp was still standing there, his hands lazily tucked into the pants of his suit, eyes still glimmering. I raised my eyebrows at him, breezing past on my heels like I didn't have a care in the world. Hearing him fall into step behind me, I narrowed my eyes when he ducked around me into the open doorway of his office. I had to walk past him to get to my end of the floor. He propped himself up against the doorframe, arms crossed, leaning like he didn't have a care in the world or any work to do.

"Fucking Edward Cullen. Stop whipping around me like that." I bit out, clutching the printed report to my chest.

"Been avoiding me, Chuck?" Tripp arched an eyebrow, one end of his lip curling up.

"Unlike you, and apparently everyone else here, I actually do work." I tapped the report pointedly.

Tripp continued to smile at me, but it looked more like he was baring his teeth in a snarl, ready to rip the heart out of another young girl at any given moment. "And unlike your boyfriend who takes calls from and makes plans with his ex-girlfriend on your family's dime."

My face fell at his words, but he had already turned and began to stroll across his office to stop at his desk, propping himself up as David had only moments ago. I immediately crossed the threshold, my quest to avoid Tripp like the plague falling by the wayside. "What the fuck are you spewing off words about now, Tripp?" I asked, practically slamming the heavy door behind me, effectively sealing us in his office. My gaze flitted around, taking note of how sterile and impersonal it remained after a few weeks of working here. "Who are you, Patrick

Bateman? Would it kill you to have a painting on the wall, or I don't know, a photograph on your desk?"

He continued to grin at me in a sort of feral delight before speaking. "David's friend, Victoria. You forget that I went to business school with David. I know Victoria. She was his girlfriend through most of prep school, Princeton, and business school. Judging by the look on your face, you had no idea she existed."

Tripp wasn't wrong. David had never mentioned her, not once. I tried to school my features, though my stomach continued to do its ironic anxiety tumble, while dreadful thoughts whispered in my ear. "Not everyone is as nefarious as you. There aren't secret ulterior motives for everything David does."

He arched a dark eyebrow, pushing off his desk with his foot, stalking toward me in a matter of seconds. He stopped just short of me, reaching out with his hand and plucking the report from where I had been hugging it and dropping it to the floor beside him. I opened my mouth to protest, but he interrupted me. "You want to talk about ulterior motives, Chuck? What are you doing all alone with me in my office? Why'd you close that door? Little Winchester wants to pick up where we left off the other night?"

"Why did you come here, Tripp? Was it really to work at WH or was it to weasel your way back into my life? Leave me alone." I whispered the last part, and a part of me was screaming at myself to step backward, back slowly away to the door, to safety, the way you're supposed to avoid a predator in the wild. But I continued to stare at him, my chin tipped up slightly to meet his eyes. I could easily make out all the sharp planes of his face. I found myself studying the pattern of his stubble, waiting on bated breath for his answer. Like maybe it would absolve me—after all these years, I would finally know. I would finally understand why twenty-year-old me wasn't enough for Tripp, for my mother—why I wasn't enough for anyone.

Tripp continued to study me for a moment, and his usual piercing eyes darkened before he was on me, a hand wrapping around the back of my neck and his lips pressing against mine as they had at the Forbes party. His tongue parted my lips with ease and invaded my mouth to meet mine in a gentle sweep as his free hand found the hem of my dress and skimmed the underside of my thigh. And for another moment, I let him. Shame and regret washed over me suddenly, and I jerked back, bringing my hands to his chest to push him off me back toward his desk, stumbling slightly on my five-inch heel. He stared at me, his complexion flushed beneath his three-day-old stubble. He was panting slightly, arms out straight behind him clutching his desk. His ice blue eyes had clouded over entirely—they were stormy and dark as he surveyed me.

"Does he know about us?" Tripp arched an eyebrow arrogantly.

"I would hardly call this an *us,* Tripp. In fact, there is no *us.* Just a continuing lack of judgment on my part." I averted my eyes, sure my cheeks were also flushed as I pulled on my sleek ponytail to ensure it was still intact. I ran my hands down the front of my dress, smoothing it. Tripp's hand had been moments from snaking up it before I had the foresight to end this transgression and slap it away.

I turned, looking back in time to see Tripp sneering and shaking his head in what looked like disbelief. "Not *this* us. Whatever the fuck you want to call *this.* I call it the you prolonging-my-blue-balls us. But I'm asking if he knows about the *us* we were at Brown."

The us we were at Brown. Unbidden, memories of that 'us' snuck across my mind. Meeting Tripp for the first time when I was a freshman, clutching a cup of stale beer in my hand at a frat party as he stopped a conversation midway to introduce himself; the way he placed his palm on the wall behind me and leaned in, seemingly hanging on every word I would say; the way no one else but Deacon ever had and no one did again until David. A twenty-year-old Tripp chased me through a frat-sponsored corn maze until he finally cornered me and grabbed my hand, dragging me into the corn and pressing his lips to mine. I giggled and ran away back to my sorority sisters with my heart beating a mile a minute. Sloppy drunk kisses under hot club lights with loud music pounding in my ears and endless laughter as we sat together on the worn couch in his frat house, trading sips of our drinks and making fun of everyone around us—that was *us*...

I scoffed loudly, even those memories were tainted now. It was my turn to sneer, and I snorted loudly. "Tripp, there was no *us* at Brown. You slept with me for points on a bracket after my mother died." The words came out as a hiss, and I looked down to the nearest end table, reaching down to grab the nearest item which turned out to be a box of tissues before whipping it at his head.

Tripp raised his hands to cover his face, jerking backward to avoid the tissue box. His tie was askew and wrapped untidily around his neck from the movement. He shook it off, then peered down at the offending box. "Charlie, we need to talk about that. It's not what you think it was."

I felt my mouth drop open in disbelief, and my blood began to boil. "Not what I think? You seem to be conveniently forgetting the part where I called you the day of my mother's funeral and you didn't have the decency to even call me back." I snatched a pen that was sitting on the end table, whipping it directly past his head.

He took a step toward me, and I took one back, pressing up against the door. "You know I cared about you. It's not what you think. You were one of my best friends," he said.

"You never cared about me." I hissed again, moving forward to grab my report from where he had tossed it on the floor. "And now I don't fucking care about what you have to say."

I turned on my heel, clutching the report to my chest before slamming the door in his face again. I returned to my office, shutting the door quietly behind me, thankful for the safety of the enclosed glass room now, and thankful my father, Deacon and David were locked away at the opposite end of the floor. I stayed there, reading and re-reading the same lines of the report—again—for the rest of the afternoon, tears burning behind my eyes. I blinked them back furiously, until my gaze landed on the lone family photo I kept in my office. My mother, young and alive, was smiling up at me. But the closer I looked, the more I noticed her smile didn't meet her eyes. All the things we were too busy or too stupid to notice. I continued to stare at her, trapped in time in this photograph while the silent tears trickled down my face. I was certain of one thing: she would not be proud of who I was becoming.

———

My heels clicked on the worn stones of the sidewalk, Taylor tugging me ahead insistently as we made our way to meet David, Deacon, and stupid Tripp at Victoria's private room. She had shown up at my house after her shift at the hospital, seemingly high on life after some sort of wildly successful tumor removal, the likes of which she assured me she would probably never see again. I had allowed her to dress me in an Alexander Wang Shapewear Mini Dress she mysteriously happened to have in the garment bag she had shown up with. Taylor insisted I wear it, running her hands along everything in my closet before pulling out an oversized blazer dress I often wore to work and putting that over my exposed shoulders. Never mind that she was wearing some sort of metallic confection again. This time, it was a form-fitting pink dress that shimmered under the light. Her blonde hair had been tied back in a messy low bun.

During dinner, she badgered me into revealing to her why I had been so quiet. Leaving out the Tripp of it all, Victoria and David's lie by omission made a convenient scapegoat. Taylor was usually the person I could tell anything to—anything in the entire world. But not this. Those were the worst moments of my life, the moments I had been the worst person, all wrapped up into one pretty little Tripp-shaped package. Being young and dumb, trying to fuck away the memory of my mother only to have allowed myself to be used for some ploy, to have had my insides scraped as a result, and to allow him to touch me again when I had something so much more, something so special with David. I was certain a psychiatrist would have a field day with my recent behavior.

We arrived at the door of Opus, a doorman standing patiently with his arms clasped behind his back when Taylor finally extracted herself from our linked arms. "Good evening. We're here to join Victoria, secret ex-girlfriend of David Kennedy. Private room. We should be on the list." Her voice was a low, joking purr as she continued to look at him.

I rolled my eyes, shaking my head at her choice of words. She had narrowed her eyes when I told her but seemed inclined to give David the benefit of the doubt. The doorman stepped back to grab a leather clipboard off the podium standing there, his eyes flicking down. "Taylor Breen and Charlie Winchester?" His words had caught on my name and he looked up at me, seeming to stand straighter for a moment when our eyes met. I flashed him a small smile, the one I had been taught to perfect over years. *Winchesters were approachable.*

"That's us, thank you." Taylor smiled sweetly, reaching her hand out behind her, fingers wiggling, waiting for mine. I stepped forward, lacing my fingers in hers, and she once again pulled me along as she walked behind the doorman.

Opus was like any other bar or lounge in this area of the city. All obsessed with the roaring twenties, looking like a place Jay Gatsby would frequent and that Nick Carroway would find himself intrigued by all the surroundings and interesting patrons. The low buzz of conversation filled the room, as we walked along the bar behind the doorman toward the back where the private rooms are. I kept my head angled down, my hair falling in front of my face somewhat like a shield, Taylor continuing to urge me along with gentle squeezes of her fingers. Had I been like my brother, I would have walked through the bar, head held high, signature Winchester chocolate hair and forest green eyes glinting mischievously.

Deacon, in his supreme douchery, had been known to wink at anyone who he caught looking or staring at him. Our father didn't approve of that sort of behavior—*showboating*, he called it. But he also never approved of my attempts to remain unnoticed and hidden. Even though the Forbes cover was not that long ago, it has gotten worse since then. Prior to that, we had been a notoriously secretive family, who despite having amassed enormous wealth in the last few decades, lived on the periphery. No one ever really bothered us too much, but now, it felt like we were at the forefront of every Chicago publication.

The doorman came to a sudden halt in front of an open archway, gesturing for us to walk through with his arm. Both Taylor and I smiled at him in thanks, stepping through and around the corner. The telltale click of our heels against the polished hardwood was drowned out by the thrum of music and laughter. I could distinguish David's laughter and Deacon's amongst the din. My stomach tightened at the thought of confronting David's past when I had continuously proved myself entirely unworthy of him and knowing Tripp would be sitting there smugly made it even worse.

Rounding the corner, Taylor and I found ourselves in a spacious room, cognac leather couches lining the walls with a stone table raised in the center of the room. Buckets of ice with champagne and other bottles of what looked to be every type of liquor available. Deacon was leaning back against the couch closest to us, having already discarded his suit jacket. The top buttons of his dove gray button up were undone, and the sleeves pushed up on his forearms, as he swirled a glass of scotch in his left hand, the other gesturing animatedly to Tripp, who sat beside him.

I glared in annoyance as I took him in. He really did look like a movie villain, all dark and sharp edges. Though I supposed, in this particular movie, I would also be considered a villain. The thought settled around me, nausea rolling in my stomach. On the other side of them, two women I assumed were Victoria's friends were sitting with their knees angled into one another, laughing together. I noticed the one farthest from us, the only redhead in the sea of blonde women in Victoria's entourage, continuously flitted her eyes toward Deacon over her friends' shoulder. Two others sat on the opposite couch, nursing what looked like Vodka Cranberries, both blonde and a picture of southern beauty and manners—from the way their hands were clasped to the way their feet were hooked at the ankles, not a hair out of place.

David and Victoria sat across the room on the couch that lined the wall farthest from us. Too engrossed in conversation, neither looked our way when we entered the room. I saw Taylor still, as she took in the sight, her eyes drawn in their direction almost imperceptibly before she turned to Deacon, holding her arms out widely and expectantly.

"Deac! Come say hi!" Her voice was louder than normal, containing a commanding quality that pierced the air. I knew what she was doing.

Deacon turned, his forest eyes alight with mischief as he took her in, his eyes roving over her bright pink dress in appreciation. "My two favorite girls, come on in and get a drink." His eyes moved to me, a small familiar smile replacing the feral grin he bestowed Taylor. "You both look beautiful."

I rolled my eyes, resisting the urge to button the loosely hanging dress and to disappear amongst the boxy fabric. David and Victoria still had yet to look our way. I swallowed, forcing myself not to stare at them and wondering why I had to feel so small—why couldn't I allow myself to go over there and say hello? It's what Taylor would do, what Deacon would have done. God knows it's what Tripp would have done. He was still sitting beside Deacon, not sparing either Taylor or me a glance when we entered the room, surveying everything with that maddening air of indifference, thumbing absentmindedly through messages on his phone.

"That's not how you treat your favorite girls," Taylor chided, tipping her chin at Deacon. Her voice continued to get louder than necessary and contained a tone that would take up all the air in the room. Her gaze landed on David again, eyes flashing briefly with anger before she looked back at Deacon and gestured to the bottles on the table. "Why don't you be so kind and pour us each a drink?" She flashed a smile at him, grabbing my wrist and pulling me closer to the couch David and Victoria were sitting on.

Settling in beside me on the leather couch, she continued to grip my wrist. "Tripp. Hello." This time she bared her teeth instead of smiling.

Tripp looked up, a lazy smile as he took us in. His eyes traveled openly over both of us. "Taylor. Charlie. Looking good as always."

"You look adequate." Taylor smiled back, tight-lipped. She turned to stare at David and Victoria—again. "David, hi. Thank you for taking time out of your busy schedule to welcome your guests. I'm not sure if you had etiquette lessons as a child like Deacon and Charlie. I didn't either, but I picked up a thing or two. One thing I did gather is that it's quite rude to not say hello to someone upon arrival."

Deacon choked loudly, attempting to hide it with the obnoxious rattling of the bottles smattered across the table while he poured two drinks for us. "Taylor!" I hissed, shaking her hand off my wrist. "That was also quite rude."

She shrugged, crossing her arms, settling back onto the couch. Her smile still in place, Taylor stared unblinkingly at David. He had turned from Victoria, concern etched across his features along with confusion in response to her words. "I'm sorry, Taylor, I hadn't noticed you there. But I'm glad you're both here."

"I'll bet you didn't." She remarked, arching an eyebrow of her own before making a carry-on gesture with her hand and turning away to accept the drinks Deacon was offering. Victoria and her friends looked back and forth between the three of us like we were a particularly interesting tennis match. David turned to look at me, a soft smile playing on his face, almost in apology. He held up a hand and mouthed one moment to me before turning back to Victoria.

I smiled stupidly and nodded, trying to indicate it was no big deal. But maybe it was. My stomach knotted uncomfortably, and I tried not to look at them for too long, my eyes skating over Victoria without picking any one feature to land on. Tripp and Deacon relaxed further onto the couch, continuing their conversation, but Tripp's eyes bounced to me every once and awhile from over Deacon's shoulder. As usual, he wasn't giving anything away in his features.

Deacon raised his eyebrows at us, handing us the drinks he had made. I brought it to my lips to take a small sip, nodding along with whatever Taylor was saying. She leaned in affectionately, wrapping an arm around me. Her chin resting on my shoulder, she whispered into my ear loud enough to be heard over the music but not for anyone else to hear. "I'm sorry. I know these things make you uncomfortable, and he should know that, too. He should go out of his way for you. That's what you deserve."

David did know that. I opened my mouth to respond but hesitated, not wanting to give Taylor the ammunition to launch a hate campaign against David furthermore. I shook my head, too, aware of how warm the room is, how loud the music got, and how sticky the leather couch felt against my bare legs. Even in the small room, tucked away from the restaurant, from the rest of the world, it all felt like it was too much all over again. I grabbed Taylor's hand, squeezing it while I leaned against her forehead with the side of my head. "It's okay. I know you're just being protective. Try not to rip David's head off. I promise I'll talk to him later."

Taylor nodded before clinking her glass against mine and smiling wickedly at me. "In the meantime, we might as well enjoy ourselves."

David stayed engaged in his conversation with Victoria, so much he didn't bother to pay any attention to me. I had stayed with Taylor, our hands clasped as we leaned our heads together, whispering and laughing loudly while we consumed drink after drink. Deacon and Tripp had moved on to talking to some of Victoria's friends, seeming perfectly content to ignore the two of us as well. Peals of laughter were falling from our lips, and we collapsed against one another in hysterics, recalling a time I visited her when she was in boarding school and we had gotten so drunk we fell into the Olympic trial swimming pool reserved for elite athletes. A loud, jarring noise sounded out of her ridiculous glittered Jimmy Choo clutch. Concern flashed across Taylor's eyes, and she held up a finger before rooting through the clutch, extracting her hospital pager.

"Fuck, fuck, fuck!" She hissed upon seeing whatever numbers were flashing on the screen, grabbing her phone in her other hand before pushing herself off the chair and practically running to the doorway.

I watched as she ran away, her metallic outfit so out of place with whatever was happening in her world right now. My stomach tightened uncomfortably at the thought of something shaking cool, unflappable Taylor. She is closer to me than almost anyone else in my life, and the thought of her hurting briefly overshadowed the anxiety that had continued gnawing at my bones all night. I dropped my shoulders at the thought of being stuck alone in this room, ignored by everyone around me. In spite of myself, my eyes shot to Victoria, studying her intently. She was leaning toward him, her attention rapt. She was slight but muscular. The honeysuckle blonde hair fell from behind her ear to frame her face just so. The waves of her hair were certainly natural. She looked like she had been in saltwater all day. Her skin appeared sun-kissed, and her slightly upturned nose had a smattering of freckles across it. She's perfect.

I felt the leather seat sink beside me, glancing sideways to see Tripp sitting down where Taylor had just been. His suit jacket was open and the top buttons of his blue dress shirt were undone, his eyes dancing wickedly in the low light. I turned back immediately to my glass, both hands now gripped around it like a lifeline. I tapped my thumbnail against the sweating glass, desperate to be anywhere but here.

"So there's Victoria," Tripp said, throwing the statement out into the air between us where it hung unanswered. I said nothing but nodded slightly, continuing to tap my thumb against my glass. I snuck a glance at Deacon, but he was talking to some redhead, engrossed in conversation, and I knew he was lost to me for the evening.

"I take your silence to mean he never mentioned his years-long relationship with her. I wonder why that is?" Tripp continued, leaning backward. I felt his arm snake across the top of the seat behind me. Once again I'm twenty, drifting aimlessly through an in-between world. I continued my silence and stared determinedly downward, tapping my heels in sync with my thumb. I felt constricted and heated with the additional layer on, tempted to strip away the blazer attached to my dress.

"Oh, come on Chuckles, you're not upset are you?" He leaned forward, almost taunting me, grabbing my glass from my hand and draining the remaining Vodka. He was breathing right beside my hair. I glanced over and saw the stubble growing in along his jawline. It looked like it could cut glass. His eyes caught mine and my stomach dropped. I couldn't make eye contact with him without remembering what it was like when he was inside me. Shame crept over me that had nothing to do with David this time. I'm young and naive again, wandering through an in-between world, hoping to find anything—anyone—to ease my pain. "I mean, she's hot in an obvious way, Chuck. But you're worth more." Tripp continued on, beginning to pour us each another drink from the many bottles that were littering the table in front of us.

"That's not a compliment, Tripp." I broke my silence, my voice embarrassingly small, barely discernible over the music.

"Come on, Charlie! There are two people in this room worth more than millions, and you're one of them. If that's not a compliment, I don't know what is." Tripp shook his head indignantly, like I had no concept of wealth.

"It's not a compliment, Tripp," I repeated more forcefully through gritted teeth, grabbing the glass he was handing me. Our fingers brushed, and the familiar electricity shot through my arm. I am not a stupid twenty-year-old anymore. I glanced upward, raising the glass to my lips, tucking my straight hair behind one of my ears with my other hand. David was gesturing wildly as Victoria leaned into him, laughing wildly like she had never heard anything so funny.

I felt unmoored. Unanchored. Suddenly, I am the spare child again. A daughter left behind by her mother to carve a path amongst men alone. I am twenty again. Closing my eyes, I leaned back into the leather bench, finding Tripp's arm had taken up residence behind me. I felt the heat from his arm radiating through my blazer dress, adding to the flush creeping across my neck and cheeks. My back stiffened immediately, as if a rod had been jammed into my spine. Tripp laughed loudly, setting down his glass. "We've been a lot closer than this, and recently, Chuck. I wouldn't worry about contact through a few layers of clothing."

I shook out my shoulders like I was shaking out a deep chill.

"Stop it, Tripp. I mean it. All of it. Whatever games you're playing, I'm not interested."

He surveyed me lazily, shifting back with his arm still outstretched. "What games?"

Rolling my eyes, I turned to face him. "You know exactly what I mean. You sit here and watch for a moment of weakness from me, and then you pounce. It's like you're a fucking hyena. All of this bullshit about caring about me and things not being what I think. It's all a game to you."

Tripp's face was impassive, and his eyes had grown cold and distant, making them difficult to read. He was silent as he sipped on his drink, occasionally looking around the room. Finally, he rested his eyes on me again. "You look good in that dress, Chuck."

I remained in my seat, pointedly ignoring Tripp and returning work emails in an attempt to look busy, occasionally taking a sip of my drink until Taylor finally returned from the page she had taken what felt like years ago. I looked up at her, noticing her eyes were clouded. Her hair looked like she had been tugging on it or running her hands through it repeatedly. She sat on the other side of me, our legs touching. I handed her my glass and dropped my phone into my open Chanel clutch. "Everything okay? Something happen at the hospital?"

Taylor swirled the liquid in the glass a few times, watching the soda bubbles rise to the surface and the ice clink against the sides. "The patient I was telling you about earlier? She died tonight. She must have had a blood clot. One must have detached from the sutures. No one's fault. It can just happen. But she was only twenty, and I promised her she would be okay. We're never supposed to do that but it was a flawless surgery. I have never seen margin lines that clean on a tumor."

I placed my hand on her leg, leaning into her shoulder. "Do you want me to take you home?"

Taylor raised the glass and took a small sip. "No no, I'll go. You stay. I should go into work and put in an IV to flush out this alcohol. I have to do some paperwork, and I should talk to her family."

I was ready to leave, and all my bodily cells were screaming at me to find a reason to go. "Honestly, I'm ready to leave. I want to go." Taylor eyed me shrewdly as I gazed at David, still engaged in conversation with Victoria. "Go give Deacon our tab. I'll say goodnight to David, and let's get out of here."

Fortunately, Tripp had moved on and seemed to be preying on another one of Victoria's friends. I stood, adjusting the lines of the open blazer dress before ducking around the table to walk toward David and Victoria. Neither looked up as I approached. Taylor was right, Deacon and I had taken etiquette lessons as children. My etiquette teacher had told me it was rude to clear your throat and to interrupt in general for that matter but when bidding goodbye it could be considered appropriate. I placed a hand on David's shoulder and plastered a smile on my face to highlight my genetically perfect smile. *Billion dollar teeth.* "I'm sorry to interrupt, David. I'm going to take Taylor home. One of her patients died tonight, and she would like to go."

David reached up instinctually, covering my hand with his much larger calloused one. He turned his head, finally looking at me, his eyes dark. "Is she okay? I'll come with you." I narrowed my eyes, a bitter remark forming on my lips when I felt Victoria's gaze on me. She was now leaning her elbow on the arm of the couch, propped up with her cheek resting in her hand, only accentuating those maddening natural waves of hers. My etiquette teacher had also taught me it was incredibly rude not to make introducing yourself the first priority in conversations. But David didn't deem it important enough, so I ignored my instincts for a moment further.

"No, that's fine. You stay and keep having fun. I'm going to call a town car and have her dropped off on my way home. I'm not needed here and some emails just came in from work." I smiled balefully at him, blinking rapidly to keep the tears of anger and frustration that were threatening to spill over.

David blinked rapidly at my words, standing quickly. "Not needed here? Charlie, it's eleven on a Friday evening." He was still holding my hand, his thumb stroking the back of it.

"It's not eleven on a Friday evening in Indonesia," I lied, pulling my hand back. I needed to leave. I wanted my mother.

"I'll walk you out," he insisted, confusion spreading across his face. His hand was still open in the air.

I stepped back, holding my hand up and shaking my head, still wearing my moronic smile. If being a Winchester had prepared me for anything, it was attempting performance. "No need, David. You stay, please." I turned to face Victoria finally, locking eyes with her. My stomach dropped. She is absolutely beautiful. Her eyes, like David's, were a deep brown. I could imagine them blending seamlessly into one another's lives along the Carolina coastline. I held my hand out to her, the stupid smile beginning to hurt my face. "I'm sorry I didn't get a chance to formally introduce myself, I'm Charlie."

Victoria surveyed me, a small smile playing on her lips. "Oh, I know who you are. The elusive Charlie Winchester! I hardly recognized you when you walked in since you aren't photographed as much as your father and brother. When David's parents told mine at the club back home you two were dating, I didn't believe it. On the other hand, David didn't even go over and say hi to you, are you sure you're dating? Is this just some bizarre PR stunt for your company?" I cocked my head and arched an eyebrow, blanching while Victoria laughed at what I assumed she thought was a good-natured joke. Before I could speak, David glanced at her sharply and stepped to the side, wrapping an arm around me. I shifted under his grip, distancing our bodies from one another.

"Victoria, I can assure you this is absolutely real. Just because I didn't interrupt my conversation with you to greet Charlie, this is somehow a PR stunt? We're adults. I can guarantee we're both secure enough in our relationship that a little thing like that won't get in the way. I'm sorry I didn't have a chance to introduce you two earlier so you could get to know her," David said, a sharp edge to his words as he spoke to her. He turned and looked down at me, his eyes soft as he ran a hand through his hair, pushing it back off his face.

"Oh, I didn't mean anything by it. David, you know I was joking." Victoria laughed waspishly, smiling tightly and running an appraising eye over me. "It's nice to meet you, Charlie. Great dress."

"It was a pleasure to meet you as well, Victoria. I hope you have a wonderful visit in Chicago." I turned, angling out from under David's arm. "I'm going to take Taylor home now. Goodnight Victoria, goodnight David."

I turned immediately and made a beeline for the doorway, walking pointedly past Deacon and Tripp. I could vaguely hear David excusing himself behind me when I ducked around the corner into the busy main area of the restaurant. Taylor was just beyond the glass front doors on the curb, rocking back and forth on her heels, arms wrapped around herself while she waited for the town car. Footsteps and David's voice sounded out from behind me, "Charlie, what the fuck was that?"

Anger, anxiety and embarrassment whirled in my stomach, blending together as I whipped around, coming to a halt right in front of the doors. My eyes burned as I beheld David standing there, a hand reaching out like he meant to grab my shoulder to prevent me from leaving. His eyes were dark and his usual dancing irises weren't sparkling with happiness. "I could ask you the same fucking thing, David."

He blew out a frustrated breath, running the hand that had been suspended in midair through his hair, pulling on the ends of it. "She was just kidding. It's her sense of humor."

"Oh!" I shrieked, tossing my hands up in the air. "Is it her sense of humor?! Well how the fuck was I to know that, seeing as you didn't even care enough to say hi to me tonight, to spend any time with me after inviting me here, let alone introduce me to her. I guess I missed my opportunity to learn about Victoria and her fucking *sense of humor*."

David stepped toward me, holding out a hand again. "Charlie, let's go somewhere private where we can talk. You can't be seen this upset."

My face burned with embarrassment at his words. A Winchester could never be caught having a private moment in public. It felt like just another reminder of all the things pressing in around me. All the things my mother tried to escape. "Where can we talk? That's pretty fucking rich seeing as you haven't spoken to me all night. Too busy thinking I'm a secure adult without any feelings. Too busy enjoying Victoria and all that her sense of humor has to offer."

He blew out an exasperated breath, taking a step closer to me and lowering his voice. "Let's be adults here, Charlie. You're clearly very upset with me, and that's okay. Let me go get my jacket, and we can go to your place and talk."

"You left me to sit there all night." My voice cracked, and the inevitable tears began to spill from my eyes. "You know how uncomfortable situations like that make me. How alone I feel. How big it all feels. How anxious....you knew and you paid no attention anyway."

"You were with Taylor!" David's voice raised, and he stepped forward again, reaching out to grab my hand. I jerked it out of his grasp in a childlike display. He let out a puff of air before continuing. "Charlie, work with me here. Adults talk things out. Be a fucking adult. They don't make scenes in public restaurants, it's the exact opposite of what you should be doing."

I stepped backward again, my skin hot while anger and humiliation raked against me. My heel hit the glass door, and I groped behind me for the handle. "Then I guess I'm a child," I whispered, pushing the door open behind me and stepping out into the night where Taylor stood on the curb. I turned my back to David and walked toward her, whose eyes surveyed me sadly while she held her arms open for me, beckoning me forward.

———

The town car pulled up in front of my townhouse after dropping Taylor off at the hospital. She hadn't said anything to me after welcoming me into her arms and rubbing my back in an attempt to soothe me while the tears from my fight with David continued to fall from my eyes. We had sat in companionable silence in the back of the car, leaning against one another as we wove through the city streets. Tears streamed down my face while an uncomfortable ache sat heavy in my chest. My phone had vibrated almost constantly in my clutch, but I left it unanswered. I murmured my thanks to the driver, stepping out onto the curb and gently shutting the door behind me.

Pulling my keys from the quilted inside of my purse, I looked up and my stomach dropped. Tripp was sitting on the stone steps leading up to my front door, his arms folded across his chest in something that seemed like annoyance. Resisting the urge to shriek out loud, I shook my head, striding past him. "I don't have the energy for this, Tripp. Crawl back to whatever gutter you call a home."

"Quite the fight you and Kennedy had," he said. I could tell he had come to stand behind me, his breath on my neck. "Don't worry, Deac paid off the manager, and all phones were checked before anyone left."

"Great," I muttered, embarrassment searing through me. I shoulder-opened the door, tempted to slam it in Tripp's face, but he had already crossed the threshold into the foyer with me. "Can I help you?"

Tripp held his hands up in surrender, an annoying grin on his face while his blue eyes roved around my home. "Far be it from me to come and check in on you. I don't see David breaking down your door."

I chucked my clutch on the sideboard pressed up against the wall that ran along both the living room and kitchen, kicking my heels off haphazardly as I did so. One flew and landed with a soft thud when it hit the couch, the other skidded under the coffee table, its trajectory only slowed by the high-pile rug. Part of me had hoped it would hit Tripp in the kneecap.

I padded into the kitchen on my bare feet, going straight for the wine fridge nestled under the granite countertops. I could faintly hear Tripp's footsteps behind me. He was likely walking around the living room, judging all my possessions and decorating skills. "Yeah, well, David was a little busy, wouldn't you agree?" Tripp said nothing, my back still turned to him while I uncorked a bottle of wine. Grabbing two glasses from where they hung under the gray cabinets, I poured a generous amount into each.

"Pouring me a glass of wine? It's almost like you want me to stay." Tripp remarked, his mouth curving to one side. He was leaning against the wall just behind me.

"I'm many things, but what I'm not is rude to someone in my home," I smiled tightly, raising my eyebrows and handing him the glass of wine, "however unwelcome they may be."

Our fingers brushed when he accepted the glass, the tips of his almost engulfing mine. I jerked my hand back, holding it up before shaking it out like I was trying to rid my hand of an undesirable substance. Tripp smirked before swirling his glass twice like a pretentious douchebag. He brought it to his lips, taking a small sip before speaking. "I don't think I'm unwelcome at all. I came to see if you were alright."

A laugh tumbled from my lips. "Tripp Banks, doing something without an ulterior motive? Sure." I pushed myself up to sit on the countertop, crossing my legs at my ankles. Another laugh rose in my throat. Here I am, sitting on top of the counter with the man whose tongue I had allowed to brush against my own not twenty-four hours ago behind the back of the man I love but concerned about propriety and the proper way to cross my legs.

"David was wrong tonight, Charlie." Tripp's voice was uncharacteristically low when he spoke, catching me off guard. I looked up and our eyes met. He was studying me, his piercing eyes swirling and much darker than usual. He jostled his wine again before bringing it to his mouth and taking a sip. I watched as his jaw moved, the sharp edges accentuated by the dark stubble lining them. "You shouldn't be with someone who ignores you like that. You should be with someone who–"

"Someone like who, Tripp?" I asked, my voice sharp. "Someone like you? Someone who participates in horrifically demeaning board games with their fraternity brothers?"

Tripp puffed his cheeks before setting his glass of wine down on the sideboard beside my discarded Chanel clutch. Walking toward me, he pushed up the sleeves of his blue button down, revealing muscular forearms. He placed his hands on either side of my thighs on the counter, his eyes never leaving mine. "I told you that wasn't what you think. Will you let me explain?"

I could feel the warmth of his hands on either side of my bare thighs. I squeezed my ankles together, as if I could create more distance between us. His face was inches from mine. I sniffed lightly, his cologne was so unlike David's, whose cologne reminded me of the ocean, like it's the essence of who he is in his soul. Tripp's scent was something almost...darker. It reminded me of dark, overgrown forests where you could barely see in front of you. I had never developed a nose like Deacon's, but it reminded me vaguely of spices. "I don't care what you have to say. If by some miracle, there was more to this story, you've had seven years to explain yourself. I don't recall ever receiving an apology phone call or letter."

Tripp continued to watch me while I drank my wine. "I didn't write those points on the board, Chuck. I wouldn't have done that to you. I went downstairs when you had fallen asleep, and I told the guys we had slept together...but it was out of excitement. I thought something might have been starting between us for real that night. They wrote it on the board, not me. Don't you remember what I said to you? I said I had wanted this for so long..."

I lowered my eyelids, a scoff rising in my throat. I shook my head slightly, the echo of the words he had whispered to me years ago ringing there. "Oh, that's such bullshit, Tripp! Even if that's how it happened, you still participated in whatever that game was and that's fucking disgusting."

Rolling his eyes, Tripp cocked his head, not a strand of dark hair falling out of place. It was so unlike David's unruly waves. "You don't think your dear big brother participated in anything like that? Your precious David? I was a kid. I'm not saying it was right, and I'm not saying I'm proud of it. But I didn't use you to win some bracket. And I didn't get your message. I didn't even know about it until too much time had passed. Post heard it and deleted it. He thought he was doing me a favor."

A cackle escaped my lips. I had forgotten Tripp's brother was named Post. "How brutally fucking east coast and elitist does your family have to be to name their children Tripp and Post?"

"Easy. That's a bit rich coming from you, no? You were just on the cover of Forbes. The title of the article was *The Next Great American Dynasty*." Tripp's voice dripped with sarcasm and irony, a dark eyebrow still arched on his forehead.

"Not by choice. I'm from the Midwest, it doesn't count." I bit out, taking another large sip of wine.

Tripp leaned in, his forehead just a few centimeters from mine. The only thing separating our faces was the wine glass I had left poised at my lips. "By the time he told me, it was too late. Too much time had gone by and–"

I cut him off abruptly, "You've had seven years. We live in the same city. You know my brother. You know David. You know so many people in my circle. I don't care."

"But knowing this...knowing that I didn't do it, that I never meant to hurt you...it changes things, doesn't it?" He whispered, something like pleading in his eyes. It looked out of place compared to the usual mischief and ire that resided there.

"Aren't you David's friend? Why do you keep doing this?"

I ignored his question, my own voice dropping to a whisper.

Tripp paused, his gaze traveling over my face. "Yeah, he's my friend, but you're–"

"I'm what? What am I?" I asked, bitterness lacing my words.

"Someone I've thought about for a very long time." Tripp answered, his words low and his voice gravelly. His eyes landed on my lips, tracing them behind the wine glass I was still holding there like a shield.

We continued to stare at one another, the silence growing heavy around us. I swung my legs to the side of the counter and jumped down, knocking his arm out of the way. "I'm going to bed."

"Is that an invitation?" Tripp's voice was lilting, and that stupid grin had reappeared on his face.

"Absolutely not. Get the fuck out of my house." I gestured with the wine glass to the front door before turning my back on him and walking up the staircase to go to my room.

"Night night then, Chuck." Tripp called from the bottom of the stairs, dryness lacing his words. I raised my free hand over the top of my head, gesturing vaguely before turning down the hallway. As I shut the door to my bedroom firmly, I realized I probably shouldn't have left Tripp free to wander my house. It would be my luck I would wake up and he'd still be there, having supplanted himself on the couch to drink more of my wine. His words continued to ring in my ears. *It changes things, doesn't it?*

I stood in front of my bathroom mirror, studying myself while I continued to sip from my wine glass. My eyes were rimmed red from crying, my hair hung limply around my face. I wondered briefly what Victoria looked like when she cried. Probably not like that. She would remain the epitome of southern beauty. She would be perfectly composed, the way I could never manage to be, much to the disappointment of everyone in my life. I looked like a twenty-year-old who drank too much and caused a scene with her boyfriend. Which, I suppose, was true. Except I was no longer a twenty-year-old who had just lost her mother, desperate to cling to a boy for comfort and salvation. I was twenty-seven, still motherless, but maybe there was absolution for my actions now.

A knock came from my closed bedroom door, and I shook my head, puffing my cheeks in frustration before leaving the bathroom and yanking the door open. Of course Tripp didn't fucking leave. "What?" I asked sharply, planting myself firmly in the doorway to block him from my bedroom.

"Are you okay, Chuck?" He asked, his voice low. If I hadn't known any better, I would have detected genuine concern there.

"I would be better if you would leave my house," I answered, abandoning my post in the doorway and turning back to Tripp. I moved across the room, dropping on my side of the bed and propping myself up against my bed frame. I stared resolutely at the wall in front of me, clutching the stem of my wine glass tightly.

Tripp leaned forward, his hands in his pockets before he took a measured step into the room. "I'll ask again. Are you okay, Chuckles?"

I turned to him, irritation flaring across my face before everything I was pushing down inside me tumbled out in some form of sad word vomit. "No, I'm not okay. David lied to me. Deacon ignored me all night once he found a girl to take home. Victoria is a bitch. Taylor, possibly the only friend I have in the entire fucking world lost a patient tonight. My father is an emotionless void of a human. My mother chose to kill herself rather than spend another second longer in our company, and oh! Guess what? You, the source of the most embarrassing moment of my life, won't leave my fucking house."

Saying nothing, Tripp crossed the room silently and rounded my side of the bed before he dropped into a crouch. I could see his face in the corner of my eye as I blankly stared ahead of me. "I was your friend, once upon a time. I could be again, if you needed. Just for tonight. You can go back to hating me tomorrow."

I turned to him and found myself sucking in a breath. There was an earnest, almost boy-like expression on his face. It made him younger and softer, like the person I used to know. The person I confided in—*once upon a time.* Twenty-year old Charlie would have shifted over in her bed and patted the empty space beside her, and she would have stayed up until the sun rose telling stories about her night and laughing away any tears.

"Are you proposing a truce?" I asked, half-laughing at the absurdity of the situation, but I found myself moving toward the other end. I pointed at the new space with my wine glass before turning back to stare at the wall again.

I felt the bed shift beside me under Tripp's weight, and my body tensed momentarily before I settled back against the headboard again. There was nothing weird about this. We used to do this all the time. It was like we were just two friends again, even if it was just for the night.

"Been a while since I've been in your bed, Chuck," Tripp spoke, and I could tell the annoying lilt was creeping back in.

"Just be fucking normal for once, will you? Talk to me like a regular person. The person you used to be. The people we used to be when we knew each other." I answered quietly. Maybe Tripp had a point—there was an *us* at Brown. But that didn't mean *us* us, it was just the people we were before.

Tripp shifted beside me, and I looked over my shoulder to see him propped up on his palm, grinning at me. "And what would those people have done in this bed?"

I looked at him pointedly before setting my wine glass down on the bedside table. I found myself rolling over to face him, mirroring him and propping my own head up. It felt like maybe there was an invisible line somewhere, and maybe I was crossing it. But in my mind, just for this moment, I was just twenty-year old me, and he was just the Tripp I knew. I knew what those people would have done. "Tell me a story."

His icy eyes widened in shock. Those words hadn't been spoken between us in years, but once upon a time they were just a part of our routine. Whether it was on the shitty couch in his frat house, the tiny bed in my sorority, or the ostentatious king bed Tripp had in his frat bedroom—our nights would end with the two of us laughing at and mocking the world until we would fall silent, and one of us would ask the other to 'tell a story.' I lost count of the stories we told over the years we knew one another. But they were never stories of a motherless girl who was never enough. And I wanted to hear one of those stories at this moment, to pretend for just a moment longer, I was someone else. "Okay, Chuck. I'll tell you a story."

My eyelids fluttered, and a heavy, wine-induced headache pressed against the back of my skull. Moonlight filtered in through the windows, and I could see it reflecting across the doors of my closet. I sat up suddenly. I never slept on this side of the bed. Whipping around and confirming my worst fear, Tripp was lying next to me. He was splayed out on my usual side of the bed, his shirt removed at some point but his suit pants still on. My stomach churned and a metallic taste rose in my throat. I pushed down the urge to vomit, remembering clearly the story Tripp had begun to tell me—a stupid one about him and his brother from when they were kids.

At some point, we opened another bottle of wine, and I could see the empty bottle sitting on my dresser—its presence was accusatory and unnerving. I told a story in return, how Deacon almost got suspended at prep school. I didn't know when I fell asleep, and I didn't care. I just knew I was horrible, unworthy of not just David's love but anyone's. Did my mother know she was leaving behind a daughter who was so careless with others and herself that she would let someone else into her bed? Maybe she knew the kind of person I was the whole time. Maybe that's why it was so easy for her to leave. I wasn't twenty. I was twenty-seven, and this was a colossal, unforgivable mistake.

There was a moment last night—a fleeting one—but it was there, when I looked over at Tripp and studied the way the moonlight illuminated his eyes, making them look endlessly fascinating; the way that the cut of his dress shirt hugged the broad ridges of muscle across his body. I wondered, for just a moment, what it would be like to reach out and touch him; what it would be like for our bodies to move together, if it would be the same as it was all those years ago.

"Get up," I whispered, my voice cracking. Tripp didn't stir. I hesitated to reach out and touch his bare shoulder; the bone jutted out against the muscles of his back. "Get up," I said again, forcefully.

Tripp shifted slightly, one arm coming to rest above his head as he flipped onto his back. He continued to breathe steadily, and now the moonlight was reflecting across the ridges of his abdomen. His hair was unkempt and splayed against the pillow. He almost looked like twenty-two-year-old Tripp. *Almost.*

"GET UP!" I shrieked, pushing myself backward off the bed. I was still wearing my dress from the restaurant, having discarded the blazer somewhere. I backed up a step, my exposed shoulders hitting my closet. Clutching my hand to my chest, I tried to focus on my breathing against the erratic beating of my heart and the tsunami in my stomach.

Tripp startled, pushing himself up in immediate response to my words. "Chuck, what's wrong? Everything's okay. We must have fallen asleep. It's okay, it's–"

"Get out." My voice was low and even but determined. I raised my hand with one finger pointing toward the door. "For the last time, get out, Tripp."

"Charlie, it's okay. It's nothing. Nothing happened." He pushed off the bed and came to stand in front of me. His hair was falling across his forehead now, and his eyes looked blurry with sleep.

I shook my head, continuing to point at the door. "Leave, Tripp. Get out. Leave me alone."

Tripp cocked his head back, causing the moonlight to shift across his eyes. My gaze fell on him, and I noticed that his eyes looked dark and sad. I could feel the hurt that sending him away caused. "You got it. I won't stay where I'm not wanted, Chuck."

"You're not wanted here so GET OUT!" I shouted, a sob wracking my body, and I gestured again to the door before kicking his abandoned shirt at him. Shouldering past him, I crawled back into my bed, staying determinedly on this new side, afraid to move over to my usual one—afraid of the warmth he left there and how it served as the reminder of the person I was. The person I didn't want to be but couldn't seem to avoid.

CHAPTER THIRTEEN

My eyes were closed and my head tilted back, chin pointed toward the sun, my hands curved around a mug I had bought at a stall in Turkey when I was twenty-two and the warmth from the coffee radiated through them. Sounds from the street below drifted up through the treetops, I could vaguely hear car doors shutting and indistinct conversations below. I stretched my feet out underneath the Mexican blanket I had spread over my legs. I was lying out on the sectional on my terrace, hoping to sink to a place deep beneath the cushions where I would never be found. The wool of the blanket picked at my exposed legs. I was wearing a Cosabella short sleeve and boxer pajama set my father had gifted me the previous Christmas. I was certain Damien had selected it. He usually picked all of our presents, or at least mine. My father probably had no idea what I would even be interested in. I actually felt like an idiot wearing it. Deacon had told me the day our father gifted it to me I looked like a penguin and the sentiment stuck.

I had woken up to a fortunately empty house, no trace of Tripp left after our midnight screaming match, beyond the wineglass he must have washed and returned to its spot hanging beneath the cupboards before leaving. Images from the previous night, along with his words ringing in my ears, kept playing against the back of my eyelids like some annoying black-and-white movie at a drive-in. I squinted, my eyes still closed, trying to focus on the feeling of the sunlight against my face. Victoria laughing loudly with David. His refusal to acknowledge me. His face when we fought. Tripp snaking his arm behind me. Deacon laser-focused on a conquest, oblivious to me, floating unmoored in the world. Tripp propping himself up beside me in bed. My bed. The bed I shared with David. *It changes things, doesn't it?*

I could vaguely feel my phone vibrating against my leg, tangled somewhere in the sheets. I had woken up to several missed calls and texts from David, and one from Deacon. Choosing to ignore them and continue my childlike display, I made myself coffee from an ancient French press I had owned for years and sat out on my terrace, trying to block out everything from last night. Maybe it was naïve of me, but I never would have pictured David with someone like Victoria. She was every girl in prep school and college Deacon dated and every girl in my sorority I didn't get along with. Girls who I was forced into friendships with by social circles, location and happenstance, as opposed to having anything in common. I was beginning to suspect I didn't have anything in common with anyone. Tripp's words continued to echo in my head. Did it change anything? It certainly didn't change what I had done, who I had been when she died...

"Charlie?" David's voice sounded and my eyes snapped open. He was standing in the doorway, arms braced against the frame leaning forward. His hair was rumpled like he had run his hands through it repeatedly. There were discernible bags under his eyes, more than a five o'clock shadow on his jaw, and I couldn't help but take him in. My breath caught in my throat. He was wearing a brown long sleeve sweater I haven't seen that had been tailored just for him and faded khakis. He looked like a figment of my imagination. "The door was open."

"Late night?" I asked, bitterness and jealousy seeping through my voice. I pictured him returning to that room and staying with Victoria until the early hours of the morning, relishing in how adult she was in comparison to his childish girlfriend who had caused a scene and left him standing in a restaurant.

Ignoring me, David straightened and gestured to the empty space beside me on the sectional. "May I?"

I shrugged noncommittally, sitting up allowing the blanket to slide off my body revealing my penguin suit pajamas. I wrapped both my hands around my mug watching as David came to sit beside me. He picked up my feet and placed them on his lap, wrapping his large hands around my ankles. The warmth of his body offset the breeze brushing over my exposed skin.

"You didn't answer any of my calls or texts. I was worried about you," he said, running his calloused thumb across the top of my foot. "I'm sorry for how we left things last night, I would really like to talk about it."

"I didn't know what to say," I answered, tapping my thumb against the ridges in the ceramic mug. "I'm sorry for how I acted. I am. But you really hurt me last night."

David nodded, his eyes darkening while his thumb continued to paint circles on my skin. "I wasn't intentionally ignoring you, Charlie. I've known Victoria for years. Our families know one another. It's a lot of shared history to catch up on."

My eyes prickled with tears and the embarrassment of last night, both from how David had been and how I had acted, rolled uncomfortably in my stomach. "You've never mentioned her. It was embarrassing...to sit there while you were just so enraptured with her, and then she made that joke about whether we were even a real couple..."

"She's never come up, because she's not someone I think about." David turned, grabbing my coffee mug and setting it down, pulling on my thighs until I was sitting in his lap. He wrapped his arms around me and brought his forehead to rest against mine. "Yes, we have shared history. Yes, we have a lot of it. Yes, we were together, but I haven't thought of her in quite a while. To me, I was reminiscing with an old friend. I realize that isn't how it came across, and I'm sorry I hurt you. I should have been better. I know how anxious being in public makes you, especially when there are high expectations of you from others. I will be better. I want to be better for you. But I'm going to need you to let me in, to talk to me, okay? You can't just retreat into yourself and leave me standing there."

Tears had begun to run from my eyes, and I allowed myself to explore the planes of his shoulder blades and the defined ridges of his back. I felt his lips brush against my wet cheeks. "I don't think I really knew what to say. I'm not supposed to make a scene, to have emotions like that. I've never been allowed to. It's like I knew I shouldn't have reacted that way, but everything was just too much and I just felt...unseen. Disposable."

David stilled at my words. He pulled back, confusion lining his features. "Disposable? You are anything but. I meant it when I said I loved you. That you are unlike anyone I have ever known. You're my favorite person in the world, Charlie. I have never loved anyone the way I love you. I would have sat with you all night until you had found the words to explain to me how you were feeling. Next time we get into an argument, if you need to scream at me and shout at me all night, I will stand there and let you. But you can't walk away from me.

Please, don't walk away from me again." No one has ever chased after me before. Not like this.

I nodded, tears free falling. David's lips continued to cross my cheeks, the bridge of my nose, my jawline, kissing them away. "I'm sorry. I won't. I don't want to walk away from you. I want to be the kind of person who deserves your patience and love, David. I promise I'll be better, too."

He stilled, pausing where his lips were pressed against the corner of my own. "Charlie, can I ask you something?"

"You can ask me anything," I whispered in return.

"Why do you always say you don't deserve what I offer you?"

I shook my head, a sob sneaking up my throat. The thought crossed my mind at that moment to tell him—to tell him the truth. The whole truth—all the way back to my mistakes at twenty. I pulled my head back, readying the words on my tongue, even though they felt leaden. I saw how David looked at me. Like I was so much more. Like I have never been looked at before in my life. The words died in my throat, and I shook my head again, sending up another silent promise to do better. To be better. I knew for certain Tripp's words from last night changed nothing, and they never would. I wanted to put as much distance between who I had been and who I was now, and as much distance from him as possible. "Just believe me when I say I'll be better. I love you, David."

He pressed his lips to mine, his warm hands wrapping around me. "You're still coming to Figure Eight next week, right? If you're not, I need to find a new jet." David pulled back and nipped at my neck, his voice thick with laughter.

A laugh escaped my mouth despite my tears, and I shoved him playfully. We were set to leave for a week with David's family the next morning. My father came through on his promise and ensured the jet was available for David and me to take to North Carolina. In a rare display, he also made sure to clear both of our schedules of company-wide meetings for the week. I was skeptical when he told me in my office earlier that week. He had rapped on my desk with his knuckles and reminded me I needed to be available for emergencies and to be checking my email regularly.

David's eyes had lightened significantly, the amber flecks sparkling the morning sunlight. "Yes, if you'll still have me Mr. Kennedy."

He groaned, rolling his neck out before gripping me tightly and pushing to stand up, still holding me. I wrapped my legs around his waist, a shriek escaping my lips. I felt him pinch the soft material of my shirt. "Let's get you out of these, have some makeup sex, and then I'll take you for brunch. Where would billion dollar baby like to go?"

I laughed again, burying my face into the shoulder of David's soft brown sweater. I rubbed my cheeks back and forth, inhaling his scent. He smelled like the ocean. Snaking my fingers up through his hair, I tugged on the unruly waves he had left to their own devices and ran my free hand along his jawline, his stubble scratching at the tips of my fingers. Tripp's words echoed faintly in my mind as David carried me inside, laying me down on my unmade bed before slowly unbuttoning my shirt. He trailed kisses across my chest, my stomach, down to the waistband of my shorts before practically ripping them from my body, his clothes disappeared, too, and then it was just us.

Our laughter echoed throughout the room, throughout the whole house, drowning out anything else. David paused, his arms braced on either side of my head, a wave of his hair tickled my forehead. A grin so different compared to Tripp's spread across his face, like he couldn't believe what he was seeing. Resting his forehead against mine, he buried himself in me and a strangled grunt replaced his laughter. We breathed together, his lips trailing across my jaw, down to my neck where his teeth grazed my skin. I arched my back to meet him, and all at once I was certain I knew the answer to the question that had been lingering around me.

It changes things, doesn't it? It changed nothing. I was home. Home is here with David. He's my *home.*

———

The Kennedy family home sat against the backdrop of the Atlantic ocean, just north of Wilmington and Wrightsville Beach on Figure Eight Island. David explained to me when we crossed the bridge to the island that it was entirely marshland and oceanfront properties—with no commercial buildings or businesses—save for water sports. His father's practice is in Wilmington, which is where his older brother Jackson lives with his wife. Sophie and Ryan still lived at home, though the entire family would be under the same roof for the week leading up to his father's sixtieth birthday party.

The house sat back from the road beyond a circular driveway. Gardens of what looked like seagrass fanned across the front of the property. Various luxury sedans were parked throughout the drive. It looked like the quintessential beach house, albeit one that belonged to millionaires. White shuttered windows lined the house, accompanied by a veranda on each level, littered with tasteful outdoor furniture and Adirondack chairs. The white shingles looked almost the color of bone in the sunlight and three garage doors the color of walnut were off to the right side. A staircase leading up to the veranda was opposite it, with a sort of thoroughfare in the middle of the home that reminded me of an open concept resort. The ocean glittered in the sunlight beyond the home. David wheeled the Jeep he rented beyond a patch of the tall seagrass, parking it beside a black Mercedes G-Wagon. A laugh rose in my throat and slipped through my lips at the disparity between the two vehicles.

He turned his head, blonde waves catching in the sunlight, and I could make out the crinkling of the corners of his eyes from behind his Ray-Bans. He was wearing a short-sleeved pink Hugo Boss button down and worn khaki shorts that stopped two inches above his knees. The second he stepped off the plane, I could picture him here. I could clearly see exactly how David had come to be, a smile tugging at the corners of my lips imagining him walking down this driveway with ocean water dripping from him, a surfboard tucked under his arm.

"It's Ryan's. He bought it with his graduation money from our grandparents." David's voice dripped with laughter while he eyed the Mercedes we parked next to.

"How generous of them." I arched my eyebrows behind my own oversized sunglasses, laughter residing in my voice. "What did you do with your graduation money, Mr. Kennedy?"

David shook his head and echoed my laughter, turning the car off, hands still gripping the steering wheel. "I invested mine. So did Jackson. Dare I ask what you did with any gift you were given?"

Another peal of laughter slid from my lips, and though we were parked, I crossed my legs on the leather seat, the denim of my boyfriend-style shorts bunching slightly. "A ten-million-dollar trust from my mother's parents that I was only able to access when I turned twenty-five, and my shares in WH. I think Deacon bought his first Bentley the minute the clock struck midnight on his twenty-fifth, though. So they have that in common. I haven't touched my trust, yet."

He pressed his forehead down against the leather of the steering wheel, a deep laugh sounding from him. David turned his head, extending a hand to me. "Thank you for coming, Charlie. I can't wait to show you off to everyone. You ready?"

"Are you sure you just didn't want the youngest member of the Next Great American Dynasty on your arm?" I asked teasingly, reaching out to place my hand in his.

"You are going to make me look very, very good on Friday at the party." David smirked, caressing the back of my hand with his thumb before bringing it to his lips. He pressed them to my hand quickly before releasing me. "I'll come back out and grab our stuff, everyone will be around at the pool. Let's go say hi and I'll introduce you."

I nodded, nerves swirling in my stomach, although meeting new people and making a first impression was something that had been ingrained in me since I was a child. I knew exactly what to do, and I knew how to make a pleasant and memorable first impression. I jumped down from the Jeep, clutching a box of Cohiba Behike cigars for David's father from mine. I wasn't even sure where he had gotten them. He produced them from the safe in his office before David and I left earlier that day. Deacon had a fit and died when he saw them being given away. My other hand held a vintage Veuve my father had pulled from the wine cellar for David's mother. I stuck a ridiculous bow on it I found in a drawer at my townhouse.

Host gifts were step one in making a positive impression, or so I have been told. My father and our etiquette teacher drilled that into us, and I don't think Deacon or I ever arrived empty-handed anywhere we went. I would have brought something on my own, but my father seemed determined to instill some sort of Winchester impression on the Kennedys and asked me to give these gifts on behalf of the family. Deacon bemoaned both the cigars and the vintage missing from the cellar, claiming he had plans for both of them.

David stepped around the front of the Jeep, a pair of Ray-Ban's shielding his eyes from the Carolina sunlight. He held out a hand to me expectantly. "Give me those, I'll carry them. My parents are probably going to try to hug you." My eyes widened and my mouth popped open. My family did not hug. I couldn't even remember the last time I was hugged by my father. Deacon and Taylor, sure. I could show them physical affection quite easily. David grinned, taking the champagne and box from me, tucking both under his arm. "I know the Winchesters don't hug."

"I'm not going to lie to you, Mr. Kennedy." I leaned into him as he fell into step beside me. "I have only ever been taught the importance of a firm, first impression handshake."

He pressed his lips to my temple, knocking my sunglasses down with the top of the champagne bottle. They fell neatly against my nose, shielding my squinting eyes. David pressed his spare hand to the small of my back and steered me to the thoroughfare of the home. Potted plants lined the hallway, along with more Adirondack chairs. Two surfboards were propped up against the open shutter of a window. Music drifted from the open end of the archway, accompanied by muffled conversation and laughter. I could see the ocean glittering endlessly in the sunlight just beyond the glass railing of the deck that spanned the back of the home. I could make out a long, wooden walkway leading from the deck to the beach, tall seagrass swayed in the breeze. The waves of David's hair lifted off his forehead with the ocean air sweeping over us as we rounded the corner.

The wooden deck gave way to an infinity pool against the backdrop of the Atlantic Ocean. The deck wrapped around all sides, except for the one bordering the ocean. An outdoor kitchen sat under the second-story veranda that wrapped around the house, all marble and cream complementing the home itself. A stone table ran almost the length of the pool with matching chairs adorned with deep cream cushions. Beyond that, matching stone pool chairs and cushions lined the edge of the deck. David smiled at me, setting the cigars and champagne down on the corner of the countertop. His family didn't notice our arrival immediately.

Two people who I assumed were his mother and father stood under the veranda, inspecting a bottle of wine that his mom just pulled from the wine fridge under the counter. David's mother had impossibly blonde hair that was pulled back from her face in a sleek ponytail, oversized sunglasses shielding her face and a silky white caftan draped over her body. I could see the outline of a black bathing suit beneath it. David's father was shorter than him, maybe by an inch or so, with light brown hair that looked like it might be peppered with gray. A pair of Wayfarers hid his eyes, and his tanned skin was set off by the light blue short sleeve button up he was wearing with a pair of khaki-colored Ralph Lauren swim shorts.

Two men stood with their backs to us in front of the pool, each holding a perspiring bottle of beer. They were wearing nearly identical pastel swim shorts and looked to be within an inch or two of height of one another. I assumed they were David's brothers, Ryan and Jackson. Beyond them, two women were lounging on the stone chairs, heads turned to one another deep in conversation. I have seen photos of David's sister, Sophie, but not of Jackson's wife, Meredith. David turned to me, wordlessly handing me his sunglasses, revealing a mischievous glint in his eyes. Tossing me a wink, he ran across the deck into both of his brothers, sending the three of them tumbling into the pool.

Shrieks erupted from the side of the pool where water sprayed over the side, drenching both of the women sitting there. The shorter and blonder of the two stood, continuing to shriek and shake her hands out vigorously, droplets of water flying through the air. David surfaced, his hair plastered to his face and a laugh escaped from his mouth. Two other blonde heads emerged moments after, shaking their heads out sending water everywhere.

"You fucking dick!" The one who looked to be the younger of the two, which would probably make him Ryan, laughed.

"Welcome home, little brother," the remaining one smiled. Jackson stood, hauling David up with him hugging him despite his sopping wet clothes.

Another strangled shriek, happier-sounding than the last, came again from the side of the pool. The shorter blonde, who I then recognized as Sophie, was bouncing up and down on the balls of her feet, still shaking her hands out. Her hair swung back and forth in a sleek ponytail that matched her mother's exactly. She was wearing a metallic gold cross halter top bikini I was certain Taylor had just bought from Norma Kamali. A wide grin smile split across her face, and she sprinted toward me. I raised my hand, ready to deliver a firm, trustworthy Winchester handshake, but Sophie wrapped me in a hug, continuing to shriek excitedly and bounce on the balls of her feet. My eyes widened behind my sunglasses momentarily before I returned her eager squeeze. She rocked back and forth, bringing my upper body with her.

Sophie pushed back, her hands lingering on my exposed shoulders. Her eyes matched David's: brown with flecks of honey and amber that glittered as she spoke. She reminded me of Taylor. But where Taylor was all sharp planes and edges, Sophie's face was soft with pillowy features and rosy cheeks. She's beautiful. I could clearly picture her as David described her: kind, unassuming, and too good for the world around her. The smile across her face was genuine. "Charlie! I am so, so happy you're here. I could hardly believe it when

David said he was bringing you. We have all been dying to meet you since that article came out."

The sun shining down on us shone all around Sophie, her genuine happiness radiating from her. I smiled, pushing my sunglasses off my face onto my head. "Thank you, Sophie, it's so great to be here and meet you, too. Great suit. My friend Taylor just bought the same one."

"Taylor Breen?" Ryan asked from behind us. I turned to see him pulling himself out of the pool. His hair was shorter than David's and was straight, not holding any of the rogue waves I loved. Water poured off of him, and he shook out his hair before running a hand through it, exactly like David does. He is slightly smaller than David, not as broad, and perhaps two inches shorter.

I knit my eyebrows in confusion. David and Jackson pushed up on either side of him. David immediately began unbuttoning his soaked Hugo Boss shirt before balling it up and throwing it in Sophie's general direction. It landed on the deck with a dull thud, causing droplets of water to splash against both of our legs. "Yes? Do you know Taylor?" I asked in response, wracking my brain for ways they would know one another.

Ryan laughed, shaking out his hair one more time. "No no. David wouldn't tell us anything about you for the longest time. You aren't as public as your brother, but Sophie and I found her Instagram. It was the only way for us to find photos of you other than random press ones. She is gorgeous."

I cocked an eyebrow, a laugh escaping my mouth. I did have an Instagram, and so did Deacon. He is verified and took great pride in his blue checkmark. Mine's private, as per my father's instruction. Deacon's was once upon a time, too, but somewhere along the way he had really leaned into his persona. Taylor also had a public Instagram and cultivated quite a following with her posts about Chicago lifestyle and working in medicine. Her feed is relatable, funny, and beautiful. "She is that. I would offer to introduce you, but unfortunately for you, she prefers women these days."

Ryan let out a groan of laughter before shaking out his hair again and extending his free hand to me. A firm, introductory handshake—that I could do in my sleep. "I'm Ryan, by the way." He grinned easily, gripping my hand.

"Charlie," I smiled in return. David walked to stand beside me, slinging a wet arm around me, his hand splayed across my shoulder protectively. His parents had come to stand beside Ryan and Sophie. A wide smile stretched across his father's face, and his mother rested a hand over her heart. I cocked my head, ensuring my smile remained on my face while I studied her. There was something I couldn't place in her features.

The other woman who had been sitting beside Sophie joined us, one hand firmly grasped in Jackson's. She almost looked like she could be a Kennedy sibling. Her blonde hair fell in waves around her face. She looked more like Taylor than Sophie, a slightly upturned nose set off by sharp, high cheekbones. But instead of the signature Kennedy eyes they all bore, hers are a light blue. She extended a manicured hand followed by a tiny but bright smile. "I'm Meredith, Jackson's wife."

Smiling warmly, I shook her hand before turning to Jackson. I studied him while he introduced himself. He looked more like David than Ryan, with wavy hair that was a shade darker than David's. His eyes were a deeper hue without the flecks of amber honey, but their jawlines were almost identical. The Kennedy genes ran strong, clearly.

"Charlie," David said, a broad grin on his face when his parents walked over. "These are my parents, William and Amelia." They each smiled at me, and I imagined that was what David would look like as he aged. The Kennedy children were an exact replica of their parents.

"It's so great to meet you. Thank you so much for having me." I smiled, as I shook their hands. David stepped away to pick up the discarded bottle of champagne and the cigars, handing both to his parents. "From our family. My father said to wish you a very happy birthday, Mr. Kennedy. He hopes that you two will join our family for a weekend in Lake Forest whenever you come to visit David next." David arched an eyebrow in surprise, his eyes twinkling. My father had said no such thing, and anyone who knew Steven Winchester would see through that very clearly.

"Thank you, Charlie, you didn't have to do that." William replied, a warm and easy smile so much like his son's on his face. "David speaks very highly of your father. We look forward to meeting him someday soon."

The odd expression remained on Amelia's face while she watched us together, at odds with the genuine smile that was placed there. "We're so happy to have you here, Charlie. Somehow you're even more beautiful than your photos. Come with me, let's get you a drink. You have to tell me where you got that dress on your Forbes cover. It was gorgeous. And your brother...my God, he is so handsome."

Heat crept over my face at the thought of David's parents reading that article. They had at least chosen a cover photo where I wasn't dangling from the desk like a pretty marionette. Amelia wrapped her arm around my shoulders, steering me to the bar under the veranda. I laughed, thinking of the sheer glee in Deacon's eyes if he found out David's mother talked about how handsome he is. "My brother knows how handsome he is, you can just ask him. And thank you, Mrs. Kennedy. The dress came from our family stylist, but I will be sure to pass along the compliment."

Amelia brought me to the bar, offering a myriad of drinks for me to choose from. I smiled politely while she peppered me with questions ranging from where I had gone to school, what my favorite parts of work are, and what I planned to wear for William's party on Friday. As I had been taught, I continued to smile, providing answers sprinkled with humor while I asked questions in return. Over her shoulder, David was standing with his siblings and father. His arm was slung around Sophie, whose head was tipped back in laughter at whatever Ryan was saying animatedly. But his eyes were on me. A smile I knew was just for me, as I stood with his mother sipping what she called a mimosa, but I was pretty certain it was only champagne with a drop of orange juice.

I looked back at him, smiling softly in return. An odd sense of longing settled over me, a desire to belong and to settle into the familial love and comfort they all held with one another. I continued to smile at Amelia and Meredith who had now joined us, and I wondered what it would be like to make a home here.

The sun began to set, bathing the deck in hues of pink and orange. All of the Kennedys' hair managed to look remarkably more blonde in the dusk. We spent the rest of the day outside. I mostly sat with Amelia, Meredith and Sophie along the pool, and we were gathered around the stone table, an elaborate feast of lobster displayed in front of us. William and Jackson spent the afternoon preparing it. I was tempted, at one point, to open my mouth and ask David who was preparing the dinner when the two of them had disappeared inside.

I picked up the linen napkin that sat folded across my plate in front of me and began to carefully unfold it before placing it in a neat triangle on my lap. To my right, David huffed a laugh. He leaned forward. "How does one eat lobster elegantly?" He asked conspiratorially with a glint in his eyes. Laughter rang up and down the table, as everyone else pulled out their chairs and settled into their seats.

"Here," I leaned forward, abandoning the linen napkin I was still making a show of folding on my lap, grabbing one of the claws from the platter in front of us. "Let me show you." I cracked the lobster claw between my hands with surprising force, butter flying everywhere, and tore off a giant bite with my teeth.

David tipped his head back and laughed loudly, exposing the strong column of his throat. Warmth radiated down my body. He smiled widely before bringing his lips to my forehead, his hand winding around my head. "You're so perfect," he murmured against my skin before pulling away. When he said things like that, there was a small, blooming part of me that wondered if it was true. At that moment, I thought that it could be true.

I focused on my plate, wiping my hands on the previously abandoned napkin. David's mother and sister were sitting across from us, watching intently. Sophie had a small, fond smile on her face as she continued to stare over her wine glass. His mother was looking at me appraisingly, that same expression I couldn't place from earlier. Like she, too, was trying to determine if the person sitting in front of her deserved that praise—deserved David.

"I'm so sorry, Mrs. Kennedy," I supplied, doing my best to fold the butter-stained napkin. "I assure you I was raised with better table manners than that."

David's warm hand was immediately pressing into my bare thigh. "Don't apologize. You're not at a state dinner. One of the things I love most about you is who you are when no one's looking."

I opened my mouth to respond, but any words died on my tongue. My favorite version of myself is who I am with him when no one is looking, too. *I am really me—who I'm supposed to be deep down in my soul.* My mouth popped open again for a moment, but I paused and rested my hand atop his instead of saying anything.

I hoped that everything coursing through my mind was conveyed in the pressure I placed on his hand and the way I was looking at him. Sophie let out something that might have been a squeal of delight while continuing to look at us intently. Her blonde hair picked up slightly in the breeze, fluttering around her face and causing the sparkle in her eyes to stand out even more. I looked back to Amelia, still staring at us. I could see it then, understanding what was etched across her features. She was looking at David in a way I wasn't sure either of my parents had ever looked at me. If my mom had, I couldn't remember. Anything I did recall was all vacant, empty smiles from across a formal table setting. Amelia was looking at her son like he was the most precious thing in the world to her, like her heart might very well burst over his happiness.

I cleared my throat, shifting uncomfortably. The only person to ever look at me that way in a familial sense was Deacon. I wasn't sure I could stand it. "Well, be that as it may David, my father would be disappointed in my behavior, so let's just keep lobster gate a secret when we go back to Chicago."

"No lobster family dinners for the Winchesters?" Ryan asked, an eyebrow arched from down the table.

I raised my own eyebrow, taking a small sip of my wine.

"Not like this. It's actually quite embarrassing. Any family dinner we have is a fully staffed affair."

"Charlie and Deacon had etiquette instructors growing up," David supplied, looking at me teasingly.

"You never know when the Queen might deign to visit the Midwest," I said dryly, rolling my eyes at him. He continued to stare at me, his eyes darkening as they skated over my exposed collarbone. I was still wearing the black tank top and loose denim shorts I had been in earlier, just with a bathing suit underneath. The rest of his family stayed in whatever they were wearing around the pool for the entire afternoon, too.

"Settle down boy," Jackson said, a wry grin on his face. His hand was placed on Meredith's. I watched as his thumb skated over the back of it in a gentle, loving manner. David grinned lazily, turning away from me with another wink like he hadn't been caught undressing me with his eyes. He shrugged, taking a sip from a perspiring bottle of beer.

William cleared his throat, hands around his own sweating glass bottle before he knocked on the table with his free hand. They all turned to him like that was common practice. "I was going to make a speech before we all dug into the dinner that Jackson and I slaved over all afternoon, but Charlie and David seem to have taken it upon themselves to dive in."

His eyes crinkled and a good-natured laugh escaped his lips. David and I were sitting frozen like two children who have been discovered with candy before dinner before we both began shaking with laughter. "Regardless," William continued, "it's so amazing to have you all home for my birthday. Though the only one I've really been able to get rid of is David, now he's brought someone who is incredibly out of his league and much better looking than him home. We couldn't be happier you've joined us, Charlie. By the way, David is staring at you, and I don't think we've seen the last of each other by a long shot. Welcome to our home and to our family."

My laughter subsided quickly, and my eyes burned when William raised his bottle. Blinking rapidly, I raised my own wine glass. David's hand pressed into my thigh, as he kissed the side of my forehead. Ryan let out some sort of low whistle, and I continued to blink. An unwanted memory burned in my mind: Tripp's hands moving across my body. Something else was there, too. A longing that ached deep inside me, desperately trying to cling to the family I thought I had with my father and Deacon.

"I'm truly thankful you invited me into your home. The pleasure is all mine." A sharp ring sounded from beside me. It seemed to be coming from David's pocket. I frowned playfully. "Wow, David. Can't even turn your ringer off during my toast? This was my moment to impress your family."

Rolling his eyes with a gesture of apology, David fished his phone from his pocket and scowled. "It's your brother." He showed me the screen before answering. I noticed he didn't even attempt to leave the table, and no one seemed particularly bothered. "Hey, Deac. Everything okay? Uh, yeah. She's right here. Yeah yeah, I don't even think she's checked her phone. Sure, just a second."

I knit my brows, accepting the phone from David and pushing back to stand. He waved me off, gesturing for me to stay at the table. "Deacon? Is everything okay?"

"Dad said you took the jet," Deacon answered tersely.

"Yes..." I responded, my eyebrows still pushed inward. My upper lip peeled back in disbelief. "It's been on the books for like weeks. Do you need something?"

"Yes, I need the jet, Charlie," he said, like I was stupid for not realizing. "But I called Guillaume, and he said it isn't in Chicago. It's in North Carolina." Guillaume has been our family's pilot from the moment our father bought the jet and is well-versed in Deacon's antics by now.

I rolled my eyes, cognizant I was still at David's family table. David pressed on my leg to keep me seated, laughter tugging at his mouth. "Oui. Je lui ai donné congé."

"What? I need the jet. Tripp and I are going to Vegas. Why are you answering me in fucking French? Tell him you both need to come home early." Deacon spat, irritation lacing his voice. It's moments like these when I didn't find the way Deacon embraced his life to be endearing. It annoyed me to no end.

"Tout le monde mérite des vacances, Deacon." Laughter was bubbling on my lips, as Deacon grew more irritated on the other end of the line. He refused to respond in anything but English, even though both speak French fluently. "My God, Deacon. I'm not leaving early with David just so the jet is in Chicago. It's been on the books at work for like three weeks. If you can't read, that's not my problem. I don't care if you and Tripp are going to the Taj Mahal. Book a plane ticket like a regular human. There's such a thing as first class."

The line clicked abruptly. I pursed my lips, handing the phone back to David. I turned to his mother. "Mrs. Kennedy, I am so sorry. My brother has no boundaries."

"And really wants the jet apparently," Ryan answered dryly.

David turned to me, a question in his eyes, "I didn't know you could speak French?"

I nodded, my cheeks flushed with embarrassment over Deacon's ill-timed phone call. "French, Japanese, and Mandarin. Spanish has always evaded me, though."

"Impressive, billion dollar baby." David winked at me.

"I'm sure your brother is continuing the celebrations. Your father must be thrilled after acquiring Halton Entertainment." William laughed, making expert work of breaking apart the lobster on his plate.

"Being a regular old billionaire wasn't enough." I supplied dryly, catching my own eye roll before it got any further. "My father was very clear that deal would not have gone through had it not been for David. He thinks very highly of him. In fact, I think he thinks more of me now that someone like David sees something in me."

William and Amelia both laughed in that ironic parental way, like that could not possibly be true. David pressed his palm on my thigh briefly before moving on to eat his dinner. I gave him a small reassuring smile before doing as I had been taught my entire life and turning to his sister and mother, engaging them in conversation about themselves.

―――――――

My head rested in the crook of David's shoulder. I quickly swept my tongue out to wet my lips and tasted salt.. After dinner, the entire family relocated to the second-story deck. It was lined with more natural wood Adirondack chairs that surrounded a long stone fireplace encased with gas. The deck itself offered a view that somehow eclipsed that of the pool below. The tall brushes of seagrass swayed gently in the breeze, illuminated by the moon that hung in the sky above the ocean.

Amelia gave me a tour of the house, ensuring my wine remained topped off the entire time. It was exactly as I would have imagined—what a house on the ocean with a family who loved one another would look like. The house is coastal and somehow opulent at the same time and filled with so much love—from one family member to the next.

While Amelia continued to show me around, I stopped in front of a black-and-white print of him. I could see the droplets of saltwater coating his exposed hands and neck, and see how they glistened against the thick material of the wetsuit that covered his body. A surfboard is tucked under his arm, and the other hand raised in the air holding some form of trophy. He must have been around fifteen. His mother ran her fingers over the edges of the print, a proud and wistful smile etched on her features. It reminded me of the print hanging in his apartment. I found myself wishing for one, too, wishing for a home David and I could share together with our lives on display.

When Amelia and I walked out onto the deck to join the rest of the family, I moved toward David to sit in the empty chair beside him when he reached out and grabbed my wrist, pulling me down to sit on his lap. David's arms were wrapped around me, the worn fabric of a Tarheels sweater he had forced over my head cocooned around me. The entire family was all splayed out in various chairs, casual comfort written on all their faces. They had all adorned sweaters in various states of shabbiness, Sophie and Meredith had pulled their hair up in sloppy yet artfully tousled buns bobbing at the top of their heads.

David brought his lips to my ear, a soft chuckle whispering past them. "Relax. It's just us here. No one's judging you." Nodding, I leaned back, resting my head against him. He was right, no one even looked our way. Ryan's eyes passed over us briefly, a small affectionate grin on his lips before looking away.

"What are you all going to do for the rest of the night?" William leaned back in his chair, a worn dark brown quarter zip I couldn't identify covering his upper body. A sweating glass of scotch sat on the arm of his chair.

Sophie, whose body was being swallowed by an oversized UPenn sweater turned away from Meredith, excitement sparking in her eyes. She clapped her hands together. "Let's go to Dodge's!"

Meredith grunted, rolling her head back before a smile stretched across her features. "Every time we go there, I have a multi-day hangover."

A feral grin that reminded me so much of Deacon it was alarming split across Ryan's face. "Dad's party isn't until Friday, Meredith. Nothing like an old-fashioned Kennedy hangover celebration to cure you."

Amelia stood, her knit sweater falling down to expose a bronzed shoulder. She held her hands up in defeat. "If that's the case, your father and I are going to end our night here. William, let's share one of those cigars from Charlie."

William winked at me, before pushing up from his chair, scotch dangling from one hand and the other extended to his wife. "You're in for a treat, Charlie."

His mother walked around to each of her children, leaning down to kiss their heads briefly. I felt David tighten his hold on me by a fraction. She arrived in front of us, a hand reaching out to grab David's arm that was resting on the side of his chair. They shared a fleeting but knowing look with one another. Amelia turned from him, her eyes shining brightly and held her arms open to me.

"Charlie, thank you so much for coming. William and I are both looking forward to getting to know you better over this next week." I stood, opening my own arms to return her embrace, expecting a perfunctory hug. She wrapped her arms around me, kissing my cheek lightly before whispering, "I have never seen David look at someone the way he looks at you. It's like you've hung the moon. The way you two fit together..." She clutched her heart. "Keep him safe."

She pulled back quickly, schooling her features before brushing one hand across my cheek and reaching to grab William's extended hand. The whisper of her fingers continued to skate across my skin while I shook my head, blossoms of inadequacy growing in the pit of my stomach. My wine-addled brain began to water them, reminding me I would forever be perfect on paper but never as who I really am. I closed my eyes briefly before turning to Ryan, who was chugging from a fresh beer bottle that had materialized out of nowhere, thumbing through his phone with the other hand. I breathed out, schooling my features before forcing a smile onto my face. "What the fuck is Dodge's?"

David pressed his lips to my ear, a laugh rumbling in his throat. "I think you'll enjoy it."

———

Amelia was right. I was in for a treat, so to speak. Dodge's is some sort of rundown bar that's front patio spilled directly onto the sand of Wrightsville Beach. It had the look of an old, repurposed garage, with opened wide-paneled glass doors, allowing people to walk from inside the bar directly to the worn wooden deck, or directly onto the patio. The inside was littered with mismatched wooden chairs that looked like they were in varying states of decay, surrounding a small dance floor and a stage where there was a man propped up on a stool tuning a guitar. When we were waiting in the driveway for the Uber's ordered by David and Ryan, I still had on David's Tarheels sweater and asked him if I should change. A grin split across his face, and he shook his head with a laugh. He assured me I would somehow still be one of the best-dressed people there. He wasn't wrong. Half of the people there were in various levels of disheveled—some looking like they had simply thrown on a pair of denim shorts or shirt over the top of whatever swimwear they were wearing on the beach that day.

Winking at me while holding the door open, David leaned down and kissed my forehead. "I told you that you didn't have to change." He placed his hand on my lower back and began to weave through the crowd toward the bar. The rest of his family was already lined up there, chatting animatedly with the bartenders, who were arranging rows of shots in front of them.

"Do you all come here often?" I asked, smiling as I thought about David and his family blending seamlessly into this bar, not a care that they lived almost thirty minutes away in an entirely different world.

David nodded, quickly removing his backward hat and running his hand through his hair. The low light of the bar casted shadows across all his features. "We've all been sneaking in here since we were fifteen. Jackson and I brought Ryan here when he was fourteen. Our parents were thrilled, as you can imagine."

I tipped my head back in laughter, thinking about the two of them sneaking their youngest brother in, how free it must have felt. Sophie was bobbing her head from side to side, looking on the precipice of squealing. Four shots sat between her and Meredith, seemingly waiting for David and me to retrieve them. Sophie tipped her chin toward them, and David reached out to grab two for me before taking the others himself. "Charlie, this is a bit of a Kennedy family and Dodge's welcome. We can't tell you what's in the shots, but you have to take them. We made Meredith do the same thing when Jackson first brought her here." Sophie was bouncing on her sandaled feet.

"It's true. It was disgusting." Meredith leaned forward conspiratorially, scrunching her small upturned nose. "But you have to do it. It's a tradition. You can join us in victimizing whoever Ryan or Sophie brings home when the time comes."

"I guess there's nothing like drinking an unnamed shot in a dirty bar to start your night off. Thank you for including me in this." I smiled, genuine happiness painted on my face. The bar was crowded, but it was nothing like any of the events I was forced to attend. It was so...pedestrian, in the best way possible. Nothing felt too big, nothing felt too loud, and watching the way David's family eagerly welcomed me into their circle eclipsed anything else I was whispering in my mind.

"We have to. David looks ready to get down on a bent knee, so it's clearly time." Jackson raised his first shot glass, and the rest of them followed suit.

Turning to look at David, I noticed he was peering down at me. Even in the low light, his eyes were dancing. He always looked at me like it was the first time, like I was sure no one else would again. He winked at me before raising his shot glass to meet his siblings. "I'll keep her as long as she'll have me."

Sophie shrieked again, bouncing back and forth on her feet in sheer delight at his proclamation. I brought the shot glass to my lips, tapping it there while I mulled over David's words. A small bubble of guilt rose in my throat and the imprint of Tripp's mouth on mine whispered past. I would spend the rest of my life loving David the way I wanted to and the way he deserved. "I think I'll keep you forever, Mr. Kennedy." With a silent promise of atonement, I tipped the liquid back, thinking of the burn on my throat as a binding promise.

The shots *were* disgusting. They truthfully tasted like a mixture of every bad hard liquor and the bottom dregs of a mystery punch at a frat party. The entire family had started shouting and whistling after we took the shots. David's eyes darkened at my words, and the moment the shots were gone, he grabbed the back of my neck and brought his lips crashing against mine, whispering against them as he pulled away. "You know that drives me crazy. I love you so fucking much, Charlie. You're everything, billion dollar baby."

That had earned another round of whatever the Kennedys referred to as their 'welcome' drink. I was sitting at a high-top table, pitchers of beer were spread out on the table in front of us. The sweater I was wearing lay abandoned on the back of my chair, and my tank top was sticking to the thin sheen of sweat covering my skin. Sophie disappeared into the crowd that was gathered around the stage where the man from earlier was working his way through a set. I could see her on the other side of the room, sitting on a table swinging her legs back and forth talking to a group of people that looked around her age. David, his brothers and Meredith were engaged in some heated conversation that involved many flying hands and laughter. Mirroring Sophie, I swung my legs back and forth while my eyes roved the people dancing across the bar. It seemed like a mix of slow dancing couples clinging to one another, while others looked like they might belong in a club.

"You wanna dance with me, Charlie?" David leaned away from his brothers, a grin on his face. His cheeks were flushed over his tan face that seemed to have magically appeared in one day of him being home. "No one's watching you here. Just me. I promise."

I nodded, hopping off my seat and extending a hand to him before I had a moment to reconsider. David tugged on my hand, leading me through the throngs of people with his firm grip. My hair was pulled back in a high ponytail, aided by the sweat across my scalp. It flicked back and forth as we made our way through the crowd. David stopped suddenly in the middle of the sea of people, where we were shielded from view at every angle and pulled me close to him.

Wrapping my arms around his neck, my fingers began to toy with the waves at the nape of his neck. I smiled up at him, hungrily studying the planes of his face. "I love you, Mr. Kennedy."

"I love you, too, Charlie." David whispered before bringing his mouth down to mine. His tongue swept into my mouth immediately. The taste of beer lingered on his lips, and I pulled his neck closer to me, not caring for one moment where we were or who I was. He groaned into my mouth and thrust his hips into mine. I wasn't sure how long we stood there, pressed against one another in a way that was bordering pornographic, desperate for every inch of our skin to touch while we continued to devour each other. David pulled back suddenly, eyes dark and breathing heavily. "Let's get out of here."

I didn't even have time to nod before he was pulling me toward the door. David raised one hand casually over his head to his family, all erupting in laughter and whistles as he practically pulled my arm out of its socket to get me out the door. I stumbled off the worn wood of the bar patio, David weaving expertly through the throngs of customers who had spilled out onto the beach. He paused abruptly before the sand, bending down and grabbing the back of my calves to steady me before removing my sandals. He looked up at me, brown eyes wicked with lust. He leaned forward under the guise of undoing a strap on my left foot but pressed lips to my exposed inner thigh, his tongue tickling my skin followed by the graze of his teeth.

David stood, handing me my sandals and resuming his grip on my other hand. "Come with me."

"I'd follow you anywhere, Mr. Kennedy," I whispered, my toes sinking into the sand as I trailed beside him. He pulled me down the beach toward a shadowy alcove carved into the sand. The seagrass surrounding it was taller than along the rest of the beach, creating a hidden spot away from the side of a worn-looking boardwalk. The sounds from Dodge's became muffled the farther we walked. David pushed aside the planes of grass holding it for me before coming to stop in the middle of a small, sandy clearing.

My eyes roamed around, my breath catching when I realized how we were somehow utterly secluded from the world around us. The seagrass swayed in the breeze, almost to my shoulders, and we had an unobstructed view of the sky. Stars dotted it, twinkling just for us. I stopped my gaze on David, whose hand was holding mine. "This is beautiful." I breathed, before arching an eyebrow and titling my head. "Did you bring me to your secret seduction spot, Mr. Kennedy?".

David laughed roughly, taking a step closer to me and grabbing my other hand. "No. I used to smoke weed here with Jackson when we were teenagers. But I *am* trying to seduce you. Is it working?"

Taking my hands back, I pulled the hem of my tank top over my head, dropping it in the sand beside me. The breeze picked up, breathing across my exposed skin and bringing goosebumps to the surface of my flesh. "It might be."

David cocked his head to the side, brown eyes trailing over me before he practically lunged at me, wrapping my legs around him. His arm slid around my back to hold me up, and his mouth crashed against mine as it had earlier. Soon we were a tangle of tongues and limbs and I wanted to be closer than our clothes allowed. David snaked his free hand through my ponytail before practically ripping the elastic out, my hair spilling across my shoulders. The cool breeze felt like it was long gone, every inch of my skin on fire. Securing my legs around his waist, David tightened his other arm around my back before turning and laying me down gently in the sand. He pulled away, one hand reaching for the neckline of his shirt and tossing it aside along with his hat. His hair stuck up almost impossibly. I ran my fingers through it, twisting and tugging, trying to memorize the feeling of it slipping through them. I wanted to remember everything about David forever.

Eyes never straying from mine, he pulled down my denim shorts before flicking them over his shoulder, leaving me in nothing but a black and nude La Perla bra and matching thong. David paused, tracing his finger along the pattern of the lace before standing quickly to kick off his shorts. Lowering himself above me, he placed his lips on mine and began to whisper to me, "I love you, Charlie. Never in my life would I have thought I would be lucky enough to meet someone like you. Did you mean what you said? That you wanted to keep me forever?"

I pulled my head back, pushing my forehead to his, our breathing beginning to intertwine. "Yes, of course," I whispered, my eyes burning and nerves swirling in my stomach. "I know it's soon. But I love you. I love you more than I have ever loved anything or anyone, and I will spend my entire life trying to prove to you I'm worthy of you."

"It's not too soon," David whispered, pressing his lips to mine, then beginning to trace my jawline down to my neck. His breath was ragged and hot against my skin. "It would never be too soon. Not with you. Never with you."

Bringing a calloused hand down to my thigh, David hitched it around his waist and pushed into me with a sharp intake of breath. He covered my mouth with his hand to muffle my voice and began to move against my body. A piercing guilt threatened me at the borders of my mind, and I remembered that minor, fleeting moment where I wondered what it would be like to be with Tripp. But soon, all I could think of was the steady mantra of words David whispered in my ear, our bodies moving together, his skin against mine, and the stars scattered amongst the sky above us.

CHAPTER FOURTEEN

David's hand swirled lazy circles across my thigh, tracing patterns in the rays of sunlight casted across my exposed skin. We were lying stretched out by the pool at his parents' house, each of us hiding bags and bloodshot eyes under sunglasses. David and I finally stumbled home around two in the morning, finding Ryan and Sophie still awake playing some sort of game out by the pool. Both were currently lying on outrageous pool floats, eyes covered from the sun with both sunglasses and forearms. A strangled and dramatic moan would sound from Ryan occasionally. Amelia and William were in the kitchen preparing what they referred to as a very common Kennedy hangover cure. I had seen them both placing intricate champagne flutes across the breakfast bar, and I took that to mean their hangover cure meant consuming more alcohol. Aside from Hydra-V, that was a favorite Deacon fallback as well.

My phone vibrated against my leg, and I suppressed a groan. Looking over, I saw a message from my father that read: "Care to explain?" appeared on the lock screen. My stomach dropped when I opened the message, which was followed by grainy photos that were clearly taken on an iPhone of David and I pressed against one another at Dodge's. Bile rose in my throat while I studied them. They *were* practically pornographic. In one, David had my head tipped back, his tongue visibly sliding into my mouth and his hand on my ass. The rest were no better. My leg hitched around David, another where I was pulling on his lip with my teeth, and in another my hand was tucked just under the hem of his shirt. I sat up abruptly, nausea rolling in my stomach, and I continued to thumb through the photos like I could somehow make them disappear.

"What's wrong?" David asked, sitting up immediately behind me. I wordlessly handed him the phone and wished I could sink into the chair below me and disappear forever. "Oh fuck. Charlie, I'm sorry. I shouldn't have asked you to dance, I should have taken you home. In a million years, I never would have believed anyone there would recognize you."

I opened my mouth to respond, caught between wanting to lash out from my own embarrassment and wanting to remind him he had nothing to apologize for. That is what I had been talking about when we first started dating. I was cut off by a loud, sharp ring, and I knew my father would be on the other end of the line. Ryan started suddenly at the sound, another moan escaping him before covering his eyes. Standing, I moved across the deck hoping to escape down the boardwalk to the beach before the ringing started again. Preparing myself for a scolding, I fumbled as I answered on speaker. "Dad...if you'll give me a moment, you're on speaker. I just need to go somewhere–"

"Do you know how much money I had to pay the worthless columnist who took them to keep those photos out of some gossip rag?" My father spat across the line. I could picture his face as clearly as if he was standing directly in front of me on the boardwalk. "It cost me one-and-a-half-million dollars to keep people from seeing your tongue down David's throat and his hand on your ass."

I scoffed, the anxiety giving way to rage that began to simmer in my blood. It was no more than he had paid to keep news about Deacon out of the media over the years. "You just acquired another multi-billion dollar company. That's pocket change to you, Dad."

"This constitutes a breach of that contract. If you knew anything about anything, you would know that a deal like that comes with morality and indemnity. Halton is a *family* entertainment company, Charlie. They would likely not appreciate headlines indicating you and your tongue are the new pre-movie entertainment." He started shouting. "This is your family business, our legacy. What do I need to do to make you understand that?"

I felt my voice raise when I responded, despite the fact that I hadn't moved to a private location, David's family mere feet away. "I went out with my boyfriend and his family. And unlike our family, they are actually interested in spending time together. I had a bit too much to drink. I wasn't thinking. Deacon has done worse, Dad. This is fucking ridiculous." The ocean sparkled in the morning light beyond me, mockingly illuminating all the families that ran back and forth across the sand.

"You will stay in that house for the remainder of your visit. You will not set so much as one toe beyond the property line. Do you understand me?" My father's voice settled to a deadly calm as he spoke, like he was issuing instructions to a child.

A mirthless laugh escaped from my mouth, and the words that followed tumbled out before I could stop them. "Were the rules that bad for Mom? No wonder she fucking killed herself. Have you ever thought about the fact that she drowned in the family pool intentionally? There's a message there, no?" Silence greeted me on the other end of the line, and a stark intake of breath sounded from behind me. I whirled around, the phone still pressed to my ear. David was standing at the edge of the deck, his mother and Sophie just behind him. Sophie had her hand pressed across her mouth in shock, and David's mother was looking at me, hand over her heart and an echoing sadness in her eyes.

"The phone, Charlie." David stepped forward, gesturing with his hand. Rage played across his features. I wordlessly extended my hand, the phone hanging loosely from my grip while my father maintained his silence. The words hung around me, taunting me, reminding me they were out there in the world, and I would never be able to take them back. My shoulders fell, and I looked down, watching as I pressed my toes into the wood of the deck, wishing I was anywhere else. David spoke behind me, his voice unlike anything I have ever heard.

"Steven. It's David." There was a pause. "I heard her. But I'm going to stop you right now. This ends at this moment, do you understand me? I respect you as a person, as a businessman, as a boss. I will never negate or deny the opportunities you have given me, but I am not speaking to you now as an employee. You may be her father, but you will never speak to Charlie like that while she is in my family's home again. Are you hearing me?"

I continued to stare down at my feet, the edges of my toes blurring as my vision became watery with hot tears threatening to spill over. Embarrassment clawed at my exposed skin while David continued. "Do you remember what you said to me in the office before we left? You pulled me in and said you'd be honored if I were to marry Charlie, to welcome me officially into your family. I'm telling you now that when that day comes, if I am a lucky enough man for her to say yes, I cannot wait to give her far more than you're giving her right now, than you've ever given her."

There was another pause from David, and I felt a warm hand settle on my shoulder. I lifted my head, attempting to blink away my tears to see Sophie standing beside me, alongside Amelia.

"That's fine. How much did it cost you to keep the photos out? Send me your details, and I'll have a wire transfer sent to you this afternoon. I take responsibility, and you will not say another word about it." David paused, his words cutting across the warm breeze. David's back was to us, but there was a clear tension in his posture, and he didn't stop there. The rest of his family had come out onto the deck now, watching as I stood, head down again and tears pouring unbidden down my face. It was like my heart was cleaving in two. One part of me felt warm, comforted and safe—like perhaps this was what it was like to have an entire family rally around you. To care about you no matter what. But embarrassment clung to me, too. Because Winchesters didn't do this. The feelings of comfort were foreign and felt somehow sticky and out of place inside me, like they had an expiration date, or maybe the next time I made a mistake. It was inevitable and could never last.

"It's fine. Everyone will sign. We don't need you to send a lawyer. I have a house full here." David stopped speaking again before answering a final time. "I'll still be at the gala on Monday. Enjoy your day, Steven." I had completely forgotten there was yet another charitable gala sponsored by my father for Northwestern Memorial taking place the next week. Great.

A silence fell across the deck and a sob crept up my throat. I swallowed, attempting to keep it down. I looked up at Amelia, barely able to discern her through my clouded eyes. "Mrs. Kennedy...I'm so, so sorry. Please accept my apology on my behalf and on my father's."

A sound halfway between a snarl and a scoff came from David. I could feel him just behind me, the warmth of his body radiating against mine. Sophie's delicate hand was on my shoulder still, her thumb skating comforting circles. David pressed his chin into my shoulder, wrapping his arms around me. "You do not need to apologize. This is not on you."

"I'm so embarrassed," I whispered to him, but it was futile. The entire family was still standing on the deck, speechless. "Mr. and Mrs. Kennedy, I truly am so sorry."

They both shook their heads immediately, Amelia stepped forward, concern laced her features. She grabbed my hands in what I assumed was a soothing, motherly gesture. "How many times have we asked you to call us Amelia and William? You don't owe us an apology, Charlie."

The sob that was creeping up my throat escaped my mouth as a hiccup, followed by an awkward laughter. "I do, though. I should have been more careful last night I should have—"

David pulled tighter around me, his muscular forearms squeezing my chest, cutting off my words. He gently pressed his lips to my temple. His mother was still looking at me while the tears I tried to blink away were falling freely. She let go of one of my hands and reached out, her thumb pressing across my cheek to wipe away my tears. "I'm so sorry about your mother, Charlie. What a terrible thing for a young woman to be missing her mother like you must be."

Despite my best efforts, the hot tears continued to fall down my face, flushed with humiliation. I thought of my mother, floating lifeless in our family pool the way I always pictured her: a red dress drifting gently in the water, hair exactly like mine fanning out around a lifeless body. I shook my head almost imperceptibly, those thoughts were for another time. I had nothing to say. My father had somehow embarrassed me from hundreds of miles away. Maybe he had been right. Maybe I had done it all on my own.

"My father is a complicated man. I hope you won't judge him too harshly." My voice was a strangled whisper. Amelia shook her head, like she didn't have a care in the world before wiping my tears one more time. "What were you saying you would all sign, David? Please don't tell me he's making you sign NDAs."

"You know your father," he whispered, pressing his forehead to mine.

I shook my head immediately. "No one has to sign those. I'll deal with him."

William shook his head before showing me a good-natured smile, like this had all been some minor inconvenience. "Charlie, it's truly fine. If the situation were reversed, I would ask the same. From a legal perspective, it makes perfect sense. It provides a safety net and legal, binding security that ensures the incident will never be disclosed to outside parties."

I opened my mouth to respond, indicating that in fact, it did not make perfect sense, when David interrupted my thoughts. "I was actually thinking you and I could get out of here today. There's something I want to show you."

Turning to look at him, I noticed he was smiling at me expectantly. His skin glistened in the morning sunshine, droplets of water from his earlier swim covered the ridges of his abdomen and broad shoulders. Before I opened my mouth to respond, David grabbed my hand and pressed into it reassuringly.

"Oh, that sounds wonderful. Where are you planning on taking her?" His mother smiled widely, briefly rubbing my shoulder before dropping her hand like she was able to suddenly forget the last fifteen minutes had transpired.

David slung his arm around me lazily, winking down at me quickly. "It's a secret for now."

———

Waves lapped against the shore of the beach. I pushed my toes into the wet sand, feeling my feet sink down. I stood, one hand placed over my eyes to shield against the sun, a wetsuit peeled down from the upper half of my body. David was sitting atop a surfboard he had pulled from one of the garages at his parents' home before ushering me into the rented Jeep. I traced his features as best I could while he tipped his chin to the person next to him in the water before leaning down and beginning to paddle forward.

David spent the day teaching me the basics of surfing, driving us to a break in the Outer Banks he thought was best for beginners. I have surfed twice before—once on a family vacation in Hawaii and another time when I was volunteering as a researcher in South Africa during college. I managed to stand up three times, on tiny baby-sized waves before getting distracted by the proud smile David wore and promptly falling over the side of the board.

He wanted to stay out longer, and I found myself more than content to watch him. He assured me those waves were nothing special, but that wasn't what I was looking at. I was too focused on his face to notice anything else. Despite his assurances, those were baby waves. I could see how comfortable he was in the water and read the joy on his face every time he caught a wave like I was standing right beside him. A fantasy, however brief, crossed my mind of me liquidating all my shares in WH and moving us to some far off coastline where we could exist like that every day, entirely alone save for the company of one another.

David fell backward easily from his board in the shallow water and began to guide it toward the shore before picking it up under his arm.

"How'd I look out there?" David asked, coming to stand beside me, running a free hand over his face and pushing his hair back.

"Like whoever the Tony Hawk of surfing is," I said, laughter spilling from my lips. Pushing up, I wrapped my hands around his neck placing a brief kiss on his lips, tasting the saltwater on them.

"I'll take it, billion dollar baby. Any compliment from you works for me." David smiled at me. He extended his free hand, grabbing mine in his, and we began to walk across the sand to where he had parked the Jeep. The beach was littered with people, some lying down on the sand seemingly soaking up the sun and other surfers scattered across the shoreline. He had already secured the surfboards to the roof rack on the top of the Jeep before reaching behind him and pulling down the zipper of his wetsuit. "So, what did you think?"

"I think I'm pretty bad at it, but I think you're great. I'm sorry you couldn't do this forever." David had pulled down the top of his wetsuit, revealing his tanned skin, and I wrapped my hands around his waist, pressing my face into his chest. My hands explored the planes of his back, and I inhaled deeply, savoring the smell of sunlight and salt on his skin. He wrapped his arms back around me, palms skating my shoulder blades.

"Then I wouldn't have met you," David whispered, pressing his chin into the top of my head. "I wouldn't trade you for anything in the world."

His voice was soft, the words a whispered promise amongst the sound of birds, laughter, and the waves gently lapping against the shore. I pulled back, meeting his eyes. "What if I cashed in everything I owned, and we ran away? Bought us a villa on the beach somewhere? You could surf...I could....well I could do something."

David tipped his head back in laughter, the sound rich. It reverberated throughout my body and circled around my heart. "You want to run away with me, Charlie?"

I nodded, scrunching my nose at him as I smiled. I was partially kidding, but there is a part of me that wished it could be true. "I could use my riches to take care of you, you know. More than enough money to last us a lifetime."

"You want a lifetime with me?" David asked, his voice was low again. He stared down, his eyes searching my face. The flecks of amber and honey sparkled impossibly in the bright sunlight. "You keep saying these things, but I don't think you know how serious I am about you, Charlie. What if I did ask you to marry me?"

My lips parted, and any words I might have responded with died on them when I saw how he was continuing to look at me. I paused, waiting for the feelings of fear and dread at the commitment to surface, to rise up and overtake me; for the thought that someone like David could see something in someone like me to become so overwhelmingly absurd that it was laughable. But they never came. I could see my own green irises reflected in David's, and there wasn't anything swimming behind them. Just the person I am when I'm with him—the person I wanted to be—staring back at me. My lips curved upward, a tiny smile just for him. "I might just say yes then."

Joy unlike anything I had ever seen on David's face spread across his features; it was far beyond what I had witnessed when he was on the water. It was like I had stopped his entire world. His usual, easy grin slid into place, but his eyes continued to sparkle. "Stay tuned then."

David bent down, shucking the wetsuit from my legs one at a time, not a care in the world who was watching us. His eyes never left mine, the smile I loved beyond anything so infectious. For once in my life, I didn't care at all who saw either.

———

Cocktail servers wove in and out of the crowd that spilled across the deck of the Kennedy home. The doors had been left open, with partygoers moving between the main floor of the home and the deck surrounding the pool. The veranda that wrapped the house on both levels was littered with tea lights that flickered in the evening light. Cocktail tables covered in pure white tablecloths with displays of matching white flowers in gold vases were scattered across the veranda. Even the pool had been transformed with floating lanterns bobbing across the surface, and two large displays of opaque white balloons weighted down in the water that floated above the surface. The entire home had been taken over since the previous evening with Amelia instructing staff where everything was to go down to the placement of the last flower.

Leaning against the panels of the veranda, I fished my phone out of my clutch and checked for messages. I wasn't even sure why—my father maintained his stony silence since our disastrous phone call earlier in the week. I continued to monitor my email as per his request, responding to anything marked time sensitive or urgent lest I gave him any additional ammunition or reason to be mad at me. David and his brothers left for an early tee time with their father first thing in the morning. The sunlight and a soft breeze from the ocean brushed across my skin when David pressed his lips to my ear, whispering a goodbye and words of excitement to show me off at the party later.

The slit of my dress lifted with the breeze, fluttering around my feet. I rolled my eyes while I grabbed a hold of the silky material. Taylor dragged me shopping before leaving, stating in no uncertain terms that the dress I wore had to be unlike anything I had worn before, should Victoria and her family be in attendance at the party. Originally, she dressed me in a head-to-toe vibrant sequin gown that clicked when I walked and sent my mind screaming back to the rainbow fish incident at the yacht club. We compromised on an emerald green Dolce and Gabbana gown with a plunging v-neck. It was vaguely Grecian-inspired, with a twisted belt of fabric around my waist, and thigh-high slits on both sides. It was more than I would ever spend on a dress, seeing as I was never allowed to wear the same one twice. I would be donating it the moment I was back in Chicago.

Wisps of my hair flitted around my face in the breeze. Sophie asked me earlier in the day if I wanted to get ready with her and Meredith, and I agreed. Upon seeing that I intended to wear my hair as it was, she shrieked and began braiding and twisting the straight tendrils, somehow transforming it into an intentionally low messy bun with twists and braids to give it volume. I watched as Amelia circled the pool below, greeting guests warmly, the deep plum skirt of her gown swishing elegantly behind her. I couldn't tell if she was frustrated that they weren't back yet. My father would have deflected in the exact way she was, with a laugh and a wave of a hand, but his smile never would have met his eyes the way hers did. Even from my vantage point, I could see the light in Amelia's eyes and the way the corners crinkled with her laughter.

Raucous laughter sounded from below me, and William appeared through the walkway, a white captain's hat sitting askew on his head. Ryan, Jackson and David trailed after him, all looking sun-kissed and windswept, and slightly inebriated. A pang of envy shot through me as I watched William grab each of them in turn, hugging them roughly before placing a kiss on Amelia's forehead. I continued to watch despite the ache in my heart while she chastised her fully grown sons, as if they were children, for being late. My eyes burned at the sight of familial ease and comfort I would never have. David turned, spotting me where I stood pushed against the railing, gown continuing to flutter in the breeze. His face split into a wide grin, and he raised one hand to me, showing me five fingers and mouthing five minutes to me. I raised my eyebrows in response and brought the champagne that was sitting beside me to my lips.

"I would have thought I would be sick of the displays of affection between you two by the time the end of the week rolled around, but they just continue to get cuter and cuter," Sophie appeared beside me, holding a champagne flute loosely in her hand. Her blonde hair was pulled tightly back from her face into a sleek, high ponytail. She was wearing a cream-colored, high-neck silk gown that hung off her like a sheet. It was unlike anything I would ever be able to pull off.

I raised my eyebrows at her, taking another sip. "Oh, come on, you've seen him with a girlfriend before." My stomach soured, and I resisted the urge to roll my eyes thinking of perfect Victoria and how seamlessly she would have blended into this North Carolina life.

"Not like this I haven't," Sophie looked at me pointedly, gold shimmer painted around her brown eyes. She tapped her glass against mine before turning away and floating down the veranda.

I pushed off the railing, grabbing the stem of my champagne flute. I could hear my etiquette teacher's voice ringing in my ears; how rude it would be if I were to remain up here alone for a moment longer. Turning on my heel, I stopped suddenly and my breath caught in my throat.

David was leaning against the doorway, the sliding glass doors framing him on either side. His hands were tucked into the pocket of slim fitting black tuxedo pants. The single button jacket was undone to reveal a crisp white shirt, the top buttons undone.

"You scared me," I breathed, drinking in the sight of him. My former feelings of envy dissipated with every moment I stared at him.

David arched an eyebrow, stepping toward me. "You look incredible. That dress..." He trailed off, wrapping his arms around my waist. "I was wondering all day what you might be wearing and never in my wildest dreams would I have imagined this."

"That's because you have only ever had the misfortune of seeing me in whatever Sabine deems fitting." I laughed, placing my hand on his chest, so I could tuck my fingers under the open buttons of his shirt. David's skin felt like sunlight.

He leaned down, pressing his forehead to mine. "I promise there is no such thing as misfortune when it comes to you."

Before I could open my mouth to protest, he spun me around, slinging an arm around my shoulder and guiding me toward the party below. True to his word, David spent the evening introducing me to every single person he could. More people than I was comfortable with commented on the Forbes article and the Halton acquisition, smiling politely like I was taught, each time I deflected and shared anecdotes about how David was instrumental to the deal.

Victoria wasn't present, but her parents were and they seemed much more pleasant than their daughter. Like he was trying to make up for the last time, or prove something to me, David kept his hand in mine, or his palm placed on the small of my back. Eventually, I stepped away, excusing myself to use the restroom. I came up to the second floor, taking a moment to lean against the railing and close my eyes against the breeze. I found it so peaceful out there. The air smelled of sunshine, and the sun warmed my soul. I kept my eyes closed, tipping my chin up, inhaling the scent of the ocean when I heard David's voice from below me. He must have been standing just under me in the walkway leading out to the pool.

"So? You've been suspiciously silent," he said, his voice low amongst the chatter of the party guests.

"She seems wonderful. I can see how enamored you are." Amelia spoke in response.

David huffed a laugh, and I could picture his face as he spoke. "She is. But still, you aren't saying much."

There was a long pause, and I found myself leaning over even farther, like I could already detect something else in Amelia's voice before she responded. I heard a sigh before she answered. "It's not that. I think she's wonderful. I think she's beautiful and funny, and from all I've gathered, working very hard to use her privilege to make the world a better place than she found it."

"And? What's your point?" David asked, his voice harsh, cutting above everything else.

She sighed again. I could almost picture her as I would have pictured my own mother, moving toward him with her plum gown trailing behind her. "The other day...the photos. Is that what you want for yourself? The constant scrutiny?"

David didn't miss a beat, and my heart stilled. "I want Charlie. I don't see any of that. Only her."

"And what if she asks you to sign a prenup?"

"Then I'll sign it." David responded, a laugh escaping his throat, again. "I'm not entitled to any more than I've earned in Winchester Holdings."

"Do you think that's fair?" She asked. It felt like a taunt, hanging in the air. I hadn't really thought about it much. Neither Deacon nor I were ever in a position that this would come up for discussion.

A strangled sound left his throat. "What does fair mean to you, Mom? We're sitting in a multi-million dollar home, with more money than most people could dream of. Charlie does what she can. It's not perfect, but she's trying to figure it out."

"I just don't want you setting yourself up for disappointment," Amelia whispered. I knew those words weren't meant for me, but I couldn't back away. "I've never seen you like this."

"That's because I've never felt like this." David said baldly, before I heard the sounds of his shoes against the stone and he disappeared back into the party.

I pushed off the railing, unsure what to make of that exchange. It wasn't for my ears, but I couldn't unhear it, everything they said swirling in my thoughts. A small part of me felt like I was soaring. I was enough. Enough for David. But that part of me felt like it might have been eclipsed by everything else his mother had laid bare in their exchange. She was already predicting that I might hurt David, let him down the way I had demonstrated I let my father down during my visit. I stepped backward, hoping I would fade away into one of the shadows behind me when I felt my phone start to vibrate in my clutch. I narrowed my gaze at the unfamiliar number I found on the screen.

"Hello?" I answered softly, moving back into the house and shutting the sliding door gently. I had been standing on the part of the deck that came off a sitting room.

"Chuckles, how's your little visit going?" Tripp's voice sounded from the other end of the phone amongst a litany of background noise.

Rolling my eyes, anger and irritation rose up in me, the ironic lilt of his voice grating against my skin. "What do you want, Tripp? I told you to leave me alone. It sounds like you have many distractions to keep you occupied in whatever cesspool you're gracing with your presence."

Tripp laughed roughly. "The Kennedy North Carolina manners haven't rubbed off on you then?"

"If they had, I certainly wouldn't waste them on you. You have ten seconds to get to the point, or I'm hanging up on you."

"Deacon told me what happened with the photos. He said you and your dad had some blowout fight over it. I was just calling to see how you were, but far be it from me to care about you."

I paused, any words of retaliation dying on my tongue. I narrowed my eyes, combing over the few moments of conversation for any ulterior motive. Tripp Banks didn't call people to check in. "It wasn't the first time I've disappointed my father, and I'm sure it won't be the last. That disappointment has already managed to translate to David's family based on what I just overheard. Should be my middle name. So, thanks for your concern, but it's not necessary."

There was silence, the background noise having faded away. Tripp made a noise of disbelief. "You're anything but a disappointment, Chuck. Not everything I do is to be cruel."

A loud laugh, more like a cackle escaped my lips. "Pardon me, if given your history, I find that hard to believe. If you'll excuse me, I have a party to get back to."

"I can see this conversation isn't going anywhere. But regardless of what you may think of me, I meant what I said at your house, and I mean what I said just now. I care about you. You're anything but a disappointment, and no one in the world should make you feel that way," Tripp said, something like sadness in his voice before he hung up abruptly.

I held the phone to my ear for a moment longer, eyebrows knit in confusion. I shook my head, hopeful to shake away his words and the lingering doubt that was threatening to consume me after hearing Amelia's words. Standing abruptly, I brushed the front of my dress like I could brush away all the fears and doubts, before I made my way back to the party with a smile on my face that I knew would have made my father proud.

CHAPTER FIFTEEN

David and I flew back from his parents' beach home the day after the party. My father was continuing his silent treatment, and a part of me was shocked he hadn't been petty enough to call Guillaume and tell him the jet was no longer available to us at some point during the trip. But, the olive branch he had extended me after my last mistake was still waiting there on the tarmac for us when we left. Upon returning home, I immediately went to Deacon's only to find his apartment empty. It felt less like being alone, so I stayed there until it was time for work on Monday.

My stomach churned uncomfortably, as I moved through the glass doors of our building. I smiled tightly while I walked past the security desk, the click of my heels on the tile ringing uncomfortably in my ears. It was early, and I was certain my father wouldn't be in yet, and that was part of my strategy. My whole plan was to lock myself in my office and act busier than I was until it was time for the executives' meeting where he would surely have more important things to discuss than my latest fuck-up. Those dreams were quickly dashed when I stepped off the elevator and noted my father sitting in my desk chair through the glass door. My heel snagged on the carpet, and I caught myself as I fell forward on the edges of the open elevator doors. He was sitting back in my chair, arms folded causing the jacket of his tailored black suit to buckle slightly. He raised an eyebrow impassively, and I could see even from there how frosty his eyes were, and the rage coming off of him felt palpable.

I stood, smoothing the front of my skirt before crossing the hall, all too aware of the continued noise my heels made against the silence of the office and the way my father's eyes were surveying me.

"Dad, to what do I owe this pleasure? It's early for you to be here, no?" I asked, breathing out to try and quiet the erratic beating of my heart and nausea that was swirling in my stomach once again. I dropped my bag on the couch by my door.

"Sit down, Charlie." His voice was even and from the periphery of my vision I could see he hadn't uncrossed his arms.

I raised my eyebrows and tipped my chin at him. "This is my office. Would you rather we go to yours?"

He exhaled sharply through his nose, shaking his head at my words. "No. That's where you're wrong. It's my office. You have a desk here, because I gave you one. Now sit down. We need to talk."

I pursed my lips, hating that he was right. None of this was really mine. That's why I had stayed away for so long and now here I was. I sat across from him and raised my eyebrows, crossing my legs at the ankle. I was certain there would be no shades of a father talking to his daughter in what was about to come out of his mouth. "Then, I'm all ears, Dad."

"When you agreed to come home, we made an agreement that you could do what you wanted here so long as you proved you were capable of it and could handle the responsibility of your own portfolio. You agreed to demonstrate to me that this works." He paused, finally unfolding his arms and leaning forward, clasping his hands on the desk. My mouth popped open and bile rose in my throat, sensing where this was going. My palms grew sweaty where I gripped the arms of my chair. "You have shown me more than once that unfortunately you are not capable of the responsibility. Moving forward, your portfolio will be effectively dissolved and turned into a once-yearly charitable donation. You may continue to hold the role and oversee the donation–"

"Are you telling me that you want me to be a philanthropist? Like an old rich housewife would be?" My voice cracked, somehow bordering between a horrified whisper and a shout all at once. "Dad, are you fucking kidding me? This isn't fair...this isn't–"

He began to tick off all of what he considered to be instances where I had demonstrated I couldn't handle the responsibility, punctuating each item with the addition of a finger on the hand he was holding up until he had reached a sum total of three. I almost laughed at the irony, hearing his voice echo in my head as if to say "three strikes, you're out."

"First, there was the mishap with Society News and with Play for Everyone. Granted, you came up with a solution to both. However, you have consistently shown minimal regard for your position. You were exceptionally difficult at the Forbes interview and disappeared at some point during the evening when we were greeting the representatives from Halton. And now, not only have you refused to take any responsibility for your actions this past week, you were insubordinate when speaking to me."

"David was in those photos, too–" I began, but my father promptly cut me off with a gesture of his hand.

"David is not the face of a charitable fund, nor is he a Winchester." He paused, clasping his hands in the maddening way again, like he was speaking to a child. "I can't have someone who makes such poor and risky decisions to run their own portfolio. Not with the level of autonomy and responsibility you were given. I've consulted legal and it's a reputational risk, as is allowing you to lead your own portfolio any further."

"You're my dad," my voice dimmed to a whisper, his words feeling like they were crushing me and sitting against my chest in such a way that made it hard to breathe. My ears were ringing endlessly. I closed my eyes, hoping to stave off the tears that felt inevitable. For some reason, I pictured my mother behind my eyes. Her small smile, the touch of her hand on my tiny shoulder at a public event—understanding in her eyes. But those eyes were gone. "I came back here for you. You asked me to."

"And I thought you could handle it, that it was time for you to take a more active role in your family legacy. Clearly, I was wrong. As I said, you can remain in charge of the philanthropic aspects of–"

"I have a fucking master's degree. I can do this. You're my father. How do you not have more faith in me than this?" I asked, my voice raised. I knew my father could be cruel; I knew almost nothing came before Winchester Holdings but disbelief rippled through me like an endless tide. But now, I was experiencing the reality that I'd always known. I never would have imagined it could feel like this.

He sighed, wiping his face with his hands. "Yes, you're my daughter. Do you think for a moment I would leave you uncared for? As I said, you will remain in charge of the new charitable structure at your full salary. I'm being more than generous, Charlie."

I stood abruptly, shaking my head while the tears finally spilled over, blurring my vision. I almost laughed at the absurdity of his suggestion. There was no world in which I was interested in that. Not only was I seemingly his greatest disappointment and a 'reputational risk,' he didn't know me at all. I turned on my heel, snatching my bag from where I abandoned it on the couch. A small part of me hoped he might have done the right thing, the unexpected thing: pushed off the desk and come after me with open arms the way a father should comfort a daughter. But he was still sitting there, expressionless as he surveyed me over his interlocked fingers.

"No. You're being cruel," I whispered, suddenly unable to find my own voice before I turned my back to him.

"You're still expected at the Gala this evening," he said, his parting words sucking all the air out of the room before I managed to shut the door on him.

———

I felt Deacon's eyes on me for the fiftieth time that night. I had barely spoken a word since he and my father arrived in a limo to pick me up at my townhouse earlier that evening. His eyes flicked over me in concern, and he opened his mouth to speak several times on the way over while I determinedly stared out the window, hoping to look anywhere but at my father. I spoke once when Deacon commented on the black draped Alexander McQueen dress Sabine had sent to my home for me to wear. My only words the entire ride to The Peninsula were, "At least it's not sequined."

We were standing together in the corner of the ballroom, off to the side of the stage where our father was giving some sort of toast. Deacon and I both smiled politely, raising our champagne flutes in a gesture of hello when he mentioned that he was joined by his children this evening. Sucking on the inside of my cheeks, my smile was still plastered across my painted lips while the burning in my throat was kept at bay. My eyes scanned the room absently, not bothering to land on one particular guest for any longer than a moment. Taylor and her parents were somewhere in the crowd, along with David and everyone else I knew. I didn't see him yet and had declined his offer to pick me up, knowing my father expected me to arrive with him.

"Are you going to tell me what's wrong, Charlie?" Deacon asked out of the corner of his mouth, his smile never faltering.

I shrugged, "I told you earlier, I was sick today. I'm not feeling well."

His eyes flitted to me, and I felt them studying my face for any trace of the truth in my words. "You know you can tell me anything, right? You're my favorite person in the entire world, whatever it is...did something happen with David? He said you were barely returning his texts today."

"Drop it, Deacon." I stated flatly, continuing to smile blandly while our father continued to drone on. There was a dull thud in my ears, and my father's words continued to echo in my head all day. My movements felt mechanical, and my stomach felt hollow. I had never felt that alone in my entire life; I was unmoored and floating alone in the world where I was left behind by my mother and so severely misunderstood by my father it was almost laughable. I was twenty again, and I hated myself.

He opened his mouth to protest, but a round of polite applause broke out across the room, and Deacon schooled his features, immediately looking at our father and raising his glass before joining in the applause. Our father's back was to us, shaking hands with whoever was up on the stage with him. Deacon grabbed my free hand in his immediately and began to pull me toward the crowd. His smile was back on his face as we wove through the crowd, pausing to say hello to anyone of importance on our way. He came to an abrupt stop at a cocktail table, draped with a navy tablecloth and adorned with candles and white flowers. Taylor and her parents were standing there with a few people I recognized as Taylor's colleagues. She had forgone her usual bright or metallic gown and was wearing a simple black, floor-length dress that had elaborately crisscrossing straps on her back. For some reason, the sight of her shoved into a dress that seemed so decidedly un-Taylor unmoored me further. Even her hair was different, pulled into a slicked low ponytail. I cocked my head, narrowing my eyes and trying to place what felt so unfamiliar about her in that moment.

"Dr. Breen, Mrs. Breen. Great to see you both." Deacon smiled easily, extending a hand to Taylor's parents in turn. I followed suit, offering my hand to them both, pumping their arms mechanically as if they weren't people I had known my entire life.

"Charlie, Deacon. It's so great to see you. We never get to see you now that you're all living in the city." Taylor's mother leaned forward, kissing us each on the cheek in turn.

"Well, we'll have to change that, now won't we Mrs. Breen?" Deacon laughed, a lilt to his voice. My eyes burned seeing Deacon fit in so seamlessly, seeing him be everything my father wanted him to be. It never occurred to me that I might be envious of that fact until it was so obvious in my face like it was right then.

A small, coquettish smile played on Mrs. Breen's lips before she turned to me. "Charlie, Taylor was filling me in earlier about everything you're doing at the company. Come get a drink with me, you can tell me all about it. It sounds fascinating."

The dull thud in my ears was replaced with the echoing of my heart. My lips popped open slightly before I closed them again, any words dying in my constricting throat. I cleared it, bringing a hand up to my chest, scratching at my skin that felt like it was on fire. Like I was looking down the wrong end of a telescope, I could see all my failures, all my worst moments playing out behind my gaze. I was still staring speechlessly at Taylor's mother, but all I could see was me. All the things I had done wrong. All the ways I wasn't enough. *Maybe I would never be enough.*

"Excuse me," I whispered, turning my back on the table and pushing through the throngs of people. I blinked rapidly, trying to quell the tears in my eyes. The entire room felt like it was shifting beneath me, like the walls might close in and trap me there with all my inadequacies any moment. I kept my eyes trained on the ground, dodging heels and dress shoes until I reached the edge of the carpeted floor. An ornate wooden door stood in front of me, and I practically lunged for it, finding myself in some sort of opulent sitting room. I pressed my back against the closed door for a moment, shutting my eyes tightly and exhaling.

The silence permeated the room, and a small sob crept up my throat. I moved into the room, dropping down on a velvet couch that looked like it had seen better days. Leaning back, I closed my eyes, squeezing them against the tears that would take my makeup with them. The abrupt sounds of the ballroom infiltrated the silence, and my eyes snapped open. The door was now open. and Tripp was standing there, one hand casually tucked into the pocket of his charcoal suit pants, the other resting on the doorknob. He arched an eyebrow at me before closing the door behind his back, his eyes never leaving me.

"What do you want?" I asked bluntly, crossing my arms over my chest. I could feel the hot, sticky tears on my cheeks.

"Wondered where you were running off to so quickly." He crossed the room, crouching down on his knees in front of me so we were at eye level. His dark hair was pushed back, and he had allowed more than a five o'clock shadow to come in and coat his jawline. A navy shirt was unbuttoned at his neck, revealing tanned skin. He narrowed his eyes at me, and I watched as they tracked the tears on my cheeks.

"I didn't put up the bat signal for you to follow me. Usually when someone leaves a crowded party and disappears behind a closed door, it means they want to be alone." I bit out, irritation at Tripp bubbling inside my veins.

"I overheard your dad and legal talking today." Tripp answered quietly, ignoring me. My stomach plummeted at his words, bile rising in my throat.

I exhaled a sharp breath, shaking my head in anger. "Of course, you did. Why am I surprised what with your fucking vampire hearing? Do you just linger around waiting to hear embarrassing things about all your colleagues or just me?"

"What happened, Chuckles?" He reached out, placing his fingers on my chin and tilting my face back to his.

"What always happens!" I sobbed, throwing my hands up in the air. "I can't do anything right. No matter what I do, I'm never going to be right. I'm never going to be enough."

"That's not true. Who could possibly make you feel like you weren't enough?"

"You!" I hissed, bringing my eyes to rest on his. "You used me for points in some stupid game when my mother had died. And I was pathetic enough to let you."

Tripp shook his head, puffing out his cheeks and grabbing my chin more firmly in his grasp. "You're not pathetic, Charlie. I told you, that was never my intention. I am sorry. It felt like it was too late when I got the job offer at my old firm to come work here in Chicago. I don't know...I thought that I would run into you and—"

A scoff escaped my mouth that was half a strangled sob, tears flowing freely down my face now blurring my vision. Tripp whispered again. "Charlie, please stop crying." I blinked rapidly, clearing my eyes at his words. They were so familiar to me, so like what he said to me all those years ago.

I am twenty again. And I am all alone.

Instead of looking at Tripp as he is now, it was like I could see him at twenty-two. His features weren't as sharp, his facial hair not as coarse, but his eyes were always that blue, and I was seeing the same warmth he used to reserve just for me in them. His thumb stroked along my chin almost imperceptibly. He continued to stare at me a moment longer, his eyes boring into me and for one moment, I didn't feel alone. Tripp leaned forward, brushing his lips across mine, seemingly kissing away my tears. I didn't pull back when he raised his other hand and cupped my cheek softly, his tongue brushing my lips in permission. I parted my lips slightly, like it was involuntary again. His mouth might have been the only thing I could feel in that moment, everything else felt far away and hollow.

The sound of the door swinging open, and the sound of three voices I would know anywhere caused my heart to plummet and my eyes to shoot open. Deacon, Taylor and David were standing in the doorway to the room. Deacon and Taylor were wearing expressions of shock and both looked on the precipice of saying something, but their mouths seemed to be silently moving as they struggled for words. But I only had eyes for David. Confusion was etched across his features, like he was trying to reconcile what he was seeing. He knit his eyebrows before exhaling a breath and parting his lips.

"No," I breathed in horror, pushing Tripp away from me and standing as fast as I could like that would take it back. As opposed to the mechanical movements that were consuming me earlier, I was suddenly aware of every nerve in my body, every crack of a joint and twitch of a ligament as I lunged toward him. "No, no David. Please...no, no, no. This isn't what you think."

David raised his eyebrows at me, his eyes dark. He shook his head slightly, shoving his hands in the pocket of his suit pants before he turned on his heel and walked back into the ballroom.

"Charlie, what did you do?" Deacon whispered, disbelief coloring his features as I pushed past him, raising to my tiptoes to try and see where David was weaving a path through the crowd so I could follow him. I grabbed the swathes of material from my gown, hitching it up and taking off after him. I shouldered past anyone who stepped in my way without a word, somehow convinced if I could just make it to him before he disappeared, that I could set it right. I could explain, and he would understand. Wouldn't he?

"David!" I yelled, raising my voice audibly above the din of the crowd. By some miracle, he turned at the sound of my voice and stopped walking. His face was expressionless, and his hands still planted firmly in his pockets. I stopped right at the edge of the carpet, a mere foot away from him, desperate to grab ahold of him and drag him back to me. "Please, please don't leave. I can explain. I know everyone says that, but I can."

A delicate hand pressed down on my shoulder, a thumb beginning to move in what I assumed were slow comforting circles. I could see Taylor's silhouette in my periphery, but I refused to take my eyes away from David. Somewhere in the back of my mind, I knew we were causing a scene. I knew we were drawing attention, yet my feet remained rooted to the spot.

"Your father's looking, why don't we take this outside?" Tripp's voice was low as he came to stand beside me, gesturing with one hand to the door that was right behind David. I could see the city lights flickering beyond the glass of the lobby door not far beyond it.

David lowered his eyelids, anger dancing behind them. He opened his mouth to speak before exhaling through his nose again, his jaw grinding under his stubble. He stepped forward, and I reached out my hand desperate for him to grab it, but he raised his fist and swung at Tripp, connecting with his nose with a resounding crack. Tripp stumbled backward, grabbing a cocktail table to try and steady himself. Gasps and screams erupted behind us, and I lurched forward to grab David, but Deacon beat me to it. Deacon moved to push David toward the exit, but David held up his hands and shook his head, not sparing me a glance before turning and walking away. Taylor tried to grab my arm, but I hitched up my dress again and chased after him like my own twisted version of Cinderella running from the ball.

"David!" I sobbed, running to catch up with his significantly longer strides as he threw the hotel lobby door open and stepped out into the night. I wrenched open the door, assaulted by the cool night air and rain that had begun to pour at some point. *Fitting.* "David please!"

My sobs seemed to echo across every surface. David stopped on the bottom of the stone steps, and I tilted forward on my heels abruptly a few steps above him. We were almost eye-level. The rain continued to pour on us, the waves of David's hair plastered to his forehead. Raindrops were pouring off his nose, and he studied me for a moment, his face still expressionless. He shook his head and shrugged his shoulders before reaching into the pocket of his suit jacket.

Another sob escaped me, and I covered my mouth with my fingers, shoulders shaking, the rainwater and my tears coating my lips. The last time I had seen that diamond ring, it had been on my mother's finger. David stood, holding it out to me like he was waiting for me to take it. I closed my eyes, praying that maybe, just maybe, I would open them again and somehow all that wouldn't be real. But it was. David knelt down, and for one twisted moment, I thought he might be intending to use it, but he placed the ring gently at my feet before turning his back on me and leaving me standing there with the rain falling even harder around me.

I sunk down to the step, grabbing the ring and it slipped between my wet fingers as I clutched it to my chest. My sobs were silent, and I buried my face in my knees, wishing I was anywhere else—wishing I was anyone else. An arm wrapped around either side of me, and I knew deep down in my soul the only two people who could see their way clear to be with me were my brother and Taylor. My silence soon gave way to loud, gut-wrenching sobs. Deacon and Taylor both pressed their heads to mine, like they could prevent my heart from shattering, but its tiny, shattered fragments from the events that just unfolded were long washed away by the rain.

CHAPTER SIXTEEN

For the second time in two days, I found myself confronting my father behind a desk in the office. I stepped off the elevator, hands firmly planted in the pockets of Deacon's old sweater. My hair was pulled off my bare face. I didn't bother to try covering my bloodshot eyes or puffy features beneath my makeup. I wasn't sure how long I sat on the steps last night, rain soaking through, ruining my gown. At some point, Deacon and Taylor ushered me into a town car, and the three of us went back to his apartment.

We didn't speak much, and I wasn't sure I was able to form words. Neither of them asked me about Tripp but rather sat there in silence beside me while I called David over and over again. The phone rang and rang, each unanswered call punctuated by a sob. I fell into a restless sleep on Deacon's couch, vaguely overhearing him having a shouting match on the phone with someone I assumed was our father. There were endless unanswered texts and calls from Tripp on my phone, but I ignored those. I had nothing to say to him. Somehow, I had let him destroy me...again.

I turned my mother's ring over in my pocket, my fingers dancing along the edges of the cushion cut diamond and skating over the tapered baguettes on either side. The ring had come from my father's side of the family and had been commissioned to Harry Winston by my great-grandfather for his soon-to-be wife. The shock at seeing it in

David's possession almost paused my sobs last night. He wouldn't have known it existed unless my father had given it to him. That stirred something in me that I was unable to reconcile.

My father passing the ring along to David for me, welcoming him into the family was so at odds with the man who practically fired me yesterday and called me a *liability*. I steeled myself, taking a deep breath as I approached my father's office, knocking on his door. He was sitting behind his desk, eyes focused on his computer screen until his eyes flicked up at my knock. Pushing back in his chair, he crossed his arms and looked pointedly at the chair opposite his.

I raised my eyebrows at him, feeling the stretch of my puffy skin and placed the ring gently on the desk between us before sitting down. "Thought you might want this back."

"Well, it doesn't appear as if it will be sitting on your finger anytime soon." My father said coolly, making no moves to take the ring.

"Ouch." I responded, despite knowing I deserved that and more. "He must have gotten that from you. When did you give it to him?"

"Before you left for North Carolina. It seemed inevitable he would be using it at one point."

David's words to my father during the ill-fated phone call rang in my ears. I imagined my dad had pulled him into that very office and told him he would be honored if he married me. "What changed Dad? You went from giving David a one-of-a-kind family diamond to practically firing me? What did I do that was so wrong in your eyes?"

My father exhaled, finally uncrossing his arms and picking up the ring. He twirled it between his fingers, and I watched as his eyes skated over it. A regular person might wonder if he was remembering giving it to my mother, remembering what it was like to marry her. But my father wasn't a regular person and apparently neither was I. We both had our dark sides. The silence stretched on, and he finally looked back at me and spoke. "I told you yesterday, Charlie. You're my daughter, and I love you. I would never leave you uncared for and your happiness is important to me, but that was a business decision."

I shook my head, tempted to argue with him. That couldn't possibly be a real, familial love. Not the way it should be. Instead, I shrugged my shoulders in defeat. "I quit, Dad."

"That's two of you today then. David was here when I came in this morning."

"David shouldn't have to quit. I should be the one to go—" I began, but he cut me off.

"I didn't want David to leave. I didn't accept his resignation at first, but it became very clear he had no interest in seeing you or Tripp. To be frank, I personally don't care if I ever see Tripp Banks again. I called in a favor and got him a job in New York. He moves next week." He said, studying me as the tears fell, unbidden from my eyes. If there was anything left of my heart, I was sure it would shatter all over again. "Where are you going?"

Rubbing my eyes with my palm like a toddler, a strangled laugh escaped my throat. "Looks like something we have in common. I made a call this morning, too. My thesis supervisor at LSE is doing some research and needs an associate. I'm moving back to London."

I waited. Waited for him to say anything at all, to comfort me, to admonish me, to beg me to stay with my family, to beg me not to run again. We sat there in silence, it grew heavier and heavier as the time passed. Finally, I stood, a sad smile on my face. "I guess we both break things, huh Dad?"

"Your recent behavior makes me think you may want to consider a therapist while you're over there, Charlie." My father spoke after I had turned my back to leave his office. The little air in my lungs rushed out, and I braced myself to turn back around, but when I did, he wasn't even looking at me. His eyes were dark and focused on my mother's ring. Without another backward glance, I left the office and the life I was trying to forge behind.

———

David's back was turned to me. His feet were propped up on the edge of his balcony, and the ember of a cigarette he held to his lips was illuminated against the night sky. I knocked on his door for several minutes before realizing it was open and let myself in. My eyes burned at the sight of him, longing panged in my heart desperate to bridge the chasm between us. I knew he didn't want to see me, but I needed to explain, to assure him it had nothing to do with him—and everything to do with me. I reached up and rapped on the glass.

He turned, his hair pushed off his face. His eyes were bloodshot with dark blue circles underneath them, too. He exhaled a plume of smoke and shrugged noncommittally. That was probably the best I was going to get, and more than I deserved. I pushed the sliding door aside and stepped out, everything I had rehearsed on the walk over suddenly vanished from my mind.

"Talk, Charlie." He took another drag of his cigarette, not making eye contact with me. He was looking somewhere out on the water. Maybe trying to spot a boat he could use to get away from me.

"You smoke?" I asked quietly. My eyes burned, and the tears threatened to spill over at any moment. I wrapped my arms around myself, shivering, despite the summer air and wishing I was wearing more than an old sweater of Deacon's.

"I used to. It seemed as good a time as any to start again." David continued to stare out at the water and began swirling a glass of scotch on the table beside him. "Can I get you a drink?"

I let out a bark of laughter. Even when I didn't deserve it, he still maintained his manners. "I don't deserve anything from you." He met that with silence, continuing to stare out at the river.

"Please don't leave." My voice was barely a whisper above the noises of the city. "I'm leaving, I should be the one to go."

He sighed, rubbing the stubble on his chin and putting out his cigarette on the balcony before tossing it over the side. I recoiled slightly, tempted to discipline him for littering, but I had long lost that right. "It's actually a better job, Charlie."

"You can't leave Chicago. I'm leaving. I quit today." I looked down, scuffing the worn leather of my sandal along the balcony. "I saved my father the embarrassment of having to fire me. He doesn't exactly love a public spectacle."

David shook his head, wisps of his hair fell over his forehead. "I have no desire to stay here. I don't want to stay in Chicago. I...I can't stay here." His voice cracked, another piece of my soul along with it.

"David, I'm so–"

"How long has this been going on? How long have I been this fucking stupid?" His voice was rough, and he raised his glass to his lips but immediately slammed it down against the table, liquid sloshing everywhere. "Jesus Christ, Charlie! You hated Tripp. You made that clear from the very beginning. Is this why you never wanted him to work at WH?" David pulled on his hair with his free hand, the other still wrapped around the glass like he might throw it at any moment. I noticed with a pang, there were scabs on his knuckles.

"It wasn't like that!" I reached forward, desperate to touch him. I gathered myself at the last minute. I had lost that privilege. "This wasn't going on. We weren't having an affair. I never loved him. I don't love him."

"So you threw all of this away for what? Ten minutes in the coat room at a party?" He laughed harshly. "I didn't think this stuff actually happened to people in real life."

"No...no, David. I never told you the whole truth about how I know Tripp." My tears fell steadily. I could barely make out the outline of my trembling hands, still outstretched toward him. Maybe he wanted to reach for me, too, but he didn't.

"Then you better start talking, Charlie."

"Tripp and I did go to Brown together. We knew each other. He was...he was my friend. We had this sort of will they, won't they, flirty relationship. We drove each other fucking nuts. We would go to parties or to clubs, and we would make out and call it off and go home. He would always tell me I was a tease, and then he would hook up with other girls. I thought I was different. That maybe I meant something more to him. It's the oldest story in the fucking boo, and it's pathetic."

"So–" David began, anger creeping into his voice.

"I'm not...I'm not done." I wiped the tears from my eyes with the back of my hands. "In his senior year, I was walking back from the library. My dad had just called me to tell me my mom was dead. I was distraught. I ran into him. He was my friend, and he was kind to me. I went back to his fraternity house, and we drank, and he made me laugh and distracted me. We slept together." I felt embarrassment creep into my voice and across my entire body. I could feel Tripp's hands on me, and I was disgusted with myself all over again. "I couldn't sleep, and I just wanted my own bed, and I wanted my fucking mom. I got out of bed and got dressed to leave. When I was going down the stairs I saw..."

My voice hitched, and I was sobbing. I never repeated that story to anyone. "In the living room, there was a poster board; it was like a bracket. I was at the top of the bracket. At some point, my name had been crossed off. There was a number of points assigned to my name. I thought he fucked me the day my mom died for points in some fucking game, David. I was humiliated and devastated, and I wanted to die. I thought we were at least friends."

"Charlie, I still don't understand." He seemed again as if he was about to comfort me but stopped himself.

"I'm not done, unfortunately." I laughed in spite of myself. "He made it clear when he came back that he never did it. Things with my dad have been...they've been hard. He made it clear I needed to demonstrate that I could do this job. Tripp kept finding me and comforting me after all these moments of my failures, and my inadequacies. The day of the Gala, my father took my portfolio away. He told me after what happened in North Carolina I had demonstrated I was a liability, that I couldn't be responsible. He said I could remain at the company in name only and be responsible for some stupid philanthropical arm to replace my portfolio. Tripp overheard. He was comforting me."

"Why didn't you tell me any of this, Charlie? About Tripp, your family? Way back in the town car after we took him for dinner?" David's voice was low, and he was finally looking at me. He appeared older than he had two nights ago.

"I was embarrassed, David. These are the two most embarrassing things that have ever happened to me." I rolled my hands over, picking at my nails. "I just felt so wrong. I didn't want to be that girl anymore. Someone who tried to fuck away the pain of her mom dying. Someone who was so inadequate, so not enough they were practically fired by their own father. I wanted to be the person you saw when you looked at me. That girl wouldn't have any of these things happen to her."

"Charlie, have I not made you feel like you're enough? Has Deacon not? Has Taylor not? Your own accomplishments? I just don't understand. Tripp should be embarrassed. Your dad should be embarrassed. And you...I thought you hated Tripp? How could you let him kiss you or touch you at all?" David's voice cracked, and I noticed his eyes were blurry.

I lurched forward, kneeling and grabbing his hands in mine. "David, David, of course you have. None of this has anything to do with you. It was about me. I saw Tripp, and he comforted me. I felt like I was twenty again. He found me in moments when I felt so alone and so bad...I don't know what I thought. I don't know what the fuck I was doing. I thought maybe I was a different person than that sad little broken-hearted girl who had just lost her mother, but clearly, I haven't changed. But please know, it was never, ever about you. You're perfect."

David sighed, taking his hands from me and scrubbing his face. "You're not a sad little girl, Charlie. You're you...you were perfect to me. And I'm sorry about your dad. You didn't deserve that." He looked down at me, grasping my hands again, and I noticed the tear streaks on his face. "But it doesn't change anything. You cheated on me with him. You threw this away for...for what? Was I just the nice guy you marry? Tripp's the guy from your past you finally get to change? Have one last fling with? I still don't get it."

I sobbed, clutching his hands to my chest like they could cradle my heart in an attempt to shelter it from what was to come. "I can't explain it to you any better than that. But please, please know it had nothing to do with you. It had to do with me. You're not...you're not the nice guy someone settles for. You're the secret affair with the mind-blowing sex that turned into something magnificent and meaningful. You're smart and funny and challenging. You are nice, David. But you're so much more than that. You *saw* me. You're the partner who I never deserved."

David was quiet for a moment. "Did you have sex with him?"

"No!" I shouted, bringing his hands to my lips and kissing them all over, desperate to make it better. "He kissed me a few times, and we fell asleep together once. But I let it all happen."

"If I hadn't walked in, would you have?" He asked, his brown eyes boring into me. They were dull and flat.

"I don't know," I whispered. And I didn't know. I didn't know myself at all. We sat in silence, and I pressed his hands to my cheek, eyes fluttering closed as I mapped all the callouses and ridges.

"I'm still leaving, Charlie." David said, his eyes back out on the water.

I looked down, setting his hands in my lap. I knew he wouldn't stay for me, but I hoped I could have made him see he didn't have to leave his life here. "Please don't leave, David. I'm going to leave."

He shook his head. "I can't be here. Not in this apartment, not in this city, not in that office. I'm sorry you feel like you have to leave, but I can't stay."

"Deacon's going to clean out my office and desk, so you won't have to see me at the office." I snuck a peak at him again, finally letting go of his hands. He is so, so beautiful. He had been mine—and I ruined it.

"Where are you going? Off to save the world?" He turned to look at me again, and my breath caught in my throat.

"I'm moving back to London. Just some good old-fashioned nepotism."

"You have to stop running someday, Charlie," he exhaled.

I nodded. I sensed, with dread, that my conversation with David was coming to a close. That my life with David was coming to an end. I was desperate—desperate for one more smile, one more touch. One more anything. "When are you leaving? What are you doing with your apartment?"

"I'm selling it. I thought about keeping it as an investment property, but I just...I need to cut ties with this place." David drained the rest of his scotch and set the empty glass down on the table.

"I'm selling, too," I said inconsequentially. "I don't want...I don't deserve my family money right now."

David exhaled through his nose and smiled sadly at me. "Maybe we can share a realtor."

"Can I ask one more question?" I looked down at my blurred hands, picking mindlessly at my nails. David didn't respond. I took his silence for permission. "The ring. Why were you carrying it around? Were you going to use it?"

David turned to me and arched an eyebrow. "That's a bold question, Charlie. I don't really see how you can ask me that. But yes. I was. That's all I'll say about that, though." David turned away from me and stared back out at the river.

I stood, sensing it was time for me to go. The empty glass sat on the table, and he made no move to refill it. "Just for the record, David, I really do love you."

He said nothing and continued to stare out onto the water, as if searching for his own green light. I turned and with a shaking hand, slid the glass door open. I placed my hand on it, pushing down to ensure I left a handprint. I knew it would only get wiped away, but I was desperate to leave a piece of me with him. I turned one last time, peering over my shoulder to see his outline—messy hair and broad shoulders, bringing another cigarette to his lips with perfect hands that were too calloused, illuminated by the moon.

I didn't deserve him, and I never had.

ONE YEAR LATER

I craned my neck to look back at the towering skyscraper in New York City, the sunlight shimmering against the sleek planes of glass that coated it. I wished I hadn't forgotten my sunglasses. I tried to count the floors to find the thirtieth. One floor looked like it was getting more sunlight than the others, and I wondered briefly if that's because of who I would find there. My whole heart was up there somewhere.

I walked into the building, smiling politely at the security desk when I produced a badge from my oversized tote and scanned it. My heels clicked against the tile floor, blending in with all the other sounds of the lobby until I made it to the padded carpet of the elevator. I was mercifully alone. I teetered back and forth on my heels, nerves skittering across my skin. I wasn't sure what I was even doing here, but the second I stepped off the plane I couldn't resist coming to see if he looked the same as he did in my dreams.

The elevator doors slid open to reveal an office floor that looked similar to Winchester Holdings, with towering glass windows and expensive-looking furniture scattered throughout. My eyes flitted to the reception desk, and I noticed no one was sitting there. I put my head down, quickly exiting the elevator. I knew no one would look twice at me. One thing my life prepared me for was blending into expensive surroundings. I didn't exactly have a plan once I was in here, because I had no idea where his office was. I looked up quickly as I ducked around a corner to make sure I wasn't walking into a dead end, and my breath hitched.

Beyond the glass doors of a conference room, David was leaning back in his chair at the head of a long table. He was surrounded by others around the table, and he was tossing a pen in the air and catching it with his right hand. His hair was a bit shorter than the last time I saw it, and the waves falling around his ears had me longing to run my fingers through it. He had clearly abandoned shaving on a regular basis and had let his stubble grow across his face. I wanted to rub my cheek against it.

He opened his mouth and laughed at something the person sitting beside him said. I cocked my head and studied him for a moment. He looked almost the same as the last time I saw him, staring out onto the river from his balcony in Chicago, but he looked like he was so far out of my grasp. Worlds away.

My stomach dropped and began to twist into knots. Before I could change my mind, I raised my fist to knock on the glass. It might as well have been an explosion. I cringed visibly as the sound seemed to reverberate off every single corner of the office and throughout the conference room that seemed more like a glass cage to me now. Every person in the room turned in their chairs to stare at me, but my eyes immediately found David's. He surveyed me impassively for a moment, setting down the pen he was tossing in the air. He pushed up the sleeves of the tailored navy dress shirt he was wearing to reveal his muscular forearms. He had a tan. I wondered if he had been home to North Carolina recently. I raised my hand in sort of a strangled wave, really unsure what to do now. I didn't think this through. My heart started to beat frantically at a pace I was quite sure could not be sustained.

David's face broke out into a grin, and he gestured for me to open the door. Tears welled in my eyes, and I smiled widely in return, closing them briefly before pulling on the handle of the door. "I'm sorry to interrupt what looked like a very important meeting with the pen tossing and the laughter. But I was in the neighborhood, so..." I tilted my head to the side and surveyed David, my eyes skating over every inch of his body hungrily.

"How did you even get in here?" He laughed, leaning forward and crossing his forearms over his broad chest. I felt the sound right down into my soul. Neither of us seemed to care that we were speaking only to each other, and everyone else was looking back and forth between us like we were a particularly interesting game of tennis.

"I snuck past security. Don't tell," I whispered conspiratorially, winking at him. My heart continued to skip every second beat.

The man sitting beside David who appeared around our age, or maybe a year or two younger, swiveled in his chair. "Should we call security?"

David laughed loudly again, and the corner of his lip tipped upward into a sideways smile I knew was just for me. "Nah. She owns this building, actually. I'm not sure how far security would get trying to throw her out. Besides, I've seen her backed into a corner, and it's not pretty. She's feisty."

I could see the wheels turning as everyone in the room looked furtively at one another. *The* Charlie Winchester. Back on U.S. soil. Resurfaced and found at last. The man sitting beside David whirled around, and I noticed he was looking at me disdainfully. I took this to mean they were likely friends.

David studied me for a moment longer before speaking again. "Everyone else get out, please."

The authority in his voice took me by surprise. The man beside him whispered loudly enough that it was clearly intended to reach me. "David...are you sure about this? Didn't she rip your heart out? Publicly reject your proposal at a fundraiser and run off to London without so much as a backward glance?"

My stomach dropped, and I knitted my eyebrows, opening my mouth to protest, but David met my eyes and shook his head almost imperceptibly. His eyes darkened for a moment before he blinked, and they were their usually honey color. "Yeah, something like that. Now get out."

The man grunted and tossed me one more scathing look before practically tossing himself out of his chair and shouldering past me to get toward the door. "Friend of yours?" I responded dryly, stepping away from the onslaught of people leaving the table. I didn't want to get knocked over by any other members of David's fan club. They didn't need to worry, I punished myself enough for what I did to David. A year in exile, and I hardly considered my sentence to be served.

David pushed away from the desk and stood. His navy dress shirt tucked into slim fit dark gray pants and if possible, he seemed stronger and broader than the last time I had seen him. My body screamed at me to run to him and bury my face in his chest. It's been more than a year since I laid eyes on him and every single part of me was urging me forward. He shoved his hands in his pockets and tilted his head slightly, studying me before he took a few steps toward me, as if unsure what he should do. He exhaled, his eyes raking over my body.

"Jesus Christ, Charlie. You look even more beautiful than I remember. Where in the world have you been?" He said, stepping closer before peering down at me, his lips pulled back in a wistful sort of smile. He wrapped both of his arms around me and brought me to him in a crushing hug so quickly I thought he might have been afraid I would disappear at any given moment.

A noise somewhere between a gasp and a sob escaped my lips as I crushed my face into his chest. My heart was whispering a steady beat in my chest. *Home. Home. Home.* My body was on fire. I pushed back, placing my hands against the broad planes of his chest. I could feel his heart pounding through his shirt. It was almost as fast as my own, and I wondered if it was singing something similar to him.

I could feel his shirt growing damp from the tears that were escaping my eyes. I pressed them so closely to his chest like I could peer into his very soul. "I just got back from South Africa. I was doing some work with a colleague. I hopped around a bit after I finished my term at LSE."

David rested his chin on the top of my head and wrapped his arms tighter around me, not a care in the world that we were standing in the middle of a glass room. "I had dinner with your dad and Deacon last week when they were in the city. They showed me photos of a trip you took to Mombasa? Deac said you tried to convince them to stay in some sort of beachfront hut. But they didn't tell me you were coming back to the states."

"They don't know I'm here. I have a few interviews, but I didn't tell them about it." I pulled back, peering up at him.

"Interviews? For what?" David asked, meeting my eyes and seemingly refusing to look away.

"I'm sure my father won't approve but...I'm thinking of doing my PhD. I had an interview at Columbia earlier and one in Boston next week." I pressed my face back into his chest, savoring every moment of contact.

"Professor Winchester," David laughed, his arms releasing me. "Why don't we get out of here? You can tell me all about it?"

I cocked my head, already feeling empty now that his arms were no longer around me. "Don't you have work to do? Big important vice president work?"

The easy grin I loved so much slid into place on David's face, and he slung his arm around my shoulder lazily, like it was something we did all the time. "I do. But one of the perks of being a big, important vice president is that I can cancel meetings on short notice."

"Oh?" I asked as David turned me around and began to walk us toward the door of the conference room. "And what are you going to say the reason is?"

David stopped for a moment, looking down at me. His eyes traced my face, and there was something I couldn't quite read in them. "I'll tell them I saw a ghost," he winked.

————

Twirling my straw in my hands, I looked up and met David's eyes. The string light bulbs hanging from the ceiling above us caused the honey flecks in his eyes to sparkle. A smile stretched across my face that I couldn't stop. He is so beautiful, and I couldn't believe I was looking at him again after all this time.

"What are you smiling at, Charlie?" David asked easily, leaning back in his chair.

I shrugged, feeling embarrassed all the sudden. "I just feel lucky. Lucky to be looking at you again."

He cleared his throat, taking a sip of the drink in front of him. "How are things with your dad?"

I exhaled, snorting before I chewed the inside of my cheek. "Distant." And they were. There wasn't another way to describe it. "We have this unspoken agreement not to talk about anything serious ever, and he just feels further away than he ever has. If that's possible. Did he...he didn't ask you to lie to people about what happened between us, did he?"

"No. He didn't ask me to lie." David shook his head, something like sorrow crossing his eyes before he continued, changing the subject. "So, are you going to tell me about school? You said you had interviews at Columbia and Harvard?"

"I'm not sure what there is to say. I really liked working with my old supervisor, researching with my colleagues and doing a bit of teaching. Obviously, the corporate world is not for me. This, this I can do. This I'm good at." I smiled up at David, painting hearts in the condensation covering my glass. "There were two programs in sustainable development I liked the best. I wasn't trying to be...I wasn't trying anything by applying to Columbia. It wasn't because you live in New York."

David laughed, shaking his head at me like I was absurd. "New York is a big city, it's okay, Charlie." He paused, looking out the window momentarily before looking back at me with an intensity in his eyes that made my stomach dip. "For what it's worth, I think you should choose New York." Silence fell between us, and I opened my mouth to speak several times before changing my mind, unsure of what words could ever be enough.

"You know I have this dream–" I looked down, focusing on the ice slowly melting into my drink. "Well, it's not one single dream. I have dreams...I dream all the time. In my dreams, I don't...I don't do *that* to you. In my dreams, it's still you and me. But then I wake up and it's...it's just this."

David tilted his head, bringing the bottle to his lips as he surveyed me. He pushed his hair back with his free hand. They were still too calloused and worn. "Well, that's the thing about dreams, Charlie, they're not real."

I nodded my head slowly and felt tears pool into the corners of my eyes. The drink below me blurred while I clutched my straw.

David spoke again. "But I did read somewhere that dreams are kind of like the multiverse theory, representing infinite possibilities of how our lives might have played out...or might play out."

I looked up, my heart dropping into my stomach as we locked eyes. Tears fell freely down my face and splashed on the marble table below me. I didn't care that we were in public. My voice was barely a whisper. "Do you think there's a world where we're together, again?"

David surveyed me again, gently setting his beer down on the table. "I'm sure that somewhere, yeah. We're still together. If you subscribe to that." My heart somersaulted in my chest, beating desperately against my ribcage. Desperate to escape its confines and find itself in the hands of the man sitting across the table from me. Every beat, it hammered against my chest like hands beating a body bloody. Angry at me and desperate to return to David.

"I hope that in this universe, there is somewhere, or someday, where we can be *together* again. Where I can spend the rest of my life making it up to you. Where I don't ever hurt you again. I know I don't deserve it, but I hope someday you give me that chance." I looked at David through my blurred eyes. I blinked rapidly, hoping to clear my vision so I could look at him as long as possible.

David was silent. He turned and looked out the window at the traffic on the street beside us. People were walking by, laughing. Hand in hand. Comparing text messages, answering phone calls. Taxis were weaving in and out of traffic, honking loudly.

He turned back to me, staring as he raised his beer to his lips again. His face gave nothing away. The usual playful curve of his smile was impassive. His eyes still danced under the swaying bulbs strung above us. He parted his lips and uttered one word that before had very little meaning to me. In fact, it had always seemed nondescript and evasive. But now, I clung to it like a buoy in the middle of the ocean as a storm raged around me. It was as if I was twenty again, clutching to a boy for salvation in my darkest moment. But instead, I was clutching to this one word.

"Maybe."

Maybe. Maybe. Maybe.

But the story doesn't end here. On the next page, find the exclusive sneak peek to the second book in The Rich Girl Series, Lost Girl, coming June 2023.

LOST GIRL
JUNE 2023

LOST GIRL

David Kennedy was standing in the back of the lecture hall. His foot was kicked up against the stone wall, arms crossed over his chest and that worn Tarheels hat I could pick out of any crowd turned backward on his head, with blonde waves peeking out to curl gently over his ears. The words I was about to say to the students died on my tongue as I took him in, my eyes tracing the way his black t-shirt stretched over his broad shoulders and chest. Our eyes met momentarily, and he arched an eyebrow at me, the corners of his lips quivering.

My heart somersaulted in my chest with the familiar beat against my ribcage that happened every time I saw David. It always sounded the same as it pulsed against my eardrums; it was always whispering the same word. *Home.* I widened my eyes in confusion before turning back to the small group of my seminar students. I sat back against the desk in the center of the room, crossing my booted feet at the ankles and stacking the heel of the leather boots.

"As I was saying, papers are due next Friday. Physical copy in my office by four in the afternoon." My cheeks burned, and I worked to keep my eyes trained on the students in front of me instead of wandering back to David to see if he was still looking at me.

"Is it true your brother's engagement party to Noa Dahan is this weekend? I saw it in Vanity Fair." Devi, one of the senior students enrolled in the International Relations seminar I instructed on solving global issues, asked. She leaned forward in her seat, propping her chin up on the palm of her hand, the other twirling her braided curls between her fingers like a schoolgirl.

I smiled tightly, folding my arms across my chest. My heart dropped for an entirely different reason, accompanied by the usual twinge of jealousy and pang of regret whenever Deacon's engagement was mentioned. Neither of these feelings had anything to do with my brother, and everything to do with the man standing in the back of the lecture hall. It didn't help that Deacon was marrying one of the most famous supermodels in the world. Their impending nuptials and general bliss were shoved down my throat every time I turned on the television or walked by a newsstand. "I regret encouraging socialization in this class now. But yes, that's why the seminar is canceled next week. I'll still be in Chicago. Any questions about your papers?"

"Will we get to see photos of the party? And your dress?" Devi continued, a small smirk playing on her face.

"I'm sure you'll see them in Vanity Fair as well. If there are no questions about your papers, you're all fine to leave for the day. Email me if you have any questions between now and then." I gestured vaguely at the door at the back of the room before turning and walking to the other side of my desk. I took a deep breath, steeling myself for the inevitable when I would be left alone with David.

I had seen David exactly three times since I moved to Manhattan, and each was more painful than the last. The hum of conversation filled the room, and I dropped down in the worn leather chair that sat behind the desk. I made a show of gathering and stacking the papers I would need to take with me, watching from the corner of my eye as the students all began gathering their things and moving toward the exit. But I wasn't focused on them. I was watching David, as he casually loped down the stairs, hands tucked into his pockets. My heart pulsed rapidly, and the familiar words wrapped around me. I continued to look down, the words on the page in front of me blurring.

David stopped in front of my desk, the continued picture of casual elegance when he swung the chair opposite me around and sat in it, folding his arms across the back. I flicked my gaze up from the blurred page, I could practically feel my heartbeat in my throat and despite my best efforts, my eyes roved over him hungrily. I drank in everything about him—the sharp planes of his face, the stubble lining his jaw that he never seemed to shave anymore, and the lines surrounding his eyes that betrayed the time that had elapsed since we first met. I hoped it meant he had things to laugh about, to smile about, things that made him happy—even if those things weren't me.

"It's been a while, Charlie." David smiled easily, leaning forward even farther. The lines around his eyes crinkled, and I wanted to run my fingers over them. "You look great."

I looked down, not thinking there was anything particularly special about the crisp, white shirt I tucked into a leather skirt this morning and paired with knee-high boots. But that was David. He always saw the things in me I couldn't; he always offered me what I would never deserve. I raised my eyes to meet his, my stomach plummeting when I caught that familiar glint of sparkling honey in his eyes.

"You too," I whispered, continuing to trace every part of him. The words hung in the air between us, growing thicker with every passing moment.

The last time I saw David played out behind my eyes. I breathed in and out, not moving my eyes from his, feeling the rain slicking my skin and my heart shatter all over again when I remembered what it felt like to see him walk away; what it felt like to live without David, how noticeable and visceral his absence in my life really was. It was an obvious hurt that smarted at me daily, but for some reason I was picturing the empty seat at Thanksgiving that he should have occupied at the first Winchester family Thanksgiving in Whitefish since my mother died. The invitation from my father, and the promise of David being there to fill some of the space she used to occupy, the idea of our family slowly healing, had been so tantalizing that I thought about it constantly in London. But when the time came, without her, without David, all it really ended up being was a giant, empty house with three broken people inside.

Shaking my head, willing the memories to disappear, I felt a fake, moronic, Winchester smile slide into place. "What are you doing here, David? Don't tell me you're enrolling."

A wry grin appeared on his face, and he took his hat off, running a hand through his hair before placing it back on. I felt a pang in my chest. It was such a distinct, David mannerism, and it was so at odds with the way he carried himself in the rest of his life. "No, but if I had more professors like you, I might have considered a few more years in grad school. I actually missed my flight—I was going to just get on the next one, but Deacon said you were taking the jet home this afternoon? Is it alright if I catch a ride with you?"

My heart somersaulted at the thought of being in close proximity with David for an extended period of time. "Can you really catch a ride on a private jet?" I laughed. "But uh, sure, of course. I have a meeting with my supervisor shortly. Guillaume called me earlier to let me know he's landing at Teterboro at five-fifteen. Do you want to meet there?"

"No point driving separately, Charles. I'll pick you up around three?" David stood, his strong hand grabbing the back of the chair and swinging it back around again.

I arched an eyebrow, eyes skittering over the veins and calluses that adorned his hands. "You keep a car in Manhattan?"

"You never know when you might miss a flight and need to drive with your former girlfriend to a private airport," David knocked on the desk with his knuckles, his smile never faltering. "I'll see you later, Charlie."

"My address –"

"I know where you live. Thanks," he smiled at me one more time before turning away and walking back up the stairs. He came to a sudden halt on the first landing, shoving his hands in his pockets before he looked back at me. "Tripp will be there."

The statement hung heavily in the air between us, sucking all the air out of the room—exactly like Tripp would have. I swallowed; a nudge of regret eating away at my insides. There was nothing I could say to change what those words meant to both of us. "I know." David nodded, saying nothing in response, before looking away from me again and leaving me sitting there with nothing but my own failures pressing in on me.

I continued to stare at his retreating form, my heart in my throat as I watched him throw open the door to the lecture hall, sunlight illuminating his silhouette like he was some sort of angel on earth; and I couldn't help but think of the last time David walked away from me—how different things would be if I could have made him stay.

ACKNOWLEDGEMENTS

First and foremost, thank you for sticking with Charlie until the very end. But as I said, her story isn't over yet. The Winchesters have many more galas and events to attend, Charlie has more bad decisions to make, and Deacon has more custom suits to be tailored. I hope you enjoyed the sneak peek of Lost Girl, and as you can see all our favorites—or least favorites depending on where you stand with Tripp—are back to cause chaos in a new city. I can't wait to see what damage they can do in Manhattan.

It's hard to believe I'm writing the acknowledgements section of Rich Girl. This story was born one night early in the pandemic while I sat on my ancient, practically dilapidated IKEA couch, using my old Macbook Pro that I was constantly afraid would die or overheat and burn me, whichever came first. This story, and these characters, have come a very long way, and I am endlessly proud of them. But the characters nor this book in its entirety wouldn't have gotten to where they are today without so many people who I owe the world to. I wish I was Charlie Winchester—not really though—so I could shower you all with lovely, opulent gifts, but my endless gratitude will have to do.

Krys Merryman and imPRESS Millennial Books, I don't know where this book would be without you—or where I would be without you—but thank you for believing in it from the beginning and helping me expand this world in ways I never thought possible. Being able to say I was your first publishing client is such a joy, and I am still sometimes in shock that you wanted to take this risk with me, but as I've said, you're stuck with me so no looking back now.

Benjamin, this book was dedicated to you, and you were the first person who ever set eyes on this story. You believed in it from the very beginning. Despite the way you knit-pick my words, you will forever be my alpha reader and first person I run things by. Thank you for always reading the random excerpts of my work and never straying past the highlighted line where you were to stop.

I had many friends who bolstered my confidence as an author and in this story specifically, but Emily, thank you for picking me up off the proverbial floor when I was second-guessing everything. Your voice notes saved me, and the day you read this story and sent me live reactions will forever live rent free in my head.

Kelsi, you were the second person who saw any part of this book, and though this book was dedicated to you, too, you've been my number one fan from day one. You will be the first person I hire if I ever make it big.

There are also many stages that a story goes through behind the scenes beyond editing, like beta reading and advanced reader copies, and I owe so much to everyone who participated in those pieces, too. Christina, thank you for your thoughtful eye and always catching when I used the word "had." I really need to get a new word and stop being obsessed with Deacon, David, and Tripp's hair. But as you said, they've got great hair. To all the advanced copy readers, thank you, thank you, thank you. Nothing made my day more than seeing your reviews and getting to connect with you all about these characters and this story.

And finally, thank you to everyone else in my life: my mom, who I am so fortunate to have such an amazing relationship with, my family, and all my other friends. You all believe in me when I don't believe in myself, and a million thank-yous would never be enough.

Now, let's see what happens to the Winchesters in New York City.